The Right Side of Wrong

Books by Reavis Z. Wortham

The Red River Mysteries
The Rock Hole
Burrows
The Right Side of Wrong

The Right Side of Wrong

A Red River Mystery

Reavis Z. Wortham

Poisoned Pen Press

Poisoned
Pen
Press

Copyright © 2013 by Reavis Z. Wortham

First Edition 2013

10 9 8 7 6 5 4 3 2 1

Library of Congress Catalog Card Number: 2012952558

ISBN: 9781464201462   Hardcover
        9781464201486   Trade Paperback

Poisoned Pen Press
6962 E. First Ave., Ste. 103
Scottsdale, AZ 85251
www.poisonedpenpress.com
info@poisonedpenpress.com

Printed in the United States of America

This book is dedicated to my best friend of over 30 years, Steve Knagg. He has been there in all weather, through thick and thin, and always had my back. After reading my first still-unpublished manuscript, he handed it back and walked away, speaking over his shoulder, "Now that you have that out of your system, go write a good novel." He was right. The next one was *The Rock Hole*, which he, and many others, pronounced satisfactory. Thanks, Woodrow.

Acknowledgments

Success in this business doesn't come easily, and usually doesn't arrive overnight. Of course the author creates the manuscript that eventually becomes the novel in your hands, but that's the easy part. The rest is dependent on those who toil behind the scenes.

My wife, Shana (who I affectionately call The War Department in newspaper columns and magazine articles) is always at the forefront of this process. Other than having to live with me, she reads the manuscript at least four or five times. She is the love of my life.

Now that the Red River series has advanced in plot, complexity, and character development, others have become part of the process.

Thanks to our great friend Ronda Wise, LVN, my first go-to source for all things medical. After many years as an ER nurse, and raising four girls and a covey of grandchildren, she's seen just about everything. My second medical source is my old friend, Dr. Duane Hinshaw, D.O. Besides keeping this biological machine running, Duane recently took his valuable time to explain gunshot wounds and prevented a terrible mistake in the second book of the Red River series, *Burrows*.

Others read and reread this manuscript, and will hopefully be available in the future. Thanks to my oldest daughter Chelsea Wortham Hamilton, high school English teacher and book addict, and her husband Jason. They are experts in continuity and

Chelsea despises adverbs and the passive sentence; Lori Cope, whose OCD in proofing works to my advantage, allowing her to catch the little things that we all miss; finally, my sister-in-law Sharon Reynolds, who also proofs my manuscripts and is so concerned with my sanity that she is convinced The War Department should sleep with a baseball bat beside the bed. Guess she doesn't know what resides under the mattress on that side.

And thanks to all the Readers including Mike Miller (my "sounding board"), who took a chance on this new series.

December 29, 2012
Santa Fe, NM

Chapter One

Constable Cody Parker's phone jangled him from a sound sleep at one in the morning. Without turning on the light, he stumbled out of bed and into the cold hall where their phone rested in an alcove cut into the wall. He answered, and two minutes later hung up without saying anything other than "okay."

Carl Gibbs and his wife, Tamara, were fighting again and, as usual, it had reached a climax well into the night. Being a referee for the combatants had become so commonplace that the young constable automatically dressed in the darkness to keep from waking Norma Faye any more than he already had. Irritated, and in no big hurry to drive into Slate Shoals at that time of the morning, he propped himself against the icebox, took a long gulp from the neck of a milk bottle, and flipped on the porch light to blink in surprise.

It was snowing.

Cody, the young half-Choctaw constable, was born across the river in Grant, Oklahoma. He was raised in the tiny rural community of Center Springs, Texas, ten miles away on the other side of the Red River, where it snowed only half a dozen times in his entire twenty-four years of life.

He recalled the old stories of deep snowfalls and harsh winters thirty years ago during the Great Depression, but accumulating snow had become rare in northeast Texas. Ice storms were a more common occurrence, sometimes piling up to more than a half inch on trees, power lines, and paved roads, knocking out power and causing problems for weeks.

The weatherman said it'd be cold and drizzly. Missed again.

Collar already up against the chill, Cody set his Stetson, took a deep breath of fresh arctic air, and hurried across the yard to his two-tone red-and-white El Camino.

Most folks in Center Springs called it a half-breed truck.

Snow squeaked underfoot with an unfamiliar sound. A small avalanche fell from the vehicle's roof when he opened the door. He dropped heavily into the seat and twisted the key.

Silence.

The battery was deader'n a doornail.

He grunted in frustration. Jumping it off from Norma Faye's red, Plymouth Belvedere wasn't an option in the darkness and freezing weather. Instead, he tromped through ten inches of soft powder to take Norma's car.

The Plymouth started right away with a low grumble. He impatiently punched the high heat control button, knowing he'd be colder than a well-digger's butt for several minutes before the thermostat opened enough to send warmth flowing from the vents.

Cody wasn't comfortable with the unfamiliar new car and the awkward push-button gearshifts on the dash. He preferred a traditional shift lever on the steering column where it belonged, but his new wife's car was his only choice unless he cranked the John Deere and drove the tractor across half the county.

It wouldn't be a bad idea to check the tractor's battery when he got back, either. All this snow guaranteed stuck cars before the day was over.

The snow-covered road was unmarked when he pulled onto the highway. Already frustrated to be out in the worst winter storm in thirty years, Cody unconsciously pressed the accelerator as his anger escalated. He followed his headlights through the storm. Most of the big snowflakes blew over the windshield, but enough began to accumulate that he turned on the wipers.

Minutes later the thermostat opened, the car warmed, and the defroster cleared the glass. The radio's tubes finally warmed enough to blare Jimmy Gilmer and the Fireballs from the speaker. He cranked "Sugar Shack" up to a wide-awake level and squinted through the foggy windshield. A quick swipe cleared a circle to see through.

The snow-covered farm road wound past dark houses illuminated by pole lights, dark barns, and bare hardwoods. Finding the cutoff was difficult. The world slept in a thick coat of white, but he finally recognized the fork divided by a cluster of out-of-place pine trees.

Someone else had been out. An earlier oncoming car had left a U-turn at the fork and cut barely distinct, half-filled tracks, which led the way and gave him something to follow.

Who the hell is out driving in this so early?

The two-lane farm road straightened. He sped up again. The Plymouth's wipers fought a losing battle with the heavy, wet flakes.

Over a small rise, his headlights lit a dark car parked in the oncoming lane, engine idling, blowing white exhaust into the cold air. Behind it, the still noticeable ruts showed an awkward three-point turn, twenty yards from a narrow bridge spanning a spring-fed stream. Obviously he'd been following that car's tracks.

Something was wrong with the entire black-and-white scenario. The sedan was parked in a deadly position. Nearly blinded by the heavy snowfall, a driver coming from behind would only have a second to see the road blocked by a dark car. The only warning would be the taillight reflectors, if they hadn't already been covered by the heavy snow.

I need to check on this.

Taking his eyes off the road to find the shift button, Cody punched it with his thumb and dropped into a lower gear. Quick as a wink, the sudden downshift caused the rear end to break free. He glanced back up to see heavy, black trees pressing in on both sides.

His tires completely lost their grip as he passed the idling car.

Shit!

The other car's windows were fogged all around. The driver had wiped his own circle to see through the windshield. A shadow moved in the back seat behind the driver.

The window slipped down into the door.

Cody gripped the wheel tight as a vise. He steered into the skid taking him toward the ditch, knowing there was no chance to stop the inevitable.

Shitshitshit...

In the other car, a shotgun barrel with a bore big as a stove pipe poked out of the cave-like open window. The primordial fear of the unknown took Cody's breath.

...what the...!!!???

The muzzle belched yellow fire.

Millions of falling snowflakes halted in the brief light.

The image was burned into Cody's memory when the flash momentarily lit the driver's face. Large nose, flat top haircut, and oddly enough, a pair of sun shades resting on top of his head.

...sliding, out of control...

The glass in the Plymouth's door exploded as a full load of 12-gauge pellets barely had time to spread.

Cody instinctively ducked and lost his battle with the skid.

The base coat of ice extended onto the Lower Pine Creek Bridge, but Cody didn't make it that far. The Plymouth shot off the road and punched through the deep snow covering a thick tangle of blackberry vines in an eruption of white. It plunged downward toward the creek with a sickening metallic crack. The drop was steep, but not straight down. The creek bottoms sloped enough for Cody to try steering the car toward a brief opening in the leafless trees that flashed in his headlights.

A mature pecan tree crumpled the right front fender. He rocketed between it and an even larger red oak, which would have folded the car like a tin can had he struck it head on.

Cody pushed one foot hard against the floorboard for stability and the other pumped the useless brake. He fought the wheel to guide the car, but it was nothing more than fruitless determination.

"Goddlemighty!"

What started out like a maneuver in slow motion quickly became a brutal thrashing when Cody realized he was going much too fast. The terrain proved tougher than it looked under the coating of pristine snow. The car jackhammered over hidden logs, hummocks and tangled patches of blackberry vines. The tail swerved and broadsided a thick grapevine that disappeared into the limbs high overhead. Big as Cody's forearm, when the thick vine snapped, the leafless trees overhead thrashed as if a giant's hand had given them a shake. He squirted between more tree trunks, hit a log buried in white, and lifted off into a sudden three-foot drop.

"Shit!"

He stiffened his elbows, knowing what was coming. For a brief moment, something soft and unseen wrapped itself around him, feathery.

Airborne.

The front bumper nose-dived into the frozen ground in an explosion of snow and black dirt. The hood crumpled as it was supposed to, instead of slicing backward and taking off Cody's head. The windshield dissolved into an opaque web of tiny cracks. Momentum sent the rear end into the air and the car flipped once, slamming end over end, stopping with a gut-wrenching bang on the wheels, mere feet from the half-frozen creek.

Silence.

Chapter Two

Cold.

Cody swam through an incredibly chilling fog and struggled awake. He'd never felt anything so numbing in his entire life, not even the time he almost froze to death while elk hunting one clear, Christmas morning as the sun peeked over the Colorado Rockies.

The bedroom was frigid as that high mountain morning. Cody fought to wake up and tell Norma Faye to put another quilt on the bed, or to turn up the heat in their little frame house. He was always after her to turn up the space heaters. For some reason, his wife didn't feel intense cold as much as her husband.

Still cold.

Surely she must be uncomfortable by now.

He stretched out a foot to nudge his wife awake. At least he *tried* to extend his left foot, but it must have gone to sleep on him, because his muscles refused to cooperate.

"Norma Faye."

It came out a softly mumbled, "Naaaafayyy…"

Cody wanted to turn his head so the pillow wouldn't muffle his voice. Fighting unusual grogginess, he slowly realized something was seriously wrong.

He wasn't resting on a nice soft pillow in his house just north of Chisum. A hard and smooth object pressed sharply into the right side of his head. Even worse, he couldn't move to alleviate the pressure.

Surprise jolted Cody fully awake. He blinked to clear his vision and squinted at the nearest barely lit object that didn't belong in their house.

He was looking at an open car door.

He blinked again.

It didn't change.

I must be dreaming.

Now why was there a car door in his bedroom? His eyes took in the broken window, frosty pieces of shattered glass on the arm rest, and a tree limb protruding through the door's interior fabric.

That ain't right.

He squeezed his eyes closed, waiting to clear his mind. When he cracked them again, the strange world within view was startling. No *wonder* he was cold. Snow was everywhere.

Cody picked up sensations.

He moved his eyes. At first, the right one didn't focus properly. Everything was *sideways*. His brain finally adjusted for the light and the strange angle. Cody longed to straighten up and find out what was happening.

Light? Where was light coming from? Good Lord. That's a headlight reflecting off the snow and I'm looking out of Norma Faye's Plymouth!

Because the door was open, the much dimmer dome light was also on, spilling onto the ground, reflecting enough for him to see the nearest drift was disturbed, scarred with debris and clots of black dirt.

Something violent had occurred.

Maybe an explosion.

Maybe a car wreck. He was in the wreckage of Norma's car.

I'm not in bed. I've had an accident!

Then he remembered and once again tried to sit up. "Norma Faye?"

When his feeble whisper barely reached his own ears, Cody knew he was in serious trouble. He couldn't move.

Paralyzed! Oh my god, I've broken my neck!

Only his eyes blinked. Nothing else responded.

The cold penetrated deep into his bones as contradictory sensations sharpened his mind.

Wait a minute. He knew one thing for sure. *People with broken necks can't feel anything at all.*

All right, then.

Fighting to organize his thoughts, Cody closed his eyes and desperately concentrated on being calm. He couldn't lose it. To panic now signaled the beginning of the end. Stay clear and rational to survive.

Think!

Well, if I panic, at least I can't run screaming through the woods and get lost and die.

He opened his eyes again to take stock of the objects in his limited field of vision.

Help!

He noticed his breath as it created a temporary fog.

Think or die!

All right, thinking, or trying to think with that stinkin' radio still going. The music was unrecognizable through a wall of static. *Why didn't I turn it off?*

Wait! Someone shot at me.

He recalled the skid, the window rolling down on the other car, the shot, the final loss of control, the car flipping like a carnival ride gone wrong.

The wreck didn't kill me, so what about the guys with the gun? Maybe they didn't hit me, but that window blowing up in my face likely convinced them that I'm dead, or so near dead that it wasn't worth the trouble to finish the job.

Breathing through his mouth, Cody probed with his tongue to see if any teeth were missing. He almost laughed. It didn't matter if all his teeth were scattered like Chiclets on the dashboard. He couldn't *move*!

A high, piercing resonance filled his ears.

What's that?

He listened, and realized the sound originated from his own throat. It was the sound of a wounded animal. He'd heard it before, from men in Vietnam who thought they were dying.

Calm down and think! Take stock. What do you know?

Well, most likely his nose was broken since he was breathing through his mouth.

Blink.

Both eyes were functioning normally once again.

Blink.

The wind soughing through the creaking trees and the muffled sound of chuckling water told him the car had nearly landed in the creek. He'd fallen a long way. It might take hours for a passing vehicle to notice the tracks where he skidded off the road and hours more for help to arrive, if ever. A rescue party would probably find his rock-hard body frozen behind the steering wheel.

I need to move.

He was paralyzed! How *could* he do anything?

Oh sure, I can think warm thoughts.

Think!

Okay. Hypothermia wasn't an immediate concern. He was dressed for the weather. Because the car was so cold when he left the house, he was still wearing his coat and gloves.

His forehead throbbed from cracking against the steering wheel sometime during the carnival ride through the woods. Luckily it wasn't bleeding too much. Or maybe it had stopped.

Cody thought about that.

Bleeding out from several different places was a distinct possibility, but since he was paralyzed he'd never know until it was too late.

Could he bleed to death before freezing?

No, not when it's so cold. He recalled stories about people who avoided death in the wintertime because blood froze over a wound, sealing it as effectively as if it were cauterized. His own Great-Uncle Melvin survived grievous wounds during the Battle of the Bulge that same way in the intense Belgium cold.

So, I won't bleed out. I still have to worry about freezing, though. Maybe they'll find my tracks soon.

He moved his eyes. There was his shoulder, and his left arm dangling by his side. His right hand lay in his lap, limp and empty. Both legs appeared to be unbroken, but that was a guess and nothing more.

Nausea welled. A wave of dizziness washed over him and he lost consciousness.

When Cody came back, his nose was numb and his ears had lost all sensation. His field of vision hadn't changed while he was out. The door and the trees in the background remained the same, but something was different.

Darker.

Heavier clouds.

Snowing again, covering his tire tracks. They might never find him! Panic rose, but he fought back.

A single tear leaked out and coursed down his cheek.

Think positive.

All right. The headlight is still on. So is the dome light. Maybe someone will see me down here as they pass.

The lights flickered as something shorted out inside the dash. They blinked several more times. When they steadied, the radio static that had been a steady background noise was silenced.

Snow fell once again, a repeat of the near white-out storm that met him that morning. With the radio dead, Cody heard the hiss of heavy snowflakes landing on the trees, the car, and the existing snowpack. He hoped someone had already found the tracks, or maybe saw the accident occur, and were even now organizing a rescue.

Time passed. A dim glow across the creek began to define the snow-laden limbs. Dawn that cloudy morning was only minutes away.

He heard a sound. Not a tree creaking in the wind. It was different...*alive!*

Someone is out there.

"Here!" Cody's attempted shout barely came out a whisper.

Soft footsteps moved around the opposite side of the car. Cody desperately wished to turn his head, move a finger, anything. He most likely appeared dead, and that might cause his rescuer to move even more slowly. "Help," Cody whispered. "Can you hear me?"

The sound stopped.

Listening.

Then it resumed, coming around the front of the car. Cody waited for the person to step into view. A strange snuffling noise reached his frozen ears. He raised his eyes as far as possible to glimpse a frightened, unkempt dog. It was one of those unfortunate animals abandoned in the country by owners who didn't have the guts to put the unwanted dog down, or the sense to know that throwing him out near a farmhouse was a slow death sentence.

With a rush of horror, he realized the huge pit bull had been attracted by the smell of blood. The gaunt animal survived by eating whatever it found.

"Go away. Get out of here!" He barely breathed the words.

The scent of fresh blood drove the starving dog mad. The only thing keeping the dog from immediately attacking was the puzzling and unsettling moans coming from the man, even though he hadn't moved, and that worried it also. Though it sensed he was injured, the man might still be a danger if he wanted to hit, or use the stick that made noise.

It whined and shuffled uncertainly in the snow. The worried animal sensed security in the car. There was familiar warmth in there, too, and shelter from the wet snow.

It crept forward, raising its nose again to sniff past Cody, and then reached toward the gloved hand that was dangling out of his sight.

Cody heard the dog lick tentatively at his bloody fingers. He knew what was coming. "No!" he gasped again, but there was no force behind it.

The dog licked again, reveling in the taste of fresh blood. The rich, life-giving liquid had dripped into the snow. The dog sniffed at the red stain and eagerly lapped at the frozen blood. It bit at the icy clots, cracking them in his teeth like dry dog food.

It wasn't enough. Food!

Bolder now, the desperate animal became more aggressive.

Cody tried to scream away this unimaginable horror.

The result was still another weak utterance not much more than a sigh.

Belly rumbling, the dog took Cody's glove in his mouth and tugged.

No no no no no no...

Shrieking soundlessly, Cody watched his unfeeling left arm pull away and then drop again to his side. Bolder still, the dog bit again and yanked, trying to remove the hand.

The dog hadn't been comfortable in weeks and the thought of a full stomach was nearly driving it crazy. It planted its feet and jerked. Cody's weight shifted and gravity slowly took over.

This can't be happening!

At the sudden movement, the dog tucked its tail and fled a short distance. It whirled in a flurry of snow and watched the man fall heavily into the snow.

Cody landed hard on his left side with his feet still inside the Plymouth, legs tilted upward at an odd angle. His head bounced when it slammed sharply onto a half-buried log in the snow. Sparks flashed before his eyes.

His field of vision was suddenly reduced by more than half. The left side of his face was buried in the icy fluff. Only his right eye revealed his surroundings, the opposite bank of the stream, and the left front tire buried in black loam and dirty snow.

Now that thing has me out of the car! Oh god oh god oh god! My eye's fixin' to freeze harder'n a marble.

The dog approached from behind. Cody closed his eyes, and hoped his weakened system would kill him soon. His mind raced. Wild animals always went for the softer parts first.

Oh Jesus please please don't let me see him chewing I couldn't stand it if I saw it with anything *in its mouth oh please please please I wish I were deaf, too.*

But the dog didn't immediately tear into him.

The one-time pet walked forward on stiff legs, ready to run again. It smelled life in the man that made mewling sounds even though, curiously, he hadn't moved.

Drawn by something as powerful as hunger, the dog crept slowly to the car, stretched carefully over the still body, and lifted its front feet onto the doorsill.

It sniffed.

Quivering, it squatted, moved its back feet nervously on the ground to gain a secure foothold, and jumped into the front seat. The dog moaned in relief as its cold feet touched the still-warm cloth and shivered with delight, soaking up Cody's residual body heat.

What is that thing doing?

For the first time since he was a boy, Cody cried.

Through his terror and silent sobs Cody heard the dog growl, low and menacing.

Muffled swishes more sensed than heard flowed over Cody's prone body. The musty smell of wild animals enveloped him. A pack of wild dogs, once pets themselves, had also scented the blood and wanted it all for themselves. Feet and legs swarmed over Cody and they attacked the first dog.

Suddenly, the world exploded.

Well positioned, First dog fought with determination. The snarling dogs climbed over Cody, but First dog fought back.

Blood flew.

Cody squeezed his eyes shut and desperately willed himself to move, to crawl away, but his damaged body refused to respond.

Overcome with rage, hunger, and bloodlust when they couldn't get into the wrecked car, the excited pack turned on each other. They stumbled over Cody's body as the fight escalated beside the car.

Cody clenched his eyes again as the savage battle rolled over him. He knew their legs and bodies were on his own, but there was no pain with the sensation, only pressure and movement. Snow flew as they sought purchase in the white fluff.

A large toenail tore Cody's cheek open. He felt pain there, and wished he couldn't.

The battle raged until weaker members of the pack yelped in surrender and retreated. Three others tore a smaller shrieking dog apart only feet away from Cody's head. His panic took it all in, while peripherally seeing First dog standing in the driver's seat snarling his defiance at the intruders below.

Emotionally numb, he wished for a quick death. *God I hope they go for the throat so I'll die quicker.*

The victorious alpha dogs of the pack stopped fighting. First dog growled down at them one final time and they feigned disinterest, examining the feast of their former member and the still man's body.

A German Shepherd stepped forward, sniffed at the fresh wound on Cody's cheek, and licked. Bolder, it licked again, and then opened its mouth.

The sharp crack of a rifle startled the pack. The German Shepherd was blown sideways. It kicked twice and was still. A second, almost instantaneous shot caught another dog behind the ear, flipping it end over end. At the third report, First dog leaped through the shattered passenger window and disappeared in the opposite direction. The remainder of the pack scattered and vanished into the gray morning.

Thank God.

Footsteps squeaked in the fresh snow and stopped beside the car.

A gravelly, time-worn voice was the sweetest thing Cody had ever heard.

"You alive, son?"

Chapter Three

Twenty-four hours later, Cody Parker lay in the stark light from a single ceiling fixture. Heavily bandaged and sleeping peacefully in the white enamel-painted, 1930s iron bedstead, his foot twitched.

"That's what we've been waiting for." Dr. Ernie Patterson rubbed his large belly, sighing with relief. "He ain't paralyzed."

Beside the porcelain sink hanging on the wall, Miss Becky Parker raised her right hand and breathed a soft exclamation. "Hallelujah! Praise Jesus!" The tight bun of gray hair she wore on the back of her neck was an outward example of her devotion to the Word clasped in her hands.

Norma Faye sat beside the bed where she'd been since they brought Cody into the hospital room. She laughed in relief, wiped tears from her eyes, then took her husband's limp hand again on top of the covers.

At the foot of the bed, Constable Ned Parker choked down the lump in his throat and stifled the sob that threatened to break through. He cleared his throat, blinked his blue eyes several times, and stared at the bare metal of the crank handle on the bed where many hands across the decades had worn away uncounted coats of paint.

Ned said a silent prayer of thanks.

Everything was monochromatic on that cold winter afternoon. Snow still coated Chisum under a smooth blanket beneath the slate-grey clouds. Inside the hospital room, the white walls were painted with glistening enamel. Tiny black-and-white tiles covered the floor and spread into the hallway where they echoed the quiet footsteps of nuns going about their nursing duties.

The only decorative color was the framed print of a bearded St. Joseph on the wall above Cody's bed.

Half leaning on her husband's bed, redheaded Norma Faye was a burst of color herself. She absently rubbed Cody's right hand which was barely healed from his near-death encounter in the Cotton Exchange two months earlier. He breathed slowly, deeply, from the drugs dripping into his arm.

Ned pondered the round, grey-haired doctor beside him. "That means he's gonna live, right?"

Dr. Patterson lifted the thin blanket to reveal Cody's feet. He took an instrument resembling a fountain pen from his pocket and pulled the dry nib along the sole of one foot, smiling at the tiny reaction.

"Well?" Ned had no patience with doctors, and Ernie Patterson had gotten on his nerves years earlier. Ned felt Patterson should have used some of the money he made as a doctor to straighten his mouth full of crooked teeth.

But it wasn't Ernie's appearance that truly annoyed Ned, or his slow response to the question. It was the place and the situation itself. Ned didn't like hospitals, period.

The nuns in their habits flowed down the halls holding steel trays full of things Ned didn't like the looks of, and didn't understand. He didn't like the glass bottle dangling from a chrome stand by Cody's head, or the tube leading into the crook of his left elbow.

Ned hated needles as much as he hated a crooked lawman.

"I believe he'll be fine, but he won't be hoeing any corn for a good long time." Dr. Patterson replaced the blanket and slipped the pen into the pocket of his white coat. "I suspect most of the paralysis will be gone in a few days. His spine was bruised pretty badly in the wreck, but he's already getting the feeling back in his extremities. That little dab of movement is a good indication the damage to his spinal column was only slight, so yes, I think he'll make a full recovery."

"He'll be fine." Miss Becky squeezed her Bible tightly and gave it a slight shake. "He's on the prayer list at church, and I know the good Lord will take care of him."

Ned thought for a moment. "Well, why ain't he awake?"

"I still have him knocked out, Ned. He may look pretty good, but that wreck damn near killed him. Sorry Becky, I meant, it nearly killed him."

Ned scowled. "He don't look good to me at all for a feller who flipped a car after he was shot at. His head must be a mess under all them bandages."

A thick dressing made Cody's face look lopsided. Two stitches closed the toenail cut on his cheek and a small cut on his scalp. His broken nose was also taped. To Ned, it appeared there wasn't an inch of the young man's face that wasn't damaged.

"Something slapped him pretty hard and he has a little frost-bite on that left ear, but it'll heal all right. I've checked his eyes, and we don't think there's any damage to his sight. We're lucky there. He'll look better when the swelling goes down."

"He needs to rest now." Norma Faye used her free hand to tuck a renegade curl of long red hair behind one ear. They'd been married for less than a year, but she'd settled into the family faster than anyone expected, despite the scandal she and Cody had created when they started seeing each other. "Where's James and Ida Belle?"

"Downstairs with the kids." Miss Becky's thumbs uncon-sciously worried at the worn leather of the Bible's cover. "They'll be up directly, when we leave. Top and Pepper wanted to come up here in the worst way, but one of them nuns said kids weren't allowed on this floor."

"I'll bring them up later if I want to." Ned scowled and fiddled with the stained felt Stetson in his weathered hands. "Nuns or not."

Norma Faye always wanted the kids close. "Where are they now?"

Ned shifted from one foot to the other to ease the ache in his knees. "Either in the waiting room, or outside throwing snowballs, I reckon."

"Top had that case he's been carrying. They're probably playing secret agent, like on that television show they've been watching."

The idle conversation was a relief valve, of no consequence, but it briefly took their minds off Cody's condition.

Worn out from sitting at the hospital since they brought Cody in, Norma Faye softly stroked Cody's hand with her painted fingernails. Miss Becky didn't like such vain foolishness one bit, though it was slightly less sinful than makeup, in her opinion, but she held her tongue.

"You need for me to do anything, sweetie?" Ned hated to stand around and do nothing. "I'll bring you some dinner if you want, later."

Norma Faye smiled, the corners of her eyes crinkling. "I'm not a bit hungry. They have a little café in the basement if I need anything, but I want to be here when he wakes up."

Patterson grunted and flipped a page on Cody's chart. "He ain't gonna wake up for a long while. I'm gonna keep him sedated until tomorrow at the earliest."

"Hon, you go on home and get some rest. I'll sit with Cody tonight." Miss Becky didn't intend for it to come out like an order, but it sounded like one just the same.

Norma Faye didn't take her eyes off her husband. "That's all right. I'd sit around the house and worry if I did, instead of sleeping. We'll stay here together, though, if you want to."

Relief washed through Miss Becky at the offer, and the bond that had been a long time coming finally solidified. "I believe I'll do that." She placed her Bible on the tiny counter beside the sink and removed her car coat and scarf. "Norma Faye, you go downstairs and get you a sandwich. Go on. Right now. I'm gonna sit right here with Cody while he sleeps and talk to the Lord for a bit."

The redhead had never seen Miss Becky take charge with such authority and truthfully, she *was* hungry. She slipped quickly out of the chair to let Miss Becky sit beside Cody. "I'll go meet James and Ida Belle. I bet the kids want something, too."

Miss Becky's hand lingered on Ned's coat sleeve for a moment as she and Norma Faye switched places. "Daddy, you said you wanted to see O.C. Why don't you run on over to the courthouse for a while and then come back by here before you go home. Cody's liable to be awake by then even though Ernie here said he'd sleep all night."

Dr. Patterson frowned, though he didn't say a word. He'd known Becky Parker since they were kids. He was two years younger, and she'd always treated him like a baby brother.

Surprise registered on Ned's face. His full-blood Choctaw wife didn't usually order *him* around, and seldom in front of anyone else. But the idea was sound. Ned wanted to visit Judge O.C. Rains about the attack on Cody.

Norma Faye stopped beside him and took his arm to walk with him down the hall. Ned started to leave, and then paused. "All right then, but y'all call over to the courthouse if anything changes."

"I will." Miss Becky studied the doctor. "Ernie Patterson, I've knowed you since we were kids. You put down that chart and tell me every little thing that's wrong with this boy, and don't give me any of them ten-dollar words when you're-a-doin' it."

"Well, Becky, there isn't much more than I've already told you."

"Tell me again what you know and what you think. I'll sort it all out in my mind in a little bit."

Dr. Patterson sighed. "Well, we dug out a couple of buckshot pellets in his left shoulder that didn't do much damage except to the tissue. The wreck threw him around in the car and his spine got hurt. It's like it's bruised, or stunned. These things can be temporary, or they can be permanent. I was pretty worried at first, and thought he'd be paralyzed, but now it looks like his body is coming to. I think he'll be all right, but it'll take time and we'll have to watch him. Now, that's all I know and I can't tell you anything else."

Ned put on his hat. "He's lucky he ain't dead. I intend to find out who did this and bring them in. Patterson, you be sure to call the courthouse if anything goes wrong."

Miss Becky'd had enough. "Ned, you go on. Norma Faye'll feed the kids and James and Ida Belle will be up here directly."

Constable Ned Parker took one more look at Cody and gladly escaped the room. He intended to get to the bottom of what had happened out on that country road.

His wife's voice chased him down the hallway.

"Now, Ernie, I believe you're leaving something out and I want to hear it. How bad are them holes in his shoulder and don't you lie to me…"

Chapter Four

Bitter cold and Ned Parker blew together into the Lamar County courthouse through the glass and brass doors. The foyer smelled of law books, wood polish, and bleach. He had a clear line of sight down the tiled hallway and into the open courtroom. Judge O.C. Rains scowled down at a sullen defendant from his high perch behind the bench. Ned's footsteps echoed on the hard walls as he approached the judge's court.

Ahead, a slouching young deputy, J.T. Boone, straightened up and faced outward toward the approaching constable. Ned unbuttoned his barn coat as he neared the courtroom door. Inside, Judge O.C. glanced out to see his old friend coming down the hall.

"Your Honor?"

O.C.'s attention shifted from Ned back to the attorney and his sullen defendant standing below. "Hum?"

"My client pleads not guilty."

"And he wants a trial, I assume?"

"Yessir."

The judge glared down at the disheveled man slouched in front of the bench. Badly in need of a haircut and shave, the defendant wiped his enormous nose with the back of a cuffed hand and frowned at his worn-out brogans.

"Carl, you want twelve people in this town to hear your little wife tell how you beat her with...," he glanced at the charges through a pair or reading glasses perched on the end of his nose. "…a *singletree*? Good god, man, I wouldn't hit a *mule* with a singletree."

The wooden crossbar of a horse harness was the equivalent of using a two-by-four.

"You don't know what that woman's like, O.C. She'll *provoke* you."

"You'll address me as Judge or Your Honor, Carl, or I'll slap a contempt of court on you so fast it'll make your head swim. I don't care if you *are* a fourth cousin. Tamara don't weigh much more than a sack of flour and she ain't no bigger than a minute. Now, if there'd been a *hame* close by, the charges might not be…"

The conversation drifted over Ned when he was no more than four feet away from the courtroom. He paid little attention to the discussion, even though the mention of a much smaller piece of curved wooden horse collar was wildly out of place in a courthouse. He nodded hello to the soft-looking deputy who frowned and partially blocked the door.

"You'll have to remove your hat to enter the courtroom, Buddy."

The experienced constable stopped and immediately felt his face flush as heat exploded throughout his body. Ned's icy-blue eyes settled on the stubborn and quite possibly slow-thinking young man standing in his way. "*What'd* you say?"

Though the constable's voice was low, it obviously reached the judge's ears. O.C. held up a hand to silence the two men before him.

Annoyed by the elderly farmer standing before him in overalls and a stained, well-used canvas barn coat, Deputy Boone pointed a finger. "I said take your hat off. You can't enter the judge's courtroom with your hat on, Buddy."

It was almost too much for Ned to take. He drew a deep sigh to gather himself. "Son, I don't know who you are, but you're still too wet behind the ears to tell me my manners. Now first off, my name ain't *Buddy*, and if you call me that again, I'll slap you so hard you'll see stars."

When the deputy's face hardened, Ned pointed a finger right between his eyes. "Now, about my hat, young'un. I been in and out of this courtroom since your *daddy* was draggin' at the tit, and I knew what to do way back before then."

"You still have to remove your hat to enter the judge's courtroom, old timer. You ought to know something like that," Boone continued, as if he hadn't heard Ned's response.

This time Ned's eyes flashed, and from across the courtroom O.C. watched as something bad was about to happen to his new bailiff. Instead of intervening, O.C. expected the young man to learn a lesson about people.

Ned reached for the leather sap in his back pocket, but realized what he was doing. The stress and worry over Cody and his brutal attack weighed on him more than he realized, and he didn't need to be whacking on a discourteous deputy with the leather-covered chunk of lead. Taking a deep, calming breath, he moved closer to the deputy and opened his canvas barn coat to reveal the tiny constable's badge pinned on his shirt, right beside the wrinkled gallus of his overalls.

"Now you listen real good, son. My name is Ned Parker, not old timer, nor Buddy, nor Mr. Sonofabitch! I've been constable of Precinct Three since nineteen and thirty, which means I was raised by folks who taught me manners, something I can tell *you* don't have."

With mounting fury, he stabbed a stiff finger in the bailiff's chest and pushed close enough that he stepped back. Ned's presence suddenly filled the deputy's view as if a mad brahma bull had just charged into the courthouse.

"I had already intended to take my hat off, when I go through there and not one second sooner, because my manners tell me a man can wear a hat indoors in the hallway of a public building, if he wants to. Now, you got exactly one second to get out of my way or I'll walk right over your prissy little ass."

The bailiff squinted at the badge and he found himself afraid to meet Ned's flashing eyes. He flushed and stepped to the side.

Ned brushed past, nearly knocking the bailiff off balance with his shoulder, and removed his hat as he entered the courtroom.

O.C. held out a hand to stop Ned from sitting in the galley, and addressed the prisoner standing below. "All right, Carl, you get your wish. Trial is set thirty days from today at nine in the morning, so you get to tell your side of the story. Until then, you can post bail or sit in jail. That's up to you."

"What's my bail?"

"One thousand dollars. Now, we'll take a twenty-minute recess."

"Damn, O.C., that's too much!"

"Watch your language. Now it's two thousand."

"Oscar! We're kinfolk!"

"You pronounce that name one more time and I'll make it three thousand!" O.C. rapped his gavel, threw it down with a clatter, and stood to leave the courtroom.

"All rise!" Boone called from over Ned's shoulder.

O.C. pointed at Ned. "My office." He disappeared through the back door into the hallway.

Ned passed the bench, glared at Carl for fighting with his little wife, and tailed O.C. into the hallway. The judge was already standing in front of the courthouse's only elevator when Ned joined him.

"I thought you were fixin' to shoot Boone." O.C. pushed the button and the bell dinged almost immediately.

"Who?"

"That new deputy out there."

"So that's his name. Yeah, I thought about caving in his damn fool head, *Oscar*."

Before O.C. had time to scold Ned for using his Christian name, the elevator creaked to a stop and Jules the elevator man opened the doors. Old Jules, as he was known, had served as the elevator operator since before anyone could remember. He once told Ned that his mama was born a slave on a plantation in southern Mississippi.

He waved a greeting from his perch on his wooden stool beside the control panel. "Mr. Ned, Judge O.C."

They stepped aboard and waited for Jules to close the doors, then the accordion safety gate. He pushed the button with an arthritic thumb and for once stepped beyond his own self-established boundaries. They usually talked of his eleventh wife, Lily, but there was sadness in his watery eyes. "Mr. Ned, I'm worried plumb sick about Mr. Cody."

"He's gonna be fine, Jules." Ned gave him a familiar pat on the shoulder. "And you can call him Cody. He'll earn a Mister when he grows up some more."

"Nawsir, Mr. Cody's jus' fine by me, if that's all right. You let me know if there's anythang I can do for him. I'll send him a mincemeat pie if it'll make him feel any better."

"I'll check with him and see what he's hungry for, when he wakes up. The doctor says he'll be fine."

The shaky elevator vibrated to a stop and Jules opened the gate and door. "You want me here in twenty minutes, Judge?"

Without wondering how Jules knew he'd called a recess, O.C. nodded. "Twenty it is."

"All right then."

For the first time in several months, Judge O.C. Rains didn't have a wire flyswatter on his desk when Ned followed him through the office door.

O.C. scowled and threw his robe over the back of a quarter-sawn oak chair piled with papers. "Close the damn door. Were you raised in a barn? That outside office is colder than a well-digger's ass." He stretched back in his matching wooden desk chair and folded his fingers across an almost flat stomach.

Ned always thought O.C. was poor as a snake. Most people said the cantankerous old judge was slim, but to Ned's eye, he was too skinny to be in good health. "I reckon it's because there's over two feet of snow on the ground and the temperature is still in the teens."

"Yep. Haven't seen weather like this since before the war." O.C. pondered the snowdrift on the granite windowsill.

"Who's that little pissant you got working for you out there?"

"Aw, don't be too hard on the kid, Ned. J.T. Boone's so green the sap's running out of his ears, but I figured to let him help me out here for a while until he gets some experience."

"If he lives long enough."

O.C. sighed. "Ain't it the truth? One of these days he'll learn how to stay out of the way of irritable constables. I believe Sheriff Griffin will have him out of my court room and in a car purty soon. How's Cody?"

Ned pitched his felt hat on O.C.'s cluttered desk and sat in the only chair that wasn't full of stacked papers. His eyes burned for a moment in the presence of his lifelong friend. It was the only emotion he allowed himself, other than a barely-corralled temper.

He cleared his throat to relieve the ache. "He…" Ned paused when his voice broke, swallowed, and tried again. "He ain't worth a fiddler's fang-dang right now, but Doc Patterson says he'll be fine after a while. His arms and legs are starting to work, but he still ain't awake."

Choking down a lump in his own throat, O.C. unconsciously twisted back and forth in his swivel chair. "He's tough. I went by to set with him this morning before I came in." O.C.'s speech pattern wandered without conscious thought or restraint between his college education and country roots. "That redheaded wife of his was sitting beside the bed, holding his hand and talking quiet to him. I don't think she even knew I was standing in the door. She'd been there since they brought him in, but I'god that little gal was fresh as a morning shower."

They sat in silence for several long moments. Ned took off his coat as the temperature in O.C.'s office burned away the chill. Resting both elbows on his knees, he laced his fingers and studied the purple thumbnail he'd injured when he slammed a garden gate on it.

The judge twiddled his thumbs and rocked in nervous habit. "It was an ambush. Some of the boys came in after they investigated the scene and towed what was left of the kids' Plymouth out of the creek bed."

"The boys" were O.C.'s constables and the few highway patrol officers he trusted. One or two Chisum sheriff deputies were thrown in the mix the judge relied on, but he was cautious with them since they answered to Sheriff Griffin. Neither man in the chilly, cluttered office had any use for the sheriff, who was more politician than lawman.

O.C. continued to rock in the creaking chair. "They found what was left of the car tracks in the snow."

"How'd they do that?"

"The ground wasn't completely froze when the car drove over the snow, and it packed the tracks down into ice. The falling snow didn't completely cover the tire marks. In the daylight you could still barely see the ruts. So they used a broom and swept the loose snow away to where it melted under the exhaust pipe and then refroze when they left."

"I'll be damned."

"Yep. It sat in the road for a *while*, waiting for Cody to come by. When he did, somebody put a load of buckshot through the side glass, then drove away as pretty as you please."

"How'd they know it was Cody in the Plymouth? I'd imagine anyone after him was probably lookin' for that half-breed car of his instead of a red four-door sedan."

"Jack Smalls is the best investigator in Lamar County, and he was helped by W.B. Graves who's a good man from the Texas Rangers. They decided that the shot came almost too late. Jack figured he was waiting for the El Camino and didn't recognize Cody until he was almost past."

"Prob'ly the only reason he lived."

"I'm sure of it. It's a miracle most of the pellets missed, but it was enough to do the job. Cody's a lucky man."

Ned's face reddened. Someone had nearly killed a member of his family and his dander was up. "He wasn't found by no highway patrol. I heard it was somebody we don't know."

"Yep. Feller old as Methuselah named Tom Bell happened along while a pack of wild dogs was fightin' over what they reckoned was Cody's dead body. The story I got was that Tom came across a set of half-covered tracks skidding off down into the creek. They was fairly fresh, so he stopped and went down to check.'"

"What makes you think he didn't do the shootin' hisself?"

"'Cause Tom carries a beat-up Winchester carbine, killed two of them dogs that was about to eat Cody, then drug him up the bank to his truck. I don't see how he did it at his age, but he's tough as boot leather. Drove him into town, too, straight to the hospital door like he knew what he was a-doin.'"

"I don't recognize the name."

"You won't. He only moved out there to Center Springs a week or so ago. I doubt you've seen him yet. I hear he's bought the Buchanan place not far from your house and intends to fix it up."

The information was startling. The Buchanan house was within hollering distance from Ned's farm, and he didn't know anyone had moved in. "That place is about to fall down, but I don't reckon he'll do much fixin' if he's that old."

"Like I said, he's in pretty good shape. I imagine he'll go at it pretty slow."

"What was *he* doing out on that road that time of the morning? That don't smell right to me."

"I didn't think so neither, 'til they called up here a little bit before dinner and cleared him. W. B. told Jack everything about Tom's story checked out with the Rangers. He cain't sleep but two or three hours at a stretch, and when he woke up before daylight, it was snowing. He's lived his whole life down in the Valley, and he ain't never seen snow except on television and in movies.

"His pappy brought him here to Lamar County when he was a baby. That figures to be about eighteen eighty or so, if my cipherin' is right. But they left for south Texas before he was big enough to crawl. Anyways, he wanted to get out in the snow that mornin'. Said he drove over toward Slate Shoals 'cause he thought the country might be close to like what he'd left, and that put him by the creek at the right time."

Ned's brow wrinkled. "Sounds kinda fishy to me, O.C. God-damnit, who the hell goes around in the dark of the mornin' to look at snow?"

"Well hell, Ned, you'd argue with a fence post," O.C. shot back. "I reckon a man who wakes up about the same time as you and ain't seen snow in his whole life might want to get out in it first thing of a morning. There was enough light for him to see to shoot, so it wasn't like he was out driving at midnight. The boys say he's all right. And unless I hear something different, or you find out something I don't know, his story'll *stand*."

The white-haired judge was sympathetic toward his childhood friend who stared stubbornly at his hands. "Ned, he saved Cody's *life*. That boy mighta froze to death, or been et by them hungry dogs if Tom hadn't come along when he did."

Ned felt a little better. "Well, all right then. I'll drop by there in a day or two and thank him."

"You do that." The relief was evident in O.C.'s voice. "But you'll have to wait a while. He's already left for the Valley again to handle some business."

"That sounds like runnin' to me."

"Naw, I talked to W.B. about it and he said it was all right. W.B.'s word's good as gold to me. My boys are still investigatin' and when Cody wakes up, we'll talk to him. Maybe he'll remember something they can use."

Ned rubbed a rough palm over his bald head, as he did when frustrated, or thinking. "I'll do a little looking myself."

"I know. Maybe you'll find something out. I want somebody's ass in jail for trying to shoot one of my constables, and not because he's Cody, neither. You be careful yourself. We don't know why they tried to kill him, and they may have it in for you, too. You've been on the wrong side of *that* fence before."

"Well, I ain't worried, but I'll see what I can find out."

"I know you will, but bring them in and I'll deal with 'em."

The silence hung heavy between the two men for several long moments as they remembered the same incident with heavy hearts.

"They hurt that boy, O.C., and I intend to do something about it." Ned stood and picked up his hat.

"I know."

"I tell you, this world's gone to hell in a handbasket. The outlaws are getting out as fast as we put 'em in jail, and now that they're doing away with chain gangs, we're gonna have more trouble than anyone ever bargained for."

"You ain't a-kiddin.'" O.C. shifted his weight and the chair creaked. "You didn't see many men come back for a second round on a road crew. It cured a lot of meanness over the years."

"It did. I'll bring 'em in if I can, but you understand they don't deserve a spot even on a chain gang for something like this. Some people just…"

"…need killin'. Shut the door behind you."

"I always do, and quit ordering me around like a pup. I've had enough of that already this morning, between your new deputy and Miss Becky. You mess with me, and I'll open a couple of winders out here on my way out."

"Don't forget your coat, you damned fool. You'll catch double pneumonia out there and won't be worth a nickel to me if you're sick. And besides, I keep smelling cow shit and I bet it came in with you."

Ned slammed the door and O.C. chuckled.

He loved to jab his old friend.

Chapter Five

Pepper tugged at her pony tail like she wanted to pull it out by the roots. "I hate hiding out in this damned stupid tree."

My eleven-year-old, near-twin girl cousin and I were about to go crazy with nothing to do. Pepper cusses worse than any man I ever heard, and it keeps her in trouble more times than she can count. Sometimes her breath smells like Lifebuoy toilet soap when she comes to visit.

The snow was long gone two months after Uncle Cody got out of the hospital and weather had warmed up enough for the trees to leaf out.

We were sitting in what passed for our tree house so Miss Becky couldn't put us to work cleaning house or hoeing in her garden. The house was clear from our perch, but Miss Becky couldn't find us through the leaves, though I didn't doubt she had an idea where we were.

The summer before, I nailed a few planks across two limbs in the giant red oak on top of a little hill a hundred yards from the barn. When it was finished, the disappointing tree house was nothing more than a platform, far from what I'd imagined.

For the past month I'd been trying to talk Pepper into building a bigger tree house with me. I wanted to use the wood stacked up under one wing of the hay barn that was from another barn Grandpa tore down before we were born. The oak planks were hard as iron, and driving a nail through them took about fifty hits each. I knew that from experience, because from time to time I got an urge to build things.

I wanted a sprawling tree house like I read about in *Swiss Family Robinson*. I'd been working through that book for about two weeks and liked it a lot, other than the folks back then tended to talk loud all the time. When they said something, they cried this, and then they cried that. We don't take much to hollerin' in Lamar County, unless it's when Miss Becky is calling us for supper.

Our tree house came out to be a triangle, since we'd started cutting boards to fit the fork of the tree near the trunk and it widened out a considerable ways. We were sitting on the first platform in that red oak, and I was thinking about starting another halfway around the tree, where two limbs grew straight out from the giant trunk. But then I'd still have two flat spots and no walls or roof.

"I'm tired of this," Pepper complained.

"Well, that's 'cause you're a girl. I intend to build this house in six levels, with swinging ropes and running water and a roof that we can sit under when it rains."

"You don't know nothing about that. We'll build a bunch of damn floors that look like a piece of splintery pie and pretty soon you'll get tired too. Let's find something fun to do instead of sitting here on our asses and talking about building shit."

"Like what?"

"Well, we can play secret agent some more. I love that new Johnny Rivers song."

We watched Secret Agent every time it came on TV. I'd decided I wanted to be a spy, and made a secret agent case like the ones they advertised on the commercials. Miss Becky had a small stained pasteboard suitcase I made up with compartments to be like those guys on television. I'd even cut a hole in one end and wired Miss Becky's German camera to shoot pictures out of the case. It worked pretty well and I'd already shot some pictures of people who didn't know I was doing it.

Uncle James brought the little camera home from Germany when he got out of the army. He sent back a lot of other stuff too, that I wanted to use in my spying, like the giant glass radio that could pick up broadcasts from across the oceans. When I was real little, he sent me a windup tank that I still kept in a box under the bed.

Pepper's mood was taking the wind out of me. "We've played secret agent so much lately that I'm getting tired of it. Besides, I'm out of film. I still have that roll that needs developing. I shot the last few pictures in town the day it snowed and Uncle Cody got hurt."

She gave up on pulling herself bald and hung her legs off the wide of the tree house. "Well, I'm tired of doing nothing."

"Let's make some tom-walkers."

Tom-walkers are tin can stilts made by punching two holes in the sides of #10 tomato cans with a nail with a piece of long string through them, forming a loop. To use them, you stand on the upside-down can and hold the long loops in your hands to pull them up tight to your feet.

"Naw, I don't want to walk around on top of some old tin cans…wait a minute." She held up a hand to make me stop talking. "Is somebody shooting?" We heard guns going off nearly every day, so it wasn't a big deal, except the hard thumps came quickly.

I stood up to see through the new leaves, toward the south. "Naw, that's somebody hammering on something, you dummy. It sounds like it's coming from the Buchanan place."

"Don't call me dummy, butthole."

The hammering wasn't long and steady like ours. Each time it started with two soft hits, and then three more hard ones. "Let's go see what they're doing." I stepped carefully off the boards and onto a long limb that stretched out and down, almost to the ground.

My dog, Hootie, was waiting for us. He'd already checked the pasture for birds and was lying beside the trunk. We straddled the limb like a horse and worked our way down until our weight lowered it enough for us to drop the last six inches or so. I was particularly careful, since I fell out of a tree back in November and broke my arm. It had healed all right, but it was still a little stiff at times.

With nothing else to do, we tore off across the pasture toward Center Springs Branch, the clear water namesake for our little country community. The barbed wire fence barely slowed us down and we sprinted across the empty two-lane highway. Hootie ran circles around us, jumping and playing in excitement.

Even though the Buchanan place sat on a little rise, you couldn't see the house from the highway because of all the woods growing thick and tall. Beyond the trees, a worn-out plank corral rotted down right beside the barn that needed a lot of work.

Pepper and I had been all through the two-story house a bunch of times, because it had been empty for so long. I never asked anyone, but it looked to us like the folks who once lived there just up and walked away one day, leaving everything behind.

Inside, we found rotting clothes, pots, pans, dishes, rusty bedsteads and even a three-door oak icebox, the kind where you put a chunk of ice inside to keep things cool. It stood nearly as tall as the top of my head, and one time Pepper dared me to get in it. She closed the door and left me in there for five minutes, kicking and screaming to get out. When she finally yanked at the latch to open the door, I was mad and crying. I intended to fist-whip her when my feet hit the floor, but I had an asthma attack so bad I couldn't do anything but suck on my puffer for half an hour.

That was all before the Incident that started only a hundred yards or so from the Buchanan place.

I shivered at the recollection. It was the first time we'd been so close to Center Springs Branch where we'd been taken by The Skinner less than a year ago. What folks called our "emotional scars," and the very real scar burned into Pepper's shoulder, were barely healed on both of us.

We still talked about it some, when folks weren't nearby, and that helped us feel better.

The hammering continued to draw us like a magnet.

We walked past the sagging barn, where the owner once kept mules and horses to pull his plows. A stiff, dried-up harness hung from one of the warped rafters, and beside it was a newer set of leathers. There were still a few folks in Center Springs who knew how to hitch up a plow horse. Grandpa was one of them.

Even though it was 1966 and people were flying around in space capsules, Grandpa used Lightning to break up the garden twice a year, more to keep in practice than anything else.

A wiry white-haired man in Wrangler jeans and a western shirt was bent over the porch with his back to us, driving a nail into the wood with hard strikes of his hammer. A black hat hung on a nail beside the door, and I immediately knew he was as close to a real cowboy as any man I'd ever seen.

He somehow knew we were behind him and tensed for a second when we stopped. He took a couple of nails out of his mouth, turned around, and smoothed his thick white mustache with a forefinger. "Howdy, young'uns. Who'r you?"

Pepper jabbed a thumb in my direction. "This is Top and I'm Pepper."

"With that cotton top of his, I suspect I should call y'all Salt and Pepper. Y'all twins?"

"Nossir, cousins, but we're right about the same age, though I'm a little bit older than him."

"Only by a few days," I argued.

"Who's that?" He pointed to Hootie, who sat down right by his feet and stared upward like he was waiting for a biscuit.

Hootie was a good judge of character, and if he went that close, then I figured the man was all right. "That's Hootie. He's my bird dog."

"He's a fine looking pup. Who do you belong to?"

I didn't want to get into one of those tangled family explanations, so I piped up before Pepper could start unraveling our whole string. "We're Ned Parker's grandkids."

He nodded. "That'd make you kin to Constable Cody Parker, too."

His voice was soft, kinda raspy way in the back, but it was strong and you knew he had a whole lot of bottom in him. That's what Grandpa says about anyone who's solid, and not frail or sickly.

"Yessir."

"Good to meet you. You in law work, too?"

I gave him a grin for his ribbing. "Some day."

"I bet you're right. I'm Tom Bell."

Mr. Bell didn't carry an ounce of fat under a thatch of thick, white hair, and still had every one of his own teeth, that I could see. He stuck out a leathery hand and I shook it with a firm grip, like Uncle Cody taught me. He let me know that he was satisfied with the way I shook.

He had a set of downright interesting peepers. They were wide and glassy, as if he was fighting mad. But at the same time, even though they might bore a hole right through you, his eyes didn't appear dangerous...right then.

On top of that, I didn't see a hint of a smile, but he didn't look aggravated or anything. You could bet your boots that he'd have that same look even when he was mad enough to spit nails. He was a matter-of-fact man, and all business. I knew men like him in Center Springs.

I took an instant liking to Mr. Tom.

He clasped Pepper's hand with both of his for a moment, a little softer. "Y'all c'mon and let's sit a spell. I need to blow for a minute." He waved a hand toward four straight-backed, cane-bottom chairs on the new part of his porch. On the opposite side, all the boards were gone, and spider webs connected the floor joists with the dirt below them.

The front door was open to the living room and revealed the most cluttered house I'd ever seen. There were all manner of household items stacked up head high. Furniture, a trunk, farm tools, harnesses, cowboy clothes, saddles, walking sticks, and fishing and hunting gear all looked like it had been pitched out of a truck to land right where it was. Some of it was out of place in our part of the world, because as he told us later, everything in the house came from the Valley.

He meant the Rio Grande Valley way down south, the Texas border between us and Mexico. I'd heard of it, and was surprised to hear a white man say he'd lived down there. I thought the whole place was Mexicans. From time to time someone came back from a visit down there with a truck load of watermelons, cantaloupes, or fruit like oranges and grapefruit that we couldn't grow up in *our v*alley up on the Red River.

Above us, raw new rafters waited for boards to shade the porch. The sun shot straight through and made it warm and comfortable. Mr. Bell lifted the dipper from the white enamel water bucket beside his chair and took a long, loud swaller. He sounded like a horse, gulping down that water, and Pepper's eyes crinkled when she got tickled at the noise. A big faded sticker on the side said, "Federal Enamel Bucket as Advertised in LIFE."

He pitched the last few drops out in the yard and offered the dipper to me before he sat down. I wasn't thirsty, but I dipped out some cold water from around a floating chunk of ice, and drank to be neighborly. I put the empty dipper back in the bucket.

It annoyed Pepper that I didn't hand it to her. "You could have offered me a drink."

"You know where it is."

Mr. Bell's eyes twinkled. He tilted his chair back on two legs against the unpainted house boards. "You two sound like me and my sister when I was your age, son. She was a ring-tailed tooter if there ever was one."

"That'd be *her*." I jerked my thumb at Pepper. Before she could work up a mad, I changed the subject. I'd heard Mr. Bell's name when Grandpa and the other men were talking about Uncle Cody's ambush. "Are you the one who saved our Uncle Cody?"

"Depends on how you look at it. I found him in that creek bottom a few weeks ago. I reckon it was the doctor saved him after he got to the hospital, right? How's he doing?"

"He's fine," Pepper said. She had a real soft spot for Uncle Cody. "He's home now and getting better every day."

"You shot them dogs that were about to eat him."

Mr. Tom didn't say anything for a minute, like he was choosing his words carefully. Then he nodded at me. "He was in a tight and I did what was necessary to get him out of it. Never liked to see a lawman in any kind of trouble. Goes against the grain, right?"

Being "in a tight" was an old fashioned phrase from up on the river that meant someone was in trouble. I was surprised to hear it used by a man who'd lived somewhere else all his life. "Did you know he was the law when you shot that dog?"

The skin around his eyes flickered at the question. He didn't expect a kid to turn the conversation back around to clear up a point. "Nossir, I sure enough didn't. But I saw his badge right quick when I picked him up, along with that pistol on his hip."

"Well, Grandpa says you saved his life. He'd been dog-et, or froze to death, if it hadn't been for you."

"I did what was necessary. You'll do the same, once you get growed, when the time comes."

We sat quietly until I finally found something to say. "You rebuild this whole house?"

"Yep. I intend to bring it back to the way it was when I was a baby."

Pepper's eyes widened. "You lived here? That must have been a hundred years ago."

He didn't bat an eye. "Sure did. That was over *eighty* years ago, instead of a hundred, but I wasn't much more than a tadpole when we left. I'd barely lost my tail. My daddy took a notion to live down in the Valley and that's where we stayed until I bought this place a few months back and decided to retire here, right?"

"Retire from what?"

"Work."

Pepper didn't like it that he kept his personal life to himself, but I didn't want her to make him mad.

"What you're doing now looks like work to me. I can help you if you want."

"You know anything about construction?"

"He thinks he does." Pepper spoke up. "He's always building something. Grandpa says if he don't quit wasting his lumber he's gonna wear his tail out."

Mr. Bell's eyes softened. "I reckon we'll have to save your sitter. You'll need to come over here and help me drive a few nails, then."

"You mean it?"

"Sure do. I can always use a good hand, 'cause there are certainly things a man my age cannot do, but a young person can, right?"

"Can I help too?"

He gave Pepper a steady gaze. "Can you use a hammer too?"

"Nope. I'll bend the nail every time."

"She don't hold the handle right," I pitched in.

"That's all right. She can do other work, then. Missy, I imagine you know tools, and you can fetch for us if we need it, right, and measure?"

"Sure."

"Well, y'all need to ask your grandpa, so he'll know where you are. Your folks don't know much about me and a stranger moving into town is always suspicious until everybody gets to know him, right? Now, you two run along and tell your grandpa where you've been and that it'd be a pleasure to visit with him. He and I'll meet up sometime soon and get to know one another."

We were dismissed, most likely because Mr. Tom wanted to get back to work. "I can bring my own hammer next time."

"That'll be fine. A man ought to bring his own tools to a job."

"I don't have any tools," Pepper said.

"That'll be fine, too. You bring yourself and I'll put you to work, if Miss Becky says it's all right."

I stopped on the end of the half-finished porch. "You know Miss Becky?"

"I make it a point to know about my neighbors, son."

"So you knew who we were when we got here?"

"I had an idea."

I didn't want to leave. For the first time in my life I was fascinated by someone other than Grandpa and Uncle Cody. But he was already measuring another 2x6 with a tape and a thick yellow carpenter's pencil.

He was through sawing the joist before we were halfway down the overgrown lane full of green grass and weeds. The sound of hammering followed us back to the highway. Hootie loped ahead, sticking his nose into every clump of grass he found. A pair of quail whirred out from under the overgrown barbed wire fence beside the two-lane track in front of us.

"You didn't cuss one time while we were talking to Mr. Tom, right?"

Pepper grinned at how I made fun of Mr. Tom's mannerisms. "Course I didn't, dumbass, right? I liked that old son of a bitch too much to cuss around him, and besides…," she shivered. "Did you see his eyes?"

Chapter Six

The next morning, Miss Becky cracked two eggs into the iron skillet on the stove as Ned came in from feeding the cows. "Did you meet that new man who moved into the Buchanan place?"

"Yep, seemed like a nice enough feller."

"I hear he was borned there."

"How'd you know that?" Ned was annoyed that she knew just as much as he did.

"Lizzie told me when I went visitin' yesterday. Poor thing lays in that bed all day with her mind a million miles away while Harold sits on the porch and spits. She said her family knew his daddy and mama when they lived here, but that was so long ago she could barely remember."

Ned grunted. "Well, she seems to remember a lot when she wants to. How could her mind be a million miles away when she knows more about what's going on than us?"

"It comes and goes. We're all in and out over there every day to make sure she's all right. Harold ain't much for changing her, nor bathin' her neither."

"Well, I'll go over myself and see if I can lay eyes on this feller."

"You do that, and see if he wants to come to dinner. We need to be good Christian neighbors."

"Umm humm."

Half an hour later, Constable Ned Parker pulled his sedan in front of the Buchanan place, stopping several yards short because of the lumber and building materials stacked there. He killed the engine and studied the completely new, rebuilt porch. Instead of immediately getting out, he waited to see if any yard dogs were laying under the porch. Country folks knew better than to get out of the car at a strange house.

The front door was wide open, and a lean old man in jeans and a faded blue work shirt stepped across the threshold. Ned's first impression of Tom Bell was of leather and steel.

"Get out!" The man plucked a well-worn, wide-brimmed black Stetson from a nail on the outside wall and settled it on his head. The color was a surprise, because no one in Lamar County ever wore a black hat, preferring the traditional silverbelly with a three-inch brim, not the four-inch size like the one on Bell's head. Even the crown was taller than those on the Lyndon Johnson style hat Ned, Cody, and the rest of the Center Springs men wore.

Ned stepped out of the car and crossed the distance. "Ned Parker."

They exchanged a firm, appraising grip. Two sets of strong eyes met under a warm spring sun.

"I'm Tom Bell, Constable."

"The kids said you knew who I was."

"Like I told them, I make it a point to know my neighbors."

"That's why I'm here. I wanted to meet you, too, since the kids was already over here bothering you a few days ago."

"They were no bother. Both seem like good youngsters. It was a pleasure to visit with them."

"They're a couple of outlaws I need to keep an eye on." Ned studied the new porch. "I meant to drop by a while back, then when I did, you wasn't here."

"I had to go to the Valley to finish up some business. I only got back to the house last week."

"Well, I want to thank you for stepping in and gettin' Cody out of trouble. I oughta be ashamed of myself for not doing it before now."

"You bet. It was a sorry piece of work to do that boy the way they did. I wish it'd been them that night instead of dogs. It'd be a pleasure to shoot the ones that tried to kill him."

You'd do it, too.

"Well, we owe you for what you did for Cody. He'll be by directly to thank you hisself."

"The kids tell me he's doing all right."

"Yep. That redheaded wife of his had him up and around pretty quick, and he gets better every day. I imagine he'll be back to work before you know it."

"That's good."

They stood in comfortable silence as Ned appraised the new construction.

Bell kicked a short piece of wood toward a small fire in the yard. "Kinda airish today, for so late in the spring."

"It is that, but it ain't as cool as it was when you met Cody."

"I'd call that morning downright chilly. He ain't been constable long, has he?"

Ned frowned. "Nope. He got elected in my place a few months ago, when I retired." Tom glanced at the badge on his shirt. Ned answered the unvoiced question. "The judge put me back in again around Thanksgiving."

"You don't hear about too many constables being *appointed* where I come from. They're usually elected."

"You're right. Judge O.C. Rains does things a little different in this county. Probably won't be another one appointed, neither, but he did it and I'm glad. I hear you're trying retirement now, too."

"If you can call this retirement. I've been working twelve hours a day since I moved in. That's your house up there on the hill, the first one this side of the creek bridge, right?"

"Sure is…been the family home place since grandpa built it. I heard this Buchanan land was sold. Glad to see you putting it back together. Looks like you had some building experience."

"Figured the Chevrolet wearing a red light and a long antenna parked in the yard was yours."

It annoyed Ned to have Tom Bell turn the conversation back around in the opposite direction he intended to go. O.C. was convinced Bell was a good man, but Ned needed to find out for himself. He still couldn't shake the feeling that there was a lot about Tom Bell he needed to know. "I see you decided to rebuild the porch first."

"Yep. I knew I'd spend considerable amount of time here. I intend to work my way through this, one small bite at a time."

"That's the way to do it all right. A lot of folks bounce around from one place to the next on a job like this."

"I like a plan."

"I can see you do." He tried again. "The kids say you're from the Valley."

"Yep. Two stores in a little community this size is unusual. I traded with Oak Peterson a few days ago, since the post office is in his store. That's where I get my retirement check. I might drop by the domino hall one of the days. I'd like to sit in on a hand of forty-two. They don't have any trouble in there, do they? Since the county is dry I'd imagine drinking stays on yonder side of the river."

Ned was surprised at how good the wiry gentleman was at deflecting his questions. No matter how hard he worked to bring the conversation around to his interests, Tom easily directed it to other topics.

"Aw, every now and then some knothead gets aggravated over a game, but I don't never get called in for it. I imagine a bottle or two shows up when they take a notion, but you're right, most the drinkin' is done over there in Juarez. The problem is the drunks always drive back home."

"Juarez?"

"Yep, that's what we call the beer joints across the river there in Oklahoma. It's the same as Juarez…"

"Across the Rio Grande," Tom Bell finished the sentence for him. "I know it well. We call them cantinas down in the Valley, but I imagine you have another name for 'em up here."

"Yep. We call 'em joints, or honky tonks."

"They're all the same. There's always a certain amount of drinking going on near where men live and work."

"You lived in the Valley a long time?"

"All my life."

"The kids said you was born here. The place changed hands a few times, but the last few years all it's been is squatters moving in and me having to tell them to leave."

"I can tell it's been empty a long time, but the bones are still good. That's cause the roof held. Your squatters must have kept the holes patched. Had it leaked, the whole place would have rotted, and as it was, there were still a few places that let the water in. It'll make a good house when I'm done, good enough to finish out my days, what's left of them."

"You live by yourself?"

"My wife died thirty years ago. Never saw the need to get remarried. How do y'all get along with others up here on this river?"

Ned immediately understood the question. "It stays quiet here in Center Springs. They have trouble from time to time in Chisum, between the coloreds and the whites. Usually they stay to themselves and we do the same. I believe most of the trouble comes from that fool Griffin, who was elected sheriff a while back. Before him, it was Sheriff Delbert Poole who kept things stirred before and after the War." He thought for a minute. "You ain't kin to either one of them, are you?"

"No. I am not."

"Well, there's good and bad folks on both sides of the fence. Across the river, the Indians pretty much stay to themselves." Ned elected not to mention that Miss Becky was full-blood Choctaw. "Mostly Choctaws, but there's a good mix of Cherokee and a few Comanches. Every now and then you'll hear about trouble between one tribe or another, but it stays up there. About the only trouble we have from Oklahoma are the beer joints across the river bridge. Down here it's mostly bootleggers."

"I'd like to stay away from trouble, and entanglements, if I can."

"You aren't expecting any trouble, are you Tom?"

Shaded by his hat, the man's eyes flickered. "No. There's a certain amount of trouble around every man, it's the nature of things, but I'm too old to entertain such foolishness now."

"You ain't wanted for anything, are you? No warrants from way back?"

Ned never took anything for granted. He almost learned the hard way, back in 1932. He'd gotten a call of a machine gun firing down in the bottoms on the Texas side of the river. Green and full of himself, Ned drove down through the fields until he heard the unmistakable chatter of an automatic weapon.

He parked his car on the dirt road and forgetting his revolver on the seat, slipped down the steep river bank to find a Model A parked on a sandstone ledge. Ned never did figure out how the man got the car down there, but sure enough, he was blasting away with a drum-fed Thompson. At the time, it was still legal for a citizen to own a machine gun.

He was already down the steep bank when he realized he was unarmed at the same moment the well-dressed man noticed him. Ned did the only thing he could think of. He held up his hand in greeting, and walked slowly across the pitted riverbed. He introduced himself as the local and very new constable and politely asked the man to put away the Thompson and leave.

After visiting a few minutes, the round-faced man loosened his tie and studied Ned for a long moment. The tension broke when he pitched the machine gun into the back seat.

Ned relaxed as he watched the man get behind the wheel and close the door. He flashed a quick smile and thanked Ned for his courtesy. "I'll go now, but you're probably the first and only law that'll ever run me off, and that's 'cause you treated me with respect. I like you, Ned. You can tell everyone that you met Machine Gun Kelly. Good luck in your new job."

Without another word, he drove off. Ned never forgot that lesson.

Tom Bell chuckled. "No, I don't have any warrants. I retired to live out my last days up here. How's your Mexican situation in these parts? I thought about hiring a hand to help me out for a while."

"A few come through, following the crops, but mostly its local people we hire. I haven't heard anyone speak Mexican in years. Do you speak it?"

"Had to, growing up in the Valley. They're mostly hard working people, like the rest of us, and I know I can trust them to see a good job well done."

"Well, there's a good man I know named Ivory Shaver who lives in the bottoms. He picks cotton for me in season and he'll give you a full day's work for your money. I'll let him know you're looking when I see him up at the store."

They paused again and studied the trees around the house.

"So you still farm, Ned?"

"Yessir, some. The constable's job don't pay that much, and the government gets part of that."

"I know what you mean. I might borrow a breaking plow, if you still have one, to start me a little garden right over there."

"I'll do more than that. The next time I hitch Lightning up to break up our garden, I'll walk him down here and do the same for you." Lightning was one of the last surviving plow horses in Center Springs.

"I'd appreciate that, but I'll pay you."

"No need. We're neighbors, but you bein' from down south, you need to know we don't put our gardens in until right after Easter, else a frost'll bite everything back."

"That's good to know. I need to get used to frosts and such. It's a deal, but I still expect to pay you."

"We'll talk about that some other time."

They examined the land under their boots and brogans.

"Well, I reckon I'll get on up to the store. I hope the kids don't get in your way. Top said you told them they could piddle around with you, so you let me know if they get to be a bother."

"They won't be. I enjoy visiting with young people. Reminds me of how life should be, right?"

"All right then, good to have a new neighbor." Ned felt like he was the one who'd been questioned, instead of the way he intended the visit. It was a feeling he'd never experienced.

They shook. Tom stood in his busy yard full of building materials and watched Ned turn the sedan around. When he was straightened out, Tom threw up a hand to wave goodbye before returning to work.

Ned left, feeling fine about his new neighbor he'd learned nothing about, and wondering who he'd been talking with.

Chapter Seven

Deputy Sheriff John Washington was waiting for Ned on the side of the two-lane road not far from the little community of Direct, pronounced Dye-rect. The almost mythical black deputy from Chisum, he usually handled issues among his people on the south side of the tracks, but was always willing to help his good friend Ned whenever the constable called.

The radio transmission only an hour earlier was cryptic. "John, meet me at Reeves' store in Direct. I'll be there directly."

Instead of waiting at the store, though, John stopped a hundred yards away. He knew the presence of a black deputy might attract attention, especially since he was a mountain among men. The familiar sight of a sheriff's car on the side of the road barely turned heads, most of the time.

Direct was another shrinking farm community about the size of Center Springs. The name came from a traveling preacher who held a revival there back in the 1880s. He was so shocked at the depravity of the little hardscrabble community that sold liquor and tolerated cathouses, in his sermon he shouted that if the residents didn't change their ways, the whole kit'n caboodle would go "Dye-rect to Hell!"

His sermon must have done some good, in John's opinion, because the community was usually quiet whenever he was called out to help Ned. He hadn't been there more than five minutes when Ned's sedan stopped on the highway beside him. Cody was driving.

Ned rolled his window down. "Did you bring an ax?"

"So that's why we're here. You know I keep it in the trunk with my shotgun."

"All right, then. Foller us."

Cody accelerated and John smoothly pulled in behind them. They traveled only a couple of miles before Cody steered onto a red rock road leading south. John was surprised, because most of the whisky-making took place down on the river, in the opposite direction.

The road wound through the country, past farms and pastures that gave way to thick hardwood bottoms as they neared Sanders Creek. Gravel became dirt and John was surprised to see an increase in shacks full of folks that looked like him. He didn't know any colored families lived in that part of the county, and it concerned him. Keeping up with his people was part of the job.

As they passed the last house, far enough in the country that John wondered if it was still in Lamar County, half a dozen barefoot children dressed in not much more than rags stopped playing in the yard to stare in open-mouthed amazement at the *two* cars on their skinny little shaded road at the same time.

At the sight of a uniformed colored deputy driving the second car, their screams of excitement brought out still more children. They popped up in a surprising number of places, from under the porch, out of barrels, and from small doghouse-like structures made of rusty sheet iron and cast off boards. John slowed to wave and try for a head count. An attractive but tired-looking woman in a shapeless shift appeared at the open entry to the house, a baby on her hip and a pig at her feet.

She didn't register any emotion whatsoever at the sight of the black deputy waving through his open window. Vowing to come back for a visit, John accelerated to catch up and the house disappeared in a cloud of red dust. The ground sloped toward the creek bottom and the dirt road petered out into nothing more than dim tracks leading into a meadow. It reminded John of the last time he and Ned busted up a whiskey still.

Killing the engines, the men stepped out of the cars without slamming the doors. "None of these tracks look fresh, Mr. Ned." John quietly opened his trunk and took out both an ax and his shotgun. They'd polished their routine through the years. Only Cody's presence changed things. John handed the ax to Ned.

"No, they don't, but that don't mean the still ain't back there. Cody and me'll foller this little path here. John, slip around back past them shin-oaks and we'll catch 'em in the middle."

Without a word, John stepped around a briar patch and disappeared into the trees. Ned gave him a few minutes, hefting the double-bit ax in his hands and staring back the way they came.

Cody watched John's huge frame disappear into the woods. Only months before, he and the big deputy shared a horrific experience in the Cotton Exchange, and Cody felt they had reached a different level of their relationship. Inside the Exchange, they faced a monster, and during that time, they shared the same fears and emotions, conversing in a way that brought the two men together. Cody was surprised that since that time, John had fallen back to their old ways of talking, and his traditional, respectful ways of dealing with the Parkers.

He wondered if John's actions and demeanor were real, or if he felt the need to put on a false front for society's sake. Cody didn't want that. He wanted John to be a true friend, and not just one when no one else was looking.

"Your Uncle Ben told me on the phone that he ran across a still down here last week while he was looking for a good place to catch crappie."

"We're sure a long way from his house." Cody examined the surrounding trees, looking for anything out of the ordinary. Redbirds flitted through the branches, and a bushy-tail squirrel calmly loped along the limb of a wide pecan. He relaxed. "He usually takes a cane pole down under the Sanders Creek bridge and fishes there."

"That's what I thought, too. I don't know why he's stringing off down here. I suspect it might be for another reason, but I'm not inclined to say yet. The thing that makes me wonder about all this is him calling me in the first place. Ben don't usually get mixed up in anything that don't pay him back in some way."

"They might have cheated him on the price of a gallon of whiskey."

"Maybe." Ned abruptly stepped out toward the woods without another word. Cody quickly fell in behind. A clear path wound through the shade beneath thick pecans and oaks. Thickets of brambles forced the path to change direction until another tangle bent it once again. Both men were familiar with such trails that could have been made by deer, cattle, or people. Ned suspected this one was made by deer and then temporarily widened by shoes. It was like any other trail stomped down by fishermen heading for a good, deep hole in the creek, but he wasn't convinced.

After a ten-minute walk, Ned glimpsed a boiler through the thin understory trees growing in the dense shade. He stopped and sniffed the air like a wary deer. "I don't smell no smoke."

Before Cody could comment, John stepped into the clearing on the other side of the still and waved. "There ain't nobody here."

Relieved, the three met beside the cold tank in the small natural clearing made by a massive oak that had fallen in the not too distant past, leaving a huge hole in the overhead canopy. Cody kicked around the stomped-down grass. "Nobody's been here for a while."

"Ben didn't say they were cooking when he ran across it."

"Maybe he scared them off," Cody suggested.

"Could-a happened." Ned tapped the side of the boiler with the head of his ax. It rang hollow. "I don't believe I've ever seen anybody set up a still and then leave it behind. This is a good one. There ain't no reason they couldn't have taken it with them and fired it up again somewhere else."

Cody put his hand against the cold metal and examined the apparatus. He'd seen a lot of disassembled stills through the years after Ned had broken them up, but he'd never seen one all set up and ready to go.

The round boiler was chest high, big enough to hold five hundred gallons of mash. From the top, a copper line dropped into a box called the "thump keg," designed to prevent what moonshiners called "puke" from boiling over. From there, the line ran to a water bath in a cooling tank covered by a wooden box. A long coil of copper, called the worm, condensed the clear liquid in the loops until it distilled pure 180-proof white lightning.

John scanned the surrounding woods. "I don't like this Mr. Ned. You notice something else about this setup?"

The two older lawmen were suddenly very alert. "Yep. Saw it right off."

Cody was getting frustrated by his lack of experience. "What?"

Ned copied John's posture and faced outward. "There ain't no car tracks in here, and I don't see any way to get one through all these trees. Nobody's gonna haul whiskey out by the gallon the way we came in. They'd have to carry this stuff along the trail before they skedaddled. Nobody does that.

"They usually find a place where they can drive between the trees, or they'll cut down a few to make a little road wide enough for their cars. This don't look right."

"I thought this might be Doak Looney's still," John said. "But I believe I've changed my mind. There ain't an empty jug in sight, no wood is cut and ready to use, and there ain't no trash piles I can see."

Picking up on their nervousness, Cody rested his hand on the butt of his pistol. "How long you think it's been since a batch of whiskey left here?"

"They ain't. Look under the boiler. There ain't no ashes, nor any signs of a fire."

"What kind of deal is this?"

"I don't know."

A blue jay shrieked, its harsh echo a familiar sound.

"Mr. Ned, if I was already shot, I'd say this was a trap. But if somebody's waitin' on us, they sure are taking their own sweet time about it."

Ned's thoughts flashed back to Cody's wintertime ambush. His eyes flicked from shadow to shadow. Finally, he realized his sixth sense hadn't kicked in, and the hairs on his neck weren't sticking up.

It wasn't a setup. So what was going on?

"Let's kick around a bit, but y'all keep an eye out." Ned stepped away from the trod-down grass and walked slowly along the length of the downed tree. The lower limbs on the trees were lobbed off to better clear the space as they assembled the still, but they were piled in a rotting stack in the middle of the clearing.

The lawmen split up. None of the three knew what they were looking for.

The surrounding woods were far from silent. Birds called, squirrels chattered in anger at the men's presence, and a slight breeze soughed through the limbs.

John finally stopped deeper into the woods, fifty feet from the clearing. "Mr. Ned, you want to take a look here?" They joined him beside a pile of freshly turned dirt. The cleared patch of ground had only a scattering of debris on top. "I believe sumpin's buried here."

His hands in his pockets, Ned studied the disturbed ground. He toed a clod. "Cody, run back there and get the shovels out of the trunk. I got a bad feeling about this pile of dirt."

The feeling was well-founded. John and Cody knew they'd find the secret after the first blade full of soft sand proved the soil had been recently dug to a considerable depth. Cody still wasn't up to full strength and he stopped to rest while John kept digging. Minutes later, he stopped when his shovel encountered something much harder than loam and sand. Cody joined again and digging carefully, they uncovered two decaying bodies lying one atop the other. The stench roiling from the shallow grave drove the two lawmen back.

On the other hand, Ned had the unusual ability to use the velum, the teardrop-shaped flap in the back his throat, to close off the passages to his nose. He was one of the few people in the county who could block smells with this strange reflex, while breathing through his mouth and keeping his hands free.

He stepped forward to stare downward into the grave. Holding his breath, John stuck the blade of his shovel into the ground and wiped his face with a white handkerchief. "I swear Mr. Ned, there's been a terrible lot of killin' around here these past few months."

"Yeah, and I'm getting a belly full of it. Y'all reckon its Doak Looney planted in this hole? We ain't seen him for a long while."

Cody faced away from the shallow grave and thought about the corpses they'd uncovered. His stomach clenched and he choked down a gag. "Hard to tell, but I imagine we'll know once they're out of the ground." He started back toward the cars. "I'll go radio this in and get some help out here."

"I can think of only one reason for this." John watched Cody disappear into the trees.

"Yep, someone got rid of the competition before these boys could start cooking whiskey."

Chapter Eight

It didn't take me and Pepper long before we were at Mr. Bell's house pretty regular. I've always loved building things, but I found out quick that I had a lot to learn.

He put me to work the first day, finishing his porch. I'd showed up right after breakfast. Mr. Bell was already working, adding a rail around the outside. He had a small lumber-scrap fire going not far from the house, and I could smell the rich pine burning long before I came up in the yard.

"I'm ready to work."

He was sawing slow and steady. With one more solid push, he cut through the board and about three inches dropped off. He bent over with the ease of a much younger man, picked up the chunk, and pitched it into the fire.

He noticed the hammer I'd slipped through my belt. "I can see you are, young man. Grab the other end of this new porch rail and give me a hand."

He'd already marked where it went on the posts, so while I held up my end, he set a nail with two taps, and then drove it in with three strong blows. "Now, drive in your end."

Mine didn't go so well. The nail wouldn't cooperate, and when I finally got it started, I had to hammer on it a dozen times. His patience surprised me. He held the rail level and watched as I rassled with the nail, but didn't say a word until I was finished.

I was embarrassed to meet his eyes, because I'd given him the idea I knew how to build, but he picked up a tape, measured the distance between two posts on the opposite side, and then read the tape a second time. He laid another two-by-four across a set of wooden sawhorses and marked it. He stuck the pencil in his pocket, measured the board again, and then quickly cut it with a handsaw.

"Measure twice, cut once. Have you ever heard that?"

"Nossir."

"Well, you do that, and you won't have many mistakes, and you won't waste wood, right?"

I'd already realized that he didn't want an answer when he said "right." It was like Mr. Ike, who said "listen" all the time. It was the way some people talked. Up at the store the men told stories and every now and then the teller might say, "So-and-So got all riled up about it, and you know how he talks, he said…" Then all the men listening nodded their heads and grinned, because they knew how So-and-So talked, and that's what made the story interesting.

"Grab your end and let's nail this one up, but this time use *my* hammer laying there."

I could tell a difference the minute I picked it up. The poll was deeper and the face was half again as wide as mine.

This time he let me drive the first nail, and it was twice as easy.

He was satisfied. "The right tool for the right job. That goes for all things in life." I held out the hammer when I was finished, but he shook his head. "I have another one right over there. That'n's yours."

An hour later we stopped to judge our work. Mr. Tom grunted in satisfaction. "Doing the porch first is backwards, but I wanted to get it wrapped. It looks good. Now, are you afraid of heights?"

"Nossir. I've built tree houses, and not too long ago I fell out of a tree and broke my arm, but I ain't afraid to go right back up."

"What'd you fall out for?"

"Grandpa and Uncle Cody were in a shoot-out not far away, and I was watching."

He studied me until it became uncomfortable. I needed to keep talking. "There was this person killing folks and cutting off their heads. When Grandpa caught up with the killer, well, I didn't want him to get away, so I climbed a tree to see where he was headed in the river bottoms, and I got excited and fell."

"Have you climbed any trees since?"

"Yessir. We've been working on our *Swiss Family Robinson* tree house for the past while."

"Well good. I'm glad to hear you've learned to overcome your fears." He pointed upward. "We're gonna roof this place today, and I can use your help. We'll do the porch roof first and work our way up. It'll be good practice for a young'un with a new hammer, then we'll tackle the house."

When Uncle Cody and Pepper finally drove down the road looking for me an hour later, we were both high off the ground. We'd already finished the porch roof and laid the first line of shingles along the front edge of the house.

Uncle Cody got out of the El Camino and tilted his Stetson back to look up at us. "I heard all the hammering and knew Mr. Bell couldn't be going that fast all by himself."

We stopped. Pepper was awful tiny from up so high and it made me laugh. I could tell it made her mad, because she never liked to be laughed at.

I noticed Uncle Cody wasn't wearing his boots. He had on a pair of brogans like Grandpa's everyday shoes, jeans, and a work shirt. He was also wearing his Colt .45 automatic pistol. Without saying anything, Uncle Cody threw a load of shingles up on his shoulder and came up the ladder.

"You don't need to be up here," Mr. Bell said. "I doubt you're healed up enough yet."

"It's all right. I'll take it easy." Uncle Cody must have seen the funny look on my face. "We know each other. Mr. Bell came by the hospital more times than I can count, and we've visited a bunch since then."

"I want to help," Pepper said.

Uncle Cody waved a hand. "Come on up here."

The four of us worked out a system where Pepper and I laid the shingles straight and the men pounded the roofing nails in with one or two hits each. We were a good team and the whole thing moved quickly.

Even though we were busy, every now and then I'd see Uncle Cody kneeling on the roof, looking all around from our high perch, as if checking for something. Then I realized why he was still wearing his .45 while we worked, because he still wasn't sure if the people who shot at him were coming back to finish the job.

You couldn't see much from our perch, parts of the highway through the trees to the north and that's about all. The other three directions were nothing but woods. There could have been a booger-bear sneaking up on us and we'd have never known it.

We could hear, though. Cars swooshed past on the highway, mourning dove cooed from the trees, and quail called from the hidden pastures and meadows. Cows were always mooing not far away, but we didn't pay them any mind.

The country-style roof only had two sides, angling up from the porch to the ridgeline, and then down the other side. It was simple work, and the day finally warmed up enough to be called hot.

Before you knew it, we were finished with the front slope and back on the ground.

Mr. Bell picked up a few short pieces of lumber and pitched them into the fire. "I sure appreciate y'all's help. Once the other side is finished, I can get started on the inside."

Uncle Cody wiped his sweaty face with a bandana, reminding me of Grandpa's habits. "Well, you can't work on an empty stomach. Kids, get in the back of the truck and you climb in up front with me, Mr. Bell. It's dinner time and I 'magine Miss Becky has the table set."

"Well, I…"

"She's expecting us."

"In that case, let me get my hat."

I was hungry all right, so Pepper and I climbed over the El Camino's tailgate and we drove the short distance to the house.

Uncle Cody was right. Dinner was ready when we got there, and I smelled it all the way out in the yard. The table was loaded with my favorites: creamed peas, pinto beans, green beans, stewed potatoes, creamed corn, chicken, chicken fried steak, and homemade biscuits.

Mr. Bell took his hat off when he walked into the steamy kitchen and Miss Becky hugged him like he was kinfolk, even though she'd never laid eyes on him until that minute. I guess him saving Uncle Cody made him part of the family, and he settled right in.

Grandpa was up at the barn and came in right behind us. He was glad Mr. Bell was there, because he was grinning from ear to ear.

"Sit right there at the other end of the table, Tom." Grandpa settled into his chair at the head and we filled the rest. There wasn't much talking, because we were all hungry. Mr. Tom put away more than his share. He didn't shame us, though. We all ate like field hands too. Shingling is hard work, and I didn't realize how hungry I was until we dug in.

As usual, the phone rang halfway through dinner and I thought Grandpa was gonna throw his fork at it. Miss Becky hurried into the living room and answered.

"Daddy, it's for you."

"Who is it?"

"I didn't ask. You know that."

He sighed his way from the table as the talk quieted down, partly so he could hear, partly because we wanted to listen, too. There wasn't much to hear.

Two minutes later he was back in the kitchen. "Constable Parker, you ready to get back to work?"

"Sure 'nough."

"I need to go pick up a prisoner from Roxton and take him to Dallas."

Mr. Bell put down his fork. "Mind if I tag along?"

Grandpa frowned. "Tom, I'd enjoy the company, but this is law work, and I cain't take no chance you gettin' hurt. You can ride with me one night when I have to make the rounds, if you'd like."

If it hurt Mr. Bell's feelings, he didn't show it. "That's all right. I'll finish my cake here and get on back to work."

Uncle Cody plucked his hat off the rack beside the door. "We can drop you off on the way out."

"No need. I'll walk my dinner off."

"You ready?" Ned asked.

"Sure," Cody set his hat and started for the door. "Who we picking up?"

"Carl Gibbs. They got him after he blacked Tamara's eye last night and lit out to hide at his mama's house. A sheriff's deputy is holding him 'til we get there."

"Why can't they take him in?"

"Because I want to, that's why."

From the tone of Grandpa's voice, I knew he was done talking about it.

"Cody Parker, you ain't going nowhere until I give you some sugar." Me and Pepper snickered when Miss Becky grabbed Uncle Cody and gave him a kiss on the cheek. It broke up the tension in the kitchen.

Uncle Cody wasn't embarrassed to be kissed by her in front of Mr. Bell, but instead of saying anything, he and Grandpa hurried off the porch with Miss Becky hollerin' for them to be careful. The house got really quiet after they were gone, and before long we were finished eating and Mr. Bell struck out on foot for his house.

Pepper went into the living room and clicked on the radio. The Beach Boys were singing when we laid down on a pallet made of quilts and took a long nap.

It was the first day we'd worked like a full hand to rebuild a house, but it was far from the last.

Chapter Nine

John coasted to a stop in the bare yard. The sun was hot, and he'd driven with the windows of his cruiser open all the way from Chisum. His sweaty shirt stuck to his back, but he didn't feel the heat because he was smiling at a gaggle of kids watching from the shady porch.

He got out, opened the back door, and lifted out two brown paper bags full of groceries, bought by money from his own pockets and from the worn billfolds of Ned and O.C. Rains.

"Howdy!" he called through the gaping door. There were no screens on the house, and insects flew in and out without impediment.

The slender black woman he'd seen days before on the way to the abandoned still stepped out and shaded her eyes with one hand. The baby on her hip wore nothing but a cloth diaper.

"I'm John Washington." For the first time in years he found himself admiring a woman. He liked the way she cocked her head and knew she was taking stock of what she saw.

She raised an eyebrow. "My man ain't here."

"That's all right. I can see him later." John stopped at the edge of the porch and set the bags down. "Y'ain't got no dogs here, do you, that'll tear into these here bags?"

"We can barely feed ourselves, let alone dogs."

"Good." He smiled and motioned toward the kids. "Y'all come on and help me unload these groceries. We need to move fast, before the ice cream melts."

"Ice cream!" They charged the car. The older children grabbed the heaviest bags and started back toward the house.

"Hold it!" The woman shouted and the kids braked to a stop. She frowned and rested her free fist on a hip covered by a shapeless house dress. "We cain't pay for no ice cream, ner other groceries, neither."

"It's already been bought."

"We ain't takin' no charity, not from nobody…not even a nigger in a uniform. What you want?"

John waited in the middle of the yard, both hands full. The raggedly-dressed children stood around him in a protective circle, as though to defy their mother's wrath against a uniformed Santa Claus. There wasn't one shoe among them.

"It ain't charity. It's from Mr. Ned Parker to pay you for some work you're about to do, and for some questions I have to ask."

"I ain't turning in no kinfolk to y'all."

"Ain't asking for that."

"I don't work for no Parker."

"You do now."

"What's he want?" She frowned again. "Uh uh, I don't do that, not even when we're hungry."

John felt his face flush. "We ain't asking for nothin' ain't right. Let me get up there in the shade out of this hot sun and we'll talk. I ain't a-kiddin'. This ice cream's done rode from Chisum, and I imagine it's pretty soft already. Let the little'uns eat while we visit a minute."

"My man'll be here any time."

John understood. "I'll stay right out here."

She finally came to a decision and sat primly in a straight-back wooden chair. The cane bottom was almost rotted out, but it held her slight weight. She bounced the baby on her knees. "All right."

The kids squealed again and charged up on the porch. In seconds, the paper bags were ripped to shreds as they pawed through the canned and dried groceries. In the bottom of one bag, two sweating and soft square cartons of chocolate Mellorine brought even more shrieks.

"Y'all go get something to eat out of," the woman said. Two of her oldest girls ran inside.

John grinned down at the smaller kids, and picked a piece of grass from a girl's thick black hair. "I figgered they'd like chocolate." He sat on the lip of the porch, just in the edge of the shade, with his back against a gray post.

"They like anything sweet."

Two shirtless little ones climbed up in John's lap. He figured they were around three or four, and knew one was a girl by the braids in her short hair. When a toddler saw them, he wanted up too. He soon lost count of how many there were, because they were as busy as a bag full of kittens.

The oldest girl appeared to be about seventeen. She dipped melting ice cream in to a variety of utensils, ranging from cups to bowls. Small hands reached out eagerly, but she followed a system that worked downward by age. The boy and girl quickly abandoned John's lap and joined their siblings, leaving him with the toddler. The oldest girl finally handed John a cracked bowl with little blue cornflowers around the outside edge. He glanced around.

"They all eatin', 'cept the baby there in your lap. I'll feed him some after I've had mine."

His bowl contained one small scoop. The teenager handed her mama a brown bowl. The woman picked up the fork that rattled on the edge. "I know you."

He met her tired eyes.

"You the one saved them two little white kids down on the creek a while back."

"Yep."

"You took up with that old constable."

"I work with him."

She took a bite, scraping the ice cream off the fork with her teeth. "That why you here?"

"Yep. Did you hear about them two was killed down the road a piece?"

"Don't surprise me. They was cars going in and out—and my first thought they's up to no good."

"That's what I'm talking about. Somebody set up a still way back up in the woods down there, and then some others came along and left 'em in a shaller grave."

"So *that's* why you here?"

"Partly. I saw y'all when we went by, and figgered you might need some help. I also figgered you might have seen who's been driving in and out, before we showed up."

She snorted like a colt. "A-course I noticed. There ain't no door or screen on this sorry-assed shack, so I hear everybody that comes by."

"You know what they look like?"

"The dead'uns?"

"Or them that did it."

She stabbed the melting chocolate with the tines. "I watched the moonshiners come and go, but they didn't come by much. They only made a trip or two. I knew what they was doin' down there, 'cause they had a truck with a tarp coverin' the back. Don't nobody cover nothing like that 'less they don't want anybody to see what they got back there."

"Could have been anything under that tarp."

"But it weren't." She tilted the bowl and drank the cool chocolate.

"What about the others?"

"Four of 'em. Three was greasy-looking no-account white mens. The other'n was big, like you, only white, and he wore shades."

"Would you know 'em if you's to see 'em again?"

"Yeah, they slowed once to get a real good look while I was hanging out clothes one day. I's facin' the road, and gave 'em a good look right back."

John dipped his finger in his bowl and let the baby suck on it.

"You got kids?"

"Ain't married."

"You handle 'em like you know what you doin'."

One little girl draped herself over John's big shoulder. He could tell they were all starving for love. He patted her hand, and gave the least one another chocolate-covered finger to lick.

"I know about kids. My sister has two. You from around here?"

"Not really. We moved here from Jefferson when I was car-ryin' the oldest girl there, Belle. My husband Walter said things might be more better for us here than back on the Caddo, but he was wrong, as usual. It's as hard here, as there."

"What does he do?"

"Sheeeiiittt. I don't know. I ain't seen him in a year. Probably laid up with somebody else." When she realized that her story was blown, she stopped.

"How do you get by?"

She ducked her head, but didn't say anything for a long minute. "We manage."

"Well, you got a job now. Mr. Ned'll send a truck by to get you."

Her eyes flashed. "I ain't no field hand."

"Well, there's a difference in a *hired* hand, and there ain't no shame in working a field. Mr. Ned pays good wages for a day's work. He'll pay them older kids, too, the same wage."

"Who gonna watch these little 'uns?"

"Bring 'em all along. There's always a young gal or two who'll watch 'em while everbody works."

"Maybe I don't want to."

"I guess you figure a car's gonna drive out here from Chisum to give you money, or a job at the soup factory. It's a *job*, and it'll make a difference here."

She stared at the empty road. "I heard the shots."

"When them fellas was killed?"

"I figger it was about that time. Them four drove past, and then a while later there was a whole bunch of shooting, a lot more than it takes to kill two people. Then, they drove back past with only two in the car. Two more was driving the first truck."

"That must have been it, then."

"Shades stopped for a minute."

John waited.

"He got out of the car and came up here in the yard, pretty as you please, like they was decent folks out on a Sunday drive and stopped to ask direction. Said he liked what I had and was I interested in sellin' any of it."

"Sellin' what mama?" a girl asked.

She studied her for a moment. "Eggs."

"We ain't got no chickens."

John saved her. "So what did you tell him?"

"I told him to get on out of here. Then he offered me five dollars and some reefer to go along with it. Said he'd come back later and bring some more, but I had a butcher knife tucked here in the back of my belt and I took it out. That sharp cuttin' edge backed him off right quick."

"Reefer?"

"A joint, you know, weed."

"They been back?"

"Nope. They left real quick and I ain't seen 'em since."

John used his spoon to rake the last of the sticky chocolate from the bowl and fed it to the toddler. "Was that good?"

The sticky face belied no expression at all. He struggled to get down. John lifted him off his knee. The toddler wandered off to examine the other empty bowls scattered on the rough porch, hoping his brothers and sisters had left something.

"Well, I know more than I did when I got here."

"About what?" She gave him a quick smile.

John liked the dimples in her cheeks. "About a lot, I guess."

She noticed all the bags and cans scattered on the porch for the first time. "Belle, y'all get these groceries in the house, then go on out back and pick us a mess of greens. I saw some fatback in one of them sacks. It'll taste good for supper."

She gave John a hard look.

"We have a good truck garden out back. That's where we get most of what we eat, but sometimes it don't stretch far enough, 'specially this time of the year when things is jus' startin' to come up."

"I figgered you had a garden. Y'all ain't starvin'. You're just po'."

"That's how I've lived my life."

He rose. "All right, then. I might be back from time to time, but don't be surprised when a truck comes at daylight to pick y'all up."

John rubbed a couple of little heads and stepped into the sunshine. When he got to his car, the woman's voice stopped him.

"John Washington!"

He stopped and rested his arm on the roof of his car.

"My name's Rachel Lea."

He grinned. "Good to meet you, Rachel Lea."

"Not all these kids is mine."

When John raised his eyebrows in question, she gave a laugh. "Belle and Bubba there, the two oldest are mine. The rest belonged to my sister. She and her husband got killed six months ago and I took 'em in."

He waited.

"She liked makin' babies!"

John chuckled and opened the car door. "So it's you and them kids here all alone."

"I tol' you the truth. Husband run off a while back and good riddance, he weren't no'count, nohow." She lifted a hand. "Next time you come by, you stay for supper, John Washington. I believe I'd like to cook you a bite."

"I might do that."

"Where'd you say all these groceries come from?"

He didn't want to tell her that Judge Rains and Ned had given him money when he told them he planned to drop by. They were constantly buying food for people with little or no means, but it was always quiet.

"Folks that care."

Chapter Ten

O.C. idly studied Frenchie's backside as she left their back corner booth and worked her way down the long, narrow café, refilling coffee cups and visiting with her regulars.

"What are you watching that thing for?" Ned took a cautious sip of his coffee and studied the remnants of scrambled eggs on his plate. "You're too long in the tooth to do anything with it these days."

"I know it, but I ain't dead yet. It don't hurt to look."

"She catches you at it, she's liable to knock your fool head off."

O.C. chuckled. "She hasn't noticed for the last twenty years. I don't reckon she'll pick up on it now."

Frenchie stepped up to the pass-through into the kitchen. "Four eggs, scrambled, hash, toast, bacon! Homer's hungry this morning!"

Potts the cook shouted from the smoky kitchen. "Comin' up!"

The air soon thickened once again with the aroma of frying bacon and mixed with cigar and cigarette smoke hanging low in the air.

Only half a block from the courthouse, the cafe had been their unofficial meeting place for years. Good coffee, better hamburgers, long, dark, and narrow, it was the perfect place to visit and still keep an eye on who was coming in and out the front door. The counter was once a bar back in Chisum's wilder days, and the mirror behind shelves full of foodstuffs and advertisements was original to the building's construction. On good days, the bell over the wooden front door jingled every few minutes.

The back door without a bell stayed busy as well, but the customers there were colored.

From Ned's position in the booth, he could see through the batwing doors and the mostly empty rough lumber tables at that time of the morning. By noon they'd be full of colored men and women laughing, talking, and eating greasy burgers, fries, and thick chicken-fried steaks covered with cream gravy. Frenchie served them the same food as her white customers, only they were required to eat in the back.

During that busy time, she shut a solid door beyond the batwings to further divide the café, not because she wanted to, but because those in the front demanded it. The Indians from Oklahoma were also expected to eat with the coloreds, and none of it set well with the white constable who was married into a Choctaw family.

Ned and O.C. sipped their strong, bitter coffee in silence, until Potts thumped a steaming breakfast through the order window. "Homer's up!"

"I heard it weren't Doak we dug up last week," Ned said.

"No. That's a fact. It was a couple of old boys from Red River County moved in to start a new business. Somebody didn't like it, and they explained their opinion with a thirty-eight."

"That'll do the job."

"You don't reckon Doak had anything to do with it?"

Instead of answering, Ned noticed dried blood all over the back of the little finger of his left hand. He'd poked a hole in his finger with a piece of bailing wire that morning while he was feeding cows. He wet his right thumb by dipping it into a small water glass on the table and rubbed at the crust. He had to repeat the process twice to get rid of the blood. When he finished, he took several long sips of coffee to rid his mouth of the coppery taste.

O.C. waited.

Ned finally seemed surprised he hadn't yet answered the question. "Why no, Doak's a lot of things, and he's a sorry son of a bitch, but he ain't no killer. Somebody else done for 'em."

"Any ideas why?"

"Nary. Moonshiners don't usually kill one another. This is something else. It might have been over a woman for all I know."

Ned watched John Washington come in out of the alley to get coffee. He waved. The uniformed deputy stepped up to the dividing entrance, but no further. "Mornin', Mr. Ned. Mr. O.C., I'll be by directly at your office, if that's all right."

O.C. twisted around at the sound of John's deep bass voice. "Sure 'nough, I don't have court 'til one today. Why don't you come have a seat and let's talk now?"

John shook his head with a grin. "I imagine I'll need to come by the courthouse." He recalled a few months earlier when he had important information for O.C. and had to come through Frenchie's front entrance.

Close to a panic for the first time in his life the day he learned the Skinner's true identity, John drove to Frenchie's café hoping to find O.C. having coffee. The Skinner had been spreading terror throughout Lamar County for months, first killing and skinning animals, and then graduating to humans. He finally set his sights on Ned's family.

The judge was there all right that afternoon, straddling a stool at the counter. Anxious to the point of carelessness, John nearly jerked the screen door off the hinges on his way in. The white customers bristled at his entrance, and Wilber Meyers, a mechanic at the Ford house and the toughest man on the north side of town, tried to stop John from coming in.

The big deputy snapped Wilber's wrist like a matchstick and was drawing the heavy sap from his back pocket when Judge Rains stopped two others who mistakenly thought they could beat John senseless.

He hadn't been back through the front door since.

"Nope." Ned slid over. "Come set here with us."

Obviously uncomfortable, Deputy Washington came in and quickly slid his huge bulk into the booth with his back to the café, as if the giant could be inconspicuous.

It didn't work.

Several of the café's customers frowned at his entrance. "Damn niggers." Two men in greasy coveralls threw money on the counter in disgust and left.

John took off his Stetson, but there was no place on the table for it. He started to lay it beside one of the dirty plates when a slim hand appeared and took it from him. Frenchie placed it upside down on the counter, beside those belonging to Ned and O.C. They always put their own Stetsons there to block customers from taking the two empty stools beside their booth.

It allowed them to talk without someone sitting close and listening.

Frenchie set a thick white mug in front of John and returned to her counter. He ran a thick index finger through the mug's handle with barely any room to spare. His broad face widened in a soft grin. From behind the counter, Frenchie gave him one in return.

Daring anyone to say a word, O.C. glared down the length of the café through the cigarette and bacon smoke. The remaining customers focused their attention back to what they were doing, but the café's buzz became ominous. "What did you have to see me about?"

Instead of immediately answering, John glanced to the side to see how close the nearest customer might be. Ned noticed the collar of his shirt was worn through after years of scrubbing.

Keeping his back to the café, John rested his meaty forearms on the table that groaned slightly under his weight. "I picked a feller up at Sugar Bear's last night and took him to jail. He was drunk, but there was something else not right about him. His eyes was funny, and when I checked his car, the trunk was full of marywana."

"I knew that stuff was gonna make its way down here for good," Ned said.

O.C. grunted. "Well, it's here all right. Mostly they're finding one of them funny cigarettes every now and then. Except for them bales you found a while back under the creek bridge, Ned, I don't think I've seen much more than a pinch of the stuff at one time."

"I've been seeing it here and there." He ran a hand over his bald head. "But I haven't needed to take anyone to jail over it."

O.C. knew Ned's penchant for dealing with issues on his own. More times than either of them could count, Ned had the opportunity to arrest young people for their stupidity, but instead, he sent them home with a stern lecture and the threat of jail the next time they jumped the fence.

Late one night in particular, Ned answered a call about a group of men shooting dice behind Oak Peterson's store. He parked his car a distance away and eased through the darkness, hearing muffled laughter and the sound of bets going down. When he peeked around the corner of the store, a huddle of young men near the opposite corner were shooting dice by the glow of a pole light.

Ned stepped into view and lit them with the flashlight in his hand. The other rested on the butt of his revolver. "All right boys, everybody set still."

All eight men jumped in alarm, then settled back when they recognized Ned's voice behind the light.

"Damn! Ned, you 'bout scared us to death!"

"Howdy, Uncle Ned."

He was startled to realize all eight of the crapshooters were kinfolk. He shook his head in disgust, recognizing nephews, cousins and one brother-in-law. "If this don't beat all."

"You gonna take us in?"

"I ought to, because this is the sorriest bunch of peckerheads I've seen in a long time."

He didn't arrest any of them, but for the next three months every ditch and fence row he pointed out in Center Springs, and every yard owned by a widow woman, was mowed and trimmed to his approval. He hadn't caught any of them shooting dice since.

John blew across his coffee and took a careful sip. Hot and sweet. "Well, I dug around some more and found out them killin's at the still might have something to do with this stuff. The story around our joints is them two been cookin' whiskey both in Red River County and across the river for a while, but was run off Little River by some boys who was starting to grow marywana up there."

"You know that for a fact?"

"Nossir, Mr. O.C., I don't. All that's hearsay, and a couple of them folks don't rightly tell the whole truth all the time."

"Lyin' don't know no color." O.C. held up his near empty mug for a refill.

"Ain't that the truth? Anyways, he said they was a bunch workin' for some white boy with big muscles who sold it to him. They offered him a job to deliver it over to another feller in Sugar Bear's parking lot. If he did a good job, they'd give him a full-time job shippin' it up here from the Valley, and that it was coming through Chisum."

"What does this have to do with them boys we dug up?"

"A lot."

John paused when Frenchie appeared at the booth, popping her gum and giving them all a big grin. "Breakfast is over. Y'all want some pie? Fresh made."

"Sure do." O.C. watched her refilling the other mugs. "I'll have peach, if you got it."

"You'll get what I bring you." She winked and headed toward the kitchen.

"Them two was making their shine too close to a marywana crop up there in Oklahoma. This top feller was settin' up his own business by growin' it in the woods up there, but he intends to get a pipeline goin' from the Valley on somebody else's dime, and then undercut them with his own supply. I reckon the shiners might have seen more than was healthy for them. They left and hadn't no more than set up shop on the creek, when they was killed."

"Burying them right there don't make no sense," O.C. said. "Somebody was sure to find the still and kick around like y'all did until they ran across the grave."

"Maybe that's what they wanted," Ned suggested. "For them to be found, but after a while, when them who had been driving up and down the roads was forgot. It was a warning, and a finish to what they'd started across the river."

"And what they wanted to finish with Cody." Ned still couldn't figure how the ambush fit in, but he was sure they were connected and it was getting to him.

"They only problem was who's livin' on the road." John sipped the steaming coffee and didn't even flinch at the hot liquid. "I've said it before. Folks look like y'all don't hardly notice my people, less they want something, or they're looking to pick 'em up. I went back and visited with one of them families we passed going in. The one y'all gave me some money for. They remember the car, and the men driving it. They described 'em to me. The same big muscled-up feller that wears shades, and one of 'em sounded like..." John checked over his shoulder again. "One of 'em sounded like J.T. Boone."

"Why, he's a deputy."

"Yessir, but he ain't always smelled right to me."

"But no one's spoke his name?"

"Nossir, that's why I'm-a tellin' you right now."

Ned and O.C. exchanged glances across the booth.

"All right, then." O.C. drummed his fingers on the table. "Y'all keep looking, and we'll see what we find. But be careful. Anybody who'd kill two men and bury 'em for what they know ain't nobody to trifle with."

Frenchie arrived at the table, balancing three thick slices of pie. John held up both hands. "No ma'am. Not for me, but thanks anyway."

"Go ahead on, John."

"Mr. O.C., I *might* come in here from time to time, and I *might* have coffee with y'all back here in the back booth, but *eatin'* is a whole 'nother thing. Miss Frenchie, can I have one of them slices of coconut in the back?"

Her eyes crinkled as she grinned at John. She slapped the other two plates between Ned and the judge. "Sure enough, hon, and it's on the house."

John nodded goodbye and slid out of the booth. Ned reached out for the last slice of coconut pie. O.C. snorted and stared miserably downward. "I don't even like cherry."

Chapter Eleven

Ned left Chisum and drove across the Red River to Juarez. The people who tried to kill Cody nearly three full months ago were still running loose, and Ned intended to find out who they were and why they wanted him dead. Nothing happens in small country communities without someone knowing about it. He learned long ago there's always a leak, and all it takes to find that leak is to poke around for a while until someone says something of interest or lets something slip.

A word or two might lead to another source, an individual with a small scrap of information that led to still another scrap until he was able to piece together a complete quilt. He'd done so over a hundred times throughout his long career as constable of Precinct 3.

Juarez, nicknamed after the border town south of the Rio Grande, was a scattered settlement of stark cinder-block honky-tonks on the north bank of the river in Oklahoma, only five miles from Center Springs. Positioned to the right of the highway, across the bridge that marked the state line, Cody's squatty joint was smack in the middle of several dives with sawdust floors, financed by generations of hard-drinking, hard-fighting men who worked a variety of jobs twenty-five miles along either side of the river bottoms.

The rough joints were magnets for trouble. Men were beaten or sometimes killed in the dirt parking lots amid haphazardly-parked cars, or inside the ugly buildings themselves, where sawdust covered the filthy floors and soaked up the blood spilled in fights and cuttings that happened nearly every weekend.

Of course Ned was out of his jurisdiction in Oklahoma, but it wasn't the first time he'd crossed over to investigate Texas crimes. A river dividing the states didn't do a thing to keep criminals on one side or the other. Ned was seven years of age when Oklahoma was still considered Indian Territory, and a lawman uncle told him it was a well-known fact that a man could get killed quick as lightning once he crossed the river.

Lamar Country residents cut their teeth on stories of outlaws and Indians who fought, hid out, and died up in the rough, lawless territories. Ned, whose family ties reached back to Cynthia Ann and Quanah Parker, the famous Comanche warrior, had long ago lost count of the men he helped arrest in Oklahoma towns as far north as Tulsa.

He killed the engine in front of The Sportsman's Lounge and listened to the sedan's hood tick as it cooled. Against the advice of his family, Cody bought the bar right after he came home from Vietnam only eighteen months earlier, but kept it after he was elected constable.

Few constables could live on what the county paid.

Ned farmed. Cody ran a joint.

He considered taking his shotgun in, but since he wasn't after any specific person and it was full daylight, Ned settled for the .38 on his hip and the little star pinned onto his shirt pocket. The pump twelve meant business, and he wasn't in that particular mood right then.

The jukebox was blaring a new Buck Owens song about having a tiger by the tail when Ned stepped through the metal door into the dim, smoky interior. He moved to the right so he wouldn't be silhouetted in the bright doorway.

Ned waited as his eyes adjusted to the darkness.

A dozen men were scattered in the smoke-filled room that reeked of spilled beer, stale cigarettes, and unwashed bodies. One was so drunk he could barely lift his head.

Low-wattage fixtures and colorful neon lights advertising Jax, Hamms, and Miller Highlife flickered behind the bar and on the walls.

Bar hounds were always easy to identify, in Ned's opinion. Greasy hair, khaki pants, cigarettes rolled into t-shirt sleeves or bulging the pockets of western snap shirts, and scuffed brogans were common.

Faces always registered their time spent drinking. Eyes wrinkled and squinted by cigarette smoke gave them a sorry look that said they had no use for anything or anyone outside the joint.

Nothing felt right from the moment Ned walked in, and it raised goose bumps on the back of his neck.

The bartender glanced at the Texas constable, and then cut his eyes to the only guy in the honky-tonk wearing a flattop.

Bulging with muscles, the man wore a tight western shirt with the sleeves rolled over thick forearms. He slipped on a pair of dark shades before crossing his arms over a massive chest in both a challenge and a show of indifference to the constable's presence.

Two customers at the bar watched the mirror behind the bartender to check who was coming in. Recognizing Ned, they returned to their half-finished beers. Leaning back in a chair behind them was Philip Fuller, a no'count who lived in Garrett's Bluff, west of Center Springs. At least four times in the past two years, Ned had arrested Philip for drunk driving, trying to get home through Center Springs after spending all his money there in Juarez.

Philip glared at the constable for a long moment before thumping his chair down on all four legs and wrapping both hands around a sweating can of beer. He ran shaky fingers through black Vitalis-slick hair before breaking eye contact.

Ned didn't recognize Philip's companion, or most of the other men sprinkled around the tables. They watched Ned from the corners of their eyes.

The slim bartender in a faded shirt moved down toward Ned's end of the room. "Mr. Parker, haven't seen you in a long time. How's Cody?"

By then Ned's eyes were accustomed to the room's dim light. He crossed to the empty end of the bar and rested his left elbow on the worn mahogany surface to face outward. "I'm fine, D.A., Cody's better. I reckon he'll go back to work before long. Has he been in since the…accident?"

"Nossir. He's called a couple of times, but that's all. He's letting me keep the place open while he heals up."

"He oughta shut it down and sell this stink hole. It's a nervous place for any decent man. You don't look too steady yourself. Anything wrong?"

"Nossir." D.A. glanced at the liquor bottles behind the bar. "Can I do anything for you Mister Ned? Get you anything? I mean, how about an RC or a Co-cola?"

"Naw. I ain't thirsty and unless you can tell me who ambushed Cody, I don't know what else to ask you for."

"I wish I knew. I truly do, but I don't have any idy."

"Has anyone talked about it in here?"

D.A.'s eyes flicked again toward the customer wearing shades, and he swallowed loudly. "Why sure. That's pretty much all these boys have talked about, except for baseball and pus… uh…poontang, Mr. Ned, but it don't look like anyone knows who done it."

"Umm hum. Howdy, boys." Ned's voice carried over the jukebox. "Y'all heard anything about Cody's ambush?"

The barfly nearest Ned shrugged. "Naw, just he was shot at and missed." His partner mimicked the shrug and stared into his beer.

The jukebox went silent as the song ended. The beer cooler hummed in the background.

"That's better," Ned said. "Now I can hear without all that noise."

With a snicker, Flattop stood and dug in his pocket for change. He smirked at Ned from behind his shades, and then sauntered to the jukebox to feed a handful of coins into the slot. He punched several buttons. The selection lever grabbed a record and flipped it onto the spindle. The player arm lowered the needle. It hissed and popped for a moment before settling into the grooves. Music again filled the bar.

"That's better." Flattop rolled his thick shoulders. "I'd rather hear Whispering Bill Anderson than a lawman, any time." He sauntered back to his table, grinning all the way.

"Who is he?" Ned felt the early edge of heat rising in his face.

D.A. absently pointed with a beer opener in his hand. "Name's Vince Whitlatch, Mr. Ned. Ain't from around here. Showed up a couple of months ago with money in his pocket and a chip on his shoulder. Says he works for Red River Freight, but he's in here a lot of the time and he's whipped everybody who stood up to him and…"

"I don't like people talking about me." Whitlatch returned to his table and dropped heavily into a chair. "It ain't nobody's business who I am and what I done, especially not from Texas law standing behind a little bitty badge."

"I believe I've heard about you." Ned was glad Whitlatch had chosen "Still," a relatively quiet song. It wasn't as loud as the one playing when he entered. "I'm asking around, that's all."

"Ask on your side of the river."

Ned's face flushed, but something about the man's attitude, and something else he couldn't put his finger on, made him cautious. "No need to get all riled up, buddy."

"I'm not *riled*, yet, *buddy*."

Their exchange crackled in the smoky air.

"Well, don't let yourself get that way."

"I'll damn sure get any way I want to."

"You *better* cool off. I was talking to D.A. here."

Whitlatch suddenly slid his chair away from the table and hung his arm over the back in an attitude of feigned relaxation. "I'm cool."

Behind him, two wiry men in the corner stood and drifted toward the bar. Philip Fuller and his friend caught the movement. They threw several bills on the bar, jumped to their feet, and hurried out the door.

The oldest of the two with Whitlatch settled onto one of the recently vacated stools. His younger friend eased down the bar to stand closer to Ned and pushed a pair of horn-rimmed glasses up onto his nose. Others at the scattered, scuffed, and heavily varnished tables watched the scene play out. Ned wasn't sure if they were with Whitlatch, or merely interested in the show.

Whitlatch grinned. "You're losing business since this law blew through the door, D.A."

D.A. nodded quickly. He roughly polished a glass with a stained cloth. "That's all right. Ned's kin to Cody. He won't care."

"I know who he is, and I don't give a shit."

Virtually on his own, Ned was more and more concerned, but he knew better than to show it. He should have told someone where he was going. The constable felt too old for these kinds of throw downs, and he'd noticed over the last year that his nerves were getting the best of him. He controlled his breathing to slow the anger pulsing in his temple.

The first to lose his temper lost the battle.

Ned didn't intend to lose.

Instead of being pulled, he pushed. "Hey Flattop, what have you heard about Cody nearly getting killed? I got a sneaking suspicion you know something."

Whitlatch's smirk faded. "I ain't even met the guy. It sounds to me like he was messin' around in somebody else's business, like you. Whyn't you go somewheres else?"

"I like it right here."

"I don't. Leave."

The order triggered the man in glasses to push away from the bar toward Ned. "You stay right there, feller."

The man nervously adjusted his glasses again. "You can't tell me where I can go."

D.A. picked up a bottle of vodka and tilted it toward the glass already in his hand. "Hatch, why don't you stay right there with Dean? That way I won't have to walk up and down behind this bar to serve you boys. It'll save me a few steps."

Events were quickly spinning out of control, as they do in dark bars among rough men. Tension raised a new coppery odor in the room and Ned wondered what he'd stumbled into. He intended to visit with a few people in Cody's bar, hoping to gain a lead or two. Now here he was in the middle of a rising storm.

It made no sense.

The room went silent again as the record changed. The opening rift of "Secret Agent Man" blared from the speaker.

Whitlatch chuckled and stood. Feet planted in the sawdust, he was solid as an oak. "Old man, it's time for you to get back across the river where you belong."

"Sit down, feller!" Fist fighting was out of the question with a man his size, despite the heavy sap in Ned's back pocket. He rested his hand on the polished wooden butt of his .38.

Both Hatch and Dean shifted uncertainly at the bar, then decided. Dean pushed at his glasses and they started toward Ned. To his dismay, three others stood and watched Whitlatch, apparently waiting for orders.

D.A. reached under the bar for the sawed-off ball bat lying next to a .38 and the door opened, spilling an intense shaft of sunlight into the dim room. Not taking his eyes off of Whitlatch, Ned was peripherally aware of the man who entered the bar.

Backlit, dust rose from the sawdust floor under the boots of a lean and slightly bowlegged figure wearing a wide cowboy hat. "Well, howdy, Ned. I'm surprised to find you in such a place."

Ned instantly recognized the raspy voice.

With the stranger's arrival, the tension stabilized. He stepped inside as the door slammed shut. Without taking his eyes off the room, he smoothly bent and unplugged the jukebox. The colored lights went out. Inside, the vacuum tubes quickly faded and the song dragged to a stop.

The newcomer hooked a chair with the toe of his boot and pulled it away from the table between himself and the customers. "There. That's better. I can't stand that noise. Hurts my ears." His raspy voice was clear and sharp in the sudden silence. "My word. I've walked into a...situation here."

Whitlatch used his index finger and pulled the shades down on his nose to glare over the top, noting the stranger's black Stetson, and most interestingly, two belts disappearing under a sport coat, the lower one thicker and hand tooled. "Who are *you*, pops?"

"Tom Bell."

Chapter Twelve

Ned's momentary relief drained away, leaving him empty. Instead of being in charge of his own situation and safety, he found himself worrying about the much older man.

Tom Bell glanced around the room. "I dropped by for a beer, but it looks like I've interrupted you boys in a serious discussion."

"This ain't none of your bidness."

Tom appeared to grow six inches in response to Whitlatch's challenge. His unusual eyes widened even more, as if gathering light in the shadowy honky-tonk. "I don't know who you are, son, but I'm not accustomed to being talked to in such a rude fashion. Where I come from, men treat each other with respect."

"Tom…" Ned warned.

"This don't look quite right." Bell moved a little closer to the middle of the room, slightly behind Whitlatch, who didn't like the realignment one little bit. "It's unsettling to see men squared off against one another, especially if one of them is an officer of the law, as Ned is, right? But it is a bar, ain't it, where if memory serves, there's always a certain amount of *discomfort* between drinkers and the law. I guess that's the nature of things, right?"

Whitlatch straightened and again flexed his shoulders to make himself more antagonistic. It had always worked before and people quickly backed down. "Get back over there, or better yet, get the hell on out of here before you get hurt, pops."

Somehow, the power had shifted and Ned couldn't figure out why. Tom should have been nervous, but he seemed *energized* by the standoff. "I told you my name, Mr. Shades. What's yours?"

"Name's Whitlatch, and I'm your worst nightmare, you son of a bitch!"

Bell didn't change expression and his voice remained strong. "Oh no, son. I have a lot of years behind me and nightmares are an old friend. I doubt yours is even a *chigger* on my ass, son. Now, you listen, because I'm sure Ned there is tired of talking to men who are wearisome as a horsefly.

"I don't like to come into a bar with the intention of having a cool beer, and instead find a pissant like you giving lip to an officer of the law. That don't set right with me." Tom moved again. Ned realized he intended for the men to turn, putting them off balance because now Tom had created the same pincer maneuver they'd planned for Ned.

But then Tom actually stepped *toward* Whitlatch. Despite his admiration, Ned's unease doubled and he kept an eye on Whitlatch's friends.

Don't he know those other guys are with him?

"Now Ned is doing what I'd be doing if a family member of mine was shot and left for dead, right? He's looking for answers, and I am too, 'cause I'm the one that found Cody that night and I knew something smelled wrong from the get-go. Cowards ambushing a lawman gets stuck in my craw and I don't like it one little bit, right?

"When I walked in here Ned had his hand on his gun, and that means he feels threatened. Well, that ain't right, son. It don't hardly seem fair, either, six against one, so now I figure to even things up a mite for my new friend here."

Whitlatch forced a snicker. His toadies chuckled along with their boss.

Tom advanced again, still addressing Whitlatch as if he was in a classroom instead of a dingy cinder-block Oklahoma bar. "Oh, I wouldn't take this situation lightly, son. You don't know what I'm capable of. Ned doesn't even know yet. We only met a short while back, so let me tell you a little something. I'm from down on the Rio Grande, and this crummy little *Juarez* of yours here ain't even the tiny white dot on chicken shit for mean. Those Meskin towns have the corner on mean, let me tell you. Some of the locals kill for a livin'.

"Anyway, I don't like the odds in here one little bit, so here's what I'm gonna do. I'll step outside with your friends over there and leave you and Ned to talk it out, and when he's done, y'all can go on about your bidness, if you can, while I get that cold beer I came in here for."

With the deftness of a magician, Whitlatch produced a switch-blade and snapped it open. "That won't be no match. He's nothing without that big nigger of his to back either one of you up."

The air in the smoky room thickened. At the same time Ned unsnapped the strap on his holster. For the first time in his life, he cocked the pistol before drawing it.

It seemed impossible, but Tom Bell's eyes widened further than his usual large stare. He suddenly *radiated* menace. "Oh, no, son. Now you've changed the game."

Tom slowly raised his left hand to smooth his well-trimmed mustache. With the other, he pulled his coat back a bit and rested his palm on the hand tooled gun belt just above a well-oiled pistol. "Put that knife away and let's be done with this little discussion."

Whitlatch's own eyes narrowed at the sight of the automatic in the holster. The odds in the deadly game had changed.

Tom waited, whip thin and coiled. "This little showdown is over, son."

Whitlatch licked his lips and lowered the knife in his hand.

The sport coat returned to cover Tom's pistol. "I'm through talking, and I'm tired of looking at this little gang of half-assed bad guys. Y'all get out of here, and when we get ready to leave, I don't want you in the parking lot a-waitin' on us, neither, right?"

Whitlatch did his best to stare the man down, but those wide eyes looked insane to him, and he knew insanity very, very well. Tom Bell wasn't wearing a badge, and to wear a pistol outright was a shock. He'd bet a dollar to a donut that he was half a second away from getting shot.

Three heartbeats later he held up his free hand, carefully folded the knife, and slipped it into his back pocket. "All right, Tom Bell. We'll leave, but you understand it'll be me and you one of these days."

Ned spoke up. "That sounds like a threat to me, Whitlatch. I intend to tell Sheriff Clayton Matthews what I heard in here, so he'll be watching on this side of the river. I'll be waiting for you on my side. If anything happens to this man, even if he falls off his porch and it's his fault, I'm coming after you."

Whitlatch slowly settled his shades back into place and built a thin grin. "You two old men watch yourselves."

Tom met his gaze. "Always do. That's how we got to be old."

With practiced insolence, Whitlatch motioned to his men. Bright light flooded in as they opened the steel door and left. Whitlatch stopped at the threshold. "I'll see y'all some other time."

The door banged shut.

Tom joined Ned at the bar. On the other side, D.A. straightened up and rolled his head to pop his neck. He took a deep breath and smiled. "What'll y'all have?"

Tom appeared to be surprised at the question. "Well, that beer I came in for, of course."

Ned carefully uncocked his revolver and snapped the leather strap back into place over the hammer. He wanted to ask Tom about what was under his jacket, but changed his mind for the time being.

"I'll have that Co-cola now, too."

He was mighty thirsty. His questions could wait until they were back across the river.

Chapter Thirteen

A month later, Miss Becky was sorting a load of clothes for her new washer when Ned came through the screen door. After more than forty years of marriage, washing clothes suddenly bordered dangerously close to enjoyable for a woman who'd been filling a round tub washer by hand most of her life.

Right after they were married, Miss Becky used a pair of laundry tubs to scrub Ned's overalls. The galvanized tubs he bought tenth-hand down at the cotton gin worked for years, until he came home one day not long after the war with the freestanding round washer. She was delighted with the wringer attached to the top, but she still had to roll the machine out on the porch, fill it with water heated to a boil on the stove, and then rinse with cold water drawn from the tap under her rough kitchen counter.

The new washer directly attached to water and electricity made the common chore a pleasure and kept both Ned and Top in clean clothes brightened by liberal applications of Mrs. Stewart's bluing. Now all she needed was to get someone to run water lines up through the plywood kitchen counter top and install a sink so she could get rid of the two WWII era dish pans.

She was already thinking about a clothes dryer.

Ned couldn't get used to the loud machine in the kitchen. Its constant hum, slosh, and gurgling weighed on his mind every time he entered the house, and this time was no exception. Ned laid two Chick-O-Sticks candies on the table. It was his custom to bring something from the store each time he went, whether it be candy, apples, cantaloupes, or even onion sets or tomato plants, if the season was right. It was his way of supporting the small businesses with the loose change in his pockets. This time he'd been to Arthur City, and the little store there didn't have much more on the shelves than candy and tobacco.

He hadn't even taken off his hat when a car pulled into the long driveway in front of the house. Through the screen door, Ned watched Cody's El Camino slowly crunching across the gravel.

"Looky who's here."

Miss Becky immediately went to the Frigidaire and removed a bowl of leftovers. "I bet he's starving."

"He has a wife at home. I imagine he eats enough."

Cody honked when the car stopped.

"He ain't coming in to eat." Ned stepped outside.

Cody called through the open passenger window. "Come go with me up to the domino hall. I got a call that Carl Gibbs is there and drunk as a skunk."

"I'll be back directly, Mama." The screen door slapped behind him and Ned joined Cody in his El Camino. He settled in, trying to fit his round frame into the tight front seat. "You need a haircut."

Cody grinned, knowing the curls over his collar bothered Ned. It was a far cry from the Boy's Regular that Top wore, or Ned's crown of hair trimmed short around a bald pate. The truth was, he intended to go up to his Uncle Buck's front porch barbershop that same morning, but the call had interrupted his plans.

For Ned's sake, Cody lowered the volume on the radio so the Beatles singing "Eight Days a Week" wouldn't annoy him any more than he already was.

Ned twisted the knob even more, to silence the radio. "What'd Carl do this time?"

"He's trying to start a fight with anybody he can drag in. Neal called from the store and said we might want to get over there."

Neal Box owned one of the two wood-framed general stores bracketing the rough domino hall. His store was originally the

Center Springs courthouse that fell in disrepair and was in danger of rotting away. Neal bought the one room building, moved it next to the domino hall in competition with Oak Peterson's store on the opposite side, and after a facelift, stocked the shelves with bread, canned goods, feed, harnesses, and other small farming implements.

"You feel like fooling with this today?" Ned watched bodark fence posts flash past his window. Cut from the hard wood of scraggly bodark trees, the usually crooked posts defined the fences of northeast Texas. "I'm not completely sure you're healed up."

Cody liked to drive fast. "I'm fine. For a while there I got tired easy, but I'm feeling good enough to think about taking the kids fishing up on the Little River."

The ancient Kiamichi Mountains were worn to nothing more than what could be truly called foothills. The rolling, heavily-timbered country was fractured with rocky streams full of smallmouthed bass and fat blue catfish.

"You think that's a good idea? There ain't much up there north of Cloudy if y'all get into trouble."

"You took me up there from the time the top of my head reached your belt. Nobody'll mess with me up in Oklahoma." Cody steered into Neal's bottlecap-paved parking lot. "I thought we'd do a little bank fishing in a couple of those holes you showed me."

"Well, it might be smart to stick close to the house for a while until we figure out who it was that took a shot at you."

No one was outside of the domino hall when they stepped out of the El Camino. Cody settled the Colt 1911 in the holster on his belt and trailed Ned up the three plank steps. The doors and windows were open to catch the breeze and everything inside seemed normal.

To Cody's knowledge, the building had never seen a coat of paint. Though nothing was, or had ever been, for sale inside, the exterior was colored with a variety of advertisements from RC and Double Colas to Ideal Bread. A vertical four-foot metal Orange Crush sign was nailed haphazardly on the west side, not particularly for advertisement, because the bottle itself had been discontinued forty years earlier, but to cover a large hole in the wall.

Half-a-dozen discarded tables with mismatched chairs crowded the single twenty- by-twenty-foot room. A cold wood stove occupied one corner. Bare light bulbs dangled on frayed wires above each table. Three tables sat empty, with loose dominos scattered across the worn surfaces amid empty spit cans and ashtrays.

The other three were in use by a dozen players, squinting at the dots through thick cigar and cigarette smoke. At the only table to the left of the door, and obviously drunk, Carl Gibbs sat beside a scraped and dented metal cooler. The last time Ned saw Carl, he was standing before Judge O.C. Rains that snowy day after Cody was ambushed.

Carl cleared his throat and spat on the floor. "Who called the laws?"

"Howdy, men." Ned stepped onto the rough plank floor and as a courtesy, was careful not to stand directly behind any of the players.

Cody rested one hip on an empty table near the door, tilted his Stetson back, and watched the play at Carl's table.

A domino slapped the scarred pine surface. "Dime."

Another slap. "Made a nickel."

The scorekeeper marked an X on his pad with a pencil sharpened with a pocket knife.

Carl drained a Jax and pitched the empty can out of the open window behind him. He flipped open the lid of his metal cooler and fished around in the ice and water for a replacement.

Cody leaned toward Ned in a stage whisper. "That's what I call drinkin' in public. You'd think he'd act right since he's out on bond."

"We're setting right *here*, Carl."

The drunk squinted at Ned. "I see all ya'll."

The Parker men exchanged grins while the players laughed loud and long. The drunk's smart response was the equivalent of drawing a line in the sand. At that point the only recourse was to take Carl in, but the mood was still light, and neither of the constables wanted to make more than the situation warranted.

"This ish Oklahoma beer. You cain't get drunk on three-two, besides, I bought it at your place, Cody." Carl dug a church key out of his shirt pocket and levered two triangle-shaped holes in the top of the dripping can.

Ned shot his nephew a disgusted look that spoke volumes. Instead of catching Ned's eye, Cody kept his attention on Carl. The man had a nose like Jimmy Durante, and its size always fascinated Cody. "Why don't we go outside and talk about this?"

"Cain't, we're winning." Carl tilted the freshly-opened can and sucked down half the contents in one long draught.

"No y'ain't." Steve Perkins shook the rocks with a disgusted look on his face, shuffling them for the next draw. Somewhat of a dandy, Perkins lived alone in a tiny two-room house up behind the cotton gin and only worked when he needed money for groceries. You could tell it, too, from his smooth hands to hair slicked down with HA hair oil. "We ain't won a hand since you cracked that first beer."

"Thass'cause you don't shake 'em good enough."

"Come outside with me for a minute." Ned motioned for Carl. "You've already been in jail for beatin' on your wife a while back. Let's talk about this so we can all go home."

"When I'm good and ready. Besides, she provoked me. She'll do that y'know, provoke ya into almost anything."

The Parkers exchanged looks again. Along with his recent arrest for assault and battery, Carl's admission guaranteed a conviction in the coming trial.

Their conversation was interrupted by a Chevrolet sliding to an abrupt stop in the parking lot. Through the open door, Cody recognized the person who stepped out in a cloud of dust and slammed the door in fury. "Uh oh."

The men inside went completely silent when Carl's wife, Tamara, stomped up the steps and blew into the room like a tiny Texas cyclone.

"Careful," Cody said. "She's got her ears laid back. I believe she's mad."

The players chuckled.

Ignoring everyone else in the domino hall, Tamara waved a revolver at her husband. "Carl, you *son* of a bitch!"

They reacted as if a mad bobcat had fallen through the roof. Cody would have preferred the bobcat. Chairs clattered on the pine floor as the lighthearted mood vanished and men scrambled out of the way. As if there was no one else in the domino hall, Tamara aimed her fury on her soon-to-be ex-husband. She didn't notice the two constables nearby.

With what appeared to be a practiced move, Cody casually reached out and stripped the gun away in one motion.

Tamara yelped when the trigger guard scraped against her index finger. She glared around the dismal room, suddenly realizing there were others nearby.

"You wait a minute, gal." Ned stepped between the two. "We're here to take care of your problem, so cool off."

Cody expertly popped the cylinder, slapped the ejection rod with his palm, and dumped the loads onto the floor. He pitched the empty revolver to Ned and walked around the table. "Tamara, you stand right there and don't do or say nothin' else. Stand up, Carl. I'm gonna put some cuffs on you so we can sort this out."

He fully intended to cuff Tamara also, for waving a pistol, but he wanted Carl out of the way first.

"I ain't a-goin'."

"Yes you are."

Tamara pointed a finger at Carl's face. "Do what they say, you son of a bitch!"

"You done said that, Tamara, now back off." Ned knew they had to move quickly before things accelerated. "Stand up, Carl."

"Nossir."

Shouldering Tamara out of the way, Cody grabbed a handful of Carl's grimy collar and yanked him to his feet. Carl swung an elbow back, catching the young deputy in the chest. Cody staggered back and regained his balance.

Chairs skittered on the dirty floor as they scuffled back and forth. Cody didn't want the arrest to turn into a fist fight, so he worked hard to get the drunk in a headlock. Terrified that Cody'd get hurt again so soon after getting out of the hospital, Ned kicked a table out of the way and grabbed Carl's arm to twist it behind his back.

Carl swung a fist at Ned, who ducked under the blow and pushed both struggling men against the wall. Planks cracked under the impact and metal signs on the outside rattled. The wall bowed outward, almost collapsing into the parking lot.

"Owww! You're tearing my ear off, Cody!"

"Well, quit fighting."

"I ain't fighting, I'm resisting arrest."

"Well, give up, you idiot."

"Let me go!"

Finally getting a good grip on Carl's head, Cody planted his feet, and with fresh leverage, banged the drunk's head into the plank wall.

"Owwww! You're a-hurtin' me, Cody!"

"I'm about to hurt you worse if you don't get them hands behind you!"

Carl stomped Ned's foot and he hopped backward with a curse. Before he could get back into the fray, Tamara leaped onto his back, nearly driving him to the ground.

"What the *hell!!!???*"

A banshee shriek nearly ruptured his eardrum. Ned reached back and grabbed a handful of curly brown hair. He yanked, and Tamara flew over his shoulder to land on her back with a dusty thump on the floor.

"Girl, what the *hell* are you doing?"

"You're hurting my husband!"

Ned suddenly found himself in the type of domestic argument that was often fatal to lawmen trying to help. "We ain't hurtin' him! We're gonna take him to jail until he sobers up."

"Let him alone!"

"He's drunk! We're taking him in, so you back away until we get the cuffs on him!"

Ned spun back to the fight. Cody had Carl on the floor, one hand twisted behind his back, and cuffed his left arm with a ratcheting series of clicks. Ned hurried over to put his knee on Carl's neck and grab his free arm.

"Awww Ned! You're breaking my neck!"

"Quit fighting!"

Ned twisted Carl's stiff arm and he shrieked again. Before Cody could lock the cuff around the drunk's other wrist, they were hit with what felt like a freight train as Tamara climbed on the table and leaped into the struggle. Ned staggered and Cody lost his hold on Carl's arm. He landed on his back with a thud, but managed to use his knee to catch Tamara's falling body as she rolled off Ned's back a second time. With a grunt, he bucked and threw her halfway across the domino hall.

Ned gave Carl's cuffs one last squeeze, finally clicking them into place. Furious, Cody launched himself off the floor as Tamara roared back for a third round. He shoulder-blocked her, lifted the enraged little woman off the floor, and threw her onto the ground like a calf.

Ned joined the battle, but it was like trying to hold a mad coon twisting inside its own skin. She squalled and bit him as he bent her arm back.

"Let go, Cody. I got her!"

For some reason, Cody didn't release his grip on her other arm. Ned's fear increased as she flailed around. This was the type of oddball fight that could reinjure Cody's barely healed spine. "Turn loose. I got her. Make sure Carl stays down."

"I cain't, Ned!"

"I said turn her aloose!"

Frustrated, Cody locked Tamara's arm straight and twisted it around to show Ned the straight razor in her hand. "I told you, I can't!"

"Hang on to her, Cody! Hang on!"

Like a rag doll, Tamara dropped to her knees and arched her back. Getting enough leverage, she threw her head back and busted Cody's lip. Tired of trying not to hurt her, he grabbed her belt, lifted her completely into the air and slammed her face first onto the plank floor. The razor rattled across the boards and the fight was over.

"Dammit woman, settle down!"

Still face down on the floor, Carl shouted over his shoulder as Ned finished cuffing her free arm. "See! See! That's why I had to use a singletree on her. Like I told O.C., the bitch'll provoke ya!"

Chapter Fourteen

Tom Bell was standing beside his truck when Ned exploded through the door, pushing Carl ahead and ignoring his complaining.

Tamara came boiling out behind them, cussing a blue streak and threatening her husband for getting her in trouble. Cody had a good grip on the cuffs behind her back and yanked her when she kicked sideways like a cow, trying to get in a good lick on Carl, but she missed.

Cody kept her out of kicking distance, but he doubted Carl'd have felt it anyway, because by then the alcohol had kicked in and he was drunk as a skunk.

They thundered down the steps. Tom Bell grinned up at them. Ned shoved Carl toward his car. "Howdy, Tom, you got here just in time."

"Seems like you Parkers are in some kind of trouble every time we run across one another."

Cody laughed. It was obvious he was having fun with the fight, though his shirttail was out and his face was flushed red. "This ain't no trouble, a little family disagreement is all."

Tom crossed his arms and leaned back against the truck. "I ran out of nails and figured Neal might have a few that I could buy. Then the domino hall looked good to me and I decided I'd like to sit in on a game or two, but it don't seem as friendly in here as Ned led me to believe."

Ned opened the back door of his sedan and threw Carl onto the seat. He slammed it and joined them. "This don't happen too often. These two go at it pretty regular, but it usually ain't up here by the store. Cody, you gonna stand there holding her all day?"

"She needs to cool down for a few minutes."

"I'm all right now." Tamara panted with exertion.

"You say that, but your eyes tell me different." Cody kept a tight grip on the cuffs.

The fight finally hissed out of her all at once. Her knees trembled as the adrenaline wore off. "I have to sit down."

"All right. I'm gonna put you in my El Camino, but you behave yourself and sit there until I get in. I don't want to rassle you anymore."

"I'm done."

Cody deposited her into the seat as his radio squawked to life. "Cody, you there?"

He reached across the woman, who had suddenly begun to cry. Ignoring her tears, he stretched the cord across the cab, straightened up, and keyed the microphone. "Go ahead, Martha."

"Cody you holler at Ned and y'all run over to Floyd Lake. There's been a drowning and someone there's calling for y'all."

"That's barely four miles out of Chisum. Who's calling for a constable? I imagine the Sheriff's Department or the police need to handle that'un."

"James Parker is there and asked for you."

Cody went cold. He knew James and Ida Belle had taken the kids to the town lake for a little fishing and a picnic. "Martha, you tell me the truth. Is it any of my family that drowned?"

He released the talk button and Martha was already speaking. "Oh god, Cody, I didn't mean to scare you. It ain't your family, they're all right. James saw the whole thing, and it was him called it in from the bathhouse. Your people are fine."

Cody put his head on the cab's roof for a moment to collect himself. "All right, then. We'll be right out."

He paused for a long moment. "Ned, we have to roll. There's been a drowning and they've called for us." He sighed. "Tamara, for shit's sake, cool off and quit chewing on my microphone cord."

◇ ◇ ◇

They arranged for John Washington to meet them at the turnoff to Lake Floyd to pick up Carl and Tamara. They'd switched cars and were in Ned's sedan. Tamara rode in the front seat with him while Cody sat in the back with Carl. The precautions were unnecessary, though, because Carl passed out before they got on the highway, and Tamara wept for the entire drive.

John was waiting at the rock sign beside the turnoff. "Floyd Lake" was carved deeply into a limestone slab quarried far from Lamar County. The only thing under their feet was sandstone and red clay.

"You want me to follow y'all out there?" John agreed to take them to jail while the Parkers investigated the drowning.

Floyd Lake was off limits to coloreds, and Ned knew the sight of John near the small lake might set off a firestorm with relatives who were already shocked and grieving over the drowning.

"I don't believe so." Ned and John drug Carl's limp weight out of the sedan and stuffed him into John's car. Tamara wiped her face and slid in beside him, cradling his flopping head as much as she could with cuffs on. She wiped his hair and kissed his forehead.

Ned shook his head in disgust. They'd be at it again before the week was out, and it'd probably happen in the middle of the night, interrupting his rest.

The trouble on Floyd Lake started back in the winter of 1935 when the park was finished by the Civilian Conservation Corps. After completion of the 1,000-acre lake, the Corps wanted to transfer ownership to the state parks board, but a committee led by then Sheriff Delbert Poole refused to allow the transfer of the land, because the proposed swimming facilities under the state park service would be open to anyone—black, white, or red.

Poole and a number of the long-gone city leaders didn't want to drink water coloreds swam in, so they blocked the transfer and the parks department gave up. After that, the lake was the municipal water source, but it was almost ignored by the City Council and most disturbances were handled by the local constabulary.

John knew full well why Ned didn't want him there, but he flashed the Parkers a grin. "I'll take these two from here. Y'all let me know what happened."

Glad to be relieved of Tamara and Carl, they pulled up to a crowd surrounding the funeral home ambulance. Two boats were already on the sun-drenched lake, dragging for the body. It surprised Ned, because the lake was owned by the town of Chisum, and they were notoriously slow at responding to incidents at their own water source.

The milling onlookers parted as the lawmen made their way down to the rickety boat dock. It was a scene they'd seen all too many times. A woman shrieked on the nearby grassy bank, surrounded by several children that favored her. A number of shocked faces watched the men as they approached.

They hoped they could help, but as unfortunate tradition dictated, lawmen usually arrived too late to do much more than take reports and try to assist the living.

The dead were already gone.

James met them beyond earshot of the grieving family. Top and Pepper hung close, away from the crowd and weeping woman. "Dad, I know there ain't much you can do, but I figured you oughta be here anyway. I don't believe I've ever seen anything so terrible happen so fast, and weren't nothing anyone could do."

He paused to gather himself.

"We were sitting under that tree over there, eating our dinner, when this family here came up in their little boat. Didn't none of them have a life jacket on, but nobody out here was wearing one today, the wind was so still.

"They came up to the dock here, and the daddy set the kids out one at a time. Then the mama got out while he steadied the boat. When she stepped off, the boat shot out from under him and he fell out and hit his head on the corner post there.

"Ned, that feller went in the water as slick as a snake and he never hardly caused a ripple, and he ain't come up yet."

Cody nodded his head toward Top and Pepper. "They see it?"

"Sure 'nough. Everybody was watching them get out of the boat because they had a whole stringer of perch and were holding it up."

Ned stared across the still lake and felt his heart sink. "My Lord. The angels come and get you just...that...fast."

Chapter Fifteen

Miss Becky was stirring a pot of boiling rice when I came in for breakfast. She always considered rice a breakfast food. Long before the water cooked out of the pan, she shut off the burner and put a lid on the pot. It sure beat the corn flakes Grandpa liked to eat before she put eggs and bacon on his plate.

She kneaded the biscuit dough resting on a plywood bread-board. I had never seen her hands idle. They were always busy as all get-out with sewing, cutting vegetables from the garden, or washing.

"It's nearly dinnertime and you're just now stirring this morning. I guess it's 'cause you flopped around most of the night, little man. I heard you all the way in our bedroom."

"I was having bad dreams."

She rolled the dough flat with a glass rolling pin. "They weren't about the Rock Hole, were they?"

"No ma'am." Those dreams I had about the swimming hole were bad for several months, but they finally led Grandpa and Mr. John to save us from the Skinner, a killer who terrorized people in Center Springs over a year earlier. "These are about a big ol' dark building and people with black hair. They keep trying to catch me and lock me up in caves."

Some of us Parkers had always been either blessed or cursed, however you wanted to look at it, with a vague ability to see the future. Unfortunately for us, the dreams seldom made sense, and we usually couldn't figure them out until after something occurred. Then everything was usually clear, but always too late.

She used a biscuit cutter to remove round disks from the dough, and dipped each one in lard before crowding it into the pan. "Sounds like the Cotton Exchange. That place burned down, and good riddance. I'm thankful to the good Lord that Cody and John got out of there before it fell."

"It ain't the Cotton Exchange." I thought about it for a minute. "I was using my secret agent briefcase outside there in the hot sun and taking pictures with it of dark people talking. I don't know what all this is, but I wake up feeling like I'm in trouble or something."

"You ain't in trouble, hon."

"I know that, but I still feel like something bad is about to happen. There's kids in the dream, too, and it looks like one of them old timey movies with Model T cars, and horses, and people who look Indian."

Miss Becky paused, turning something over in her mind. "I want to ask you something, but you don't say nothing to nobody after we're done here. There ain't nothin' wrong, but there's some stories and feelings that needs to be left alone."

"Yessum."

"In these dreams, are there colored people with the Indians, and are there little children that ain't right?"

By that, she meant retarded, because that's the way our people talked about anyone who wasn't right, the way they called some kids Mongoloid.

"No. They're Indian-looking people."

"What about them horses? Do they act normal?"

I couldn't figure out what she was talking about. "They're horses."

"Does it look like when me and your Grandpa were young?"

"I didn't say y'all were in the dreams."

"I know, but was it around that time?"

"I can't say."

Great-Grandpa could put his finger a time or two on things that he dreamed and understood, but his visions weren't dreams. They were real, like the time he and Great-Grandma were hurrying out of the bottoms in the wagon to get the doctor for his mama. Before they crossed the creek bridge in broad daylight, a wooden coffin floated across the dirt road. He knew what had happened, reined in the horses, and went on back home, because he knew his mama had already died.

She was gone when they got there.

"Where's Grandpa?" I didn't want to tell her about the angels, either. I had to study on that one for a while. I'd dreamed they were wrapping someone up with their wings so they wouldn't get hurt in a hailstorm, but I couldn't tell who it was that was in trouble. I thought it was Uncle Cody in the car wreck a few months earlier, but there wasn't any hail that night, only snow, and we usually don't dream of stuff after it happens, so I didn't want to worry Miss Becky about angels, 'cause I knew she'd have to take us to church and pray on it.

"He went with your Uncle Cody up to the store."

The rice was still soupy and full of juice when she dipped a bowl full and sweetened it with sugar. "Eat this. Pepper and Ida Belle will be here in a little bit."

"I remember one dream real clear, though. It was about Mark Lightfoot."

She brightened at his name. Mark Lightfoot was full-blood Choctaw, and I met him up at the feed store in Hugo. He came to live with us for a while when his whole family was murdered not far from Grandpa's house. His no'count daddy went to jail, and nobody could find any of his relatives. I think Grandpa and Miss Becky were about to try and adopt him when some of his Choctaw kinfolk showed up in the yard one day and took him away.

"What was it about?"

"Not much, but he was talking about you and wanted some of your biscuits." Mark loved her cooking, and while he lived with us, he must have growed three inches. "We talked for a while, but I can't remember what it was about, and then an

Indian with his long hair tied back threw a handful of powder onto a fire and Mark disappeared."

Miss Becky closed her eyes and moved her lips in a quiet prayer. "Well, let's hope he's doing all right. Was there anything else?"

I still had angels on my mind, but I kept that one to myself.

I was on my hands and knees beside the pasture, crawling up on a red bird sitting on the bottom strand of the bobwire fence, when Uncle James' car pulled up in the drive and Aunt Ida Bell and Pepper got out. For once Hootie wasn't interested in what I was doing. He was dozing on the front porch and out of my way. Aunt Ida Belle pulled a bag full of clothes out of the back seat and went inside the house.

Pepper walked over to where I was within ten feet of the bird, but she didn't sneak. The red bird cheeped, flipped the line, and was gone.

I stood up, frustrated. "What did you do that for?"

"What? What were you doing?"

"I was sneaking up on that bird."

"What's in your hand?"

"Miss Becky's salt shaker."

"What are you doing with that?"

"Uncle Cody told me that if I could sneak up and shake salt on a bird's tail, it'd let me pick it up."

Pepper snickered. "You ignernt shit! That's what adults tell us, but it ain't true. You can't sneak up on a tee-tiny bird like that and shake salt on it. It'll fly away every time. What they're trying to say is if you can get close enough to shake salt on it, you're already close enough to catch the stupid bird, and that's all."

I was suddenly embarrassed when I realized I'd been had again by an adult. I held the shaker down low beside my leg, to get it out of sight. I felt like giving her a punch in the kisser. "What are y'all doing here?"

"Mama had some clothes that needed sewing, and our machine is on the fritz, so she came over to use Miss Becky's treadle."

Electric machines sometimes have problems with their motors, but Miss Becky's foot-treadle Singer always worked.

I noticed the pocket on Pepper's jeans was full of something. "What's that?"

With a grin, she tugged out a little transistor radio covered by a leather case. "Listen." She flicked the ON dial with her thumb and Sam the Sham was counting in Spanish. Then his song "Wooly Bully" started.

"That's a nasty song," I told her.

Pepper turned it up. "No it ain't. It's about buffalo."

I wasn't sure, but she usually knew more about that stuff than I did. "Where'd you get the radio?"

"It belongs to Christine Berger. She got it for her thirteenth birthday, but the battery ran out and she didn't have a new one, so she let me borrow it for a while if I'd put a new one in. Look, it has *seven* transistors, that's the best, and it has a *marine* band, too, so you can hear about the ocean."

"Let me see it a minute." She handed me the radio and I slipped the case off, then used my thumb to pop off the back.

"Hey, what the hell are you doing?"

She snatched at my hand, but I jerked it away and held the open radio to my nose to take a deep sniff. Of all the smells in the world, I loved to smell the plastic and transistors best.

"Gimme that back. You're the damnedest thing I've ever seen."

"Here." Instead, I put the radio back together, but not until after one more sniff. The Beach Boys were trying to get Rhonda to help them when I gave it back.

This time Pepper slid it into her shirt pocket so we could hear the music. "Well, what do you want to do?"

"Look at these." I took a package of pictures out of my back pocket. "Miss Becky had these developed at the drugstore. I took 'em with my spy camera."

The pictures were stapled on one end, and bound inside a fold of yellow cardboard. The first shot was fuzzy, but you could tell it was Pepper standing on the front porch.

"I don't remember you taking that one."

I grinned. "That's how you use a spy camera in a case. This is the first one I took and you didn't know it, but it's a little fuzzy."

She flipped to the second photograph. Miss Becky and Grandpa were sitting at the table, and you could tell I shot through the window screen. The third picture of Grandpa asleep in his rocking chair was much better.

"These are boring."

"The snow pictures are next."

She flipped to the next one showing everyone standing outside St. Joseph's Hospital, looking worried. It was the morning we went to visit Uncle Cody after his wreck. "Did you take these through the case?"

I swelled up with pride. "Yep. I got better at holding it still and figuring how to aim."

The last three shots were clearest of all. One was Pepper making a snowball. Another showed the street covered in snow. The last picture was Pepper making a snow angel in front of the courthouse while we waited for Grandpa to come down from visiting with Judge Rains.

She handed them back and I stuffed the booklet into my back pocket. "I'm bored."

I grabbed my BB gun that was leaning against the porch, and Hootie stretched and trotted along behind us. "Let's go to Mr. Tom's." We hadn't been over there in several days, though the sounds of constant hammering told us he was still working on the house. It was quiet that morning, though.

We walked down the hill and along the gravel drive to the highway, then darted across the cement and the bar ditch into the trees on the other side. Hootie ran ahead and then locked up in a point when he smelled quail hiding under a dead limb half-covered with last year's berry vines.

I stepped up like I'd seen Grandpa do, and the little hen exploded through the dried vine and whirred away. I threw the BB gun to my shoulder and sent a shot after it.

"You better be glad you missed that bird," Pepper said. "It ain't quail season and she'll probably make a nest to set pretty soon. Grandpa'd wear your ass out if you'da hit it."

She was right, and I felt bad about shooting, but it didn't seem right to let a flushing bird go after Hootie made such a good point. "Well, it's almost impossible to hit a flying bird with a BB anyway."

"Colton Jenkins hunts them with a twenty-two."

"I've heard that, but I don't believe it. You can't hit a flying bird with a rifle, especially not one as little as that, besides, it's dangerous, there's no telling where that bullet will go."

"Well, they say he does."

For my entire life, I'd wondered who "they" were. "They" were always telling people stuff that was both true and untrue.

We continued through the woods, intending to intersect the two-track road leading to Mr. Tom's house. It didn't take us long to get there, and the silence told me Mr. Tom was gone.

I wanted to turn around and go back home, but Pepper got that light in her eyes again. "Come on. I want to look around while he's gone."

Walking around the house by ourselves didn't seem right to me, even though we'd been over there so much helping him work. The outside was finished, though not yet painted. The foundation was still open, but the floor joists in a couple of rooms resting on fresh new bodark posts were straight and level. I knelt to see if there were any critters under the house, but the only thing under there was Hootie sniffing around.

Everything in the still air smelled like fresh-sawed pine, and sawdust caught in the grass like yellow snow. There were still stacks of lumber covered with canvas tarps in the yard. The scrap lumber fire was almost completely out, though a tiny wisp of smoke rose straight up.

Pepper climbed the porch steps and peeked through the new windows. Mr. Tom hadn't gotten around to hanging curtains yet, and the living room was wide open to the outside. "There's that trunk still sitting in the middle of the floor."

"So."

"I've been wondering what's in it."

"Oh no. You stay out of that house. That's Mr. Tom's trunk, and when he wants us to know what he has in there, he'll tell us."

She left the window and stopped in front of the wooden door. She gave it a push, and it silently swung open. "Ooops." There was that Betty Boop voice of hers, and every time she used it, we got in trouble. "Look, the door is open. He didn't lock it when he left. I bet we oughta to go in and make sure everything is all right. You know, bandits could have come around and robbed him."

I stayed right where I was beside the dying fire, and didn't move. "Don't go in there." We'd been in the house a hundred times in the last few weeks, but it didn't seem right to go in while Mr. Tom was gone.

She peered inside and called in a singsong voice. "Mr. Tom! You've got company! You home?"

I expected to find his truck rolling down the dirt drive at any time.

Pepper stepped inside. "We're here to help clean up some of this sawdust."

Her voice was barely audible, and I was shocked to find myself standing at the base of the new porch steps. "Who you talking to?"

"Nobody, you idiot. He's not home. Come on! Don't you want to know about him?" She came back to the door. "He doesn't tell us anything. I bet there are some papers in the trunk that'll let us know what he did down there in south Texas. I bet he was a cowboy, or a big rancher. I bet that's it. He owned a giant ranch down there like the Ponderosa in Bonanza, and then he sold it and came back up here."

Her eyes widened. "The trunk is probably full of money from the ranch. He hasn't moved it since we first came here, because it's probably full of twenty-dollar gold pieces and it's too heavy."

And there I was, peeking in the doorway. "You think it's full of gold?"

"He's probably a bank robber that got away with a railroad payroll. That or cash money, what else?"

"Probably clothes." Like filings drawn to a magnet, I found myself standing beside her.

"He'd have moved it to the bedroom by now if it had clothes in it." She kicked the trunk, and we could tell it wasn't empty. Pepper dropped to her knees in the sawdust and put her hands on both sides of the battered lid. "Well?"

I couldn't take my eyes off it. I was so nervous I was shaking. "Okay, raise it up and let's take a peek. Then we go."

Her eyes flickered, and she knew she'd won. The lid creaked when she raised it up, and she had to use some muscle. "Wow, this lid is heavy!"

Lying on a stack of leather-bound books was a hand-tooled holster holding a pearl-handled, cocked .45. I recognized it as a Colt 1911, like the one Uncle Cody carried, but this one was so worn and oily it made me think of a water moccasin laying there.

Then we found out why the lid was so heavy. Held against the inside curve with leather straps was a rifle like I'd never seen before. It wasn't in one piece, because the trunk was too short, but the barrel, breech and stock all fit neatly into the curved space. Several magazines were stacked in one corner beside the books, all fully loaded with ammunition.

Eyes glassy with excitement, Pepper reached out and caressed the pistol's handle. "Do you want to hold it?"

I knew better. Guns had always been around us, and Grandpa kept his service revolver on top of the television. The adults allowed us to move them if they were in the way, but we had to have permission to take one out of a holster. We knew it was wrong, but the trunk's power had almost total control over the both of us.

A carved box was nestled on top of a worn Bible beside the pistol. I was reaching for the Colt when Pepper lifted up the box. She carefully opened its lid, and discovered a black-and-white photograph a much younger Mr. Bell with his arm around a beautiful dark haired woman who looked Mexican, or Indian.

Underneath was a badge on a folded red silk handkerchief that smelled like perfume.

My hand stopped short of the pistol. "That's a Texas Ranger badge."

"How do you know?"

"I've seen them up close. Turn it over. It's stamped out of a Mexican peso, and if it's real, writing will still be on the back."

She did, and there it was. "Wonder what he's doing with this?"

"He must be a Ranger."

Texans think Rangers walk on water, and to actually hold an authentic badge, and to know the man who'd worn it, was something close to a holy moment.

I hadn't noticed, but though Pepper's radio was still on, it had gone silent. Then, the first harsh chord of "Hard Day's Night" filled the room. It jolted me like a charge of electricity. I glanced out the door. Mr. Tom's truck flickered through the trees.

Pepper noticed my reaction and recognized the truck. "Shit!" She quickly closed the box's lid, dropped it into the trunk, and stood up. That's when I saw the tracks of our tennies in the fine sawdust on the floor beside Hootie's paw prints. They all led from the door and into the house, and I hadn't even seen him come in.

She slammed the trunk lid, then rushed to the door and slammed it too. "What are we gonna do?"

I took one look at the truck flickering through the trees. "Out the back! Hootie!"

Completely familiar with the house, we shot through the living room and into the kitchen. Hootie came sliding around the corner and met us the second Pepper yanked the back door open. We ran onto the much smaller back porch and I tripped over a paper bag full of finishing nails. It exploded, scattering them everywhere.

Neither of us touched the steps, and in seconds raced across the tiny back yard to disappear into the woods. We charged down a deer trail and didn't stop running until we were well away from the house.

"Did he see us?" Panting, Pepper bent and rested her hands on her knees.

"I don't think so, but he'll know somebody was there, because we left tracks on the floor."

She slapped at the sawdust on her jeans. "What do we do?"

"Hope he doesn't say anything."

We took off down the branch, and I felt bad, because we'd somehow betrayed our new friend.

I corrected myself.

We'd betrayed a Texas Ranger.

Chapter Sixteen

My knees were still shaking when we finally snuck around the pasture and met Grandpa in the yard.

"I'm going by your Uncle Ben's house for a minute, y'all want to go?"

He should have known we'd been up to something by the way we acted, but I reckon he had other things on his mind. Pepper mumbled something about a headache and went in the house. I couldn't think of a good excuse not to go.

When we got there Aunt Sylvia was hanging dingy sheets on the sagging clothesline out back. The open windows caught the breeze, and the curtains were sucked against the rusty screen wire. Chickens and one raggedy turkey scratched in the dirt yard behind her. Thirty yards away, a sow grunted in the hog pen. The smell of soured water and mud filled the yard.

For the first time I could remember, I wondered why they didn't bother to paint their house. It wasn't a bad looking place. A coat of paint would have spruced it up.

We parked on the side of the house and got out. Aunt Sylvia had a mouth full of wooden clothes pins when we walked up. She took them out, dropped them into her apron pocket, and gave us a grin. "What are you boys up to? Y'all out cattin' around today?"

Grandpa stopped beside an overgrown rose bush and stuck his hands in the pockets of his overalls. "Working. Where's Ben? It's too early to plow."

Grandpa never planted a single seed in either the garden or a field until after Easter, and he didn't think anyone else should put in a crop until then, either, because of the danger of frost.

Aunt Sylvia didn't answer for a moment. She absently ran her red fingernail through my white hair. "Cotton Top, I have some Dr Peppers in the icebox. Why don't you get a couple for you and your Grandpa?"

Cotton would have stuck on me, but we already had kinfolk with that nickname, so they settled on calling me Top, for my name, Texas Orrin Parker. Yeah, we already had a Tex, too.

He nodded that it was all right, and I climbed up the rickety porch steps and went in through the loose screen door. There was rust everywhere. It had eaten holes in the screen, and colored the white porcelain sink a crusty reddish color. The water faucet coming out of the wall under the window had almost rusted through and hung on by a promise. Rust even grew through the worn enamel coating of their rattling and wheezing icebox.

I opened the stained door and found very little food. Half a pan of biscuits, a full bottle of milk, and a dish with a soft stick of butter were the only things on the top shelf. The second was full of Dr Peppers and Miller Highlife beer.

It was mostly beer.

The bottom shelf contained only two bowls covered with foil. Miss Becky's icebox was always so stuffed with food that you could barely add another fried drumstick, and you'd never find beer in her house.

I grabbed two lukewarm Dr Peppers and slammed the door with my knee. We always had a drawer right beside the refrigerator that contained a lot of junk, tools, and always a churchkey. There wasn't one beside the icebox, so I opened drawers to find an opener. Uncle James screwed a fixed opener on Aunt Ida Belle's cabinet, like the one on the cooler up at the store, but I didn't find anything like that, neither.

I crossed the kitchen with the bottles in hand, intending to call through the open window and ask Aunt Sylvia where she kept her opener. Through the screen, I saw her and Grandpa standing real close together between two lines of clothes, hidden from the road by her flat sheets.

I thought at first he was kissing her. The thought made my head reel, because that wouldn't be right, but their heads were real close and they were talking. Their voices barely carried into the house, lifted by the morning breeze.

"I'll be gone by the time he gets home."

"You sure you want to do this?"

"I'm sure, and so is he. We'll never be able to come back to Center Springs again, because Ben will kill Leon when he finds out we've run off together."

My head spun again. I only knew one Leon, and he was married to Aunt Rose, Uncle Ben's sister.

The two married-in people were running off to leave the brother and sister behind.

I'd heard about people running off together. That meant they were married to other people when they packed a suitcase and disappeared, leaving behind everyone and everything they owned.

"He sure will. I wouldn't put it past Rose to come looking for *you*, too."

"It don't make no difference. I'm done with Ben, and Leon promised me a house on a hill somewhere far away from here."

"The grass ain't always greener, girl."

She rubbed her hands on the stained apron tied around her waist and wiped a stray strand of bleach-blonde hair out of her eyes. "It'll be a sight greener than what I've got here. Look, I didn't sign on to raise chickens. I want more than a shack up here on this old river. I want to see the lights. I want to go dancing on Saturday nights where everybody ain't kinfolk. I'd like to have concrete under my feet every once in a while, instead of sand and mud."

Grandpa took off his hat and rubbed his head. "Sooner or later, them lights will get tiresome and you'll have to come home and do dishes and sweep and cook and make the bed. It'll be the same thing, just somewhere else with somebody different."

"It'll be better than here, with him."

"Well, hanging sheets on the line don't look like you're going anywhere."

"I wanted to leave him with a clean house. I've washed his clothes, folded the towels, and swept the floors. It's the least I can do after twenty years."

"How are you getting gone?"

"Leon will be here in an hour or so."

"Where's Ben?"

"He went to town. He won't be back 'til dark."

"I reckon I'll have to come back tomorrow, then. He won't be in a good humor, either, when I get here. He told Neal up at the store he wanted me to stop by. Something about what he found in y'all's barn."

They didn't have a phone in the house. A lot of folks in Center Springs that didn't have phones left word up at the store if they wanted to talk to someone. If it was an emergency, they drove to the person's house.

"I know what he wanted." Aunt Sylvia took another sheet out of her laundry basket and threw it over the line, like everything was normal. "It wasn't this here barn behind the house. Ben was feeding in the back pasture and followed a set of fresh tracks leading to the hay barn down there. We haven't used it in years, and he was curious about the tracks. When he went inside, he found a pile of full 'toe sacks stacked against the back wall."

There wasn't nothing unusual about 'toe sacks in our part of the world. We used them for everything from dog beds to hauling anything you could stick in the burlap bags. Grandpa perked up, though. "What was in 'em?"

"Said he knew what was in 'em as soon as he stepped inside because he could smell it. They was full of dope."

"Marywana? You know that for a fact?"

"Yep. He brought one sack to the house. Little Ben said that's what it was. He knows a lot about that stuff. When they went back out there the next morning, the rest of it was all gone."

"How many sacks was it?"

"I don't have any idea. They didn't say and I didn't ask."

"Well, I knew it'd finally get up in here, but I never expected to hear about *sacks* full of that mess in this county so soon."

She gave him a funny, half smile. "Ned, things are changing fast these days. It's been here a long time, but you ain't run across it yet."

"I guess I will before much longer, then. Where's that sack Ben brought to the house."

She grinned wider. "It's gone."

"I figured as much."

"Little Ben smoked some of it last night, and then he left and took the rest with him."

"What'd you tell me that fer?"

"I thought you might like to know."

"I'god, you beat all." Grandpa must have already expected me to be on the back porch. "Top, what are you still doing in there?"

I waited a beat. "I can't find a bottle opener."

Aunt Sylvia moved the same strand of hair out of her eyes. "There's one on top of the icebox, hon. Can you reach it?"

"I'll use a chair."

"Then get on out," Grandpa called. "You don't need to be messin' around in there."

"Yessir."

I knew their conversation would be over when I came back outside, so I took my time pulling a creaky wooden chair across the cracked linoleum. The opener was right where she said it was, so I pulled the caps and put it back where I found it, because it was expected. Adults were always telling us kids stuff like that, like we didn't have good sense.

There was a little red lard can up there without a top, and when I put the opener back, I knocked it over. Half a dozen cigarettes scattered up there in the dust. I recognized hand rolled cigarettes, because a lot of the men in Center Springs still rolled their own from white cotton bags of Bull Durham, but these were different. Each one was wrinkled, and twisted together at the ends.

Grandpa and Aunt Sylvia were farther apart when I went back outside. I handed him one of the bottles and sat on the back porch steps to drink mine while they finished talking. It didn't take long before he put his empty on the steps and I could tell he was ready to go.

He reached into his pocket. "He hasn't finished that drink, so here's two cents for the bottle."

Aunt Sylvia laughed. "Two cents won't make a bit of difference come tomorrow morning, Ned."

"I know it, but that ain't our bottle." He put two pennies in her apron pocket. "We're even."

The breeze came up and Aunt Sylvia's dress flapped around her legs. "Even?" She wasn't wearing sensible shoes like everyone else in Center Springs. She had on a pair of high heels that were trying to bury themselves in the damp ground.

She held a wet towel between them and they said a lot for a few seconds without saying anything at all. It was strange, but I knew something was going on.

"You be careful, gal."

"I will, Ned." She surprised me by standing on her toes and giving him a quick peck on the cheek, marking him with her bright red lipstick. "You take care of things around here. We'll be checking back from time to time."

He rubbed the mark on his cheek. "Don't you do it. Don't come back. Keep going and don't get caught. You don't need to be around here for a long while."

Instead of answering, she came over to the porch where I was sitting, bent over, and kissed my forehead, marking me too with her red lipstick. She rubbed it away with her thumb while Grandpa rubbed his own cheek clean. I was so surprised, I didn't know whether to thank her or run away. She took my head in her hands and gave me a grin that made her eyes crinkle. "You mind your Grandpa and Miss Becky."

My attention disappeared down her neck and into the top of her blouse that was cut lower than most that I'd ever seen.

I could see a little bath powder between her big titties and it smelled pretty good. "Yessum."

"Let's go, boy," Grandpa said gruffly. His voice sounded hoarse. "I'll come back in a day or so to talk with Ben and Ben Junior."

"He's eighteen. He'll be fine, Ned. And I don't much care about the other'n."

"I was talking about the marywana."

"Oh, well, all right then."

"Y'all be careful. C'mon, hoss."

We climbed in the truck, and I wondered why Grandpa was so quiet on the way back to the house.

It didn't make sense to me for him to be sad. Running off sounded like a great adventure and I hoped to run off some day myself, and be a cowboy.

Chapter Seventeen

When Cody walked into the house, Miss Becky and Norma Faye were sewing on a quilt suspended from the ceiling on a frame that was more than a hundred years old. He pitched his hat on the television and settled into Ned's rocker.

"Let's go fishing."

Miss Becky stopped what she was doing. "My lands, I haven't been fishing in a coon's age. I'd like a mess of fish."

"It's supposed to rain tonight, so I imagine they'll be biting. Ned went to Tom Bell's house to see if he wants to go with us. They'll be here directly." He watched them sew for a minute. "Where are the kids?"

"Down at the pool, I reckon. They had their crawdad poles the last time I saw them." Miss Becky stopped sewing. "Top's having dreams again."

"Uh oh," Cody said. "That's never good."

"He said they was about horses back when Ned and I were y'all's age."

Cody rocked and closed his eyes. "Have you ever said anything to him about when that happened…"

She immediately knew what he was talking about. "No, I ain't, and I ain't gonna be talking about it with the youngun's."

Norma Faye had never heard that tone in Miss Becky's voice before. "Can I ask what?"

The room filled with uncomfortable silence. Cody and Miss Becky waited for the other to say something. Finally, Norma

Faye broke the deadlock. "Well, y'all don't have to talk about anything I don't need to know about."

"It's about our dreams." Cody rocked and hoped Ned would hurry up.

"She needs to know." Miss Becky slid her needle into the fabric so it wouldn't get lost. "Ned's family had the Gift for as long as they can remember. I ain't gonna get into this too deep, but right after we got married, one of his kin whose name I won't call, found he had both that Gift and another one that helped people pass on to be with the Lord. It got him in trouble with the law and Ned had to help him out of it. Before it was over, some people in town wanted to lynch both of 'em, like they did that colored feller just before I was borned."

The brutal lynching of a wrongly accused Negro man in Chisum at the end of the nineteenth century was a sour reminder of how mob violence could quickly destroy innocent lives.

"It's a story you won't believe, and I'll tell it to you one of these days when the time is right, and now it ain't. Anyways," Miss Becky continued, as if they hadn't gotten off track, "Top dreamed about dark buildings and dark people, but he said it wasn't the Exchange."

"We don't much dream about what happened in the past, just what's coming."

"I know that, but he was telling me the other morning."

Cody sat straighter with a start. "I just remembered something. Before Christmas I dreamed about snow and rivers and Mexicans."

Miss Becky's face told her feelings. "You was shot in the snow, and nearly wound up in the creek."

"May be part of it, but creeks ain't rivers, and there weren't any Mexicans around. Wonder if it has anything to do with Top's dreams. Mexicans are dark."

"So are coloreds."

Norma Faye shivered. "I wish y'all didn't have that."

"So do I."

The screen door opened and Ned came into the living room, along with Tom Bell. "Y'all ready?"

Miss Becky stood. "Howdy, Tom. Y'all crank this frame back up and we will be there in a minute."

Cody went outside to call the kids and to let the sun warm the chill he felt when they were talking about dreams.

Chapter Eighteen

Uncle Cody gave his rod tip a twitch, cranked the open-faced reel twice, and twitched again. Squatting on the bank of the creek not ten feet away, I watched his Rapala lure swim toward us.

My own bobber didn't move much at all, unless you counted the sluggish current. "I haven't gotten a bite."

Pepper's rod tip twitched and bowed hard toward the river's surface. "Got one!"

Her head covered with a colorful flour sack bonnet, Miss Becky expertly moved the tip of her cane pole to the left, making room for Pepper's fight. "Yank him in!"

Sitting beside Miss Becky, I couldn't help but notice that Norma Faye had on makeup and lipstick, something most of the women in Center Springs didn't use, and she sure was pretty. I'd been watching her off and on while we were fishing, and wishing she'd come over and sit by me for a while.

Grandpa put his pole down and made his way to stop behind Pepper, in case she needed him. He waited behind her, hands holding the galluses of his overalls. On past about twenty feet, Mr. Bell gave his bobber a little jig, but kept his eyes on Pepper's line cutting through the smooth water. A fat crappie rose and flashed in the sunlight. As usual, she forgot to reel and pulled it up on the bank by turning to run.

"Lordy, gal!" Uncle Cody hollered and laughed. "You do that every time. Use that reel you have there and your fish won't always be sandy!"

Grandpa reached out and grabbed about two yards of loose line to help her land the speckled crappie. "You're like your grandma there when she was about your age. She'd have ten feet of line on her cane pole and instead of lifting the tip, she'd turn and run up the bank, a-dragging them poor ol' fish in the mud."

Miss Becky flashed him a grin from the shade of her bonnet. She never went outside in the sun without covering her head. Old folks knew any type of covering, whether it be a bonnet, hat or cap, kept them cooler than having the sun beat down on an unprotected head.

Grandpa put his brogan on the flipping white perch to hold it still until Pepper grabbed its bottom lip. The rest of us went back to fishing while they slid a stringer through its gills and lowered the fish into a deep hole close to Miss Becky.

Mr. Bell checked the worm on his hook, and then plopped it back into the water. "I sure appreciate y'all asking me to come along. I haven't been fishing in a coon's age. You know, we couldn't fish this way down in the Valley."

"Why's that?" Grandpa asked.

"Too many snakes and not much water."

Uncle Cody cast again and let the lure float in the slow current for a minute, waiting for the rings to disappear. He says fish'll swim up and look at the lure for a while, trying to decide if it's good to eat. "You know, me and Lane Miller went fishing last fall and learned something about snakes."

Lane Miller was one of Uncle Cody's running buddies. The last time I'd seen him was when we went dove hunting. Lane was laughing, because their friend Steve had shot himself in the foot only a few minutes before we got there. Those guys always thought it was funny when anybody got hurt, if it wasn't too bad.

I'd seen them howl one time up at the store when Jimmy Foxx, one of the Foxx brothers, walked around too close to the back of his truck and barked his shin on the trailer hitch he already knew was there. While Jimmy Wilson cussed and rubbed his shin, his brother Ty Cobb and the rest of the guys laughed so hard tears ran down their faces.

Uncle Cody said it was because they'd all done it at one time or another, and to them, it was funny. "Me and Lane couldn't fish that day without being covered up with snakes."

Pepper shivered. She hated snakes worse than spinach.

Uncle Cody twitched his rod and reeled twice. "Me and Lane were out on Hap Martin's pool that morning, working some lily pads growing near where the draw comes in, when this water snake swam by with a half-grown frog in his mouth. Well, I got to thinking, we weren't doing much good with crawdads, and if snakes were hitting frogs, maybe a bass might like one too.

"So when the snake got close enough I scooped him up with a net to get the frog out of his mouth. He wouldn't let go, and I didn't want to kill the poor thing, so I grabbed him by the back of his head and tried to pry the frog out of his mouth."

Pepper shuddered and Grandpa, who also hates snakes with a passion, joined her in a sympathetic shiver.

"That snake hung on like a snapping turtle, so when Lane wasn't looking I snuck a half pint of snakebite medicine out of his tackle box…"

"Snakebite medicine?" Miss Becky perked up.

"Yeah, you know, he had half a pint of J.T.S. Brown in there."

Miss Becky shook her head at the thought of them having whiskey. Me and Pepper grinned, because we know our Uncle Cody.

"Well, anyway, since both hands were busy, I opened the bottle with my teeth and then I poured a good slug of whiskey around the frog and in the snake's mouth.

"Hooooweee! He like to have twisted out of my hand, then he let go of the frog and I pitched him out into the pool. That snake thrashed around in the water for a good five minutes before he disappeared. I threaded the frog on my hook and threw it out there, but I had to give it up."

"Why?" Miss Becky asked.

"Well, lordy, I couldn't fish for all the snakes offering up frogs for trade."

Acting aggravated because she'd been snookered, Miss Becky waved a hand at Uncle Cody and pulled her bonnet down a little to hide her smile.

Brush popped a ways down on the other side of the creek. Two men in overalls came out of the woods and picked their way toward the bank. Both wore beat up felt hats that mostly shaded their faces. Neither acted friendly, nor waved.

We sometimes liked to fish that part of the creek where there were several deep holes and a big wash under the bank, so I didn't think nothing of anybody else fishing over there, because it had happened before.

"Can you tell who that is?" Grandpa asked.

Uncle Cody waved in greeting. "Naw, they're too far down."

We knew they saw us, but neither one so much as raised a hand in response. I could tell it aggravated Grandpa. "Unfriendly, ain't they?"

"Umm hum." Uncle Cody reeled slowly.

We could hear them talking across the water, but I couldn't make out the words. They sat down on a blow-down log, but neither one put a line in the water.

I could tell Grandpa and Uncle Cody didn't like it a bit that they hadn't spoke. We watched our bobbers for a few minutes in the silence of such rude behavior.

After a while, Norma Faye cleared her throat. "I've never had trouble with snakes, but the last time I went fishing, I caught something most people haven't ever hooked in their lives."

"What's that?" Uncle Cody was surprised that she had a story.

"Me and Darla Watkins were drift fishing for catfish in a big lake outside of Houston late one night when I hooked something that bent my rod completely double. It felt like a tire on the other end and it took me nearly thirty minutes to pull it up from the bottom, since I didn't want it to break off."

The whole family nodded right along, because we knew better than to horse a big blue catfish out of the water. The line would break sure enough.

Pepper jumped in, not wanting Norma Faye to get one up on her. "I bet it was a turtle. That's what they do, they lay down deep there on the bottom and you have to drag them in or break the line. I've had that happen before."

"No missy, it wasn't." Norma Faye tilted her head and pushed her red hair back. "But I wished it *had* been. It took a while, but I finally hauled it up close to the boat and you know what I'd caught?"

We all stopped fishing and minding our bobbers to hear.

Mr. Bell absently jiggled the end of his cane pole. "What was it?"

"Yeah," Uncle Cody said. "What was it?"

"Well, Darla Watkins recognized right off. I'd done gone and caught myself a *body*." She paused and waited. When no one said anything, she went on. "The dead body of a *man*, bobbing there in the dark beside our boat, and let me tell you, it was spooky."

We shuddered in horror. It had never occurred to me that Norma Faye had had a life before she and Uncle Cody got together. I knew she was married to Calvin Williams and that he was mean as a snake, but to think she'd lived down in some exotic place like Houston, and had found a dead man, was almost too creepy to think about. Apparently, I wasn't the only one surprised.

"What did you do?" Grandpa asked. I remembered he'd helped haul a body out of the Red River not too long ago.

"Why, Grandpa, we didn't have a Body License, so we threw him back. We caught five more the same size before the night was over."

We were so surprised none said anything for a minute. Then Uncle Cody threw back his head and laughed loud and long. Grandpa snickered, and Pepper frowned, because she'd been caught a second time in five minutes and didn't like the idea of adults getting the better of her.

Miss Becky shook her head, and then I realized her shoulders were shuddering. At first I thought she was crying, but I realized she was laughing. She gave Norma Faye a little push on the shoulder with her big hand, and right then I knew that everything was all right between them.

On the other side of the creek, one of the men snickered and one of them mocked our laughing. Grandpa's ears got beet red, and it was easy to see he was getting a mad on for sure.

Pepper stepped a little closer to me to whisper. "Them two are assholes."

It always scared me to death when she cussed around adults, but she was so good at it, they seldom heard. "Look at Uncle Cody."

He stood stiff as a bodark post. His shirt was unbuttoned, and I knew his .45 was under it. I was sure glad he had it on. Those two men were scary.

After a while, one of the men unrolled the string on the tip of his cane pole and plopped a bobber into the water. The other one didn't do nothin' but sit across there and stare at us.

The day was pretty, and the shade keeping the sun off our necks was cool and solid.

Miss Becky raised the end of her pole to see if she still had any bait left. "Well, y'all sure have been pulling my leg, that's for sure. Top, this reminds me of when your mama was a little older than you. She liked coming here."

Everyone on the bank quieted down, because we usually didn't talk about Mama or Dad. They were killed in a car crash several months earlier, and it hurt to bring them up.

I felt like I had to say something. "I didn't know she liked to fish."

"She did when she was a teenager. Remember Ned, we had to walk a foot log to get over the creek. She was scared every time." She laughed at the recollection. "She always took her shoes off and moved as slow as molasses until she got halfway across, then she almost ran and skipped the rest of the way."

I couldn't imagine Mama ever laughing. Her last years were filled with depression. Dad never let loose of her, though, and did everything he could to help her get well.

"Your daddy taught her how to walk a log when he started hanging around, and them two were always running off to fish, or pick berries or picnic. My lands, I never knew two people who enjoyed each other so much."

The wall of new and painful images rolled over me in a wave. I couldn't imagine my parents young, or having fun. Life had beaten them down to a quiet couple who spent their evenings alone, Mama in bed with the shades drawn, and Dad in the living room, reading.

Pepper kept her eyes on the bobber, but I knew she was waiting for me to say something. I was at a loss for words, thinking about them as youngsters. It was Grandpa that broke up our dark thoughts.

"One thing your grandma didn't tell you was that your Daddy was wild as a March hair when he was growing up, and I spent most of my time trying to keep him out of trouble. One time, when him and his cousin Dale were younger than y'all, they were fooling around somewhere here in the creek bottoms when Dale had a pain and needed to go outdoors. He dropped his overalls to squat down in the grass beside a dirt road, and something bit him right on his little bare butt.

"He thought it was a snake and it scared him to death. He jumped up, pulled up his overalls, and took off running for the house with your Daddy chasing right behind. Every now and then Dale got scared and dropped his overalls and squatted down so your Daddy could check out his snake bite. He got on his hands and knees to look, but Dale couldn't wait, so he jumped up and ran for the house faster than ever. A little further along, they went through the same thing again with him squatting in a dirt road and your Daddy squinting at his little old white butt. They finally got to the house and found out he wasn't snake bit, he'd only squatted down on a sharp stick that stuck his bottom."

It was like the Red Skelton show on television. We were all laughing big when Uncle Cody's rod bent nearly double and he reared back to set the hook with a grunt. Before I knew it, mine did the same thing and the two of us were fighting big catfish.

They went on the stringer before you could say Jack Robinson. It went that way for the next few minutes, and then things settled down again as the fish moved off. We waited for the next bite to start.

I smelled the fish on my hands and the mud under our feet. I wished Uncle James and Aunt Ida Belle were there with us to tell some stories of their own, but she wasn't much on fishing.

I knew Pepper didn't care, though, because if they'd been with us it would have been, "Pepper do this," or "Pepper be careful," or "Pepper why are you doing that?" It was enough to unnerve a preacher.

Uncle Cody edged closer to Grandpa. "Those two over there haven't moved an inch, and that feller ain't pulled his line in one time to check his bait."

Grandpa grunted. "I know it."

It made me think to check my own hook. The bait was gone. Sometimes little bream will nip a worm off your hook without moving the bobber. I reeled it in and reached toward the coffee can full of worms, when Mr. Bell threw a holler at me.

"Hey, son, have you thought about using chewing tobacco for bait?"

I hadn't heard that one. Once I caught a crappie on a piece of pink bubble gum, but that was all. "No, sir."

"Well, you might want to think about it. Course you'll need a club for that technique. You want to try?"

"Sure."

"Find you a thick stick, and I'll cut you a piece of this Day's Work plug here in my pocket."

Limbs were on the ground all around us. Everybody concentrated on their fishing while I put down my rod and went to find a good one. Pepper joined me, because we were about to learn something new. When I passed Grandpa, I saw he was staring hard at the men across the creek.

We found a stout limb on the other side of Miss Becky and carried it to Mr. Bell. He had a chunk of fresh tobacco in his hand. "Here, drop this in close to my bobber."

I followed his instructions and we squatted down. I watched the line leading down into the water. "What now?"

"Why, you wait."

"For what?"

"In a little bit those fish are going find that chew, then you give them a few more minutes."

Pepper frowned. "Then what."

"Why Little Missy, when that catfish comes up to spit, you whack him 'tween the eyes with your club."

That must have been the funniest thing the adults had ever heard. I knew we'd been had, but it was Pepper that threw a fit. She stomped off toward the woods, cussing under her breath.

"Pepper," Uncle Cody called. "Stay close by."

She was as sulled up as a possum. "Why?"

"You might slip into the water and drown."

She still didn't get it, so I had to explain it to her. "He don't trust those two guys over there, you dope."

"Kiss my ass," she mouthed.

"Tom, I swear," Grandpa shook his head and snickered. "I'd a thought they'd heard that before. That joke's older'n both of us put together."

"Ain't it the truth," Mr. Bell said, and then set the hook on the biggest catfish we caught all day.

I was starting to feel guilty about what we'd done to Mr. Bell, what with sneaking in his house and peeking into his trunk, when a stick snapped behind us. Uncle Cody threw his rod on the ground and spun. In a flash the .45 appeared in his hand, pointed at Mr. Washington who was picking his way down the trail to where we were.

He pretended not to see the pistol that Uncle Cody put back under his shirt pretty quick. "Howdy, everbody."

Grandpa was surprised. "John, what's the matter? What are you doing here?"

"I been lookin' for y'all. I knew you said you's going fishing, and I knowed you likes this stretch of the creek, so I come on down when I couldn't raise neither of y'all on the radio. We got a phone call said a body was found hanging in a barn out here. Mr. O.C. sent me out to tell y'all, and to help."

"My lands!" Miss Becky put her hand on her chest like she was having a heart attack. "Do you know who it is?"

"Yessum. Howdy, Miss Becky, Miss Norma, sorry I didn't speak when I got here." He was embarrassed he'd forgotten his manners.

"No need to apologize, John." Miss Becky stood straight, waiting for the bad news. "Who is it?"

He cleared his throat. Grandpa knew why Mr. John was hesitating. "Go on. You can say."

"It's Benjamin Winters."

Miss Becky gasped. "My Lord, kinfolk."

Grandpa shook his head. "Which one? There's two, the daddy and his boy."

"They didn't say anything on the radio but Benjamin."

"Well, let's go, then. Y'all get in your lines."

I was numb. I'd been in Uncle Ben's house only days before, and now one of them was hung. I wondered if Grandpa had told Miss Becky about Aunt Sylvia leaving, but knew enough not to say anything myself.

While we hurried to gather everything up, Mr. John noticed them men across the creek, but it wasn't much more than a glance.

Their voices rang clear across the water. "Now that's a cryin' shame. It's a good thing them nigger lovers are leaving."

Uncle Cody answered Mr. John's unspoken question. "We don't know who they are." He spun on his heel and headed in their direction. Even though the creek was between us, both men stood up as he stomped down the bank. They might have been expecting a cuss fight, because they ducked their heads when he got close enough to talk to 'em casual-like across the water.

"You men got something to say to us?"

The meanest-looking one answered around a juicy chew. "Naw, not much."

"Well, give me what there is, then."

The other one had slit eyes. "Y'all need to watch yourselves. Don't get into nothin' that don't concern you."

"What are you talking about?"

"*You* know what I mean. We're supposed to say if y'all back off, you might find a fat envelope waitin' for you under the seat in that fancy El Camino you drive."

Uncle Cody stiffened. "You sonsabitches better stay away from my family, *and* my car, or I'll bury you somewhere only God can find you. I don't want nothin' from trash like you."

Mr. Bell joined them and the men looked afraid. They didn't answer. Instead, they left their poles and hurried up the bank and into the trees.

Uncle Cody was madder'n a wet hen from the set of his jaw, but he didn't say anything else. He motioned for Norma Faye to follow and led the way back to the cars. Mr. Bell stayed where he was, without moving, as if waiting for a charge across the creek.

Mr. John lifted the heavy stringer of fish like it didn't weight nothing. He took Miss Becky's folding chair, and followed with me and Pepper in tow. Grandpa and Mr. Bell were the last to leave the creek.

I stopped at the top of the steep bank to see what would happen next. Them two strangers stood just inside the edge of the trees, watching. Grandpa had his hand in the pocket of his overalls, studying them.

I knew one hand rested on the little .38 he carried in there.

Without another word, he pointed his left index finger at the men. First one, then the other. That gesture said more than a whole set of World Book encyclopedias.

We were in the car by the time he climbed the bank and joined us.

"Did you say anything else?" Uncle Cody asked.

Mr. Bell snorted. "Didn't need to."

They didn't get home from Uncle Ben's house until nearly dark, and by that time, Miss Becky had the fish cleaned and the grease hot. We had us a fish fry that night. Uncle James and Aunt Ida

Belle joined us and they laughed at the stories, but the adults weren't as bright as they would have been, because of the death.

I sure was proud Mr. Bell got Pepper's goat, and went to sleep long after dark, expecting to dream of catching big turtles and grinning, tobacco-chewing catfish.

Instead I dreamed of a hanging man who was dangling in a cloud of smoke and talking to me in a language I couldn't make out, because he was on the other side of the creek. It sure sounded like them Choctaw words Miss Becky teaches us every now and then, when we're sitting under the Mimosa tree after supper.

Along about two in the morning, all them fish I ate started calling for water. I got out of bed and took a good, long drink from the water bucket in the kitchen. When I went back to bed, I had another dream and forgot the first one until several days later.

Chapter Nineteen

Ned drove to Ben Winter's house in a rising south wind. It wasn't but a mile as the crow flies, but they had to zig zag along the gravel country roads leading around one pasture, then another.

He parked in the yard already crowded with agitated people. At least a dozen cars were in the way, and more were pulled off to the side of the road against the bar ditch in front of the house.

"Son of a *bitch*!" Ned killed the engine and climbed out, building a head of steam. "They've tromped on everything between here and the barn."

Isaac Reader was standing with a group of men near the front porch. Seeing Ned's Chevrolet, the jerky little man hurried across the yard, already talking well out of earshot.

"Ned, listen, listen. It weren't me that found nothin' this time. I's up at the store and heard Benjamin been found hung and I rode over here with the Wilson boys."

Cody stifled a grin, knowing Reader wore on Ned's last nerve with his talking. Within the last year, Isaac seemed to have acquired a penchant for being the bearer of bad news. It was Isaac who found Cody's brutally mutilated bird dog that set off a chain of related animal mutilations leading to a killer living in their midst.

He also found the murdered bodies of Josh Brooks and his entire family only months later.

Ned waited until the nervous little farmer was close enough for comfortable conversation in the high wind. "Isaac, do you know who found him? Which one is it?"

Ike's Adam's apple traveled for a moment. "Listen, I was told it's Benjamin, but I didn't know for sure 'til I got there."

"Well, who found him?"

"Ben."

"I'god, Ike, conversation with you wears me out. One of 'em's alive, which one is it and where's he at?"

A look of surprise crossed Reader's face. He had no idea why Ned was so upset with him. "Ben's in the house with the Wilson boys."

"I'god, which one is still drawin' air? Big Ben or Little Ben."

"Why Big Ben, like I said."

"All right then." Ned clumped up the porch, nodding to the men gathered there. He grabbed the handle of the screen door and heard women sniffling inside.

Isaac stayed in the yard. "Listen, listen Cody. He's hung in the barn, not the house."

"I know Ike, we'll get out there in a minute."

Ned let the door slap behind him and called back through the screen. "Y'all stay out here for a minute, and everybody keep out of the barn."

Benjamin senior sat on a horsehair divan between two of his sisters. His eyes were wet and red, and he didn't have his teeth in. Though it was sunny outside, the interior seemed dimmer than the last time Ned was there. All the windows were open, and the thin homemade curtains flapped in the dry breeze coming through rusty screens.

He expected to see Sylvia, but she wasn't there.

His question was answered for sure. Little Benjamin was the one they'd come for. Without a word, Ned nodded and passed on through the house, the kitchen, and out the back door. Cody fell in behind after resting his hand briefly on the weeping man's shoulder.

John was already at the barn, fifty yards behind the house. Massive arms crossed over his chest, he stood guard at the doors. Only the Wilson boys named after famous baseball players Ty Cobb and Jimmy Foxx were there talking to him. They always showed up when something was going on, like they had some sixth sense for adventure or trouble.

"I guaran-damn-tee-you he didn't hang hisself." Ty Cobb picked at a crusty in his nose. "That boy wouldn't do nothing of the kind."

Jimmy Foxx rubbed his own nose in sympathy. "I bet he got crossways with some bad folks don't live around here. There's a lot of meanness these days. That's why I carry a pistol everywhere I go, and Ty Cobb does too." He raised his shirt tail to reveal the butt of a revolver.

The sagging clothesline wires hung empty. A sow with a ring in her nose grunted from the ramshackle hog pen, hoping for a bucket of slop. No one noticed the thick aroma of soured mud.

A rusty piece of loose sheet iron serving as the roof on the hog shed was loose in the rising wind. The sharp screech was more than an annoyance to Cody. The sound of flapping sheet iron always made him feel sad and melancholy, especially if it was on an uncomfortably warm day and he was alone in a pasture somewhere.

The warped barn doors were closed. Ned pulled one open, and then spoke over his shoulder to the increasing crowd of men. "Y'all stay out here until one of us calls for you."

It was too late, of course. There had been a steady stream of horrified people through the doors, but he didn't want to deal with their questions right at that moment.

The small barn was rich with the smells of alfalfa, feed, and cow shit. Stalls and feed bins lined both sides of the hall, and rafters crossed high overhead. Light beams filled with dust motes stirred by the wind gave more than enough illumination for the grisly sight.

Little Benjamin hung from the center rafter by a grass rope that cut deeply into his contorted neck. His grotesquely protruding eyes, purplish black face, and bulging tongue proclaimed that slow strangulation was the cause of death. Hands and wrists dark with pooled blood hung at his sides.

Flies buzzed in a busy cloud around the suspended body.

The sight of the rope cutting into his distorted neck was shocking, even to Ned. "Lord God."

"How could anybody do that to themselves," Cody said aloud to himself, staring upward at a big yellow jacket nest. After his first glance, he didn't want to look at the young man.

Ned examined the dirt floor beneath the body. A straight-back cane-bottom wooden chair lay on its side. After several long moments, he surveyed the rafters overhead and the rope as it looped over the rough-sawn oak. He noticed it was tied off with a roping knot on a stall door.

"Something's wrong."

"What's that?"

"Look how high he is."

"I still don't know what you're talking about."

There was no need to worry about disturbing the soft dust at their feet. Dozens of tracks from the gawkers had obscured any tracks left by Big Ben or anyone else. Ned circled the body.

"Looky here."

He knelt near the corpse's feet. Two of the four impressions from the sharp chair legs were still clear on the floor. He picked it up and carefully repositioned the legs in the two holes.

"Now do you see?"

Cody tilted his hat back. "I must be thick."

"Nope, you're not seeing. You don't have much experience with such things. The difference between the soles of his shoes and this chair don't match up. I'd expect him to be hanging a little lower from the stretch of the rope. Might near to the ground."

"I get it now. His feet are an inch or so higher than the seat, even with his weight on the rope. He must have stood on the back."

Ned slipped his hands into the pockets of his overalls. "You cain't do it. Nobody has that kind of balance."

"So you're saying he didn't hang himself."

"Right. Somebody done it for him. I hope he was dead when they hauled him up there." He stepped around the corpse, squinting upward.

The barn door opened a crack. Light spilled across the body. John stuck his head inside. "Mr. Ned, the ambulance is here."

"Good. Send 'em in."

Carlton Evans, the oldest and most experienced ambulance driver from McGinnes Brothers Funeral Home, and his partner Harvey Glasscock, tugged a stretcher on reluctant wheels through the soft sand. Neither reacted to the sight of the body. They'd seen that, and worse, in their business.

Carlton stopped several feet away. "Howdy, Mr. Ned. Can we get him down?"

"Sure, go ahead on."

Harvey went directly to where the rope was tied off on the gate. "John, can you help me here?"

The big deputy was already moving, because he realized the two of them were needed to gently lower the body into the other man's arms. While the heavy attendant grasped the taut rope and braced himself, John yanked the long end of the release knot free with a sharp snap.

Cody stepped in to help lay Little Ben on the ground. Rigor mortis had already set in, so he was difficult to manage as respectfully as they'd preferred.

"Looky here, Cody." Ned bent over and raised one stiff arm. "Look at his hands."

"The skin is peeled off. Some fingernails are missing. It looks like rope burns."

"They are," Carlton said. "I've seen that before with people who've hung themselves. They change their minds when they don't die right away. For some reason they think everything will go black the instant the rope tightens." He pointed at the peeled palms. "This happens when they can't get air and try to hold themselves up, but it's impossible."

Ned spoke to himself. "It also looks the same when someone is hauled up by their neck, too."

"You saying he didn't do it on his own?"

Frustrated that his habit of talking to himself had let something slip, Ned waved a finger. "I didn't say nothin' of the sort, and don't y'all be telling anybody I did. I'm thinking here, that's all."

Cody checked Benjamin's pockets and came up empty. The barn door opened and Ned reared up over the intrusion, until he recognized the justice of the peace, Buck Johnson, who had come to pronounce the body.

Buck joined the little cluster of men. "Damn that wind." He stared down at Benjamin's body. "O.C. rode out here with me, but he elected not to look at another body, and I don't blame him. Not much to say, is there?"

"Not a thing."

"He's dead. All right boys, you can load him up."

"Wait a minute." They waited for Ned. "Turn him so's I can see the back of his head."

The attendants rolled the stiff body face down.

Ned knelt on one knee to get a better look. Hands on his knees, Cody bent forward.

Buck joined him. "What is it?"

"Look at the dried blood on the back of his head. He didn't do that while he hung there."

Carlton spoke up. "I've seen that a time or two when someone hung themselves and the rope broke, or the knot didn't hold. They fell, split their heads, and had to do it all over again."

Buck straightened, twisting momentarily to make his back pop. "Yeah, 'bout twenty-year ago there was a feller determined to kill himself come hell or high water. He used a lamp cord, but it broke and he fell. He had a big split on his forehead that bled like a stuck hog. Then he went to sawing at his wrists, but the knife was dull and it must have hurt too much, so he went and got a pistol and stuck it in his mouth. That did the trick."

Ned rose with a grunt and slapped the dust off his knee. "All right."

John cut off all but three feet of the rope with his sharp pocketknife and left the noose around Little Ben's neck for the autopsy. The attendants wrestled the corpse onto the stretcher, covered him with a sheet, and with much difficulty, rolled him out the door.

Ned replaced the chair on its side, exactly where it had been.

Buck examined the dusty barn. "What a helluva place to leave for Heaven from, with a slip knot around your neck."

They trailed him outside, surprised to find Sheriff Donald Griffin getting out of his car. Donald Griffin had been sheriff for nearly twenty years. He came to Chisum from Dallas, eager to get away from the city's crime and politics. He found a home in the small town, but Ned Parker had little use for the man who was as territorial as a junk yard dog. Ned felt Griffin had something crooked going on.

The two of them tended to lock horns every time they met, and O.C. usually had to referee for them when he was around, even though he disliked the man himself. Griffin liked to try and tell O.C. how to conduct his business, but the judge refused to bend. He'd handled his side of the law in his own way for years, and he didn't intend to let a drugstore sheriff get in his way.

The beefy sheriff affected the appearance of a Texas lawman from his Stetson hat, crows-feet in the corners of his eyes, and a heavy gray mustache. He carried a pearl handled Colt .45 revolver on his hip that gave rise to hidden giggles and smirks behind his back from men who preferred the simpler things in life.

"Constable Parker, this is now my case."

Ned squinted. "Which Parker you talking to, Griffin? I'm sure it ain't me, because this is my precinct and you're *wayyy* out of bounds to come out here and tell me what to do. You're a *part* of this, but not all of it."

It tickled Cody to watch the two men spar. He'd learned to dislike Griffin after the incident at the Cotton Exchange months before. The pompous, arrogant lawman caused nearly as many problems as he solved. Cody recognized Griffin's driver from the incident at the Cotton Exchange and gave him a tentative wave.

Deputy Carlton White had been in Chisum's newly created K-9 unit until his dog partner, Shep, was killed during the assault on the Exchange. Overcome by grief, White refused to train another dog and instead, became Griffin's driver. It was a decision he already regretted.

Griffin scowled at O.C., who was standing idly nearby. The judge hadn't said a word, but Griffin knew O.C. and Ned were inseparable, and he'd just as well talk to them both at the same time. "This is a murder, and I am fully empowered as a peace officer with county-wide jurisdiction, which means, Parker, that I am in charge in this unincorporated part of the county."

O.C. raised his eyebrows at the exchange. He knew Ned was about to lose, and it galled him.

Ned stepped closer to speak quietly without being overheard. "You call me by my last name one more time and it'll be just you and me out behind this here barn when everyone leaves. I know the law, but I know these people, too. I can find out more in ten minutes than you will in a week, the way you bull around. You take that boy out there on the stretcher, and you do your investigating, but I'm asking questions, too, and you cain't do a thing about it."

Taken aback by the look in Ned's eyes, Griffin found himself once again wanting to retreat from the tough old constable, but he held his ground to save face. "I planned to do just that, without you telling me I can. I imagine y'all tromped on all the evidence in there, so it won't do my men any good to look around."

"We left everything just as it was, except for the body. Go ahead on and have your look." Ned paused. Despite their mutual dislike of one another, he still wanted to find out what happened. "The dirt in there was already tracked up before we got here, and there's enough cars parked in the yard to start a used car lot, so we didn't tromp through anything that wasn't already messed up."

"I'll have my men question the witnesses, and I want a written statement from both of you two…constables. Cody, don't forget you was the one elected, not Ned. He's just appointed, and I intend to find a way around that, too."

O.C.'s famous temper began to rise, but he choked it down. They'd pick their crow, but at the right time, in the right place.

They watched Griffin stalk across the yard and flip the sheet off the body. After staring and grimacing for a few seconds, Griffin stormed into the barn. The attendants made up for his disrespect by pulling the sheet back over the disfigured face and securely tucking the corners once again.

Two more sheriff's deputies were waiting in the yard, their heads lowered to prevent the wind from snatching their hats. Ned barely glanced at them. "One of you boys keep everybody out of the barn for a while."

They looked at John.

Ned understood the silent question. "I want him inside with me, not out here."

They didn't like it. Negros should have been guarding doors, instead of white deputies, but neither wanted to argue with the man who had become a legend among the Chisum law community.

"The other one come go with me to move everybody off the front porch, and don't let anybody else in the house while we talk to the boy's daddy."

Before obeying, they glanced around to be sure Sheriff Griffin was out of earshot. He was territorial, and he'd skin them alive if he thought they were favoring the constable.

In the house, John stopped in the kitchen. "I'll wait right here."

"All right." Cody held the door and Ned led the way into the living room. Ben still sat on the divan, eyes red and leaking. Sylvia still hadn't appeared.

Sympathetic friends and family stood uncertainly in the living room. Ned stopped. "Y'all go on outside and let us talk for a minute."

It was apparent they wanted to stay inside and listen, but they stood. A bottle-blonde sister kissed Ben on the cheek. "All right. Y'all come on."

When everyone reluctantly filed out, Ned took a seat on a sprung chair catty-cornered from the dingy gray divan. "Ben, I'm sorry."

The toothless, grieving man worked his lips. "It shouldn't-a happened." The words came out mushy.

Still standing, Cody tilted his head to better understand. "Put your teeth in, Ben, so we can understand you."

He felt around in the bib pocket of his overalls, located his dentures, and slipped them in with a clack.

Ned gave his knee a pat. "Was it you that found him?"

"Yep." Sniffle. "I went to the barn and found him hanging there."

"I know. I'm sorry it was you. A man ought not see any of his family like that, especially his own kids. Now, I have to ask you some questions so we can find out what happened. When did you see him last?"

"Last night. He went out like he always does."

"Do you know who he went with?"

"Naw, he didn't say. I figured it was them new friends of his from Oklahoma."

"How come?"

"'Cause he's been running with people I don't know."

"Not boys from around here?"

"No, they was town boys, but he met them at some honky tonk over there. He got crossways with the boys on this side a while back and took to running with some others. They spend a lot of time across the river..." He stopped.

Cody felt uncomfortable, hoping he wasn't talking about The Sportsman, his honky tonk. The loose piece of sheet iron rattling in the wind was setting his teeth on edge. If he had a hammer, he'd have gone out and nailed it back down.

Ned knew he had to keep pressing. "What were they doing over there?"

Ben gave him a sad look, and then dropped his eyes. "I don't know."

"I believe you do. Y'ain't helping him none now. He's gone, and I need to know who to look for."

"Why do you want to look for anybody? Little Ben hung hisself."

"No, he didn't."

"You don't think?"

"No, and you don't either."

The room was silent.

"You *know* he didn't. He wouldn't-a done that, not even with his mama gone. Tell me what you know. He cain't get in any trouble, now."

"He got in with a bad bunch that's moving that marywana, and some other stuff. I told him to get out of it before he got hurt, that it wasn't right, but he didn't listen."

"You already knew he was messin' with that stuff?"

"Yeah."

"Then why didn't you come tell me about it?"

"I didn't want him to get arrested, and I thought I could talk him out of that foolishness, but he was making money." Ben absently waved a hand. "We ain't got much, you can tell. And then when Sylvia left, things...died around here."

A noise interrupted their conversation. Ned's eyes flashed at the annoyance. John quickly stepped into the kitchen. Cody joined him, and when he returned, Ned raised his eyebrows in question.

"It's Miss Becky and some of the women from her church. They're bringing food in."

Ned knew better than to wade into that one, even after he'd told everyone to stay out. He wondered if the deputy was still where'd he'd posted him at the back door. Most likely that little Indian woman rolled right over him.

Cody squatted on his heels and rested a hand on the battered coffee table between them to maintain his balance. A tattered copy of *Life* magazine covered a worn Bible. The headline *How You Can Survive Fallout*, barely registered in Cody's mind. "We need for you to tell us the rest you know."

"Son, I don't know much more. Little Ben had a wad of money in his pocket and he was helping haul that stuff."

"Did he put them bags in your barn?"

"No, he was as surprised as I was about that. I'm thinking them people decided to hide it in there, since they knew him." He glanced from one constable to the other. "I'm afraid they got mad when that one bag disappeared. He probably suspected it was theirs, but he should have known you cain't steal from people like that."

"Do you have any names?"

"Naw. They was all a lot older than Little Ben, and I told him they'd get him in trouble, but he said he was gonna make a killin' and then go to Dallas and buy a big painted house and live high on the hog."

"Did you ever see them?"

"Onec't, but not around here. I was getting gas in Arthur City when they rolled up from across the river with a flatbed full of hay."

The one gas station in Arthur City was on the southbound side of the highway, not a hundred yards from the river bridge.

Ben wiped his nose with a wet handkerchief. "Only I knew it wasn't all hay from the smell. The wind wasn't blowing that day, and when they stopped and got out, I could smell that stuff. Benjamin stayed in the truck because he didn't want to explain to me why he was with them, or to answer my questions, but them other two got out."

"Describe them," Cody said.

He did, and the description perfectly matched the two men who'd been watching them fish from across the creek that morning.

Only Cody didn't know the description also matched the two men trying to flank Ned in his joint not long before.

Ned recognized them, though.

Chapter Twenty

I went out on the porch to watch the sky get dark and dangerous looking. Grandpa was helping Miss Becky in the garden when it first started coming up a cloud.

They hurried back to the house to beat the rain. The strong south wind always told of springtime storms on the way. One minute it was blowing strong, and then stopped. A few minutes later, the wind again sprang up from the west, and lightning flickered in the dark clouds.

Pepper had stayed for supper. "Shit. It's gonna storm and Grandpa will make us go to that damned cellar again."

Thunderstorms didn't really make me nervous, but I remembered last year when we spent half the night in Uncle Henry's cellar while a tornado blew away everything from barns to pigpens. "Maybe this one won't be so bad."

A strong gust threatened to snatch Grandpa's hat as he wired the pasture gate shut. He always used the extra twist as cheap insurance. It drove Pepper crazy, because she hated to use both the bailing wire and the loop over the gate post.

Thunder rumbled across the pasture and the trees thrashed in the wind. I watched the big oak give before the storm, and hoped our tree house was strong enough to stand the strain of the limbs moving first one way, then the other.

Miss Becky hurried on the porch with a bucket full of fresh greens. She untied her bonnet. "My lands, I thought it was gonna catch us."

Grandpa stomped up right behind her. A sudden gust grabbed the mop hanging on the side of the house and flipped it off. "Might near did, but I don't believe there's any rain in it."

Storms came through like that sometimes, bringing heavy wind, thunder and lightning, but no rain. Other times the bottom fell out and it came what Grandpa called a frog strangler.

When no one was around, Pepper called them turd floaters.

Miss Becky was still on the porch when the lights flickered and the electricity went out. It wasn't unusual to lose power so far out in the country. While Grandpa fumed over the weather, Miss Becky lit the coal oil lamps. Compared to the electric lights, the lamps made a dim glow in the house.

The whole thing made both Grandpa and Pepper about half mad. With no light, she had to sit there and listen to the adults talk, and that kind of thing always drove her crazy.

The storm quickly blew past, and the sky cleared like nobody's business. It was full dark and there was still no power. It was cooler outside so we sat on the porch. Grandpa went to his car, rolled down the windows, and clicked on his Motorola. He'd finally gotten it fixed after several months of it working only part of the time.

Voices crackled from the speakers, but all the law business was in Chisum. About half an hour later, a set of headlights came from Center Springs, and Uncle James' Chevy turned into the drive. They parked behind Grandpa's car and joined us.

"Y'all out of juice, too?" Uncle James sat on the porch steps.

Aunt Ida Belle had her knitting with her, and she shooed Pepper out of her straight-backed chair. Mumbling to herself, Pepper sat on the edge of the porch beside me.

Grandpa grunted. "Yep. I don't know why the co-op cain't figure out how to keep the lines strung during a storm. This happens two-three times a year."

Miss Becky brought a little stool out on the porch and sat one of the lamps on it to give Aunt Ida Belle enough light to stitch by. Aunt Ida Belle was always pretty quiet and didn't say much. "Now, you kids don't knock that stool over."

"One of 'em probably will, and then the whole house will burn down," Grandpa said.

Miss Becky came back out with a pan of peas to shell and settled down on the other side of the lamp.

Another set of headlights came down the road. It was Uncle Cody and Norma Faye. He hollered when he got out of the El Camino. "This a reunion?"

Miss Becky jumped up. "I'll get some more chairs."

They threaded their way past Uncle James and the porch got crowded. "No you won't." Uncle Cody held her in her seat and went through the screen door. "I'll get them." He came back out with two more.

"Here comes Mr. Tom," I said, watching lights flicker through the trees. He parked behind Uncle James' Chevy a minute later.

"Tom, you ain't got no power yet, so how'd you know we'd all be here right now."

Mr. Tom tilted his hat back and grinned in the dim light. "Shoot, when the whole county goes dark, even us that live by kerosene knows when the lights go out."

"All except for Hugo over there."

Grandpa was pointing at a dim glow to the north. Oklahoma had power.

Uncle Cody stood and stretched. "This calls for ice cream."

"Good idy," Miss Becky said. "You run up to the store and get some ice. We'll mix everything up and have it ready when you get back."

He stepped off the porch. "Well come on, urchins. Y'all come go with me. It looks like Pepper's about to bust."

He didn't have to tell us twice. Miss Becky called through the open screen. "Y'all get another can of Eagle Brand and some salt, too. We're 'bout out."

The radio hadn't even warmed up before we pulled in front of Neal Box's general store. A crowd of locals sat on the porch in the darkness there, too. I recognized Mr. Ike, the Wilson boys, and Cale Westlake, sitting like a toad with his back against the store's wall.

He and I glared at one another while Uncle Cody went inside the interior lit by a coal oil lamp and a couple of candles. Seconds later, Neal came out with a flashlight and opened the door to the wooden ice box. He had an ice pick in his hand, and he chipped away at a big block of ice until he got ten pounds, like Uncle Cody always bought. He heaved it out of the cooler with a pair of tongs and carried it over to the El Camino.

"Howdy, kids." He had a piece of 'toe sack in his hand. He slipped the burlap into the back, and then thumped the ice on it. "Top, climb in back here."

I crawled over the tailgate as Uncle Neal flipped the rest of the 'toe sack over the ice. "You set on this here so it don't slide around on the way back to your Grandpa's house."

He left me sitting there and went back inside. Pepper stuck her head out. "Why do you get to set on the ice and not me?"

"I don't care. You do it."

We switched places by the time Uncle Cody came back out. "Shit, this is cold on my ass," Pepper said, thinking no one heard.

"Good." Uncle Cody shifted into gear. "Maybe it'll cool that temper of yours off before we get back to the house."

Ten minutes later, the women had everything mixed up and poured into the bucket, and Uncle James started chipping away at the block of ice. While Uncle Cody cranked, they covered the ice with salt.

"They're kinda nervous up there at the store," Uncle Cody said.

"What fer?"

"I heard said the Russians might have planned some sort of attack on the United States this week, and it was a coincidence that storm rolled through when it did."

"Do you believe that?"

"I don't know. They brought all them rockets and atom bombs in down there in Cuba a few years ago. It wouldn't surprise me none if they figured out a way to shut down all the electricity before they landed troops."

"The lights are on there in Hugo."

"Yeah, but who would want to invade Oklahoma?"

The men laughed.

"Pepper, if your butt has thawed out, maybe you want to sit here on the bucket while I crank."

"My as…rear's still chilly. Top can sit on it."

I didn't mind, I liked to hold the bucket down while Uncle Cody cranked. But the conversation had me a little spooked. I kept looking back toward the lights of Hugo, wondering if we were under attack.

A couple of weeks earlier, me and Pepper brought a card from school to get filled out at home. One of the five questions on the card asked that if there was an atomic attack, did they want us to run home, or stay at school.

Miss Becky checked the "stay at school" box, because she didn't want me running the mile from our school to the house through no bombing or fallout.

Grandpa went to his car and cranked up the volume on the Motorola a little more, to hear if there was talking about Russian troops marching through Chisum.

The ice cream was starting to harden when Miss Lizzie in her house across the pasture completely lost her mind.

She and Uncle Harold lived in a ragged house about six hundred yards away. Mr. Bell was talking about what job he was doing on his house, when a strange wail floated to us on the still air.

Let me tell you, it raised the hair on my neck. At first I thought it was that River Monster folks liked to talk about late at night. There were stories about an eight-foot hairy monster with big feet down in the bottoms, and that it hollered at night with a loud, long wail.

"Goddlemighty, what's that?" Uncle Cody asked.

Miss Becky came to the door. "I know that voice. It's Lizzie, poor ol' soul. Something's happened, Ned, you better run me over there."

"But the ice cream is almost ready."

"It'll have to set a spell to harden up. We'll be back here by then."

"I'll go with you." Norma Faye dried her hands on a cup towel.

"All right, hon."

"Can we go?" I asked.

"Sure," Grandpa said. I imagine he was thankful for the company.

"Are you crazy?" Pepper was appalled at the question. "What do you want to go over there for?"

"You want to sit here in the dark and worry about Russians and wait for the ice cream to get hard?"

Miss Becky came out, so it was all of us, except for Mr. Tom.

"I believe I'll stay right here and guard the freezer." He rubbed his flat stomach and frowned for a second. "No telling what them Russkies might do if they come rolling through here and find an unguarded bucket of fresh banana ice cream."

Harold's house was close enough to hit with a .22, but the road meandered around pastures, pools, and Miss Becky's little frame church, so it took a minute or two to get there.

It was pitch black in the yard, except for the light from one little ol' oil lamp on a little table beside Harold's rocker on the front porch. Our headlights lit things up and threw harsh shadows behind a ragged lilac bush, an upside-down wash pot, and a pile of rusting tin cans.

Pepper and I slid out of the back seat and followed the adults to the edge of the porch where we pulled up pretty quick, because Harold's body odor was the worst I'd ever smelled. It was rancid lard and armpit sweat.

Grandpa stopped at the steps. "You doin' all right tonight, Harold?"

Harold was sharpening his pocketknife. He spat over the rail and went back to rubbing the blade on a whetstone in his hand. Most men in Center Springs kept a sharpening stone close at hand, if they didn't already have one in their pocket. Grandpa carried a small, flat Arkansas stone in his overalls to touch up the blade on his own knife, whenever he needed it.

"I'm all right, but if you're here about Lizzie, well, there ain't nothin' we can do for her."

A scared voice came from the dark insides of the house. "Help! Who's out there? My legs is gone and I can't find my eyes! I cain't hardly see nothin'."

Uncle Cody went on up the porch with a silver flashlight in his hand. "I'll go check on her if it's all right."

Miss Becky was up the steps like a shot. "My lands, poor thing." Norma Faye trailed right behind.

Grandpa stepped back all of a sudden. I figured he'd gotten good whiff of Harold. "She's hollerin' pretty good."

Harold spat again. "Don't matter to me none. She don't know any of us anymore. Her mind is as gone as gone gets."

Pepper leaned over to me. "That man is crazier than a shit-house rat, and he smells like one, too."

Grandpa stood there in the yard, visiting like all the electricity in the county wasn't off and there wasn't a crazy lady with Old Timer's disease in the house. "Why'n't you go in and calm her down?"

"Won't do no good. She'll squall 'til she gets tired of hollerin' and then she'll settle down. I had to tie her in the bed."

"That why she's hollerin?"

"I reckon, but I tied her up day before yesterday, so I'd imagine she'd be over it by now."

"You kids get in the car," Grandpa snapped, quick as a snake-bite. I'd heard that tone before, and knew he was mad. Pepper and I took off like a shot to stay out of his way.

Pepper held her nose. "He smells like something died in his britches."

Grandpa moved a little upwind. "You had her tied up since day before yesterday?"

By the light of the oil lamp, Harold tested the sharpness of the blade by shaving the hair on his left arm. "Once."

Uncle Cody slammed the screen door open and came out on the porch like thunder. "Damn you Harold, stand up!"

The sharp crack of his voice jolted Harold from his chair. "I didn't have no choice."

The flashlight spun across the porch as Uncle Cody pitched it to Grandpa, who caught it and shined the beam onto Harold. "Put that knife down." Harold carefully folded it and laid the knife on his rocker.

Uncle Cody spun him around and snapped a pair of cuffs on his dirty wrists. "I wouldn't treat a hog the way you've done Miss Lizzie. You're headed for jail, and she's going to the hospital."

"I did what I knew to do."

"You could have fed her, and changed her, and cleaned her up."

"I been doing that for years, but when her mind went, I figured she wouldn't know. I's just gonna let her drift on and off and hoped that medicine Little Ben had would do some good."

"Little Ben Winters?"

"Don't know no other Little Ben."

Uncle Cody studied him. "What medicine?"

"We tried that new stuff to get her to calm down, and it works pretty good, but she can't hardly hold the smoke in her lungs for it to do any good."

"What are you talking about?"

"Why Cody, that stuff that Little Ben sold us. Said it was good for Old Timer's disease and would ease her at night so she could sleep."

"You talking about marijuana. You give her dope?"

"Sure 'nough. The medicine Doc give her ain't working, and it's dope, too. I bought some papers and rolled her a couple of cigarettes and she tried it. It works for a while, but I'll be damned if I can afford much of the stuff. You reckon I should have made her just chew it like tobaccer? You know she dips Garrets Snuff pretty regular, so it shouldn't be any different."

Cody squinted at Harold. "You been smoking that dope, too?"

"Yeah, right smart since it cost so much and I didn't want to waste it. I've felt pretty good the last day or so. I don't know why they outlawed it."

"Because it's dope, Harold." Grandpa rubbed his bald head beside the car, standing in the half-open door with his foot propped on the edge of the floorboard. "What you did wasn't right." Grandpa picked up the microphone on his Motorola and called for an ambulance.

The lights flickered as the power came back on, and a dim glow filled Harold's living room.

Miss Becky and Norma Faye were rushing around in there, and I knew then we'd finally eat our ice cream, but much later and that was all right.

I needed to get the stink out of my nose first.

Chapter Twenty-one

The Parkers hadn't been gone but a minute when a new sedan came over the creek bridge and rolled sedately down the straight mile of two-lane highway before reaching the house. Tom Bell heard the tires change tone when it slowed. He'd blown out the kerosene lamp on the porch and propped his chair back on two legs in contentment, waiting for everyone to come back.

His ear perked when the car slowed even more on the highway, and almost rolled to a stop down by the drive.

Its headlights were off.

It was dark on the porch, and impossible for anyone to see from below. Tom didn't move. The dim glow of the coal oil lights in the house gave little illumination to the outside.

Giving the car a quick glance, Tom slipped his hand into the small of his back and slipped his .45 automatic free. Instead of concentrating on the car below, he raised the pistol, aiming along the side of the house, to the porch steps on his right.

He waited.

The silent car idled below.

The wind laid for a moment. He heard the commotion at Lizzie's house.

A soft noise of cloth brushing against the side of the house told him someone was trying to take advantage of the sudden blackout.

With the pistol still pointed at the corner of the house, Tom spoke, softly. "Don't."

He waited.

"If I was you, I'd slip back around the house and down the hill there to your friends in the car. If you don't, I'll kill you. This forty-five in my hand will blow holes in you big enough to pitch a dog through."

Silence.

"I imagine your friend down there in the sunglasses is getting impatient. You better hurry, and I don't reckon you better come back here again. Tell him we'll be waiting."

The wind picked up again.

A minute later, he heard several soft thuds as the prowler high-tailed it down the hill and back to the dark car. When he opened the door, the dome light illuminated the interior. The door slammed, and the car roared away, switching on its lights as it gained speed.

He'd seen enough to recognize Whitlatch behind the wheel.

Tom slipped the pistol back behind his belt and continued to lean against the wall, thinking he'd need to keep an eye on Ned's house for a while.

He also wished they'd hurry back. That banana ice cream still sounded good.

Chapter Twenty-two

We'd been shooting at frogs and snakes with our BB guns, but the sun settling over the trees shoved us on home before it got too dark. Pepper beat me over the hill from the pool. She's always been able to run faster, even though our legs are about the same length.

Uncle Cody was standing beside his El Camino. "Y'all go wash your faces, and put on clean shirts."

"What for?"

He gave us a grin. "Well, there's a tent revival that Miss Becky is gearing up for, and your Grandpa's in town with Judge Rains. He ain't back yet, so y'all can either let me carry you to Pepper's house for the night, or you can go with me and Norma Faye to a powwow in Grant."

The offer was like a chance to go to Disneyland. I'd never been to a powwow, and the idea of a revival or an evening with Aunt Ida Belle sounded as good as getting jobbed with a sharp stick.

With a whoop, we charged into the house, washed our faces, and changed shirts. Miss Becky was in the front bedroom, letting Norma Faye braid her hair up into a bun. Their backs were to us. "I'd a sight rather y'all go with me to hear the preaching tonight."

We didn't say anything for fear that a conversation might suddenly turn into a change in plans. Norma Faye gave us a wink in the mirror over Miss Becky's head.

"You and Cody could go too."

Norma Faye nodded like she was giving the idea some serious thought. She brushed at Miss Becky's long, salt-and-pepper hair that reached below her waist. "We could, but I've never been to a powwow, neither. I've been to tent revivals."

Miss Becky sighed. "My mama took me to a powwow when I was little, but she died not long after."

"I didn't know."

"No, I reckon you didn't. We don't talk about it much."

"You were born in Grant, weren't you?" Pepper stepped up beside them to look at herself. "That's where we're going."

"Sure was, and we lived there until Mama died when I was six, then Papa brought us across the river here to Center Springs."

We'd never heard Miss Becky talk about my great-grandmother.

"We lived in a little holler on a creek, not far from a good spring. Papa was in Tulsa that day with some of the tribal elders, and my sisters and I were helping Mama make soap. It was our job to keep the fire going under the wash pot.

"I don't know what happened. Maybe a coal rolled out, or Mama's dress blew into the fire. She wore dresses that brushed the ground and they were forever getting dirty, or muddy, or snagged on something.

"Anyways, all of a sudden that cotton material caught a-fire and blazed up all at once. I imagine she'd spilled some lard on it, or had been wiping her greasy hands on it all day long, because that's what we used to make soap back then, wood ashes and fat, but before we knew what was happening, she was a-fire."

Norma Faye listened and slowly twisted three thick stands of hair into a bun.

It was like Miss Becky was telling a story she'd had bottled up for years, and she didn't want to stop, all the time looking through her reflection, back to a time long ago.

I imagined it might be a magic mirror, and shifted to look into the past with her.

"If you catch fire, you're supposed to drop on the ground and roll around, but Mama panicked and ran toward the house. Maybe she wanted to get to the water bucket beside the door, but her hair caught, and her's was longer than mine, because she was younger and wore it down a lot. She was a-screamin' and a-screamin.'

"Before you know it, she was all a-fire, and she fell on the ground and rolled around in the dirt, because that's all our yard was, but it was too late. Sister threw a quilt on her to put her out, but it didn't do no good."

Norma Faye put down the brush and picked up a thin black hair net that she stretched over Miss Becky's hair.

"Mama's clothes finally went out, and Neva Lou ran to get help, and left me, Geneva, and Wilfred there by ourselves. He was a little baby. Mama was black on one side of her face and moaning, and I didn't know what to do for her, so I covered her up with a different quilt and bathed her face with cold water, but every time I did, her skin came off on the rag. It was red raw underneath."

The house was totally silent. Norma Faye rested her hands on Miss Becky's shoulders. Great aunt Neva Lou was the only sister Miss Becky had left. Geneva and Wilfred both died before I was born.

"Us kids wrapped her up right there on the ground and waited with her all by ourselves that night, while she shivered and moaned. We kept giving her water when she called for it, but she was out of her head. Help finally came the next morning, but it was too late. She died that afternoon, not long before Papa got back home. I cried for days after Mama died. It wasn't long after that Papa left us with some relatives and didn't come back until I was a teenager. I swore then I'd never leave any family for no reason at all."

All of a sudden, her eyes widened. "Well my lands, now why did I go and tell that story when y'all were excited about a powwow. Y'all better get going. Cody!"

I was startled when I heard him right behind me. "Yes, ma'am?"

"These kids don't know what to do. I don't want them to insult anybody. You make sure they mind their manners, and take some dollar bills for the drum out of that red lard bucket in the china cabinet."

Pepper swelled up. "We know our manners."

Uncle Cody pulled her toward the door. "You do around here, but powwows have rules, and they're important. Now, clam up because she's probably just a hair away from making y'all go to that revival with her."

It was dark when we arrived in the little community of Grant, but the powwow was already going strong. Big generators roared and thick cables stretched across the grass, powering floodlights that brightened a pasture full of happy people. They were far enough away to keep the noise from covering the songs and events. It reminded me of only a few months ago at the Cotton Exchange in Chisum where they used floodlights for the lawmen and firemen to help Uncle Cody and Mr. John.

The whole shebang was set up not far from the lone country store that was doing a booming business. I imagine Neal Box would have loved to have something pop up like this near his store a couple of times a year. This part of Oklahoma was no different than where we lived in Center Springs, except it had Indians everywhere, and for once, a lot of them were dressed the way I expected Indians to look. Kids my age were all decked out in feathers, bells, and buckskin, waiting for their turn to dance.

Despite the warm weather, a fire burned bright in the center of the pasture. Between the parked cars and the fire, a circle of men surrounded a big drum and were beating the whey out of it with what I took for leather-covered war clubs. I liked the beat, but it didn't sound like what you heard on television when Indians were singing and doing their war dance.

BOOM boom boom boom BOOM boom boom boom.

This one was more of a strong, steady beat I felt deep in my chest. It almost made my lungs tickle, and I was glad my puffer was in my back pocket. They were singing a traditional song, but I didn't know the words, because they were in Choctaw or Comanche or something.

Then I recognized one phrase that Miss Becky taught us. *Chi hollo li.*

Some of the men at the drum were dressed like white people, but a few wore khakis and were shirtless. You never saw a grown man without a shirt on in Center Springs, and at first it didn't seem right for them to be half naked, but the Indians looked more like what I imagined.

The drums and music touched something deep inside me, and for the first time in a long while, I felt really, really good. When I caught Pepper's eye, I knew she felt the same thing and her eyes lit up in excitement. While we walked from the car to the crowd, the drummers quit.

People clapped and the men started a different song, but it sounded the same. "Why are they singing the same one again?"

"It's different, Top." Uncle Cody stopped. "The songs sound alike when you don't know the words, but I doubt they'll sing the same ones twice, unless there's a request, which reminds me, there are important rules that you need to remember."

For the next five minutes he explained how powwows worked, and what we were allowed to do. There were a lot of don'ts.

"We're not settin' anywhere, so that'll keep you two from getting in trouble with the older folks who can't stand up for long. We'll stay back here, but don't get any closer than that ring of benches, and as a matter of fact, if y'all do find yourselves away from me, ask permission if you can stand behind anyone or anything."

Half a dozen little kids chased each other past us. Uncle Cody reached out and ran his fingers through one little girl's hair as she dodged around him. "When anyone stands for songs, you stand too."

"Like the national anthem?" Pepper's head was about to spin off, because she kept trying to take in everything at the same time.

"Kinda. There are Prayer Songs and Memorial Songs we stand for, out of respect."

Frying foods, wood smoke, and cigarettes mixed with a sweet smell of boiling caramel candy gave a carnival feeling to the dry air. I soon learned they called it Burnt Sugar.

Cub scouts were everywhere, building little campfires that extended in all directions. Grownups were putting up tents for the night. There were even authentic teepees.

My nerves jangled in excitement. Uncle Cody and Norma Faye walked slow, holding hands. He was dressed in a blue shirt and khakis with his .45 on his hip. She wore jeans and a short sleeved shirt. I noticed, because women back then usually wore dresses.

Norma Faye rubbed the back of my head. "Y'all look like we're at the circus."

Pepper was almost dancing, and it was the first time since the Incident down by the Rock Hole that she really and truly acted like her old self. "I've never seen anything like this!"

I tugged on Uncle Cody's arm, taking his attention from the crowd. "I can't believe Miss Becky said it was all right for us to come out here. This doesn't seem very religious, from the way she believes."

He and Norma Faye exchanged glances. "Well, y'all know how she is about church, but that little woman knows a lot more than we give her credit for. I think she wanted y'all to understand where we come from and how our people are."

Pepper pointed. "Why are they putting money in front of that guy there?"

"It's a sign of respect. They're honoring him for some reason…"

Cody's explanation was cut off when a body flashed out of the crowd and slammed into me.

My first thought was Cale Westlake was here and wanted to finish the fight!

Cale tried to beat me up nearly a year earlier, not long after I moved to Center Springs. He was a couple of years older than me, and had it in his head that Pepper was supposed to be his girlfriend. When we got crossways at a dance, he and some of his toadies waylaid me out behind the school gym.

I couldn't believe my bad luck in running into him in Oklahoma. I braced my feet and twisted, trying to throw him off before his buddies showed up and started trying to beat the snot out of me. I heard Pepper screech, and then she ran into us, knocking me off balance and nearly throwing me to the ground. Hair flew in my face, and I butted heads with someone.

In the back of my mind, I wondered why Uncle Cody hadn't stepped in to help, but I figured he was letting me and Pepper handle our own battles.

And then I heard him laughing.

Pepper shrieked. "Son of a bitch!"

"Pepper!" Norma Faye scolded. "Watch your language."

I finally got free and ran back a couple of steps to get some space. My fist was doubled up when I spun around to find a target, but all I saw was Pepper hugging a girl. Behind them, Uncle Cody and Norma Faye stood by with their arms around each other, beaming while Pepper rassled with her right there in front of everyone.

The people walking around us weren't upset over two kids fighting. They passed with big smiles on their faces.

Something was wrong with the fight, because Pepper wasn't mad, and the person she had her arms around wasn't trying to hurt her. Then the other girl let go, pulled her long black hair out of her eyes, and held up her right hand toward me with a big grin.

"How!"

"Mark!" This time it was me who charged with tears in my eyes, and I wrapped my arms around my best friend in a big bear hug.

Ten minutes later Uncle Cody handed each of us an ear of roasted corn and we found a place to stand out of the way. Norma Faye sipped a Dr Pepper through a paper straw standing in the neck of the bottle. "What have you been up to?"

We hadn't heard from him in months and it bothered Pepper most of all, because she had a crush on him.

Mark's grin split his face from ear to ear. "Not much. Missing *y'all* mostly."

He and Pepper standing so close their shoulders brushed. It should have bothered me, but he'd become my best friend in the short time we'd known each other. Uncle Cody took him for a haircut when he lived with us, but in the months since, it had grown back to his shoulders, thick and black.

"Where you living, son?"

"Still with my aunt and uncle, up near Frogtown. They're somewhere hereabouts."

"I didn't think there was anything left of Frogtown these days."

"There ain't. We ain't got no store or nothin'. Just a few shacks and that's all." Mark was much thinner than when he lived with us, and he was wearing clothes a size too large.

Uncle Cody chewed his bottom lip. "You've lost weight."

Mark worked his way down the ear of corn from one end to the other like a typewriter. He chewed for a moment. "They don't have much money, so we eat mostly beans and a few 'taters every now and then."

Uncle Cody studied him for a long moment, and I knew he didn't like what he saw. Mark was hungry, and we didn't talk too much until the three of us had eaten two ears apiece, gritty with salt and dripping with butter. Norma Faye couldn't keep her hands off of him, and I knew she felt bad that he was so skinny.

By that time, the drum went quiet and a couple of the singers stood up and left. Not all were longhaired Indians. Some were white folks like us. Others quickly took their places and the beat started up again. A singer threw his head back and the air was filled with a sound from a time long past. Several people, both white and Indian, moved up to dance with small steps in a slow circle around the drummers and the fire.

Mark shuffled his feet to the beat. "I heard 'bout what happened to y'all."

Pepper stiffened for a moment, and then tilted her head. "We're all right."

I knew she felt uncomfortable, so I changed the direction of the conversation. "I got a puppy after you left. We named him Hootie, and he helped save us."

"A pup did?"

"He was half growed then, and he ain't much puppy anymore." While Uncle Cody talked, he kept an eye on the crowd, and I knew he was looking for something. "I do believe he saved them a second time down on the river in the fall."

"Sounds like y'all been busy."

"You wouldn't believe it." Uncle Cody took Norma Faye's hand and led her toward the dancers. "Come on kids, let's go stand over there so we can watch everything and talk without bothering anybody or getting in the way."

We threaded our way through the crowd. Pepper held Mark's hand behind Uncle Cody and Norma Faye, like a miniature version of grown-ups. We stopped beside a group of Indian men building another small fire.

I'd never seen Indians make fire, so I was interested. I expected them to get a stout limb and a bow saw to start a blaze with friction, but I was disappointed when a big bellied man unscrewed the lid from a jar of Vaseline and dipped a glop out with a big piece of raw cotton. He laid it on the ground and stuck a match to the cotton. When the Vaseline caught, he piled on small sticks until it burned bright.

The man gave me a big wink. "Old Indian trick. We don't use flint and steel anymore. We learned what was easiest."

Embarrassed that he knew what I was thinking, I went back to Mark and Pepper. For the next hour, we talked and caught up while Uncle Cody and Norma Faye stood nearby, visiting with different people.

One of them was the Hugo sheriff, Clayton Matthews, who'd been on the job less than a year. They say he wore a badge up around Tulsa somewhere, before he beat out Sheriff Post for the Hugo job. I believed he won the election because he looked more like an Indian cowboy than a sheriff. I moved closer to hear them talk.

Mark and Pepper didn't care. They wanted to whisper to each other. It was like he'd never left, but I knew she'd fall apart when we went home and realized he'd be gone from us again for a long time.

"I haven't come across anybody who looks like that, Cody." Sheriff Matthews stood beside him and they talked without hardly looking at one another. "You say he's a big man, all muscled up?"

"That's what Ned said. Built like John Washington, only white. There was three others with him in the Sportsman, and we think they might be involved in at least one killin' on our side of the river."

The obvious question hung out there until the sheriff couldn't stand it anymore. "You think it was them shot at you?"

Uncle Cody shrugged, as if it wasn't a big deal. "Maybe. I didn't get a look at anyone because it was too dark, and then I was busy trying to rein in Norma Faye's car."

"What makes you think they're here?"

"Didn't say they was. I said I figured they might be some-where's close by, since they hang out at my place a lot, or did while I was in the hospital. I don't want to try and arrest any-body. I only want to visit with them for a little bit, and try to jolt 'em a little."

Matthews grinned. "You're a-lyin'. The minute you get the chance at 'em you'll haul 'em to jail."

"Maybe, but not from this side of the river. I want to get my hands on them on our side."

Norma Faye spoke up for the first time. "Say again what he looked like?"

"Ned says muscled up, flattop, rolls his sleeves of tight cowboy shirts as high as he can, wears shades inside and out."

"Like him?" She jerked her chin toward a big man sitting on the tailgate of a dark green company truck.

It was hard to make him out in the light, but the guy was as big as Mr. John. He also made me uncomfortable, even from that distance. I was always scared of men who were greasy and tough, with their slicked-back hair or flat tops, and cigarettes hanging from their lips.

The man on the tailgate was even scarier, because he also wore a stained bandage on his cheek that glowed in the lights.

It didn't faze Uncle Cody. He suddenly set his jaw and left us standing there. Sheriff Matthews quickly tagged along. Norma Faye held us back. "Y'all, we need to stay right here."

"I want to see," Pepper complained.

"Oh, you'll see all right." Norma Faye took a deep, shuddering breath and shook her head. "I 'magine you're fixin' to see more than you want to."

Chapter Twenty-three

Based on the description, Cody instantly recognized the man in the harsh floods as the one who threatened Ned in the Sportsman. Deep inside, he also instinctively knew it was the man behind the wheel of the car that had ambushed him. His mind shifted into overdrive. The bandage covering his cheek surely hid a wound resulting from a struggle with Ben junior. There was no logic to the knowledge, nothing but a dead-solid gut feeling that felt right.

He'd finally learned to trust his instincts.

Locking in on the huge figure, he plowed through the crowd in a straight line toward the truck. Milling residents and visitors quickly moved out of his way when they saw the look in the Texas constable's eyes. Cody unsnapped the strap over his pistol. Sheriff Matthews mimicked his actions, praying they wouldn't get into a gunfight in the middle of so many people.

The giant caught sight of Cody pushing through the crowd and stiffened. The men he'd been talking to noticed his reaction and backed away like vanishing smoke.

"What's your name?" Cody demanded, stopping short and suddenly hypersensitive to the noise, crowd, and music.

"Whitlatch. What's yours...oh, wait, I know you. You're Cody Parker, that constable from Center Springs."

"Stand up!"

Matthews reached out and touched Cody's arm to calm his rising rage. "Cody, let me."

Whitlach placed the palms of his hands on the tailgate, lifted his body, and arrogantly swung his considerable bulk onto the ground with a thud. He squared his feet in an aggressive stance. "*Now* what do you want me to do, *constable?*"

Sheriff Matthews moved in front of Cody. "Whitlatch, I need you to…" He was interrupted when a scuffle broke out not ten feet away. A woman screamed as two work-hardened men grappled over an unknown slight, then the fight became real when one of the slender men punched the other with a meaty crack.

Blood flew.

As if attracted by a magnet, a crowd moved in, a living entity that immediately congealed six people deep around the combatants. Instantly the smell of crushed grass rose around them.

A knife flashed in the floodlights.

Another scream.

The crowd roared their approval amidst the country carnival smells of frying foods, cooking sweets, and wood smoke.

Sheriff Matthews and Cody turned toward the disturbance, Whitlatch momentarily forgotten.

"Shit!" Realizing what happened, Cody's head snapped back around, but Whitlatch was already gone. The gathering throng prevented Cody from responding, and when he spun in the sheriff's direction, he couldn't believe his eyes.

Two entirely different men stepped between Matthews and the onlookers, asking questions as if nothing was going on behind them.

"What county is this, Sheriff? We're looking to move to Okla…

"He's just kidding. What we really want to know is if they sell beer around here tonight, we're mighty thirsty."

Confused at the bizarre turn of events, Sheriff Matthews momentarily divided his attention between the unnaturally-casual conversation and the crowd around the fight.

Another roar went up and the crowd pulsed with movement.

"Move!" Cody charged past the two who resisted for a moment and then stepped meekly aside.

"You two stay right here!" Matthew shoved the tightly packed gawkers out of the way and pushed his way through to the fight. Bodies rippled like rings in a pond, but when the lawmen broke into the makeshift arena, both fighters were gone.

"Dammit!" Cody scanned the crowd in frustration. When he tried to locate the two who'd stalled them, he found they had also disappeared.

The maneuver orchestrated by Whitlatch's men worked so smoothly it might have been planned.

Cody was close enough to touch the men who tried to murder him, and they'd slipped away like ghosts.

Chapter Twenty-four

Half an hour later, Uncle Cody met us over near the popcorn stand. We'd missed most of the action because of the crowd ginning around in front of us.

Norma Faye stepped forward and took Uncle Cody's arm. "Was that him?"

"I think so, but they're slick. They got away. Matthews wanted to call for help so we could check the cars coming and going, but it'd take twenty minutes before they even got here. Whitlatch is already long gone."

Mark shook his head, eyes twinkling. "You Parkers are something else. You come to a powwow and find people who're trying to kill you."

Uncle Cody put his arm around Norma Faye, still keeping his eye on those around them. "You're older than your years, Mark Lightfoot. An eighty-year-old man told me the same thing not too long ago."

"What do you want to do, Uncle Cody?" I knew Pepper didn't want to leave Mark, and I wanted to stay for the rest of the powwow. She was afraid he'd take us home and then come back to look for that feller. I didn't see how that little incident would ruin a perfectly good night.

"We're gonna stay right here and have a good time."

"Good." Mark acted like he wanted to be with all of us, but it was easy to tell he was more interested in Pepper. "Cody?"

"Umm hum?"

"I know about that feller you went over to talk to."

Uncle Cody's eyes lit up. "How do you know that?"

"I've seen him around. Some of my outlaw kinfolk talk about him at night around the fire. His name is Whitlatch, and he's got a group moving marijuana up here in Oklahoma from Mexico."

The whole night suddenly focused on the five of us. I'm sure there were people around, but we'd moved into a world of our own.

Uncle Cody knelt on one knee to be eye level with us. "Do tell."

"Whitlatch drives different cars they only keep for a week or two, and then sell 'em to buy new ones. That way no one recognizes the cars, most of the time, but he keeps a green fifty-nine Galaxie five hundred that he drives sometimes."

Cody rocked back like he'd been hit between the eyes. "I remember! That's the car I glimpsed that night. Those four headlights had me half blinded, but I know those low rear fins were right there beside me just before I left the highway. How do *you* know all this?"

Mark ducked his head. "Two of my uncles was making whiskey up in the Kiamichi, when Whitlatch's men showed up and told them to shut it down and leave, or they'd kill them. We haven't seen them since, but my kinfolk have been keeping an eye on Whitlatch, because he knows something."

The simple statement identified the two men in the grave for Cody. "Out of the mouths of babes. Why haven't you told anyone?"

"Who'd listen to me? I'm an Indian kid. That's just as bad as being a nigger kid."

"Why didn't you call me or Ned?"

"Dimes are hard to come by, and I try to stay out of the way."

"It ain't anymore." Uncle Cody dug in his pocket and counted out half a dozen Liberty Head dimes. "Here, stick 'em in your sock or something. They're for you to call us whenever you need help, or if you need to tell us something. Now, tell me what you know."

Mark raised his patched jeans to reveal bare ankles. "I ain't got no socks, but I'll put 'em in my shoe, at least until I get a hole in the sole."

I heard Norma Faye make a soft, choking sound. I knew better than to look at her, because I was sure she had tears in her eyes. "Hon, put these in your pocket and don't tell anyone you have them. Cody, give him some more money."

While Uncle Cody pulled bills from his billfold, Mark tried not to look embarrassed. "They're bringing marijuana in here from some town in the Valley called Him Billo, or something. I heard they didn't want anyone to know they was up here, so they run all the moonshiners off. Them that didn't run, disappeared."

Cody recalled the corpses they dug up at the unused still. "You ain't a-woofin' they disappeared."

"They're hiding the dope everywhere they can, and then some others break it up and sell it in places like Dallas and Oklahoma City. It's up in Muskogee, and even down in Chisum. It's everywhere."

"You know for a fact Whitlatch's driving that Galaxie?"

"Yessir. Turquoise. It looks green to me, but I'm about half colorblind. I remember, 'cause that's the color of a stone the Navajo like to work for jewelry."

Uncle Cody shook his head. "Boy, you're something else."

Mark's cheeks dimpled. "Don't I know it?"

"That's enough." Norma Faye ran her fingers through Mark's long hair. "You still hungry?"

"Sure am."

"Let's all get us a hot dog."

Uncle Cody wanted to ask Mark some more questions, but Norma Faye had done made up her mind that we were eating, and that was all right by me.

The singers changed every so often, and the dancers shuffled their feet until the air smelled *green*. The grass was long gone and dust rose around us. We joined in a couple of times, but mostly watched.

The adults got to talking with some people beside us, and I had an idea, so I nudged Mark with my elbow. "Stick out your thumb."

He stuck his thumb up in the air, and I opened the pocket knife Uncle Cody gave me months before. Mark knew exactly what I was gonna do, and grinned. "Don't cut too deep."

"I don't intend to." I drew the razor sharp blade across my left thumb until blood welled. It stung for a second, but I'd cut my fingers worse a dozen times before. I held out the knife, but Mark shook his head. "You have to do it."

Pepper's eyes widened when I drew the blade across Mark's thumb, and we stuck our wounds together. "Blood brothers forever."

"What about me?"

I tried to give Pepper the look Uncle Cody gave us when we asked dumb question. "Girl cousins can't be blood brothers. Whoever heard of a blood sister?"

The question sounded better before I said it, but she snatched the knife out of my hand. "*Shit!!!*" she hissed, and I saw she'd accidentally cut herself. Her's was deeper.

Mark pulled his thumb away from mine and it stung for a second time. The thin layer of blood had already stuck us together. He squeezed his thumb with the other hand for a second, then took Pepper's cut finger and pressed them together. "You're already blood with Top, but now we are too, only it ain't brother and sister. It's something else until the day we die."

In the flickering shadows, I saw tears in Pepper's eyes and couldn't figure out why she'd cry from just a little cut.

Long after they should have turned loose, Pepper and Mark kept holding hands and whispering. The drummers changed again and I saw Mark rub the back of her shoulder where the Skinner had branded her. She must have told him about it, or it might have been an accident.

The wind laid and the skeeters got bad for a while, until an Indian in overalls threw a handful of powder into the fire, and then they all vanished like the smoke that rose into the darkness.

We left around midnight, without Mark, and I was right, Pepper cried all the way home like her heart was broke. Norma Fay's eyes were wet, too, and Uncle Cody didn't say much as we rolled through the darkness.

We didn't see Mark for a long time after that.

Chapter Twenty-five

One week later all hell broke loose not far from our house.

It was after dark and Grandpa was out on a call somewhere. Pepper and I were in the living room, trying to tune the antenna to pick up American Bandstand. Grandpa wouldn't let us watch it when he was home because he hated rock and roll music, but Miss Becky said it was alright as long as we didn't turn it up too loud.

She answered after the second ring, because we weren't supposed to pick up the calls after dark. She listened for a minute, and then sat down heavily at the telephone table. I quit fooling with the electric rotor.

She'd heard about everything on that black rotary phone, but this time she was stunned. She quickly hung up and dialed. "James, hon, you need to get over here."

It was that fast. She hung up and dialed again. The phone must have rung a long time before she hung up. Miss Becky figured we were dying to know. "Kids, there's been a bad wreck at the creek bridge and they think your Aunt Sylvia has drowned."

Memories of our visit to her house washed over me, but I didn't say a word.

The phone rang again. The community grapevine was cranking up. A car rolled up the gravel drive when she picked up the receiver and headlights reflected through the windows. "See who it is, hon."

No one had ever told me to go to the door after dark, so I knew something really bad was happening. When I flicked on the porch light, Hootie was barking at Jimmy Foxx and his brother Ty Cobb.

Ty Cobb threw up his hand in a quick wave from their truck and turned off their headlights that nearly blinded me. "Top, do you know where Mr. Ned is?" They'd seen his car was gone.

"Nossir."

"Well, there's been a bad wreck at the creek and we're looking for him. You tell him to come on to the bridge when he comes back home."

Throwing their truck into reverse, they threw gravel as they shot down the drive and turned toward the store.

Miss Becky was still on the phone when I came back into the living room. Tears rolled down her cheeks as she talked. For once, Pepper didn't have much to say. She sat there and listened to our end of the conversation.

Another car crunched up the gravel drive, and in minutes Uncle James was in the house. "What is it, Mama?"

She momentarily forgot she was talking on the phone. "James, your Aunt Sylvia was coming back from across the river with Leon Fergus. I reckon he was drunk and lost control of the car. They missed the bridge and went off in the creek, and she drowned when it flipped upside down."

He left without a word. We heard his car hit the highway. The engine roared.

I swear, our little house on the hill was a magnet for every car that came down the road that wanted to stop in for a minute, folks clucking their tongues in pity before leaving.

Grandpa came to check with Miss Becky on his way to the accident. "Did y'all hear anything?"

"Nary sound."

"We did." Pepper said.

She and I heard a pop, but figured it was somebody shooting. There wasn't a day that went by in Center Springs you didn't hear the sounds of gunfire. Most men carried at least a .22 in their trucks for varmints, and there were more than a few rusty revolvers in the pigeon holes. People up north called it a glove box, but Grandpa's were usually full of trash, tools, and papers, especially rolled up wanted posters, but never gloves.

"How many times. You know where it came from?"

I wished I could help, but what we heard was no more than a crack. "Just one, but we couldn't tell where it came from."

Grandpa knew what we were saying. One pop late in the day was nothing.

In the kitchen, he took a long drink of ice water from the dipper, then put it back beside the bucket. "Leon and Sylvia were coming back over the creek bridge from Juarez." He wiped a drop from his chin. "A car coming the other way made a U-turn past the bridge when Leon's Oldsmobile topped the hill. He was going way too fast, and swerved at the last minute. He lost control and flipped into the creek. They were trapped in the car and drowned."

He stopped for a moment. I thought he'd seen a scorpion on the wall, but there wasn't anything there. "My lord, they run off together and didn't get five miles from home. They were looking for bright lights and a big two-story house, and all they found was a dirty honky-tonk and this."

He studied the dark television screen. "This has happened before. What did y'all hear after that pop?"

"I didn't hear nothing, but the kids saw a car go past."

I shrugged when he raised his eyebrows. I hated not being able to tell who passed below the hill to our house, because Grandpa always asked who it was. "A car went by a minute later and somebody honked the horn, but we were trying to tune the tee vee and didn't look."

He sighed. "Mama, put your pistol in your pocket and watch for whoever drives up."

Miss Becky set her jaw, went straight to the kitchen, and took her .25 automatic from the drawer in the china cabinet. Grandpa was already backing down the drive when she latched the hook on the screen door.

Pepper whispered in my ear. "That little metal hook ain't gonna stop nothing bigger'n that damn monkey Tarzan carries around."

Sometimes Pepper aggravated me for real. "It might slow a bad guy down for a minute." I pointed to the loaded shotgun in the corner, and we both knew a .22 rifle stood against the kitchen door frame.

The phone rang again, and Miss Becky answered. "I know, honey. It's just awful…"

Unconsciously rubbing the scar on the back of her shoulder, Pepper hugged herself and went to stare out the south window at the ribbon of highway past the yard.

We were once again locked in the house with our grandmother and several loaded guns.

Chapter Twenty-six

Judge O.C. Rains joined the lawmen at the creek bridge. Headlights lit the scene. "Ned, Cody, y'all tell me what you got."

Knees aching, Ned had been leaning on his elbows over the hood of a car, talking with the others about what had happened. "What'n hell you doing out here tonight?"

"It don't take much to put two and two together. Even I know an ambush when I hear about one, only this time it worked. Y'all have any idea what's going on?"

Worried, Cody chewed the inside of his lip. It was beginning to get sore from all the thinking, and he figured he'd have an ulcer in there by the end of the night. "You're right, judge. At first we thought it was an accident, that Leon was drunk and ran off the road, and he was probably drunk all right, but there's a bullet hole in their windshield and it didn't come from inside."

A long line of drag marks led from the creek to the highway where Isaac Reader had used Ned's tractor to pull the car from the water.

Cody stared down at the marks as if they held a clue to the murder. "They done took him and Sylvia to the funeral home. That would have been me a few months ago if Tom hadn't showed up when he did."

"'I god, first her boy and now her. Y'all think it was Ben done it?"

"He probably thought about it, but naw, it wasn't him."

Ned unconsciously jiggled the loose change in his pants pocket. "It was the same ones who shot at Cody there. It's Whitlatch and his men, but I'll be damned if I know why."

"I do."

Tom Bell stood behind them.

O.C was unfazed at Tom's sudden appearance. It seemed as if he were expecting him.

"Whitlatch and his cronies are working with somebody in Chisum to move marijuana up here from Mexico. They're also starting a new business where they're growing their own."

Ned felt his face flush. "How do you know all this?"

"I used to be in a business down south that knew a lot about what's coming across the border. Since I retired, I kinda keep my hand in, just to know what's going on."

"Why'nt you tell us this before, Tom?"

"I only found out about half an hour ago, when a friend of mine called and told *me*. It's a good thing I got that phone put in yesterday. I have electricity now, too."

"Just what business were you in?"

"O.C., I'd rather not say right now, but I can give you the name of a couple good men in south Texas who'll vouch for me. There's one more thing, y'all ain't gonna like one little bit. The ramrod for the outfit up here ain't Whitlatch, he's just a gofer for somebody else, but I don't have any idea who it is."

"I'll find out," Ned said.

Tom chuckled. "I have no doubt you will."

"That matches up with what Mark Lightfoot told us," Cody said. "Now I believe his story. The kid knew more than us. Ain't that a kick?"

A pair of headlights appeared over the hill, underneath a revolving ball mounted to the roof. Cody crossed his arms and rested his hip against a car. "Boys, this just went sour."

Sheriff Griffin stepped out of the car, adjusted his hat, and strolled toward the accident scene as if going to the store. Deputy White still looked miserable in his role as driver.

White shook Cody's hand and spoke softly. Both men assumed positions against the car to view the continuing battle between Ned and Griffin. Ned planted his feet and waited for Griffin to close the gap between them. When he was close enough, Griffin took a deep breath to begin the skirmish and the huge form of John Washington appeared from the darkness, drawing Griffin's ire.

"Washington, what the hell are you doing way out here? Isn't this out of your jurisdiction?"

O.C. waved an arm as if at an annoying mosquito. "I sent him out." The statement wasn't completely true, yet it wasn't untrue, either. He'd sent John out to Center Springs on a number of occasions, so technically, he was still out on an older call.

John hadn't expected to be attacked by Griffin, but it wasn't a total surprise. He stayed out of the sheriff's way as much as possible, knowing Griffin had no use for his only colored deputy, and even less use for the people who lived on the south side of the tracks.

John spoke softly, with restrained respect, but his stance between Constable Parker and the sheriff couldn't have been any clearer. Either consciously or unconsciously, he intended to block Griffin from getting close to Ned. It was an instinctive ballet of territorial defiance on the empty highway.

"Nawsir, I 'spect I go where I'm needed. You know that. I heard on the radio what had happened here not far from Mr. Ned's house. Mr. O.C. talked to me on the radio a little bit ago, so here I am. And since one of our constables was shot at not long ago, I figgered I'd hurry and help a fellow lawman best I can."

Griffin struggled to find fault with the statement, but to his aggravation, John was right. Sheriff's deputies served the entire county, as Griffin's presence proved, even though John's territory was unofficially south of the tracks. The sheriff had already defeated his own argument by being there.

"We don't need every deputy I have out here," Griffin sputtered.

"I'll go."

The sheriff pondered the suggestion for a moment. "No, I'll go. Have a complete typewritten report on my desk first thing in the morning." He knew as well as Ned and O.C. that John had never written a report on a typewriter in his life, and the deadline was impossible. "I want to know why they were out here, where they were coming from, what happened, and a list of suspects."

"You'll have it," O.C. interrupted. He intended to write the report himself.

Griffin hooked both thumbs behind the hand-tooled gun belt and rocked back and forth for a moment. He hadn't considered O.C. butting in. "You people out here in Center Springs think y'all have your own little kingdom, don't you? But before long, I'm gonna tear y'all's playhouse down."

Tom Bell waited to see if anyone was interested in relaying the information he'd just given them. Griffin finally noticed the old man standing close by. "Who are you?"

"Nobody."

"You have some reason to be here?"

Tom's eyes displayed his annoyance. "Don't need one. Unless I woke up in Russia this morning, I can be anywhere I want."

"Well, we don't need any old ranchers gettin' in the way of an investigation."

"Don't worry about me, sheriff. I know my place."

Griffin hooked his thumbs in the gun belt around his waist. "Is there anything else I need to know before I leave?"

When no one answered, Griffin avoided the increasingly uncomfortable silence by flipping a hand for White and returning to his car, shouldering past the Wilson brothers. White raised an eyebrow in apology, slid behind the wheel, and they left behind a crowd of very irritated citizens.

Tom Bell watched White turn around, barely missing the deep ditch that would have without a doubt stuck the sheriff's car. "Your sheriff don't seem to be a particularly friendly feller, does he?"

"No he ain't," Ned rubbed his face. "I don't give a shit about him, but he does a good job there in town, for a City Feller."

As if those last two words explained everything, the men working the accident scene went back to sorting out the details. Thinking, Cody stood on the solid yellow line painted down the middle of the highway. He stared down the arrow-straight ribbon of concrete that disappeared into darkness. Behind him, the hill rose sharply.

"This is all coming to a head, and I can't figure out what's happening."

Ned joined him. "It seems to me Whitlatch is clearing his field before he plows."

"What do you mean?"

Tom stepped close. "He means, son, that when Whitlatch is finished, there won't be anyone left to tie him to this drug operation, or to them they've killed to get rid of the competition, right? I been keeping up with what's in the papers. Dead moonshiners, until there ain't no more whiskey stills around here. Then the drug system is set up, and when it's in place, them that worked on it are gone, along with anyone who knew or suspected anything about their comings and goings, like these poor folks here. It leaves only the hired hands on the bottom, Whitlatch in the middle, and Mr. I Don't Know Who He Is on top. It ain't nothin' new."

"Tom, how the hell do you know all of this? What ain't you tellin' us?"

He sighed. "Ned, I was a lawman down south. I came up here to retire and get out of misfortune such as this, but it looks like I moved smack in the middle of the exact things that made me old before my time."

The men standing around completely missed the dismissive comment. "What branch? Were you a constable or something?"

An extremely private person, Tom held back even more with the Parkers. They'd find out soon enough. "Can't say, as of yet, but you can call down south if you really want to know my bonafides. They won't tell you much, just that I wore a badge. Now let me help you without too many more questions."

"Well I have a couple more, if you don't mind."

Tom Bell gave Ned the briefest of nods. "I'll answer what I can."

"Why are you here?"

"I been asked to follow some drugs up here from the Valley. That's all I can say on that subject."

"You cain't leave us with that. Give us a little more."

Tom started to say more, but then he shook his head and backed up a step, as if that distance would keep him from talking too much. "I just gave you all I got to give, right now."

Tilting his hat back, Ned rubbed at his forehead. "You carried a badge, but you're out of the bidness, you know things we don't about this marywana, but you won't tell us no more."

"Only that you can trust me."

"All right, then, but we're still lawmen and we have that behind us. What can *you* do?"

Tom gave them a chilling look. "What you can't."

Chapter Twenty-seven

Cody finished draining a glass of sweet iced tea just as the phone rang. He left it on the kitchen table and answered the black phone sitting in a surprisingly ornate nook in the hall. "What?"

"You're supposed to say 'hello,'" the annoyed caller said. "Is this Constable Parker?"

"One of 'em. Which one do you want?"

"Don't matter. I's out off the Blake Creek road in the army camp, looking for some polk salet, when I ran across a barn out there that was falling down, and when I went in it I found a bunch of marijuana and white lightning hid under some feed sacks."

Cody's ears perked up. He'd grown up, along with everyone else in Lamar County, pronouncing poke salad. The tall weed was a cheap substitute for garden-grown greens. Mostly poor folks ate the free food, but those who'd been hungry in the past still had a taste for it, cooked with fatback or neck bones, and a side of cornbread.

Surprised the caller had properly pronounced the word, Cody absently wondered how long it would take to find Ned. "Who is this?"

"Uh uh. Nossir. I ain't gettin' mixed up in no drugs and whiskey. It's out there, though, if y'all want to go get it."

"Well, now wait a minute. There's a lot of country out there and more than one barn. Tighten up on your directions a little bit and help me out here."

A long sigh came through the line. "Go in through Gate Five and stay on it 'til you get to the creek. Take the left fork and foller it 'til the road peters out. You'll think you're done, but keep follerin' the track and you'll see where I drove across the meader to a barn on the right. It's might-near covered in vines and that's where it is. Now I got to go."

The line clicked for a minute, and the dial tone buzzed. He kept the receiver to his ear and hung up by pushing the disconnect button with his thumb. When he let it go and heard the tone again, he dialed Ned's house.

"What?"

Cody grinned. "A minute ago a man told me I was supposed to say howdy when I answered the phone."

"I would have, if I'd known it was you."

"Don't go nowhere. I'll be by in a few minutes to pick you up. The feller that called said he'd found some more marijuana hid out down near Blake Creek Road."

"That damned stuff is popping up everywhere."

"It's the times."

Ned hung up without another word, and Cody grinned again. *I need to tell him how to use his manners on the phone.*

Ned fidgeted once again in the passenger seat of Cody's red-and-white El Camino. "Next time we go anywhere, we're driving my Chevrolet." He pronounced it Chev-a-lay.

"I wish you'd get a new car. That wreck has so many miles on it I'm surprised parts don't fall off every time you hit a dead possum in the road."

"It don't matter none. I have more room in my car, so like I said, the next time I'm driving."

"I might think about it, if you'd get them bullet holes patched up that Jimmy Don Foster shot in it."

"Most of them are covered. Rod Post ran out of Bondo before he got finished. He'll get back to it one of these days."

Cody watched the trees flicker past. "He won't do it unless you stay on him. Go by every day until he gets it done."

Rod Post was the community's shade-tree mechanic that worked on everything from cars to tractors.

"I don't have time for that. It seems like I've been in the field every day since Easter."

"Well, it don't look right for the constable to run around with bullet holes in his car."

Ned snorted. "You say *that,* and drive around in *this?*"

"I have a car that looks good, and a truck when I need one. It's the best of both worlds."

"I like my world the way it is. Do you know where we're going?"

"He gave me some directions, and they lead out here."

"I wish I knew who called you."

"You and me both."

"I don't like it that he wouldn't give you a name." Ned hung his elbow out of the passenger window. "You'll learn soon enough that about half of what we get comes from folks who don't want to leave their names or get involved, but they want to tell us so we'll check it out. This ain't nothing new."

"Well, I still don't like it. Especially right now with it feeling like things are coming to a head."

"I ain't sayin' don't be careful. It could be a setup every time we get a call, and we need to know that. I've seen folks get careless about this kind of work, and they usually get hurt when they do. But it's our job to follow up on every call, so keep your eyes open and the wax out of your ears."

Cody left the highway and drove through Gate 5. They followed the asphalt road winding through the empty buildings of Camp Maxie, the almost defunct World War II army camp. When they were past the main areas, the road quickly took them into country being rapidly reclaimed by nature. The asphalt crumbled and as they drove deeper into the interior, it finally gave way to fine gravel, the final remaining bonding element of the low-bid paving material.

After driving through alternating woods, pastures and open meadows, he slowed so they could peer through the overgrowth.

"I remember there being a house-place in here somewheres," Ned said. He recalled when the army teemed with soldiers and civilians alike during the war years. Nearly everyone in Center Springs and nearby Chisum had family that worked in some capacity in the camp, not to mention the men who went off to other camps to complete their military training. Glancing through his window, he recalled more than forty thousand soldiers who moved through the camp on their way to war.

It was hard times, and there were even a few single women, or women whose husbands were in the army themselves, who placed red railroad lanterns on their porches or discreetly in a window, indicating they were open for "business."

The entire camp was still posted with warnings of live and dangerous ordinance. Unexploded shells from artillery practice were a common find by hunters and fishermen who were only recently being allowed back into the more remote reaches of the camp.

He couldn't help but wonder each time he considered an open meadow if it was one of the many resting places for the war supplies buried by the U.S. military after Japan's surrender. Stories still circulated of guns still in Cosmoline, entire engine blocks, ammunition, artillery shells, and food, all buried in deep holes and covered with dirt by bulldozers.

It wouldn't surprise him if they'd buried the entire contents of the army camp in those fields.

Cody stopped the car. "There it is."

A distinct set of car tracks cut off the road and across the long, green grass. It wove around a couple of short, ragged blackjack trees and one drooping bodark. Cody drove off the road through the grass and weeds, hoping he wouldn't get a thorn in his tire. The day was turning off hot, and he didn't want to be changing a wheel right then.

Ned hug his arm out of the open window. "What did that feller say he was looking for out here?"

"Polk salad."

"Stop a minute."

Cody braked to a stop. The smell of crushed grass filled the El Camino's cab. The sagging barn not far ahead was covered with vines that hid more than a quarter of the walls and roof. Tall leafy plants grew waist high against to the sides. A ragged line of bodark posts marked a long gone corral.

"What are you thinking, Ned?"

Without taking his eyes off the barn, Ned took off his hat and ran a hand over his bald head. Rotting barns and houses were a common part of the landscape in Lamar County, but this one was different, somehow ominous, even though it slumped there in the bright sunlight. The hair rose on the back of his neck. "You notice something about these tracks?"

"Nothing particular."

A cardinal cheeped and flitted across their line of sight.

"They go one way."

Cody still wasn't sure what Ned was talking about. "So."

"Look behind us at our tracks."

Cody understood what was bothering Ned. "There's two sets, theirs and ours."

"That's right. You got off of 'em a time or two. We all do. Nobody can drive directly in another set of tracks. Here on out, I see two traces. I think the car is still back behind the barn."

"Maybe he went out somewhere different."

"Might, but most everybody runs the same ruts so's they don't get a flat. Look over yonder, you cain't go out no way other than this. And another thing, we've passed a dozen patches of polk salad since we got here. We had the chance to pick us a mess of greens without driving this far into the army camp."

Nerves jangling, Cody waited, and examined the barn as a wave of fear made his chest ache. The barn suddenly reminded him of the Cotton Exchange, where he and John Washington nearly died only months before.

"There ain't none growing anywheres around the barn." Ned felt the back of his neck tickle, instincts thrumming like live wires. "It likes fence rows, or turned dirt. I'd expect it to be growing near the corral, or on the north side of the barn. There ain't none there."

"So you think this is a setup?"

"I don't know what to think, but I don't like it."

A light breeze waved the grass.

"Nossir, I don't like this one little bit. Call the sheriff's office and get us some help out here…" Ned stopped abruptly as the noise of a starting engine cut the quiet. An Impala shot through the weeds from where it was hidden by the barn. "That's what I thought! We set here so long they got spooked and flushed. Get 'im, Cody!"

Without a word, Cody handed Ned the microphone to keep both hands free. He tromped the accelerator and spun the wheel. The Impala already had a running start and was on the decaying road in a flash. A thick cloud of dust boiled from underneath as they shot away.

Cody fought the wheel, dodging scrub trees and doing his best to avoid the gopher mounds that felt like boulders under the El Camino's tires. Invisible limbs and rocks rattled against the undercarriage with the sound of shrapnel against metal.

Ned bounced in the passenger seat as he keyed the microphone and grabbed the dash for support. "Martha, you there!?"

The sheriff's department dispatcher and Ned went to school together. "Go ahead Ned."

"Me and Cody need some help out here in the army camp. We're runnin' down a Chev-a-lay and likely heading for Gate Five."

"Okay, Ned. Help's on the way."

Cody hit a high spot and Ned bounced against the ceiling, crushing the Stetson down around his ears. "Son of a bitch!"

"Hang on, Ned!" They hit the dirt road and punched through the dust cloud left by the fleeing car.

When the Chevrolet reached the broken asphalt leading toward the highway, it shot away at an angle.

"What are they doing running deeper into the camp?"

Cody glanced at the speedometer and was surprised to see the needle rising past seventy. Gravel rattled against the undercarriage. "I bet they know something we don't. What's going on?"

"It was another ambush by them sneaky sonsabitches." Ned held tightly to the arm rest on the door as Cody jerked into a sharp left. For a moment they were out of the dust with a clear view of the car running ahead. "Them cowards were waitin' on us!"

Four men rode two in the front and back. One of the backseat passengers twisted to look out of the open window and Cody had a clear look at him.

So did Ned. "That's one of 'em I tangled with in your joint a while back."

Cody finished the turn. The car sloughed to the side and they were immediately engulfed in dust once again. He gripped the wheel tightly with both hands. "You sure?"

"You're damn right I'm sure. You got close to these boys and they think you know something. I bet you a dollar they're the ones who shot at you the night you wrecked the car."

The Motorola crackled. "Ned, help's on the way. They're turning into the camp now."

The El Camino bottomed out with a bang, throwing them against the roof once again. Ned threw up an arm against the ceiling.

Cody grunted at the impact. "What are them buildings up there?"

Ned's shoulders were hunched like a turtle pulling back in his shell. "The soldiers called it German Town. They built it to practice fighting in villages during the war."

"Looks more like a ghost town to me."

The Impala made a hard right and rocketed into the crumbling "streets." Essentially a movie set composed of false-fronted buildings, twenty years of northeast Texas weather had taken its toll. The movie set streets were full of scrub brush and tall grass. Vines covered many rotting structures and the whole thing was rickety enough to fall over in a strong gust of wind.

Cody slowed, not wanting to run into the car that suddenly disappeared into a pretend village covering one hundred acres or more. He stopped in a cloud of dust only a few feet inside the artificial town. Warped boards peeled away from disintegrating walls like curls. A gaping window opened onto a parallel street, providing an open sightline through the building and out the other side.

"Uh uh. Not going in there."

"Nope." Ned agreed. "They're most likely out of that car and a-waitin' on us. They tried to lead us into a trap. Back up quick and get us out of here!"

Cody threw it into reverse and gunned the engine. The back tires spun. They had barely moved when the sharp blast of a rifle shot echoed from building to building. Both men knew it was a large caliber weapon by the heavy thump. Cody threw his arm over the seat and drove by looking over his shoulder, not trusting his ability to back up quickly by using the rear view mirror.

They found themselves rocketing back down the same dusty road, only in reverse. Another shot rang out, this time from a different weapon and most likely a handgun, then a flurry of scattered bangs chased the fleeing El Camino.

Ned drew his pistol, wishing he had the shotgun standing in the corner of the living room back home, but he was slung around so fiercely that there was no way to return fire. He needed to save his ammunition, anyway. He only had six extra cartridges in his pocket, in addition to the five loaded in the chambers.

Cody left his .45 automatic in the holster for the time being. He quickly shifted into neutral, spun the wheel and they made an abrupt 180-degree bootlegger turn. Before the car finished the maneuver, Cody quickly shifted again and the engine roared as the back tires caught traction.

A bullet plowed through the tailgate, punctured the cab's back wall, and rattled to a stop in the floorboard near Ned's feet. Then they were out of range.

Furious, Cody slammed the heel of his hand on the steering wheel. "Dammit!" He drove another hundred yards and then stopped. Both men watched over their shoulders. "Where's the damn sheriff's department?"

Ned grabbed the microphone cord and well-roped the handset from where it had fallen to the floor. Though frightened and charged with adrenaline, his voice barely quivered. "Martha, get us some help here! They're shootin' at us."

He heard the catch of fear in her voice. "Boone should be there by now."

"Well, he ain't."

"Y'all hurt?"

"Naw, but they hit the car at least once't. They's four of 'em, all white that we can tell, in a sixty-three Chev-a-lay Impala."

"All units. Shots fired in the army camp. Gate Five is your entrance."

Cody's attention flicked to the mirror. "They're taking off again."

The Chevrolet burst from behind the buildings, making a run in the opposite direction from Gate 5, further into the creek bottoms ahead. Cody yanked the wheel.

"Don't get too close this time, they might try the same thing again."

"I'm gonna keep them in sight until we get some help." A covey of quail exploded from beside the El Camino. Cody groaned when he felt the back end skew. "Aw hell. They hit us again after all and shot out one of our tires."

The tire was almost immediately flat, and he knew it was no use to push the vehicle any further. He let off the accelerator and braked to a stop. "How many ways can they get out back there?"

"Half a dozen, I reckon."

Cody killed the engine. They stepped out and moved behind the half-breed truck for cover, in case the Chevrolet returned. The sound of the retreating motor quickly faded, and they were left in the relative silence of the late evening.

The scattered quail began to call, trying to reassemble the covey. The familiar, comforting sound was for once lost on Ned. He stared back toward the east, to where a sheriff's car should be coming.

"Something's wrong about the rest of this deal."

"What do you mean?"

"Our help didn't come quick, and it'll be a while yet, I imagine. Looks to me like somebody in the sheriff's department is in cahoots with them fellers. They aimed to get here all right, but after we's both dead."

When they were sure the Impala wasn't returning, Ned holstered his pistol and once again keyed the Motorola's handset when he heard Martha's alarmed voice.

"Right here, Martha."

"Y'all all right?"

"Same as before, only now we got a flat."

"Did J.T. get there yet? He said he was close enough to hear the shots."

The two constables exchanged glances. J.T. Boone was already under their suspicion, and this didn't help matters at all.

"No."

"I don't understand…well, two more cars should be there in a minute or two."

"We'll be right here when they do. I hear the sirens now."

The next deep and very scared voice on the radio was very obviously not Martha's.

"Ned!"

John Washington's car streaked down the asphalt gravel, a giant rooster tail of dust indicating his speed. Two more chased them at a distance to avoid the dust. "It's all right, John. We're fine."

"Thank the Lord! I see y'all now! This have anything to do with Ben Winters senior being found dead?"

Ned felt empty. He keyed the microphone. "Didn't know anything about it."

"Sheriff Matthews from Hugo called. They found Big Ben's body in a ditch, about a mile east of Grant. Shot once."

"I been expecting it. Nobody's heard from him for a few days." Ned replaced the microphone on the hanger and watched John slow as he neared the disabled El Camino.

Cody crossed his arms and leaned against the vehicle. "I imagine this *is* tied in somehow. You recognized one of them?"

"Yep, and the driver too. He's the one I want. It was that feller Whitlatch, from your joint. I think I'm starting to figure all this out."

Chapter Twenty-eight

Carl Gibbs and his wife Tamara were arguing.

"I don't know why I had to go over to their house and eat tonight. I never liked Pete Fuller anyway."

"Carol Ann is my friend." Tamara stared into the night and watched the smudge pots on Highway 271 flash past as Carl drove recklessly through a construction zone. "It didn't hurt you none for us to eat a bite and talk. I swear, I'm home all day by myself and I like to visit with another woman every now and then."

"Well, I don't like it when you drag me along."

"You don't have to go next time."

"I ain't sittin' home after work all day while my wife strings off around town after dark. It ain't right."

"It's all right when you run around on Friday nights without me?"

"Sure it is. That's what men do, and women oughta be awaitin' on them at the house when they come home."

"If you think I'm gonna listen to you bellyache all the way back, then you've got another think coming, mister. I mighta said love, honor, and obey to that justice of the peace, but I didn't intend to hire on as your mama."

Steaming mad, Carl took his foot off the accelerator and drifted toward the shoulder. "I think that right rear tire's going flat. Look at it when I stop. If it's still up, then we'll drive home slow and I'll change it in the morning."

"Why don't you get out with a flashlight and take a look at it yourself. It's your car, and that's a *man's* job."

"Dammit woman! Will you do *anything* without arguing with me? Just look at the goddamned tire!"

"Don't you be hollerin' at me Carl Gibbs! You oughta respect me more."

He pressed the brake. "I'll respect you all right if you'll do what I say!"

Fuming, Tamara opened the door and stuck her head out. "It's too dark. Gimme your flashlight."

Carl handed it to her. Tamara leaned further, trying to see without actually getting out of the car. She didn't trust her husband not to drive off without her. She was right, he fully intended to do it, but his frustration mounted when she aggravated him even more by not getting out.

So he did the next best thing. Carl shifted into park, put his right foot against Tamara's rear, and shoved her out of the car. She yelped when she fell into a thick patch of sandburs.

"You sonofabitch!"

Laughing like a loon, Carl shifted into gear and shot off into the darkness. Crying and mad, Tamara gathered herself and picked the worst of the stickers out of her clothes. She stomped through the darkness along the shoulder, watching the taillights of their car disappear over the hill. She knew Carl wouldn't be back. Her only hope was for a sympathetic neighbor to come along. But at that time of the night, well after midnight, she'd be lucky to get a ride.

Driving Norma Faye's Oldsmobile, Cody Parker almost passed Tamara until he realized a lone woman was walking along on the shoulder. He slowed and stopped in his lane, watching.

Tamara stopped short when the unfamiliar car slowed. Cody flicked on the dome light, and she sighed with relief when she recognized her old friend. She leaned into the open passenger window and Cody knew she'd been crying by her puffy face and wet eyes. Both knees below her skirt were skinned from the fall, and her usually untamed hair was even more out of control.

"What are you doing out here, girl? You all right?"

"My soon to be ex-husband kicked me out of the car."

Cody studied her for a moment as she stood outside drawing a deep, shuddering breath and willing herself not to cry. He felt oddly relieved. "All right. That's the same husband that hit you with a single tree."

It was more a statement than a question, so instead of answering, Tamara opened the passenger door. She dropped into the seat, slammed the door, and the dome light went out. "I deserve that, but I'm through with him now."

"You should have done that a long time ago."

"Are you fixin' to give me a ride home, or sit there and try to be a marriage counselor?"

Cody stayed where he was.

She scratched her knee where a sticker had broken off under the skin. "Can we go now?"

"All right." Cody shifted into gear. "You gonna stay with Carl, or we gonna do this every night until I get to be Ned's age?"

"I'm finished with him."

"Good."

"Who's car is this?"

"Norma Faye's new one. We bought it second hand last week. My El Camino's in the shop, so I'm using it tonight."

"I like this one better."

"Yeah, but I don't have a radio."

"What are you doing out here, then?"

"Just looking for a car."

When he didn't volunteer any more information, they finished the trip in silence. Instead of taking Tamara home, Cody pulled up in front of her mother's house. She was too tired to argue.

"Are we finished with this?"

Tamara nodded. "Yes. I'm done."

"Good, because he's gonna kill you one day."

"I'll get Mama to carry me to town tomorrow and get an attorney."

"Good."

"You might want to drop by and see Carl when you get a chance. He has about a pound of dope at the house that he got from Little Ben before he died."

"Good lord, has everybody in this county gone crazy? Where'd y'all get the money to buy that much dope?"

"He didn't buy it. Little Ben gave it to him a couple of days before he hung himself. Said he found it in a shed or something somewhere, and he passed it around like M&Ms."

Cody felt cold. "He *gave* it to you?"

"Yeah, I wouldn't let Carl pay for it. Ben said some guys he worked for let him give pot away to his friends so they could see how good it was. He called it 'casting bread on the water.'"

Cody looked out the dark window at the quiet neighborhood. The parts fit. Little Ben was working for Whitlatch, and in an incredible act of stupidity the naïve country boy stole an entire 'toe sack full of dope to give to his friends. He paid for it with his life and those of his family, and maybe others as well.

"That little idiot. Don't tell anyone else about that. You hear?"

Tamara shrugged. "Sure, but them that he give the pot to, they already know where it come from."

"You know what I mean. I'll look into what you told me, but if those guys find out you know anything about Little Ben and the dope, they're liable to come find you next."

The murderer's plan was coming unraveled, and it wouldn't be long until everyone knew what they were doing. When that happened, they'd have to pull up stakes and light out, or it would become more of a bloodbath than it already was as they finished the job they started with the moonshiners.

Cody intended to throw them in jail long before they had the chance to get away.

She stepped out of the car in the soft darkness. "Thanks Cody. Can I pay you back some way for your help…you know…I've always liked you."

"Nope. I don't believe Norma Faye'd like that, but thanks for the offer."

She closed the door and leaned back inside. "Don't hurt Carl when you go over there. He's really a great guy."

He sighed. "I know. Now, get inside and go to bed."

She smiled, waved, and he waited until she was in the house before he left.

Mentally clicking the pieces into place, Cody drove to the gas station in Arthur City and parked out of sight from anyone driving south across the river. It was his favorite place to wait for drunks to leave the joints and cross into Texas. He hoped to see Whitlatch passing by, so he could follow the car to the drug-runner's hide-out.

While he waited, Cody studied on what he knew. Whitlatch and his men were moving in the darkness to avoid capture. They were most likely in cahoots with Deputy J.T. Boone, which allowed them to know the movements of Cody, Ned, and anyone else looking for him.

After their running gunfight in the army camp, Ned and Cody talked about the scene, and both were convinced that Little Ben Winters was murdered, hoisted by his neck. The scene was set up to look like a suicide. Ned figured Little Ben fought his murderers, most likely throwing his head back and splitting his scalp on Whitlatch's cheek, explaining the white bandage on the killer's face that day.

With a jolt of understanding, he realized the death of the entire Winters family was a cleansing. Cody glanced down at the dash, wishing for the radio in his El Camino.

Uncharacteristically out of the loop, Cody settled into the front seat and watched the dark highway. Whitlatch had been using Little Ben to help move the drugs through Chisum, hiding a large amount of marijuana in his barn without telling him. Inexperienced in his association with criminals, Little Ben found the unexpected sacked bales, and thinking they wouldn't miss it, decided to help himself.

When the disappearance was discovered, they executed the young man, just as they'd executed the bootleggers conducting business nearby. In a move that backfired, their plan was to reduce the reasons for law enforcement officials to be kicking around Precinct 3. Instead, people talked, the bodies were found, and Cody and Ned were working harder than ever to bring them in.

After Mark Lightfoot told them how Whitlatch and his men were moving through the daylight hours in a series of different cars, it didn't take long to check the used car ads in *The Chisum News* and other smaller community papers on both sides of the river. A few phone calls revealed that Mark Lightfoot was right. Whitlatch was buying at least one car a week, using them to move the drugs, and then reselling them to repeat the process.

The only thing Cody still couldn't figure out was why they'd tried to kill *him* the first time.

He was still studying on it two hours later, when Lady Luck smiled.

The Galaxie, with Whitlatch driving, passed the gas station, heading south.

Chapter Twenty-nine

The moon was bright, and Cody let the Galaxie gain some distance before he hit the highway and pulled on his headlights.

They made a delivery and are heading home, wherever that is. I have 'em now.

Not a headlight broke the darkness ahead. Norma Faye's Olds was unrecognizable, so he felt comfortable keeping them in sight. He allowed it to gain more distance, and waited until it crested the first hill that was the lowest edge of several natural tiers leading up from the river bottoms. When their taillights winked out over the crest, he stomped the accelerator to catch up.

They were still heading for Chisum when he got to the top, so Cody let off on the gas and paced them. He wasn't worried about being seen. There was often traffic between the river and Chisum, even at that late hour. Ahead, the Galaxie's distinctive round taillights were like red eyes in the night.

Twenty minutes later, the Ford slowed as it came into town, and Cody dropped back even more, glad now that he wasn't in his El Camino that would have stood out like a rocket ship under the street lights.

The Ford passed Frenchie's dark café, the courthouse, and followed the traffic pattern around the square. Cody had an idea they'd continue south on 271, past the hardware store, eventually crossing in front of the ruins of Cotton Exchange before making a final right across the tracks and out of town.

He made a quick left, then a right and shot down a residential street to get ahead of them.

They passed without seeing him parked on the side street. Cody wished he had a radio to call in and tell dispatch he was behind the suspects. He didn't expect anyone to become alarmed by his lack of communication for a couple more hours. By then he should be able to find a phone and make a few calls.

Johnny Horton was singing a love song on the radio when they reached Dallas, an hour-and-a-half later. There was enough big city traffic to trail them in the early morning hours at a comfortable distance without worrying about being seen.

The remainder of the night was a southbound trip and Cody was thankful there was plenty of gas in the big tank. The Galaxie pulled into an Esso station well after dawn, in a small town an hour out of San Antonio. He cruised on past and found a Texaco a mile down the road.

"Fill 'er up, mister?" The uniformed station attendant was cheerful for so early in the morning.

Cody climbed out, stiff and sleepy. "Sure, but don't bother checking the oil. I gotta go pretty quick."

"You bet. Regular or Ethyl?"

"Regular."

"Get that windshield for you? It's full of bugs."

"Naw. I'm in a hurry. You got a phone?"

"We do, but it ain't working. They're supposed to come fix it, but I ain't seen nobody from Ma Bell in a week. They'll come dragging in one day of these days…"

Cody tuned him out and stepped behind a pump, to be sure he wasn't standing in the open if the Galaxie passed before they were through.

"She's full. That'll be ten dollars and thirty cents."

"I thought gas was supposed to be cheaper down here closer to the coast."

The man smiled and dug his finger into a dirty ear as Cody thumbed two fives and a one from his billfold. "That's on the other side of San Antone. We're a little higher here."

Cody handed him the bills and glanced down the road. Still no Ford.

They must be taking a leak.

"Where's your toilet?"

"Round back."

He hurried around the corner and recoiled at the thick stench wafting out of the warped door set in the cinder block building. A cow lowed in the pasture full of mesquite behind him. The highway was clearly visible from his position, so he faced the peeling station, unzipped, and sighed in relief as he watered the weeds growing at the foundation.

When he returned to the car, the attendant had taken the liberty of washing the windshield anyway.

Still no Ford.

Cody dug for change. "You got anything to eat around here?"

"Naw, all we got is cokes there in the machine."

"Well, I'm hungry."

"I got some rat cheese and crackers I brought for my lunch."

"What'll you take for them?"

"How 'bout a dollar?"

"I'll give you two bits."

"Six."

"Four bits."

The attendant smiled, revealing teeth bad enough to rob Cody of his appetite. "Deal."

Cody dug two dimes from his pocket, fed one of them into the cooler and removed a Coke after it crashed into the slot. He was repeating the action when the man returned with the cheese and crackers wrapped in wax paper. Tires hissed on the highway. Keeping his back to them, Cody handed the attendant fifty cents and then watched the Galaxie pass at a leisurely pace.

They were a hundred yards away when he returned to his own car. "Thanks for the windshield."

"You bet," the attendant said and dug in his ear some more.

Cody waited until the Ford disappeared over a rise before shifting into first and giving it the gas.

Chapter Thirty

The new loop around San Antonio made it easier for Cody to keep the Galaxie in sight. Going through town would have forced him to stick closer in the unfamiliar city, and be recognized. The virtually unused loop through open, sandy desert kept the Ford in view. Cody finished his drinks and pitched the empty bottles overhanded so they sailed over the car to land on the shoulder.

Workers were still parked at various locations, putting finishing touches on the highway behind a long line of smudge pots. Cody shook his head at the high overpasses and the channels slicing the hills, instead of going over them.

They flew down the two-lane highway, cutting between shimmering fields of crops that would soon be picked by the hands of brown-skinned people. Rivers with Spanish names retreated into the distance, to be replaced with dry creeks named after animals and colors.

The sun was high when they reached the Valley. The Brownsville radio station seemed to be all Mexican music. The accordions and trumpets set Cody's teeth on edge. He turned the radio down and slowed as the Ford pulled into a Mexican café right off Main Street. Eagle Lake glistened like a cool island not far away. An open sign at the Chuck Wagon café across the street caught Cody's attention.

Home cooked foods.

A narrow alley led to a dirt lot around back. He parked out of sight from the street. The rusty screen door in the back allowed the smell of frying onions to drift outside.

Cody rapped on the wooden frame. "Is it all right to come through here?"

The greasy-haired cook with a "Mama" tattoo on his forearm grinned around a gap in his teeth and waved a spatula. "Sure 'nough. Everybody else does."

"Thanks. Didn't see a reason to walk all the way around in this heat."

"Go on through. What can I get started for you?"

"Two burgers with cheese and all the fries you can stack on a plate."

"Comin' up. Tell Cassie you've ordered and to bring you a drink."

The café was busy with a mix of Mexicans and white people, but a small table by the front window was vacant. Cody slipped into a chair with a clear view of the cafe down the street. He sighed in frustration at an "Out of Order" sign on the pay phone near the door.

"You want something to drink with them burgers?"

Cody smiled at the tired, plump waitress. "Don't phones work down here in south Texas?"

She returned the grin, and he wished she hadn't. Cassie was missing more teeth than the cook. "You must be from up *north*."

"Yep. Chisum."

"Honey, I don't know where that is. There's lots of phones that work around here, but not this one. Whadda ya want to drink? Beer or tea?"

Surprised to hear beer offered in a café, Cody had to think a minute. Where he came from up on the Red, it was almost scandalous to know there were places in the world that sold beer where teetotalers ate. "Sweet tea."

"Sweet for the sweet," Cassie flirted and gave his shoulder a little squeeze as she left to drop off a customer's check.

◇◇◇

Hours later, Cody had used up every excuse he could think of to keep the table. Cassie thought he was hanging around until she got off work, and that worried him. His tea glass was never more than half empty. She showed him the check for the burgers, then tucked it into her ample bra with another flirty grin.

"It's on the house."

Lordy, what a high price to pay.

Finally, near the end of Cassie's shift, the Galaxie's occupants left the Mexican café and got in the car. It was the first good look he had at them. Whitlatch with his bandage, big muscles, and flattop was easily recognizable. The others matched Wanted posters he had on the table back home. Their names escaped him, but he knew they were the ones Whitlatch kept on the payroll. He also recognized the man with slit eyes as one of those on the creek they day Cody was fishing with the family.

Their car had been sitting in the hot sun all afternoon, so they rolled the windows down and almost immediately pulled onto the street.

The movement was so fast, Cody was almost caught unawares. He jumped to his feet and headed for the back.

"Honey, I don't get off for another half an hour," Cassie said, grabbing his arm as he hurried toward the kitchen.

"That's all right. I'm gettin' the car." It wasn't a complete lie.

"Okay, honey." She slipped two fingers under her stained uniform and half pulled the unpaid check into view.

He knew what that mean. Cody quickly yanked a five dollar bill from his shirt pocket where he'd stashed it earlier in the day and stuffed it into her bra beside the check. "I pay what I owe."

She winked. "So do I, hon."

Cody was through the kitchen and out the door with a flash.

"I'd run, too," the cook shouted after him.

Cody jumped behind the wheel, started the engine, and shot through the alley. He caught a glimpse of the Ford on Main Street. Falling in behind, Cody had a feeling they were close to their destination. They were soon headed west out of town through dry, rough country, and he let them get ahead on the two-lane highway with wide sandy shoulders that were sometimes almost drifted over with sand.

He hung back, but it was easy to keep the Ford in sight. An hour later, the Galaxie made a hard left off the highway onto a perfectly straight, narrow road. Cody slowed, let them get out of sight, and when they disappeared over a slight rise, he hurried to catch up. As he topped the hill, they disappeared over next crest. Ten minutes later Cody was in the border town of Hembrillo. Without stopping, Whitlatch continued south between wide, sandy lots sitting empty and surrounded by thick stands of mesquite.

Cody's blood ran cold when Whitlatch finally passed under a huge sign that said *"Bienavides* Mexico."

Welcome to Mexico.

He'd dreamed of Mexico, deserts, and snow. It had all come true.

Shit.

Chapter Thirty-one

There was no way to have predicted how badly things would go when Cody hit Mexican soil.

Several cars back, he caught up as the Galaxie rolled slowly through the dirty streets of *Carreta Ciudad*. Whitlatch and the others appeared to be looking for a particular building, because he kept tapping his brakes, causing the others behind to roll bumper to bumper.

Whitlatch finally located the one he wanted and nosed into an empty parking place, cluttered with trash piled at the curb. As Cody drove past, Whitlatch tapped his horn twice. None of the occupants noticed the Olds driving slowly behind them. Their attention was on the front door of a cantina called *El Escorpión*.

Cody repeated the familiar maneuver of circling and parking to watch the Ford. He'd barely shifted into park when two uniformed Mexican police officers left the bar and waved for Whitlatch and his men. The officers briefly disappeared around the side of the building, and then re-emerged in a dusty and nondescript Chrysler.

It left quickly, followed by Whitlatch. Cody hung back, keeping them in sight through brief glimpses and reflections on chrome in the bright sun.

They drove for fifteen minutes, leaving the small city behind. Cody became concerned when they angled sharply onto a dirt side road. He barely slowed on the highway, keeping an eye on the cars as they finally stopped at the top of a slight hill. The highway was empty, so he watched over his shoulder through the shimmering heat waves and wondered what to do.

With the suspects gone, the only alternative was to return to town and call Ned. They were probably worried sick already, and he needed to let Norma Faye know he was all right. He U-turned on the rock and dirt shoulder, and started back the way he came. Ahead, two military-style trucks appeared, driving fast, and cut the corner across the desert to intersect the road behind the Galaxie.

Both vehicles had benches in the open backs, and a dozen uniformed men rocked from side to side as they bumped through the shallow ditch and onto the smoother gravel.

Cody slowed and watched the trucks full of men raise a cloud of dust until they stopped at the top of the sharp rise. Going any slower would attract attention, so Cody continued until he came to an arroyo shaded by tall cottonwoods. A faint track led toward the dry depression hidden by scrub and cactus. He left the road and threaded his way through the gray vegetation and rocks, until the car was hidden from view.

Knowing it was a bad idea, Cody killed the engine and left the door open on the Olds. He made his way along the arroyo as it meandered through weathered rock formations in the direction of the stopped vehicles. Soon he heard voices.

On hands and knees, he crept out of the dry ravine and worked his way through thick mesquites, hoping there were no rattlesnakes lying in the shade. The voices were clearer, but he only understood one side of the conversation. Moving slowly, he slipped around a thick clump of cactus and finally maneuvered into a position to see through the mesquites.

Cody watched Whitlatch cross his arms in the open on the edge of a thin hogback full of gray rocks and cactus. Shades, thick biceps, and a clean flat top, the big man was anchored to the rocky ground in a stance that signified defiance. Spread out in an aggressive line in front of the four men Cody had trailed from the Red River, the truck-load of Mexican police faced them with the clear intent of taking them in.

Cody settled back in shock. He finally got a good look at Whitlatch and the last piece of puzzle fell into place. A week before Christmas one frosty evening nearly six months earlier, Cody pulled a car over in Arthur City for what he suspected was drunk driving.

The two men inside were cooperative, but Cody couldn't get past the uneasy feeling they were up to something. For fifteen minutes, the coatless men shivered beside the highway while he ran the license plate that came back clean. The driver had purchased the car only the week before, after moving to Chisum from Odessa, Texas.

The man Cody now knew as Whitlatch was sullen, but cooperative the whole time. He didn't want to offer any information about his home town, and Cody kept wondering why he refused to maintain eye contact.

That cold day, the men spoke clearly, didn't show signs of intoxication, and there were no empties in the car. With nothing to charge them with, Cody let them go, but with the warning that he'd be watching for them in the future.

The encounter must have been significant to Whitlatch.

There in the Mexican desert, Cody grasped how little it takes to start a chain of events that leads men to commit murder.

What Cody figured was a hired gang of crooked Mexican lawmen scattered even wider in a broken line facing Whitlatch and his men. Some stood in the fragile shade, others beside the trucks. All of them held rifles pointed at the Americans.

"I don't care what you say." Whitlatch's arrogant voice was full of confidence. "We did our part. The supply line is complete and all the competition is cleared up. Hell, we damn near buried everybody that looked sideways at us. The next load is ready to go. We just want what we're owed, what you owe the boss, and our expenses to this point."

An obviously angry officer answered in rapid-fire Spanish. Whitlatch crossed his arms. He understood the language, but answered in English. "Our expenses got out of hand. There ain't but a couple of roads up there that cross the river, like here.

We had to keep buying cars every week so the laws wouldn't recognize us.

"I done told you how much we spent. Now, give me the damned cash so we can get out of this heat. I'm tired of dicking with you pepper bellies. God, I hate this sorry-ass country. What do you say, *pendejo?*"

The hair rose on the back of Cody's sweating neck when the officer answered for the first time in broken English. "All right, *señor*. We'll get you out of this heat, but it'll be hotter where you're going, *pendejo.*"

His vision was partially blocked by mesquite limbs, but Cody made out enough. On the obviously prearranged signal, the uniformed men raised their weapons.

Gunfire thundered over the arid landscape. A spike buck hiding nearby leaped at the explosions and launched into a flat out run across the desert.

Whitlatch and his men crumpled like rag dolls, shredded by dozens of bullets.

The echoes were barely gone when Cody heard a heavily accented voice behind him. "Why did you kill those Americanos, *amigo?*"

Chapter Thirty-two

Pepper and I weren't in the house when the phone call came in. We got tired of playing secret agent and went in the smokehouse to shoot dirt dauber nests with our BB guns. The tiny explosions of dried mud was always satisfying, and we figured we were doing Miss Becky a favor by keeping them from nesting in the rafters, and on the rusty bedsprings hanging high overhead.

Miss Becky's shrieks jolted us out of the smokehouse and into the yard. I'd never heard her make that sound, and it scared me to death. I heard Grandpa's voice over hers, yelling to beat the band. They'd been joking about her loud washing machine when we went outside after supper, and the terror in her voice ran down my backbone.

We raced across the yard, past the propane tank, and up the steps onto the porch. Hootie skidded to a stop behind us. Miss Becky was sitting at the kitchen table and crying even louder when we pressed our faces against the screen.

Tied to one end of the living room by a six-foot cord, Grandpa was stomping back and forth with the telephone in one hand and the receiver in the other.

He reminded me of a horse rearing up against a lariat rope. "Grandpa's *mad!*"

"Shitfire! He's madder'n a sore-tail tomcat!"

Miss Becky caught a glimpse of us and shrieked. "Oh, my God! You kids come in this house right now."

I figured there must be a booger out there fixin' to get us, so we ran inside. As soon as Hootie was in, I dropped the screen door's hook latch into place. Miss Becky grabbed Pepper and held on for dear life, like a drowning person holds a life preserver.

Grandpa stopped in the middle of the living room and quivered. I didn't know if he was crying, or furious.

Pepper pulled away and tears ran down her face. "What's wrong?"

Miss Becky reached out to me with one arm, and I let her pull me in close. "Cody's hurt bad and he's in prison down in Mexico!"

I prickled all over. Uncle Cody couldn't get in prison, not him.

We listened to Grandpa's side of the conversation. "What town are you in, son?"

He paused.

"This line's crackling bad." He sat down at the telephone table and picked up one of them giveaway Harold Hodges Insurance pencils. "Spell that."

Miss Becky got control of herself, but her deep, shuddering sobs were so strong I felt them in my chest.

"Shit," Pepper said.

"Hush, child," Miss Becky said, not really hearing Pepper's language.

We quieted when Grandpa raised his voice.

"What town did you go through on this side of the river?"

Pause.

"How bad are you hurt?"

Pause.

"*Did* you kill 'em like they said?"

He paused again. I hated being on the quiet end of a one-sided conversation.

"They ain't even gonna give you a trial?"

Pause.

"Did they say anything about bail?"

Pause.

"When are they gonna do that?"

Pause.

"It'll take us a while to get down there."

Pause.

"Damn this phone. Say that again and tell that Mexican son of a bitch to quit talking over you. I'm having a hard enough time hearing you as it is."

Pause.

"Did he just hit you?"

Pause.

"Goddamn it!"

Pause.

"All right. All *right*!"

Pause.

"I'll tell her."

Pause.

He stood. "Wait! I need to know more to be sure...hello? Goddamn sonofabitchin' bastards!"

I thought he'd slam the receiver down, but with his back to us, he slowly lowered it into the cradle. His shoulders slumped and his head dropped. Grandpa stood still as a fence post, arms limp at his sides and knees buckled inside his overalls.

His body literally shrank in front of our eyes.

Miss Becky's breath caught, shuddered, and caught again in hiccups. A lump grew in my throat, and I felt tears roll down my cheeks. The three of us in the kitchen waited, as if expecting Grandpa to melt down into nothing but a puddle on the floor, like Little Black Sambo's tiger when he melted into butter.

What came next was a complete surprise. As if inflating, his knees straightened, his shoulders squared and his head rose. He came into the kitchen and for the second time in my life, and for the first time very clearly, I saw Grandpa truly enraged. I swear electricity flashed from those blue eyes.

He actually looked bigger. "Mama, them Mexicans have Cody. He trailed a suspect down across the border. That's where he's been for the past week. I need to get down there before they kill him."

She stood up. "Go."

Chapter Thirty-three

While Pepper and I watched, a cyclone of activity churned through our little country house. Miss Becky called Norma Faye, and she was there in a flash.

And like water brought with a storm, folks flowed through the door in a steady stream. The house quickly filled up like it always does when somebody is hurt, or dies. Ninety-year-old Miss Whitney was listening in on the party line to the long distance call from Mexico. As soon as Grandpa hung up, she started the grapevine humming.

Friends and relatives brought so much food there wasn't one inch of table or cabinet space in the kitchen that wasn't packed with something good to eat. The only problem was, none of us was hungry.

Mr. John Washington slid into the driveway twenty minutes after Grandpa called him, and like the wind through a screen, he blew into the kitchen without knocking. He'd made his bones with us the night The Skinner took us, so he was treated as one of the family.

Ralston Shaver brought Miss Sweet, Mr. John's auntie, to the door. He was the healer's driver and took her everywhere she went. He didn't come inside, but she did, and for the second time in a year two colored people were in Grandpa and Miss Becky's house.

Mr. O.C. Rains, the Wilson boys, Isaac Reader, and dozens of other Center Springs residents arrived in a steady, worried march.

Grim-faced men filled the living room, talking low. Their voices rose in anger at Mexicans and drug dealers and quickly ebbed. Pepper and I stayed on the porch, out of the way beside the open window, to hear what they said.

Grandpa paced on the living room linoleum. "Cody told me they've beat hell out of him and this is the first time they've offered to let him call. I'm going down there tonight to get him out."

Judge Rains presided from Grandpa's rocker. "Let me try through the law."

Grandpa was too worried to sit down. "Hell O.C. There ain't no law down there we can trust. They've already showed us that."

"You go on then, and I'll get in touch with the U.S. Embassy and see if they'll meet you when you get across the border."

"All right, but there ain't much time. They're moving him deeper into Mexico in a day or so, to a real prison. Right now he's in the local jail. He said that stink hole was called," he read from the folded paper in his hand, "el Cell ass, or something like that."

A high pitched voice filled the room. It was Mr. Isaac Reader. "Listen, listen, I'm a-goin' with you."

Mr. John's voice was a deep rumble in the room. "You stay here. I'll go with Mr. Ned."

"Why you and not me?"

Grandpa blew his nose. "Ike, even if it don't look like it, this is law business. John's right, we've worked together for years, so I can depend on him to think the way I do if things start to pop."

"Listen, I'll be right here if you need me, then."

"I know you will."

Jimmy Fox Wilson's voice rang strong and firm. "Me and Ty Cobb will follow you in our truck. We'll be good to have around if things get rough."

It was true, they spent their whole lives running the river bottoms with guns in their hands.

Uncle James spoke up. "I'm going."

"No, you're not, and neither are you Wilson boys. I still need you here, James, and I cain't be worrying about you in Mexico, too. One family member down there is enough. You other boys don't have any business down there. You're liable to get into something I cain't get you out of."

"But dad…"

"I done spoke!"

Mr. O.C. dug in his pocket and pulled out a wad of cash. "Here, they're all crooked down there. Take this money. You can either use it for a bribe or to go his bail."

Other men in the room opened sweat-stained leather billfolds and pulled limp bills into the open. Mr. O.C. took off his black hat, dropped his money in it, and passed it around the room.

Grandpa wiped tears from his eyes. "I'll pay y'all back."

Murmurs filled the room as men acknowledged the comment.

Ten minutes later, Mr. John came out of the house carrying a shotgun in each hand. He put them in the back seat of Grandpa's sedan. The eager hands of men who lived close to the land offered several boxes of shells.

Knowing they might need heavier ammunition, Ty Cobb passed John four boxes of double-ought buck. "This is better than that number four buck y'all use. You might need a little more punch where you're going."

John shrugged. "I intend to be ready for whatever comes."

Jimmy Foxx added two boxes of .38 caliber ammunition from the supply they kept under the seat in their truck. "I know what Ned said, but do you want us to follow y'all?"

"No. Mr. Ned says it'll be me and him, but you might be ready, just in case."

Grandpa hugged Miss Becky, and then wrapped me and Pepper up with both arms. He didn't say anything for a long while. Pepper's breath was shuddery, and I fought to keep from crying.

"I love you two." Grandpa quickly stood, pitched his car keys to John, and set his hat. "C'mon John, let's go to Mexico."

Chapter Thirty-four

The next day, John drove Ned's car through the dirty streets of Hembrillo. Neither had ever been to the Texas border, and they were already tired of the mesquite-infested landscape.

"Where we going Mr. Ned?"

"Find the bridge. They say you can see the jail and that prison they call Los Cell-u-las from this side of the river."

"It don't look much like our river. This thing is a nasty color. I'd a lot rather be back home."

Ned watched the sluggish water move between thick stands of cane and mesquite. Cottonwoods lined both sides of the river, but to him, they were trash trees. He already missed the hardwood bottoms of home, and the miles of cultivated fields they'd passed while driving through the Valley made him want to climb back onto his tractor and start plowing. It was getting late in the season, and if he didn't get a crop in, he wouldn't have much in the bank come fall.

"We'll get back soon enough, once we get Cody out."

John didn't miss the curious stares. The huge black man was an oddity for sure in a town populated by Mexicans and white people. The fifteen hour trip had drained all the energy out of the two lawmen. The first couple of hours to Dallas went fairly fast. From there south, they drove on parts of the new interstate system under construction, but over fifty percent of the roads were still skinny farm-to-market hogbacks leading through every one-horse town on the route.

The road ahead turned, and the bridge appeared. Ned sat a little straighter and rested his elbow out of the window. "There it is."

"So what are we gonna do now, drive across that there bridge, bail Cody out of jail, and then go home?"

"Close enough. Foller that car and let's get over there and find the jail. It shouldn't be too hard to do in this crummy little town."

John slipped behind a dingy De Soto. The car slowed as it reached the bridge, and then sped on across when the Texas border guard waved it through. John was about to go when the guard held up a hand for them to stop.

"Let me talk, John."

"Sho 'nough."

The border guard approached from John's side as a second man stopped at Ned's window. The first guard did the talking. "Morning, sir."

Instead of answering, John nodded when he realized the man was talking past him to Ned.

"Where's your driver taking you?"

Ned leaned forward to peer around John. Neither wore their badges, but both were dressed in their Sunday clothes. "We're headed down to the jail over there to fetch my nephew."

The guard frowned. "They have him in *Las Células* in *Carreta Ciudad*?"

"I reckon so. He got word to us that's where he was, so we come down here from Chisum to fetch him."

"You've come a long way." The second guard leaned into Ned's open window, so close he smelled onions on the man's breath. "You carrying a lot of money?"

Such a personal question wasn't worth a damn, in Ned's opinion. "I might have enough for bail money, when we find out how much it is."

The first guard understood Ned's flash of irritation. "What he means is that you make sure nobody over there knows you're carrying a wad of cash. That's a mean town when you get off the main street where the jail is, and you're likely to get your throat cut if you run across the wrong person."

"We'll watch out. Where's that jail?"

The guard pointed toward an ugly, square building hulking above the squatty, two-story businesses that surprisingly resembled a tired version of Chisum's main street.

Both men had expected to find a Mexican town straight off of television, complete with adobe buildings, unpainted wooden store fronts, and serape-wearing peasants. Instead, the town south of the Rio Grande resembled every Texas town they'd passed on the way down. There was even an S.H. Kress five-and-dime, and what appeared to be a hardware store bearing the familiar GE appliance logo.

"Don't let your driver get too far from you, either. Those Mexicans over there don't care much for niggers, and they're liable to cut him."

John held his tongue.

Ned didn't like it either, but this was no time to get into an argument with the border guards, especially not with a car full of guns. "There must be a lot of cuttin' over there."

"More than you'd believe, mister. If I's you, I'd stuff that money down in my drawers and don't let any of them *Federales* there know how much you have. They'll ask for a lot more than they expect, so try to Jew them down a little. Now, one more word of advice, y'all oughta turn this car around and park it back there in the bank lot and walk across. I'll tell 'em it's all right if anybody asks. Tags from this side of the river are targets over there. One little traffic accident, or run a stop sign or something, they'll take your car. With him in the car, you're gonna be more of a target than most folks."

The idea didn't appeal to Ned, but he understood the wisdom of the man's advice. "All right. Back up there, John, and let's do what the man says."

"Yassuh, Massah Ned."

While Ned grinned and waved at the guards, John glanced over his shoulder to find the way was clear. He backed quickly and circled around. They parked the car at the bank directly across from the bridge.

The guards were talking with the passengers of a truck when Ned and John passed them in a flow of people and started across the long bridge on foot.

"Stay out of Boys Town!"

Instead of answering, Ned raised a hand in acknowledgement. He watched the muddy water roil far below. "Lordy, John, you're right. This here river ain't near as pretty as our Red."

"Sho' nuff, but there's a lot more water that I expected. I thought it was shallow enough to wade across, but it looks like a pretty good swim."

Ned barely heard the words, instead looking carefully at the Mexican crossing guards who had traffic backed up on the northbound side, going into the states. They were much more interested in who was crossing *into* the U.S. The American guards stopped a few of those same cars when they reached U.S. soil.

Without issue, they were in Mexico.

"I have to tell you Mr. Ned, I'm 'bout scared to death to be over here."

Spanish flowed over them as soon as they stepped on Mexican soil and Ned suddenly realized that communication might be an issue. "You don't speak any Mexican, do you?"

"Nossir, nary a word."

"We'll have to figger this out as we go."

"I imagine somebody in the jail speaks both." John smiled and shook his head at a young boy who held up a bundle of homemade tamales wrapped in corn shucks and tied with string. The big deputy's stomach rumbled at the rich smell of unfamiliar spices, reminding him that he was hungry. "No."

Disappointed, the boy understood the word that was the same in both languages. He returned to a blackened Dutch oven resting on a bed of coals piled in a rusted wheelbarrow.

John flashed the boy a smile to soften the refusal. "This place is built up more than I expected."

Ned pointed toward a small grocery store and a sign reading Perimex Drilling, painted on the window. "Phil Cates told me this was a dirt road border town until they took to drilling here about ten years ago. They poured a lot of concrete and now it's a company town, at least on this street."

A cross street allowed a view of the three story jail in the distance. Ned hung a right and moments later the town completely changed. Only one block off Main, the streets were dirt. Ancient wooden and stucco buildings settled into the earth.

Houses were small, dusty, and simple. Many were desperate. Chickens scratched in dirt yards. Some of the haphazard lots closest to the trees lining the Rio Grande were larger with rough corrals and tired barns.

"Mr. Ned. A lot of these folks ain't got no solid doors on they houses."

"Nor glass winders, neither."

Ned's brightly shined shoes were already dusty, and he noticed the backs of John's dark slacks were accumulating a coating of fine powder. Both were glad they wore straw hats in the bright morning sun. Dogs barked challenges, but most stayed within the confines of their own yards.

Half a dozen silent, barefoot children trailed behind them. They reminded John of his people back south of the tracks in Chisum. "What do they want?"

"Most likely to know what we're doing here." After another block, the crowd of little people had doubled. Ned stopped. "Y'all oughta go on back home."

The silent, expressionless children didn't respond. Apparently none of them spoke English.

John waved a hand. "G'on! Y'all need to git!"

"Where are you going?"

Startled by the heavy accent, Ned's attention swung to a skinny dark-haired girl near Pepper's age. "You understand American?"

"*Si, señor.*"

"I reckon that means you do."

"Yes. My brother and I both speak it."

"Which one is your brother?"

"I am."

Ned grinned down at the brown-skinned, black-haired copies of Top and Pepper.

"All right missy, what's your name?"

"Yolanda. My *hermano* is Jorge."

"Hor-hey?"

"You say George."

"All right then. Why are y'all taggin' along behind us, Yolanda?"

"Nothing else to do. Not many Americans on this street during the day, unless they're drunk or looking for a woman. You are not drunk. Do you look for a woman?"

Embarrassed, Ned exchanged glances with John. "Well, neither." He waved a hand toward the brick building that didn't look nearly as good up close as it did from a distance. "We're going over to the jail there."

Her eyes widened. "Why you going to *Las Células*?"

Ned didn't much want to tell his business to a little Mexican girl, but he might need her help. "My nephew is locked up in there, and we intend to get him out."

"You have monies?"

Recalling the border guard's warning, Ned deflected the question. "We'll see what we can do when we find out how much it'll take."

"The guards are *muy malo*. They are bad. They will steal your monies and may put you in a cell also. Do not trust them, they are…" she frowned at George. "*Como se dice corrupto?*"

He gave her a gap-toothed grin. "Crooked."

Ned despised a crooked lawman, and having to deal with criminals in police uniforms rubbed him the wrong way.

The girl took John's big hand in hers. He flashed her a smile and received one in turn. "Maybe we can use these kids. They can speak this Meskin to them guards when we get there."

"Might." Ned studied the youngsters for a long moment. "Y'all know much about this here cell…cellar place?"

Yolanda nodded vigorously. "Si. *Mucho*. All of it bad. Many peoples are put in *Las Células* by *La Guardia* and never seen again. The *comandante* is *muy malo*, very bad, and he works for the *policia*, our police. People are put in *Las Células* without a reason and stay there for many months or years."

Ned noticed their dirty feet in the coarse Mexican sand and knew they didn't own shoes. He felt bad for them, because he'd been raised at a time when one pair of shoes per year was all he got. They came with the start of school, and had to last until the summertime.

"We need to get in there and talk to whoever is in charge to get Cody out, but we don't speak the language. I'll give you five dollars apiece if you'll talk for us when we get there. Will your mama let you do that?" He figured they'd buy shoes with least half the amount and use the remainder for sweets.

Her eyes wide with the possibility of such riches, Yolanda shrugged. "She does not care. She sleeps after being up all night in the bars. How long ago did they took your *sobrino*?"

Ned didn't understand the word, but the meaning was clear. "A little over a week."

George shook his shaggy head. "He will be very hungry if he did not have monies to buy food. Did he have any?"

John was startled. "They don't feed their prisoners in there?"

"Si, they have food, but never enough. Prisoners fight for it when they eat each day. If they pay, they get tortillas and beans."

"My god, John." Ned broke into a brisk stride toward the jail. "You know they took his money when he went in. If these kids are right, that boy's damned near starved."

John recalled the fight between Cody and several bad guys up at the store nearly a year earlier. "Yeah, but imagine he's managed to get a bite or two."

Yolanda spoke sharply to the other kids in Spanish, and watched as they scattered. Then she and her brother followed the two Americans, jogging to keep pace.

Chapter Thirty-five

Me and Pepper were sitting on the edge of the porch to keep away from all the crying and carrying on. Grandpa hadn't been gone more than ten minutes when Mr. Tom Bell drove up and hurried out of his truck. "Is what I heard up at the store true?"

It was almost dark and there were still fifty men standing in the yard.

Always in charge, Mr. O.C. spoke up. "That depends on what you heard, Tom."

"That Cody is in a Mexican prison and Ned's on his way down there to get him out."

"That's the size of it."

"Has anyone called the embassy, or the Rangers?"

"I did. The man at the embassy said they'd start working on it, but it might take a while. I spoke to a Ranger captain down in Waco, and he said he'd call back as soon as he knew something. That's about all I know to do."

Mr. Tom stuck his fingers into the front pocket of his jeans. "Ned will be like a fish out of water down there."

Ike couldn't stand not being in the conversation. "Listen, listen, I said I'd go help, but he didn't want nobody except John Washington."

"I'm afraid this will get worse before it gets better." Mr. Tom kicked the toe of one boot with the heel of the other while he thought to himself. "Either one of them speak Spanish?"

"Na'er one."

Mr. Tom nodded. "O.C., you remember that envelope I gave you a while back?"

He frowned. Tom had dropped by not long after he returned from the Valley the last time. He brought a sealed envelope bearing instructions to only open it in the event of his death. "Sure do."

"Keep it handy. I'm going down there to help. I speak the language, and know those people."

A dozen hands went up to volunteer, but Mr. Tom shook his head. "Nope, I appreciate it, but I need to go alone."

Judge Raines studied Mr. Tom's truck for a minute. "Tom, that truck of yours won't make it down there and back again. You were smoking pretty bad when you came up the drive."

He sighed. "I'll get as far as I can."

Mr. O.C. pitched Tom a key. "Here, take my car. You need something reliable, and I imagine you better hurry as quick as you can."

Instead of arguing, Mr. Tom returned the pitch with his own truck key. "I'll run to the house and get a few things. I'll let y'all know what I find out when I get there."

◇◇◇

It was full dark when Pepper and I watched Mr. Tom drive to his house in Judge Rain's 1948 Chrysler. Pepper stood up. "Come on."

"Where we going?"

"To Mexico."

"Are you out of your ever-lovin' mind?"

"Well look, titty baby. Our Uncle Cody is probably being cut up by Mexicans right now, and they're probably making him eat hot peppers until his butthole burns like fire. I bet Grandpa would have asked us to go if he'd thought about all we can do for them down there."

"You're an idiot." I lowered my voice so the men in the yard couldn't hear our whispered conversation. "What can two kids do?"

"We can meet up with Grandpa and Mr. John when we get there, and handle things like phone calls. We can fetch hamburgers when they're hungry, take notes, and run errands. You've seen how police departments are on television. People are always needing stuff done. That'll be *our* job."

"How do you think we're gonna get there, even if I said your bonehead idea was a good one?"

"We'll stow away in Mr. Tom's borrowed car. We can both lay down in the back floorboard and cover ourselves with a quilt. Mr. Tom will think that Judge O.C. left some stuff in there. It won't be his, so he'll leave it alone."

"You're crazy." Despite my argument, I found myself behind her. That's how Pepper always gets me in trouble, she starts talking, I drag along behind to argue, and the next thing I know, we're getting kidnapped, or watching shootouts.

The women were in the kitchen, but the living room was almost empty. Pepper slipped inside, and came back out a few seconds later with two folded patchwork quilts in her arms from Miss Becky's quilt box. She handed me one, and we disappeared around the house, out of sight from the adults.

"Uncle James will give us a whippin' over this."

She didn't break her pace. "After what happened last summer, whippin's don't scare me none. You've had 'em before. Besides, Daddy won't whip *you*."

"For this he might."

Once behind the house, we hurried down the hill, across the highway, and ducked into the woods. We knew the trails there like city people know the roads in their neighborhoods, so even in the darkness it was easy to make our way to Mr. Tom's house. Hootie wasn't with us. When so many people showed up at Miss Becky's earlier in the day, I'd locked him out of the way in the corn crib.

We were still arguing in whispers when we reached the edge of the woods. "Everybody will be scared to death when they can't find us."

"We'll call first thing when we get to Mexico tonight. By that time, we'll have to let Mr. Tom know we're with him, and it'll be too late to bring us back. Then Mama and Daddy will know they can come on down to the border and help with Uncle Cody when he gets back across the river."

"How long will it take to get down there?"

"Aw, it doesn't take more than two hours to get to Dallas, so probably another couple of hours or so after that. We'll be there long before daylight. It's better than sitting around here and listening to them crying. You don't want to hear this for the next two or three days, do you?"

We stopped in the woods and watched Mr. Tom come out of the house and drop his heavy trunk in the back of the judge's car. When he went back inside, Pepper snuck through the yard, opened the car door, and we quickly crawled into the back seat.

She pulled it closed and we winced at the loud click as the latch caught. We waited, but nothing happened. I pushed open the back vent windows to get more air and we curled up on each side of the hump, in the deep wells of the floorboards. Pepper threw one of the quilts over me, and then covered herself with the other.

All four windows were open to catch the breeze. A skeeter buzzed overhead, looking for a way under the quilt. Mr. Tom came back outside and pitched a suitcase onto the backseat through a window. Something light hit me on the arm. I realized it was his hat.

Pepper was right. Mr. Tom slipped under the steering wheel without looking under the quilts, and started the engine. It cooled off right smart once we got on the highway and the air started moving when he sped up. I heard a quick honk in greeting, and knew we'd passed our house.

Despite my worry, I felt good about what we'd done.

We were barely past Arthur City when I dozed off under the quilt and slept until we were in Central Texas.

The only problem was, how were we supposed to know the Mexican border was fifteen hours away?

Chapter Thirty-six

Two haphazardly parked sedans in front of the crumbling brick and stucco façade of *Las Células* looked as if they'd been baking under the strong sun for years. The Texas lawmen paused in front of the Mexican jail.

The ominous building reminded Ned of The Walls unit in Huntsville. Both he and John had visited the bleak southeast Texas prison on numerous occasions. Ned wondered at the irony of relying on two children to guide them through the process of negotiating with the police. He studied John for a moment before going in. "You reckon you ought to stay out here?"

John crossed his massive arms, the material of his khaki shirt stretching across his shoulders. "Nawsir. I pretty much stick out like a sore thumb no matter where I am, so I'll stay with you and these youngun's."

"Just thinkin'…"

"I know."

Yolanda grabbed the black iron knob with both hands and gave it a twist. The thick wooden door opened into a dark interior, and she entered with George right on her heels.

Ned and John stepped inside the much cooler building, hesitating for a moment to let their eyes adjust. Only two small windows near the tall ceiling at the front of the building allowed light into the stark area. Two bare bulbs hanging from exposed wires added pale, yellow light to an equally pallid desk lamp casting few rays through a thick coat of dust.

The stink of fear and misery leaching from the peeling brick walls was almost overwhelming.

A bored guard occupied a battered desk in the middle of the room. John closed the door behind them and the young man glanced up from his girlie magazine. John quickly scanned the empty room, noting a steel door behind the desk.

"*Qué quieres?*" the guard crossed his arms. The giant Negro unnerved him so much he barely noticed the old bald man with him.

Yolanda took two steps in front of the men and spoke in rapid-fire Spanish. "These Americanos do not understand you. I am here to speak for them."

The guard turned his attention from John with a dismissive snort. His obvious insolence quickly angered Ned, who hated not understanding their conversation.

The guard's eyes finally fell on Ned. "What do these…people want?"

"They are here for to get their *sobrino* who you have locked up in this miserable place."

"Is the *sobrino blanco* or *negro*? We don't have many *negros* in our prison."

"Blanco."

"What's this gringo's name?"

Surprised at the obvious question she hadn't asked, Yolanda spoke to Ned in English. "What is the prisoner's name?"

"Cody Parker."

For the first time, the guard addressed Ned directly in Spanish. "*Cómo sabes que lo tenemos aquí?*"

He waited for Yolanda's translation.

"How do you know Cody is here?"

"He called. Said he'd bribed a guard to make one phone call home."

Yolanda gave the guard a cold stare. Somehow Ned knew the spunky little gal wasn't one bit afraid of the guards. "*La mordida.*"

The young man snickered.

"Tell him I want to see Cody and to pay his bail to get him out."

Yolanda rattled a long string of Spanish, and the Americans knew she was saying much more than Ned's simple demand. At one point her voice went up and Ned thought he recognized a couple of her words.

"John, I believe she's giving this feller a good cussin'."

The deputy's face wrinkled in a grin. "This here's a little brown Pepper."

The guard answered with an angry snap. She ripped right back into him, and he paused to think for a long moment. Ned was a little nervous, wondering if she were making some deal he wouldn't like with the man in a language he didn't understand.

The guard finally picked up the phone's receiver, the only other object on the table besides the tattered and well-thumbed magazine, and spoke for several minutes. The person on the other end had much more to say, and he listened without another word, then hung up.

"The *Capitán* will be here in *un momento*."

Seconds later, the exterior door slammed open behind them and two uniformed police dragged a sweating prisoner inside. The man in custody was so drunk he couldn't stand on his own, and they yanked him roughly across the floor. As soon as the young guard saw them, he picked up the phone and spoke quickly. With a rusty groan only seconds later, the steel door leading into the jail swung open on tired hinges A mustached guard grabbed a handful of the drunk's filthy hair with a laugh and helped haul him inside.

The door slammed shut, leaving Ned and John to wait even longer.

"A moment" the guard promised stretched into half an hour. Ned was steaming mad when the bolt was thrown from the inside.

An incredibly handsome officer appeared, looking as if he'd stepped out of a Hollywood movie magazine. Black hair perfectly cut and combed, manicured fingernails, and dimples when he smiled, the man was in direct opposition to what Ned expected.

The officer finished chewing, swallowed, and spoke in heavily accented English while wiping greasy fingers on his pants.

"I am *Capitán* Fernando Guerrera. I am the *comandante* here. You may come in now." He waved with the other hand toward Ned and John.

The children started to follow, until the officer's sharp voice brought them to an abrupt stop. "No!" was all Ned understood as Yolanda and the man dove into a hot and heavy exchange.

Again Ned's frustration increased at his failure to understand the Mexican language. Yolanda wagged a forefinger at the officer until finally angered, he spent a full two minutes shouting at the youngster. Her face registered defeat. Frightened, George drifted behind the two Americans.

Yolanda fixed her attention to Ned. "This pretty pig says that Jorge and I cannot go any farther than this room. He says there are things in there that are not fit for children to see, but he knows you don't speak our language and I think he doesn't want me to tell you what he says in there."

"Well then, how are we going to understand him?"

She shrugged.

Guerrera beamed and his dimples etched deeply into his smooth brown cheeks. "I talk good *Americano*."

"I bet," John muttered.

"We don't have any choice, John." Ned extended his hand toward the open door. "All right, then. Show us the way. You kids wait outside, I might want to visit with you some more before we leave."

"We will, because you owe us five *pesos* each," George reminded him.

"Dollars," Yolanda snapped. "They are worth more than *pesos*."

"That's right, I do." Ned brushed the boy's hair with his fingertips and they entered a long, tiled hallway.

Guerrero turned left in the weak light from frosted pendulum fixtures and led the two Americans past a number of peeling doors. Grit crunched underfoot from decomposing concrete. A large rat watched them through one of many holes left by missing yellow-green tiles. They came to a door indistinguishable from the others. The stench of sewage and unwashed bodies rolled around the nearby corner. A constant buzz of men's conversations told Ned where the cells began.

Guerrera opened the door and indicated they were to enter. Again, a single bare bulb hanging from a wire cast a harsh light. A battered wooden table sat in the middle of the room. Ned recognized stains on it for what they were…blood. One chair waited on their side. Obviously, prisoners weren't expected to sit. A closed door behind the table had never seen a coat of paint.

Flies buzzed in the still air, many more lit on the table to explore the stains. *Capitán* Guerrera rested against the dirty wall and crossed his arms. "The prisoner will come *un momento*. Do you have money?"

Ned shook his head and waved at a pestering fly. "I don't even know how much his bail is."

Guerrera shook his head. "You should have brought something to pay us for our trouble."

Fury rose hot and prickly along Ned's neck. Instead of answering, he removed his hat and wiped the sweat with a handkerchief. "We'll talk to a judge about his bail after I see Cody."

After a long moment, Guerrera translated the statement in his head. He drew a sad sigh. "Oh, no, *señor*. There is no judge. The trial is past and the prisoner has already been sentenced. He will be taken to our prison down in *Allende* where he will remain for ten years."

Ned was stunned at the announcement. Arguing was useless. Only higher authorities in the Mexican government could dismiss the charges. The officer before them had no authority to make any changes in the conviction.

The law was the law.

Only it didn't work that way where they stood south of the border.

Chapter Thirty-seven

The rusty door finally opened with a moan and Cody stumbled through, pushed from behind. Four uniformed guards followed and spread out against the wall. Hands shackled together behind him, the young constable's appearance was shocking. His black hair stuck up in a matted mess. Dark circles painted by fatigue and worry surrounded both eyes. The left was blackened and swollen almost shut. Dried blood crusted the ear on the same side, telling Ned some right-handed son of a bitch had been working on him. Clearly, he hadn't slept in a week.

Cody brightened at the sight of Ned and John. He managed a wry grin, but winced when the movement broke open a crusted cut on his lip. Blood welled. His teeth were caked with food particles, making it obvious that brushing wasn't on anyone's list.

John felt a heavy lump settle in his stomach. Ned's neck and ears reddened. He laid a big, calming hand on his friend's shoulder. Before either of them uttered a word, Cody's eyes narrowed and he gave a tiny, almost unrecognizable shake of his head. "*Ya ta hey.*"

Ned was taken aback, and John wondered if he'd heard right. Was Cody's mouth so damaged he couldn't speak?

"This is your nephew?" *Capitán* Guerrera asked.

"Yes."

"I do not think so. This *lunatico* is obviously a Mexican, not a *gringo*, or one of the *indios* from up in the mountains of

Chihuahua. Look at his dark hair, his eyes, his skin. I believe
he is *indio*."

For the first time since Ned had laid eyes on Cody when he was
only five years old, he studied the features the officer had described.
"All right, he favors y'all in some way, but he's American."

"He is *indio*."

"All *right*. He's Indian, but that'd be Choctaw, not from any
of the tribes down here. He's my kin."

"You are not *indio*."

His frustration mounting, Ned barely managed to contain
himself. "No, I ain't. But we got Cody when he was little and
raised him as one of our own. He's been ours since his daddy died,
and his no 'count mama never knew him. He calls me Uncle, and
every now and then he'll say dad, and I reckon that's what I am."

"Do you have his *certificado de nacimiento*?"

"His what?"

Guerrera thought for a moment. "His birth papers."

"I didn't think I'd need his birth certificate. It's back in Texas,
in Chisum. I'll have to send for it."

"That will take too long, my friend."

Cody finally had enough. "Hey, I'm right here."

Angry at the interruption from a prisoner, Guerrera snapped
an order in Spanish at the skinny guard with a thick mustache.
"Ordaz, silence this man."

The sadistic guard grabbed Cody's shackled hands and
jerked them sharply upward, causing him to hiss with pain as
his shoulder joints took the stress. He bent forward to relieve
the incredibly sharp pressure, his head bouncing on the table.

The room virtually exploded. "Hey!" Ned bellowed and
started toward Ordaz.

"Ned, no!" Cody shouted and gave into the pressure. The
other guards brandished well-worn billy clubs and showed they
weren't afraid to use them. The door behind Cody slammed open
at the bark and more guards poured into the room.

John yanked Ned back, putting his body between him and
the threat. With no weapon at all, Big John doubled up his

ham-sized fists and prepared to take a sure beating, knowing that at least a few of the *federales*, as he'd already come to think of them, wouldn't look the same the next morning.

"*Alto!*" Cody shouted over the rising noise of angry officers, his cheek against the table. "*Alto*, god*damn* it! Ned, John, back off!"

Hearing Spanish from Cody was almost effective as an ice water bath. Everyone hesitated. At least two of the Mexican officers were grateful for the interruption. They found themselves on the leading edge of the charge into the giant black man who'd already set his jaw for battle and appeared perfectly capable of singlehandedly clearing the room.

"Everbody calm down," Cody spoke conversationally, his wrists still high above his head. He blew a fly out of his mouth.

Guerrera spoke quickly to his men, and they warily backed off.

Ordaz released the pressure on Cody's wrists. Sure they were finished making their point, Cody slowly straightened, chin bloody from his reinjured lip. "*Capitán,* can I speak?"

Guerrera nodded, his authority reestablished.

"Since there's enough of us in here, *Capitán* Guerrera, can you please take off these cuffs so I can wipe the blood off my face. I prefer not to visit with my relatives looking like this."

After a moment, Guerrera coughed out a phlegmy, arrogant laugh. He issued a series of orders. Ordaz fished a ring of keys from his baggy pants and unlocked the cuffs.

With a flick of his wrist, Guerrera ordered the others to leave and assumed a relaxed stance against the wall. "You all may speak."

"*Yah ta hey,*" Cody said, again. He wiped the blood away with his palm and cleaned it on his pants.

The Navaho greeting startled Ned a second time. Cody and Ned called it John Wayne Indian language after seeing the movie *McClintock!* at the Grand theater in Chisum. Mixed with the little Choctaw they learned from Miss Becky, the Parkers sometimes used it when the mood was light. In this instance, though, their spirits were anything but free.

Guerrera was equally surprised, and annoyed. He was used to conversing in Spanish to keep conversations private between his men and the *Anglos* they arrested who rarely understood their language. He also used it to make deliberations difficult for Americans when they came to bail out relatives and friends.

He didn't like the reverse tactic one bit.

For a long moment, no one said a word. Then Ned put both hands in his pockets and nodded. "I reckon I don't need to ask if you're all right. You look like hell."

Cody kept his eyes on Ned, refusing to acknowledge Guerrera's presence. "This is a rough place. Glad you made it. They're taking me out of here tomorrow."

"I heard."

"To a *prison*. They tell me it's a lot deeper in Mexico."

"What's the charge?"

"The *charge* is murder and moving illegal drugs across the border."

"Who'd you kill?"

"Nobody." He cut his eyes to Guerrera, but decided not to tell the whole truth. "Whitlatch and his men were murdered in the desert and they hung it on me, because I was there when it happened."

"That's ridiculous."

"That's what I told them."

Guerrera spoke up. "Enough talking. You are not allowed to discuss the case at this time. It is over. He was caught with drugs and the pistol he used to murder four *turistas norteamericanos*.

Arguing was useless. Cody stared hard at Ned and switched to what little Choctaw he'd learned through the years. "No *na hullo anumpa. Keyu oka, keyu tanchi impo.*

No English language. No water. No corn to eat.

For the first time in his life, John saw Ned shocked into silence. What were they talking about?

"What did you say?" Guerrera asked sharply.

Cody struggled to recall the words. "*Aki,* this *ofi. Tubi, ah,* me."

Ned processed the broken Choctaw mix, especially the familiar word tubi, *kill*, and translated it into terms he understood very well, *My father, this dog will kill me soon.* Very clearly it was *get me out.*

"Son, I'm barely keeping up with you…"

"*Tubi, ah*, me," Cody reemphasized. *He'll kill me.*

"You will speak English in my *presence*!" Guerrera snapped, and slid his own chipped billy club from the ring on his belt. It slithered through the metal with a promise of pain.

Ned ignored the man. If Cody was desperate enough to communicate in a language they barely knew, he'd try to understand. "When?"

"*Tombi. Oni.*"

Ned frowned, worrying with the translation. Then he realized Cody meant "ray of light." *Tomorrow morning.*

Ned jammed a trembling finger at Guerrera. "How much will it take to get him out of here and home?"

The *capitán* smiled, showing brilliant white teeth. Here was the conversation he'd been waiting for. Now he was on familiar ground, the business he knew best, extorting money. He shrugged expansively, playing his role to the hilt. "This man broke our laws, the laws of my country. He killed Mexican citizens. He must be punished."

"The man asked how much?" John growled.

"Much *dinero*." Guerrera spread his hands as if sharing in their problem.

"Oh, so I *can* buy him out. So much for the law."

Guerrera acted sympathetic, but the hunger for money twinkled in his eyes. "It is our way here, *amigo*."

"All right. Give me the price to bail him out."

"Ten thousand *dolares*, dollars, in cash *por favor*."

That price shocked the three Americans. None of them imagined the cost would be so high. Ned only had two thousand stuffed into the top of his sock. There was no way to get the other eight thousand by daylight. It was legalized robbery, plain and simple.

"How about I give you a thousand now and take him with me?"

Guerrera sadly shook his head, feeling Ned's pain. "There are many people to satisfy. It takes much more to pay for what is...necessary."

"Two."

Guerrera's eyebrows rose. "You have that money with you? Now?"

"Of course not. I wouldn't bring it in here like this, but I can get back with it in the morning."

"I am sorry. It will be too late. Tomorrow will be probably," he spread his hands again, "*fifteen thousand.*"

In desperation, Ned rested his shoe on the wooden chair and yanked the cash from his sock. He pitched the wad on the table. "Two thousand, right now, and we leave with Cody."

The clump of money lay there, slowly unfolding. The young *capitán* licked his lips and jerked his head to Ordaz to pick it up. The younger man quickly counted the bills while John shifted back and forth to bleed off nervous energy. "*Dos mil.*"

Two thousand.

Guerrera issued an order and Ordaz disappeared through the door. Another guard took his place behind Cody. Ordaz returned empty handed in less than a minute. All eight men stood in uncomfortable silence.

The tension was too much for John. "Well?"

Again, the brilliant white grin. "Well what?"

"Is that enough? Can we take him now?"

"Is what enough?"

In horror, Ned realized he'd been robbed, and there wasn't a thing they could do about it. "You. Son. Of. A. Bitch!" He reached for Guerrera's collar.

John barked over the roar. "Mr. Ned!" He knew exactly what was happening. For the second time that day, John pulled Ned away from the man he intended to kill.

The room again filled with warning shouts and threats, thickening the fetid air with tension thick as smoke. Guerrera uneasily backed against the wall and twitched the baton in his hand.

Ned gained control and stepped back. The room quieted and everyone waited for the next scene leading to the climax. John smelled the fear radiating from the guards, who wanted to be anywhere but in the room with the furious *Americanos*.

"He's right, Ned." Cody squinted out of his good eye. "Y'all go on ahead and get out of here. Now you know how these people are. See what you can do from the outside, 'cause you ain't gettin' nowhere in here."

It was a costly lesson, but one that Ned knew he'd earned. He was ashamed, and fighting mad. "Guerrera, it'll be me and you one of these days."

"Is that a threat, *señor*?"

"It's a promise that I'll be visiting you again one day."

"Come by any time. I'll make you a guest in our...hotel."

Cody jerked his head toward Guerrera. "*Tanampi, me.*" Guerrera was *hostile, at war with Cody.* "Not you!"

Ned's blue eyes flashed at the *Capitán*. "It's both of us now. *Tanampi humma.*"

Cody noticeably sagged with relief when he realized Ned understood his situation. "Yes. *Chi pisa lachike.*"

Goodbye, I'll see you soon.

Lips tight, Ned nodded at John. "Let's go."

The big man was already prepared for a fight to get Cody free, so he was surprised that Ned backed off from the battle. In his experience, the old constable never, ever gave up.

"We're done here, John."

"Whatever you say, Mr. Ned. Cody, you hang on. We was in worse not too long ago."

"That's what I've been doing, John." Cody didn't turn his head from Ned. "*Capitán*, can I hug my uncle goodbye?"

"Of course," the *capitán* answered expansively. "By all means. Tell him goodbye. He is family."

Ned stepped around the table and Cody met him halfway. The old constable wrapped his arms around the young man and felt him tremble. Cody barely raised his arms, resting his hands on Ned's hips.

"Hang on, son."

"I will."

The hug was brief, and they stepped back.

Cody cleared his throat. "Tell J.T. Boone I'll drop by as soon as I get back home. He and I have a lot of catching up to do." He raised a lip in what could have been a smile, or a snarl. "Lot's to talk about."

Without missing a beat, Ned nodded. "I will."

Cody stepped back and put his hands behind him. Ordaz snapped the cuffs back on.

Ned took two steps toward Guerrera who was leaning against the door leading into the hall. "Move."

With an insolent gaze, Guerrera slowly shifted his weight and stepped to the side.

Their eyes were locked as Ned reached for the handle, opened it, and started through.

Cody once again spoke in Choctaw. "*Chi hollo li!*"

Still maintaining eye contact with the crooked Mexican lawman, Ned paused when he heard the rusty steel door creak open behind Cody. Footsteps told him they were through, and then the door slammed with an echo. Through two heartbeats, he and Guerrera squared off.

John's deep voice rumbled in the silent room. "Let's go, Mr. Ned."

With Cody gone, there was no reason to stay. Ned paused. "We'll speak again some day, Guerrera."

The *capitán* smiled. "I look forward to it."

John put his hand in the small of Ned's back and gently shoved. The pressure was enough to send Ned out the door. As he passed, his shoulder caught Guerrera hard enough to let him know it wasn't an accident. Slightly off balance, Guerrera placed his hand on the wall and thought about arresting Ned for assault. That thought disappeared quickly when John moved past like a dark thundercloud, filling the space with much more than the threat of violence.

Guerrera watched them walk down the hallway. The guard rose from the rickety table when Guerrera flicked his hand, and unlocked the metal door.

Ned and John found Yolanda and George still waiting in the reception area. The young guard had been talking with them, but he stopped suddenly, picked up his magazine, and winked at Yolanda.

When the lawmen were almost to the exit, she snapped a long string of Spanish that caused the guard to frown. She started to leave, and halfway to the door, she stopped and unleashed another verbal assault until he slapped the magazine down and stood. Aware she'd pushed the man to his limits, Yolanda grabbed George's hand and joined the numb Americans in the vacant, dusty street.

Back in the sunshine, the men unconsciously sucked in deep breaths of free air to empty out the poisonous fumes of misery and corruption. John felt empty, and Ned shook from fear and anger, leaning against the rough wall.

John barely registered the kids' presence with them in the street. "What was that y'all was talking in there, Ned?"

Ned took a deep, calming breath. "Choctaw."

"Didn't know you talked it."

"We don't. Every now and then when we set in the yard, Miss Becky'll teach the kids a word or saying she learned from her Mama and her people, more for fun than anything else. I've picked up some through the years, up in the Territories. Cody was always good at remembering what she said, and Top and Pepper both know some, so they like to trade words. I'm not sure I understood everything Cody told me, but I understood enough.

"John, they're gonna take him out of there tomorrow morning and kill him, not take him to a Mexican pen. I believe Cody found out where them drugs are coming from, and probably who's running the whole shebang, and it starts with some of these people. They think he knows something that'll bring the laws down on 'em, and they intend to stop it. I don't know how he found out, but he did. We have to get that boy out tonight."

John studied the building's crumbling stucco facade for a long moment. "We'll take care of this."

"I hoped that's what you'd say."

"We will. Let's go."

The kids stuck right on their heels as the Texas lawmen silently retraced their path to Main Street, each alone with his own thoughts. When they reached the bridge, Yolanda tugged on Ned's pants. "You're leaving now, *señor*?"

"Yes, ma'am."

"Did you forget anything?"

Feeling bumfuzzled, Ned unconsciously rubbed his face. "I don't know what…"

John remembered. He reached into his back pocket and pulled out a thin, worn wallet. He thumbed it open, withdrew two limp bills, and handed one to each child.

Their eyes widened, because instead of five dollars each, they held ten-dollar bills.

"Hold it, John. That was my deal."

"You done spent a sight of money, Mr. Ned. Let me do this. Besides, I might not need it later, and they shore do."

Understanding John's meaning, Ned deflated. He knelt beside the youngsters. "C'mere and give me a hug."

Without hesitation, George and Yolanda stepped into Ned's arms. They recognized the grandfather for what he was. He held onto the kids for a long moment and then released them, his eyes wet with tears. "Now listen to me. You two hide what's left of that money after you buy your shoes, hear? Don't let your mama know you have it."

"*Si*. After we buy some *pepitoria*."

"What's that?"

"Peanut candy."

"All right, then. Now, y'all go on back home."

Ned rose, dusted the knees of his pants and glanced toward the bridge. The guard who warned them away from Boy's Town gave them a smile that was more of a leer.

Understanding the implied meaning, Ned felt his temper flash once again. He choked it down and started across the bridge. "*Damn* this country, and *damn* these people."

"Looks like some of them already are." John stepped quickly to match his pace. He glanced back at the prison over Ned's hat. "What was that last thing, that *chi* thing, Cody said back there when we was walking out the door?"

Ned's eyes glistened once again. "I love you."

They crossed the river in silence. Once back on U.S. soil, John finally broke the question. "So what now, Mr. Ned?"

He wiped the tears, set his jaw, and pulled out a tightly wadded piece of paper from the right-hand side of his waistband. As John watched, Ned carefully unfolded the grimy square to reveal a crude, but detailed map drawn in thick pencil.

"He slipped this in beside my belly when I hugged him goodbye."

It was a rough but fairly accurate drawing of *Las Células*, and the X marking Cody's cell was smeared with a drop of blood.

"Like I told Cody. *Tanampi humma.*"

"What was that Mr. Ned?"

"It's a Choctaw phrase. *We'll go to war red.* Let's get our guns."

Chapter Thirty-eight

I thought Mr. Tom was fixin' to beat our butts when he found us.

Well, he didn't really *find* us. Pepper woke up on her side of the car when the sun came up and got bored, so she decided to listen to the transistor radio she hadn't yet given back to Christine Berger. When she rolled the little on/off volume dial with her thumb, the car hit a bump and she spun it way too far.

The loud, tinny sound of Chuck Berry singing "Maybelline" nearly caused Mr. Tom to lose control of the car. We got shook up pretty good in the floorboard until he stopped the car on the shoulder.

He threw one arm over the back seat and twisted around. "What the *hell* are you two doing in here?"

Had I thought of those spooky eyes of his and how they'd pop out when he got mad, I wouldn't have even given a second thought to stowing away in his car. Stowing away looked fun when The Three Stooges did it on that ocean freighter with the Russian guy smuggling watermelons, but that steaming man on the side of the highway scared the pee out of me.

Well, truthfully, I had to pee so bad I was about to bust anyway. I couldn't decide whether to get out and unzip my pants while he yelled at us, or wait until he finished. He didn't say another word, so I knew he was waiting for an answer.

We used the long cord stretched across the back seat to pull ourselves up. "Mr. Tom. I know you're mad, but can it wait until I pee?"

"That ain't fair," Pepper argued. "I gotta pee just as bad as you, but I can't just pop a squat here on the side of the road. You have to wait like I do until we get to a town or a station, or something."

"I think I'll leave you two right here and you can hitch a ride by yourselves." Mr. Tom was madder'n a wet hen, and I wasn't sure he wouldn't do it.

"We just want to help Uncle Cody and Grandpa."

"We won't get in the way." Pepper batted her eyes in a way that works for her most of the time. Mr. Tom's own eyes trumped her Betty Boop look, and Pepper quickly examined the tangled quilts at our feet.

"What exactly do you think you can do?"

"Make calls, take notes, run errands?"

Instead of answering, Mr. Tom took out his pocket watch and checked the time. With a sigh, he returned it to his jeans. "Well, it's a sure thing I don't have time to take y'all back."

He studied us on the side of that empty highway. For the first time I took stock of my surroundings through the window. The oaks were different than we had back home. They grew wide and low in the pastures. Cactus was thick in a nearby wash. Stringy old range cattle watched us through a tight bobwire fence on cedar posts.

It looked like they had a good crop of rocks to me, too.

Without expression, Mr. Bell faced the front. "There's a town about five minutes away where y'all can pee, and me too, I reckon. I ought to leave y'all at the bus station. I don't suppose you left a note or anything, right?"

"Nossir."

"We'll call your mama and daddy, Pepper, and Miss Becky for you, Top. You'll tell them what you did, but I'll take over from there."

I examined the tops of my legs.

When he shifted into third gear, Mr. Tom spoke into the rear-view mirror. "The only reason I don't give you two a good belt whipping is I did something like this myself, when I was your age."

We passed a wooden sign that said Cotulla when a rear tire blew on the hot highway. Neither of us was dumb enough to say anything. Once again, he pulled onto the shoulder and opened the trunk.

The spare was flat, and he slammed the lid.

I couldn't take it anymore. I opened both doors and peed between them, shielded from the highway.

When I was finished, Pepper stared at the doors for a long minute. "Well, shit."

I was surprised when Mr. Tom pulled a handkerchief out of his back pocket and handed it to her. "Me and Top will just look back down this highway for a minute."

He was right. We were wayyyy too far to turn back.

Chapter Thirty-nine

Las Células wasn't visible from the motor court parking lot, but the Mexican fortress-like jail was all Ned and John had on their minds that afternoon. The hot sky was cloudless. Cicadas sang in the cottonwoods along the river. The air smelled of sewage, dust, onions, and diesel.

The owner frowned when Ned checked them in and John knew it was because even down in the Valley, white and black men didn't room together. Money ruled though, and he reluctantly gave them a key.

John rested uncomfortably in one of the small chairs provided by the little motel while Ned made two collect calls back to Chisum. The first one nearly scared him to death and added another layer to a nearly smothering sense of dread.

Ned had a white-knuckled grip on the receiver. "Them two kids did what?"

He shook his head at John while Miss Becky explained. When she paused, Ned held his hand over the speaker. "You ain't gonna believe this, John, them two little shits snuck into the back of the car Tom Bell borrowed from O.C., and by the time he found them, he said he was south of San Antonio."

"Tom's coming here?"

"That's what Becky said." He returned to his conversation. "Yeah, we talked to Cody. He's in bad shape, but he's alive."

John heard Miss Becky's tinny voice shout through the speaker. "Thank God!"

"We talked to them that have him, but the police down here are as crooked as a dog's hind leg. We tried to buy him out, but they wouldn't have none of it, so we're gonna get him out the best way we know how."

He didn't want to, but figured Miss Becky had a right to know Guerrera's plan. She was silent for a long time, and he thought she'd hung up. "You still there?"

"I'm here."

"I don't know no other way. Mama, they've been pretty rough on that boy."

He heard her breathing, then a sharp intake breath. "Ned, the good lord gave us the sense to know what's right and wrong. I don't know no scripture that says you can't save our own kin."

"You know what you're sayin'?"

"Get him back."

"You know what I may have to do."

"I know, but don't you let them kill that boy, nor John, nor you. I couldn't bear that."

"All right. We're stayin' at The *El Sombrero* motor court." He read off the phone number handwritten in the center of the dial. They talked quietly for several more minutes, and then he hung up.

John was waiting for him. "What did Tom say he was going to do with the kids?"

"He's bringin' 'em with him. Norma Faye is on the way to get Becky right now, and they'll drive down here and get 'em."

"What about James? Why don't he come?"

"James and Ida Belle are both down with some sort of stomach bug. They been sick as dogs, and neither one can get out of bed. I swear, Becky needs to be over there taking care of them, but said she'd come get the kids."

"James must be *some* sick to keep him off the road."

"He tried, but he couldn't even drive to the house. He had to pull over twice in a mile to puke. The doctor came out and said that if they didn't get any better, he'd put them in the hospital by dark. It's a mess back there."

"When it rains, it pours."

"I know it. They'll tell Tom where we are, if he checks back in. We'll need to let the manager know they're coming, so they can get in if we ain't here."

He made a second collect call, this time to Judge O.C. Rains in his office in the Chisum courthouse. Though the conversation was one-sided, the deputy knew the snowball was rolling.

There were no games this time. O.C. was anxiously waiting for the call and answered on the first ring.

"It's Ned, O.C." He listened for a long moment.

John rose, opened the blinds, and returned to his chair to look out on the playground and tiny swimming pool in the center of the horseshoe-shaped courtyard. Both were empty, so he watched the cars pass on the street.

"He told me they're going to kill him tomorrow."

As he listened, his face began to redden.

"Hell no, he didn't say it out loud. The damn *Federale Coman-dante,* or Captain or whatever the hell he is was-a standing right there. Cody told me in Choctaw so the son of a bitch couldn't understand."

O.C.'s tinny voice wasn't understandable. John rose and paced the room like a nervous cat. He pulled the switch to turn on the television sitting on a stand made of metal tubing. The picture tube still hadn't warmed up by the time he crossed the room and punched a button to turn on the water cooler. It blew hot air for a time until the pump kicked in to wet the straw, finally giving some relief in the stifling room. The TV picture was starting to form when he sat back in the chair.

"O.C., I know the law as well as you, but we don't have time for all that. The sonofabitch plans to move Cody deeper into Mexico in the morning, but the boy says they're gonna kill him instead. I believe him. You should have seen his face. He's beat black and blue, he ain't et good in days, and I think we're out of time."

He told O.C. how the *capitán* stole the bail money. O.C.'s angry voice was louder at the news.

"Of course they're crooked, and you know how I am about such things. You are too. I need to tell you what I intend to do, so somebody will know when it's over. We have a plan to get him out, but it ain't exactly legal. Hell, it ain't legal a-tall! It's barely on the right side of wrong."

He spent the next several minutes outlining his plan and finally listened while O.C. talked. "Yeah, John's with me on this."

He listened some more. The fuzzy picture on the television was a soap opera, in Spanish, and John didn't like to watch the stories even in American. He rose, twisted the dial in a series of loud chunks, and found another station. It too was fuzzy, so he fussed with the rabbit ears, trying to get a better signal.

"You can call whoever the hell you want, O.C., but it won't do no good down here. This place is a regular Sodom and Gomorrah. You won't believe what you can buy, and I think that's how Cody found what he came for. He dug around and the connection leads to somebody in Chisum that I won't say over the phone, because I don't have any idea who's listening, but I know what's going on. Cody learned something, and it got him buried in this Mexican jail."

On the television, Dick Van Dyke said something to Mary Tyler Moore in Spanish, but the laugh track was the same John recognized from back home. Disgusted and uneasy, he slapped the switch with the palm of his hand. The picture shrank to a pinpoint and then winked out. He returned to his chair and settled in with a sigh.

Their guns were scattered across the worn blue bedspread. John picked up a pump Browning twelve-gauge and quickly took it apart for cleaning, which gave him something to do while listening to Ned's conversation.

"This might all go wrong, and I imagine it will, but I don't know what else to do. If anybody asks, tell 'em we did what we thought was right, and that's about all I can say."

The air conditioner's wheeze filled the silent room as O.C. talked.

"All right, then. One more thing. There's some money buried in a quart fruit jar beside the northwest post of the kitchen porch. You might need it to…for us later. It oughta be enough to do the job. I don't want to be a burden on anybody…shut up and listen! There's another fruit jar buried on the south side of the bodark tree beside the chicken house. There's enough in there to take care of Miss Becky and Top for a good long while."

The timbre had changed in his voice, and in O.C.'s also, enough that John once again felt uneasy.

"All right then. Bye."

Ned replaced the receiver and watched John clean the shotgun. "You don't have to do this. I can do it myself."

"No you cain't. I doubt the two of us can do it together, but we're family."

Ned started to answer, then stopped. He swallowed a lump and wiped his nose. "And we're lawmen, going up against lawmen."

"They ain't the law, Mr. Ned, not like we know it."

"We're gonna break the law. It's tough for me to think about doing that…again."

"There ain't no other choice."

Without conscious thought, Ned picked up a dented can of 3-in-1 Oil and a scrap of cloth tied onto a string. He squirted oil on the cloth, dropped the line through the short barrel of his .38 and pulled it through. "You stay on this side of the river. I'll get Cody out and you wait with the car so we can make a quick getaway."

"It's easy to see why you on this side of the law, cause that idea won't hold water."

"I'm trying to keep you safe, John."

"We're going with your first plan, and don't worry 'bout me. They's one thing, though. What if them Meskins shoot at us?"

"Why, we shoot back, I reckon."

"That'll come as close as anything we can do to make us the same as them."

The room was silent as they digested the implications of that statement. John's face was blank, masking his unease despite the necessity of their plan.

Ned set his jaw and placed a drop of oil to run down on the hammer strut pin, then cocked it several times to lube the hinge. "When my granddaddy was a Texas Ranger, he crossed the border into the Oklahoma territories to bring back murderers and robbers. While he was there, he did what he had to do to stay alive. I believe we'll do the same. This might not be right in the eyes of some, but to me, it's the right thing to do. In my opinion, some folks just need killin' for what they done, or *are* about to do to Cody."

Chapter Forty

It was an hour before daylight when Ned and John drove back across the dark Rio Grande in a car they'd stolen from a bar down the street. Neither man wanted to drive Ned's car across the border. They didn't figure to get back with it in one piece, and besides, by Ned's reasoning, anyone leaving their car in front of a bar all night deserved what he got.

Lit by harsh lights, a different Texas border guard waved them across the deserted bridge. It was a good thing, because they were driving a stolen car, and the back seat was full of guns covered with the now oil-stained bedspread snitched from the motel room.

John glanced past Ned through the open passenger window at the reflected lights on the mist-covered water below. His stomach tense with fear, John sighed as he accelerated across the bridge and onto Mexican soil. "That was easy enough."

"It'll probably be the easiest thing we'll do all morning... look out!"

The big deputy slammed on the brakes to avoid running over two children who stepped off the dark Main Street sidewalk and into their lane. "These damn kids down here..." he stopped when he recognized the youngsters.

"*Hola, señores!*" Yolanda hurried around to the back seat and opened the door. She and George piled inside as if they were supposed to be there. When George felt something hard in the seat, he peeked under the bedspread. "What's this?"

Instead of answering, John pulled to the curb and parked. Ned fumed. "What are you two doing here? Get out of this car and go home."

George pulled the bedspread back. "*Todeas estas armas!*" *All these guns.*

Frustrated and terrified they'd be noticed, Ned stretched over the seat and yanked the spread back over the guns. "What do y'all want?"

Yolanda shifted forward and sat on the edge of the back seat, like Pepper back home. "We've been waiting for you all night. I thought you'd be back a lot sooner than *this.*"

"How'd you know we'd be coming back?"

"Because you were," she simply said. "You shouldn't drive down that road. The *policia* are always watching for American cars when they get off the main streets. Turn here, and I will tell you where to safely park near *Las Células.*"

The men exchanged glances, and with a shrug, John shifted back into gear and eased into the ratty alley she indicated. Neither lawman would have entertained the idea of driving through the narrow aisle almost blocked with abandoned items and trash.

"Turn off your lights." Yolanda hung even farther over the seat back.

"I can't see to drive. It's dark."

"We'll go slow. It isn't far. Turn here."

With abrupt directions, Yolanda guided them into a dismal neighborhood reminding John of his side of the Chisum tracks. She had him stop in front of a brightly painted house with a dirt yard. Somewhere not far away, a goat baaed for her missing kid. The sound came clearly through the open car windows.

"This is *mi tia's* house." She translated. "My aunt's house. Your car will be safe here. *Las Células* is only two streets over, between those houses. No one will see you walking through there, and if they do, they won't say anything if you don't speak to them."

The thin ribbon of a vaguely defined alley cut past rundown houses. It wasn't inviting in the dark, and Ned wouldn't have considered it in the daylight, unless he was armed. "All right, you kids get out of this car and wait in your aunt's house. You have your money, and I thank you, but it'd be best if y'all stayed away from us now."

They were surprised when Yolanda and George bounced out of the car. "Okay. Be careful and *vaya con Dios.*" They disappeared into the darkness, running in new Red Ball tennis shoes.

Stomach fluttering, Ned took a deep breath. "You can still back out and wait here in the car."

In response, John opened the door and stepped out into rich, thick air smelling of manure, damp mud, and rotting vegetation from the nearby river. He reached through the open back window and withdrew his gun belt. Strapping it on, John realized it was the first time he'd ever worn his pistol without pinning on a badge. That morning, both he and Ned wrapped their badges in folds of paper, dropped them into an envelope, and mailed them to O.C. in the motel mailbox.

On the passenger side of the car, Ned slipped his dress belt through his leather holster and threaded what remained of the belt through the loops. He buckled it and settled the .38 into its accustomed place. He slid a second revolver into the waistband at the small of his back and dumped Jimmy Foxx's cartridges into his right-hand pocket until it bulged. The other swelled with twelve-gauge shells.

John handed one of the already loaded shotguns to Ned when he came around. His mouth dry as cotton, Ned noted that John's khakis and white shirt were almost a lawman's uniform. The strap of a canvas ammunition belt crossed John's chest. Designed for duck hunting, it was filled with twenty-five double-ought buckshot shells. His pants pockets were also full of .38 rounds.

Without another word, John led the way down the narrow alley. The first twenty yards were silent, then a yard dog opened up and before long, more dogs were announcing their passing with ferocious barks.

Frightened and nervous, they hurried past angry curses in the predawn darkness as the neighbors and owners shouted for quiet. They came out on a street one block from the jail.

"I thought she said this was the way to go."

Before Ned answered, dogs tuned up on another block and they realized the uproar was a usual occurrence for that part of town.

"I reckon this way we blend in, instead of walking out in the open on the street." A man stepped out of the alley, carrying his lunch in a syrup bucket. He either missed the two armed men wearing distinctly American Stetsons, or elected to ignore them.

"They's the same as us," John said. "He's jis' going to work."

"Good people are the same everywhere. Let's go."

They stepped into the second alley, more at ease this time. Early risers were already moving in the houses, casting shadows on the few curtains that were drawn. Most of the doors and windows were wide open, and if the lights were on, illuminating the residents sitting at tables, or standing idly and peering into the darkness.

"These folks get up early," John said. "Maybe we should have gotten here a little earlier."

"Too late to think about that now."

Unconsciously picking up their pace, they finally came to the street and found themselves in front of the imposing structure of *Las Células*. An extremely bright bulb in a single fixture over the entrance threw stark light over the same two dented cars that were parked there the day before. The wide building's corners were cloaked in darkness.

"Are you ready?" Ned asked.

Without answering, John jogged across the street and dodged between the cars, his shotgun at port arms. Praying the guard was alone, he opened the door and stepped inside. Ned was right on his heels, his own shotgun muzzle alongside his leg.

They were lucky. A different guard was dozing in the chair. John rushed across the room and rapped the desk with the gun's muzzle. "Morning."

Ned took one last look outside, and seeing no one, gently closed the door. The sleepy guard snapped awake, but his head was still full of cobwebs. His eyes cleared at the sight of the enormous tube pointing at his chest. He raised both hands.

"*No disparar!*"

Ned rounded the desk. "I don't speak that. Call back there and tell them you have a prisoner and to open the door."

Silence.

Ned suddenly panicked. "Do you speak American?"

The terrified guard shook his head. "*No hablo ingles!*"

"Now what we gonna do?" John asked. Only seconds into the rescue, and already things were falling apart.

Ned spoke to himself. "I bet if we slap him hard enough, he'll understand English better than he lets on." The outside door slowly creaked open. He spun and leveled his shotgun at a heavily armed Tom Bell.

Looking every inch like a worn out cowboy coming into a saloon for a whiskey, Bell nodded from under his big Stetson. "Mornin', gents."

Chapter Forty-one

An intricately etched and cocked pearl-handled .45 automatic rode on Bell's hip. "What are y'all doing here?"

Cradled in the crook of his arm was a nasty-looking Browning automatic rifle. A heavy belt full of extra magazines for the BAR hung over one shoulder. The light, portable machine gun was the favorite weapon of Clyde Barrow, of Bonnie and Clyde fame, and a staple of the WWII infantryman.

The old man's presence astonished Ned, but John wasn't fazed in the least. "We're fixing to get Cody out of this jail, and to kill some people if we have to. Especially a crooked lawman named Guerrera."

"I'd be proud to help out."

It was the Texas Ranger badge on his shirt that finally jolted Ned to speak. "How the hell did you find us?"

"O.C. told me what town y'all called him from, and a little Mexican gal outside with long, black hair told me y'all were in here."

"Where did you get that badge? You're gonna get killed wearing that thing."

"They haven't killed me yet, and I've been wearing it for fifty years. I figured you needed the help."

"You're supposed to be taking care of the kids. Becky said they were with you back on the other side."

"They are…I hired a woman to keep an eye on them two in your motel room, and I doubt I paid her enough for the job. But let's talk about this little situation we have here. It looks tense and I imagine you don't speak the language, right?"

"We done thought of that."

"Too late, probably. Tell me what you want to say." He pointed at the guard whose hands were still raised.

"We ain't got no choice, Mr. Ned," John said. "We got to do something and do it quick."

Never one to hesitate, Ned decided. "Tell him to call back and say they have a prisoner here. Open the door."

Bell addressed the young man in rapid Spanish. The man sat perfectly still with his hands still in the air, taking in the situation. John pushed the muzzle closer to the guard's head, and his terrified eyes flicked back and forth from the Ranger to the giant black man glaring at him over the shotgun.

Bell spoke again in Spanish, softly, and the guard got the message not to try and warn anyone on the other end. He gingerly picked up the receiver, conversed briefly, and then answered a question as Bell listened carefully. He replaced the receiver and waited with both hands flat on the table.

"Did he say the right words?" Ned asked.

"Yes."

With a fast, smooth motion borne of long practice, Ned reached into his back pocket for the lead-weighted sap he always carried. His wrist flicked. The leather-covered sap made a sickening crack behind the guard's right ear, and he dropped face forward onto the desk. A thin trickle of blood found its way through his hair.

Tom Bell nodded in approval. "Always liked the way those work."

Ned remained behind the desk and kept an eye on both doors. "You're liable to get killed here this morning."

"It don't matter, I've got the cancer anyway," Tom said dismissively. He took up a position to cover both entrances.

John waited beside the door leading into the jail. Keys rattled on the other side and it creaked open. The big deputy's huge arm shot through the opening and grabbed the first shirt he saw.

Surprise always makes unprepared people pause, to take stock of the situation, and question the reality of what's happening. It worked once again. With a violent yank, John slung a very shocked guard into the room, where he slammed to the floor. Tom kicked him hard in the side, and then in the head, his pointed boots inflicting serious damage.

Capitán Guerrera stood in the doorway, his hands held high and staring smack down the large bore of John's twelve-gauge. Abruptly awakened from the deep sleep of the virtuous on the cot in his office and unable to comprehend what was going on, the *capitán* hadn't even buttoned the shirt over his flat belly. They'd gotten a call that a prisoner had been brought in, and when they opened the door, the deputy beside him had literally flown away.

Guerrera's mouth opened and closed like a fish. Tom Bell lifted his chin and spoke quickly in Spanish. Guerrera kept his hands high and entered the room to face the deep barrel of still another shotgun and a mean-looking rifle promising a long, deep sleep.

John tugged a pair of cuffs from his back pocket, spun Guerrera around to face the wall, and snapped the metal around his wrists.

When Bell asked a question in Spanish, Guerrera's sly eyes flicked to the floor. He shrugged, buying time to clear his head. "*No se.*"

Bell leaned his forearm against the back of the *capitán's* neck, forcing his stubbled face into the gray wall, all the while keeping up a steady stream of words incomprehensible to the two Texas lawmen.

"I've trailed dope from this pig sty to Texas and right back here to you and Whitlatch. I know you rubbed him and his men out, and for my own reasons, I'm ending this business here this morning, so you can't send no more of that shit into my country."

"What's he saying, Tom?"

"Hang on a minute, Ned." Bell switched back to Spanish. "I'd just as soon gut you like a fish, but I'm about to turn you over to this man here. I just wanted you to know that I've passed the word to the Rangers, so they're about to tear your playhouse down."

Guerrera raised his lip in a sneer. "*No sé lo que estás hablando.*"
I don't know what you're talking about.

Bell's dead eyes erased the sneer and replaced it with fear. "*No me importa. Estás muerto. Dónde está Cody?*"
I don't care. You're dead. Where's Cody?

Ned's patience was wearing thin. "Where the hell does he have Cody? Have they moved him out yet?"

Guerrera shrugged. "*No se.*"

"Says he don't know where Cody is," Bell translated.

"We do." Ned was at the end of his rope. He stepped forward and drove his fist deep into Guerrera's bare abdomen, doubling the man over in a cough of pain. "I told you I'd be back." He whacked the side of Guerrera's head with the leather-covered lead sap, harder than he'd ever hit anyone before, and then in blind rage, harder once again.

"Ned."

He heard John's caution. "I ain't."

Ned tugged a handkerchief from his pocket. A handful of bullets came with it and rattled at his feet. He quickly stuffed the cloth into Guerrera's mouth. Instead of pushing it in with his fingers, he used the barrel of the .38 to jam it deep. John pitched him the red bandana he used as a handkerchief, and Ned yanked the material between Guerrera's lips and tied it firmly into place behind his head.

He rolled Guerrera onto his belly, removed the *capitán's* belt, and drew it tight around the man's feet. Finally, he bent Guerrera's legs and looped the remainder of the belt through the cuffs' short links. Trussed on his stomach like a hog to slaughter, he lay helplessly, trying to breathe through his congested nose.

"That took long enough," Bell said. "Cutting his throat would have been faster."

"I thought about it, but I ain't that far into this, *yet*. We're lawmen even though we're in the middle of this bidness. Thought you were, too."

"Sometimes the law gets gray around the edges down here." Bell's wide eyes took in the empty hallway. That one sentence spoke volumes. "Where to now?"

"Cody's cell, and that'll be the hard part."

"You know where it is?"

"We have a map."

"This gets better."

John stuck his head through the doorway and checked the area in both directions. The hallway was empty, except for a wooden table directly opposite from where they stood. When John ducked into the corridor, Ned matched his pace. Bell brought up the rear, keeping a careful watch over his shoulder for anyone suddenly appearing behind them.

Three old lawmen men crept through the stench and filth to break a fellow lawman out of a Mexican jail.

Chapter Forty-two

Ned had memorized the map, but he took it out of his shirt pocket and kept one eye in the smudged lines as they crept down the hallway. He counted doors on the right to orient himself, and breathed a sigh of relief when the marks on the map matched the actual openings they passed. The tally was correct when they reached the corner and turned right.

The prison was designed in a huge three-story square, with cells on the inside facing a bare concrete courtyard where prisoners exercised in the sunlight. The bleak outside wall of the square consisted of offices, solitary confinement cells, interrogation rooms, and unadorned spaces for everyday use, such as bathrooms, kitchen, and dining room.

Unfortunately, Cody's cell was on the square exactly opposite from where they stood, so they were forced to traverse the entire length of the left side's ground floor. The three men moved without a word. It was early enough that most of the prisoners were still asleep in dirty eight-by-ten-foot cells.

The air was thick with the reek of unwashed bodies, piss, and shit. Flies buzzed through the bars without impediment. Roaches crawled on the walls and floor, and crunched underfoot.

Their luck held. Not a guard was in sight so early in the morning. This was the hour when generals traditionally initiated attacks, when men slept heavily and were less inclined to wake quickly. No one noticed their passing, at least until a prisoner jerked up as they passed a cell crammed with so many men that some had to sleep sitting upright. A whispered exclamation caused his cellmates to stir, but the trio had already passed, moving swiftly along the corridor.

Three *Americanos* wearing Stetsons was an unusual sight in the depressing jail. Behind them, stirring sounds and murmured conversations told them that the cells were coming alive.

"Mr. Ned."

"I know. I hear 'em. It's the third cell on the right after we turn the corner."

Ten steps later, John backed against the wall, peeked around the bend, and found another empty corridor. Rats and mice darted across the open floor.

Quiet as a well-oiled watch, the determined trio ducked around the corner and rushed to Cody's cell.

"Cody!" Ned's heart beat so hard he thought it would explode.

Shadowy figures snapped awake and sat up, two and three men to each vermin-infested bunk. Someone coughed quietly. It was so dark they couldn't distinguish the inmates swinging their legs over the sides. Ned's head reeled when the floor shimmered, then waved in the darkness. It took a moment to realize people were packed in so tightly there was no empty floor space at all.

"Here." Tom handed him a metal Eveready two-cell flashlight.

Grateful, Ned found the small red spotlight button above the on-off switch with his thumb. The light clicked on and he played the beam around the cell as men covered their eyes. Roaches scurried and unidentifiable insects leaped from one man to another. None of the prisoners were Cody.

"Oh lordy. He ain't here. You think they moved him already?"

Shading their eyes against the sudden glare, the men behind the bars began to talk. Ned turned to Bell. "What are they saying?"

"Hang on a minute." He spoke in hushed tones to the men inside.

They drifted close to the bars and Ned worried that someone might reach through. Old habits learned in the Lamar County courthouse had kept him safe for years. Ned rested his hand on the pistol butt at his waist. He didn't want to risk injury from an inmate.

The whispered exchange was disheartening. Bell translated the information. "They never put him back in here after y'all left yesterday. They say he's in one of the solitary cells, but they don't know which one."

Ned groaned deep in his throat in barely contained frustration and faced the line of blank doors across from the cells.

More soft voices carried from the cell as Bell conversed with the prisoners.

"They say he wasn't walked back past here, so they don't think he's on this side, or on this hall. Ned, there's two sides on this level, and eight more in the two stories above us. There ain't no telling where he is."

"Guerrera knows."

"Oh, lordy," John said. "Now we got to go back and get him."

"Told you we didn't need to cut his throat," Ned said. "Yet."

Chapter Forty-three

Bell and the cell's occupants spoke softly as a low buzz like that of a giant beehive filled the air around them. "They'll pass the word about what we're doing, so maybe it won't get too loud too quick."

John more than heard the jail fill with conversation that almost immediately began to build. "How are they gonna do that?"

"You watch. The news will beat us back around to Guerrera, especially after I told them how we'd left him."

Anxious to the point of panic, John led the way. "Let's go, then."

Bell was right. An almost physical wave washed before them as whispered conversations passed the word. Since John still hadn't seen any guards, he reasoned this was the time when people were sleeping deeply, or they were extremely bored.

Maybe their luck would hold.

Guerrera was still trussed like a turkey when they rushed back into the reception area, but he'd managed to wriggle against the closed door. When John gave it a hard shove, the steel banged off Guerrera's head. While Bell watched the hallway and Ned covered the front door, John yanked the bandana from Guerrera's mouth, untied his feet, and released the belt.

"Spit that rag out," John ordered, yanking Guerrera to his feet. Unsteady, he leaned against John, and then feeling brave, planted his feet and shouldered him in the midsection in a vain attempt to knock the deputy off his feet.

It was no match.

Angry and sweating heavily, John grabbed his cuffed arms and slammed Guerrera face first against the cinder block wall. That done, he wrenched the *capitán*'s arms so that he bent forward with a hiss of pain, exactly as he'd ordered his deputy to do with Cody the day before.

"You listen, mister. I ain't got time to fool with you. Do what I say and keep quiet or so *help* me I'll finish breaking that jaw."

Cowed and beaten, Guerrera turned his face upward to John. His nose was broken, one eye had begun to swell, and blood flowed from a gaping gash on his chin.

"*Si. Si!*"

"Now that you're listening," Bell said. "We want you to take us to Cody right now! You know where he is, and so help me if things start to get out of hand, you'll be the first one to go down."

"*No comprende.*" Guerrera acted as if didn't understand.

Bell repeated himself in a blaze of sharp Spanish, and Guerrera finally admitted defeat. "Third floor. Back right corner. As far as possible from the entrance."

Again Bell translated the directions. This time John grabbed Guerrera's cuffed hands and pushed him out in front. "Lead the way."

Back in the hallway, Guerrera lurched right. "Uh, uh." Ned shoved the hand-drawn map under the man's nose. "We know where we're going, but you're gonna take us this way and up them stairs in the corner."

The other direction led to the same place, but at least Ned was familiar with the left-hand hallway, and he wanted Guerrera to know right off they were in control.

The overwrought procession once again moved out, hurrying toward the stairs that led to the third floor. Conversations literally buzzed like a wasp's nest.

Fuga de la cárcel! Jailbreak!

In his mid-sixties and completely out of shape, Ned was winded by the time they reached the third floor landing with their prisoner. Again in the lead, John opened the door and gave them the nod that the coast was clear. They stepped into an exact copy of the first floor, except this time open cells lined both sides of the building.

Guerrera ducked left, but John kept a tight grip on his wrists. The news had somehow already reached top floor and shabby, broken prisoners lined against the bars on the double row of cells, waiting on the raiding party.

As they passed, hands reached out to the Texans. At first Ned was frightened, but he quickly realized the prisoners wanted to get their hands on Guerrera. He didn't care what happened to the man, but at that moment, he still needed him.

At least until he found Cody.

Their luck finally ran out as they reached the next turn. A sleepy guard stepped around the corner and directly into Guerrera. Recognizing his commander, he jerked tall and straight, then recoiled at the sight of his commander's damaged face and the Americans behind him. The guard opened his mouth to yell, but John's fist slammed squarely into his nose with the force of a sledgehammer. The guard went down without a sound. Guerrera's feet tangled up with the fallen man and he almost tumbled down himself, nearly jerking John off his feet.

A hand darted through the iron bars quick as the strike of a water moccasin, and when it retreated, Guerrera recoiled, gagging, and fell backward against John.

Blood jetted from the severed artery in his neck as if from a fire hose.

"Oh my lord." John gasped in a shocked, clear voice as Guerrera slipped bonelessly to the floor.

"Goddamn it!" Ned quickly knelt beside Guerrera, grabbed a handful of hair, and yanked his head upright. The man's panicked eyes told him they both knew Guerrera had only seconds left. "That solid door at the end, right?"

Guerrera thrashed and gurgled.

"You know what I'm saying! Make it right before you die, you sorry sonofabitch! *Which* one of them doors down there?"

Guerrera jerked sideways, trembling as the same arm struck again through the bars, this time driving a sharpened blade deep into the *capitán's* side. Instead of pulling back into the cell, the prisoner worked the makeshift knife deep inside, wriggling it forcefully, doing as much damage as possible.

"God*damn* it!!" Ned hauled Guerrera's body out of reach along the concrete floor.

At the same time, John kicked hard and broke the man's arm. The entire floor came alive when the prisoner shrieked and fell back into his cell.

Without responding to Ned's desperate question, Guerrera shuddered. His eyes rolled back in his head.

Shouts in Spanish echoed down the halls. Confused guards called back and forth. Prisoners filled with vengeance cried out the same statement over and over in a cacophony of rejoicing.

Guerrera es muerto!

Guerrera es muerto!

John and Ned didn't need any translation this time.

Guerrera is dead!

"Yeah, and so are we." Bell's wide eyes blazed defiance.

Chapter Forty-four

"We need to run, Mr. Ned." John was up and rushing down the corridor before Ned thought to answer.

It was almost the same statement he'd hollered that night in the bottoms when they carried Top and Pepper out of danger. The similarity wasn't lost on Ned.

Danger was obvious. They charged down the exact middle of the corridor to avoid the forest of hands bristling through bars. The jail's designers had estimated exactly how much space was needed to safely pass between the cells, and the Texas lawmen had only inches to spare. Finally, at the corner, the cells were no longer open cages, but instead were behind solid walls.

Over the din, Ned heard shouting as the guards reacted. All attempts at being quiet were long gone. Ned evaluated four ominous blank doors. "Cody!"

"*Guerrera es muerto!*" drowned his voice.

All three men took up the cry at the same time to be heard over the discord. "CODY!"

Instead of an answer, loud thumps reverberated in the hallway as the doors beside them were kicked from the inside. "This one!" John held out his hand. "Keys."

"Dammit, they're on Guerrera's belt." Ned looked back down at the corridor to find the *capitán's* body pulled against one of the cells. Hands plucked at the corpse like feeding piranha, and above it, a bearded prisoner fumbled a key into the cell's lock.

With a disgusted look on his face, Bell rushed down the corridor. Before he reached them, the cell door slammed open, spewing a crowd of rough, desperate men.

"*Claves!*" Bell shouted.

Keys!

With an expert flip of his wrist, one prisoner ignored him, twisted a second lock, and yanked the door open. Another wave of men boiled free. It was only the beginning. Like bulls, a crowd surged toward Bell, but when he raised the BAR, they stopped. Even if they didn't recognize the big automatic rifle by name, the very design announced that it was designed to kill people in volume.

It was too late anyway. The keys had already opened another cell and quickly passed hand to hand away from the increasingly desperate lawmen trying to save Cody.

"*Alto!*" With the rifle still trained on the escapees, Bell retreated toward his men. "The keys are gone!"

Gunshots rang out around the corner.

Voices howled amidst the riot when the guards began shooting the escaping prisoners.

John set his feet and kicked the metal door. It didn't budge. He kicked again with the same results. "Cody! Back up!" He aimed the shotgun at the door frame instead of the lock, and pulled the trigger. The report hammered their eardrums, dampening Ned's hearing. The full charge of buckshot, nine .32-caliber pellets, destroyed the metal frame, but didn't completely release the lock.

"Again!"

The second shot wasn't enough either, but the third mangled the metal enough that the door sagged open.

What rushed through the door wasn't Cody. An apparition of violence exploded into view. A bald man nearly John's size, shirtless upper body completely covered in jail-house tattoos, was finally free after many, many years of torture and incarceration.

There was a reason his eyes were wide, dark, and devoid of emotion.

They were the eyes of criminal insanity.

The hugely muscled Mexican slammed into John, knocking the surprised deputy back into the cinderblock wall with the sound of a raw steak hitting concrete. He swung a fist that would have torn John's head off his shoulders had it connected, but John parried with the shotgun to block the blow.

The scarred giant's knuckles broke against the stock with the sound of a snapping chicken neck. The pain didn't faze him.

In the gray light of early morning, neither Ned nor Bell had a clear shot. It was all between the two big men, as Bell kept the mayhem at bay behind them.

The babbling prisoner grabbed the twelve-gauge, trying to lever it from John's hands. Instead of yanking and pulling, for the second time that morning John did the opposite of what most people expect.

He attacked.

Using his sole advantage, John kneed the Mexican in the groin and pressed forward, cracking the stock into the monster's cheek as the man woofed in pain. Biceps bulging, John roared with the effort and jammed his shotgun across the man's neck.

It was a fight for survival, violent and rabid.

With his adversary pinned against the wall, John kneed him again and again in the crotch until the man released his hold on the weapon. When it gave, John slammed his forehead into the prisoner's nose. Blood erupted in a torrent. John twisted the shotgun free and slammed the butt sideways into the man's broken nose again. The third time he pounded a direct strike between the eyes with the butt, driving all of his power into a killing blow. An audible crunch closed the encounter. The prisoner's legs became rubber.

He smacked face first onto the floor and died.

The deafening report of a shotgun once again echoed in the close confines. John jumped to face the next threat. He was relieved to see Ned shuck another shell into his twelve-gauge and fire a second charge into a door frame directly beside them. This time when the door opened, Cody's swollen face appeared.

Relief washed through all of them as Ned grabbed Cody in a quick bear hug.

Chapter Forty-five

The keys made their way completely around the third floor, and the freed prisoners had control. Grudges quickly settled themselves through a variety of homemade weapons pulled from hidden places. Men bled out on the grimy floors as the rampaging crowd charged the Texans.

"*Alto!*" Bell shouted. For the first time, he opened up with the BAR. The automatic rifle was deafening as he directed his fire over the prisoners' heads. They recoiled at the concussive explosions of the heavy 30.06 rounds, many dropping to the ground for safety. The much greater mass retreated down the corridor.

Bell ejected the spent magazine and slapped another into place with satisfaction. "The right tool for the job."

Cody held out his hand. "You have anything for me?"

Ned pulled the revolver from the small of his back, and handed it to Cody, butt first. Confident it was loaded, Cody hefted the pistol.

Bell fired again, ejected the empty magazine, and slammed another one home. "We gotta go!" He pointed to the way out. "The same way we came in! *Vamanos muchachos!*"

John didn't need instructions. He rushed past the three men and led the charge to retrace their path. Shrieking prisoners fled the quartet.

Heart thumping, Ned was surprised at how many cells had already emptied in such a short amount of time. Almost trotting, he thumbed more shells into his empty shotgun. Higher pitched gunfire crackled throughout the jail as the guards finally rallied enough to try and turn the tide in their favor.

Acting as a wedge, Big John charged downward past a crowd of rejoicing prisoners running before them. At the sight of the Texan's arsenal, the freed inmates sidestepped and raised their hands as they ran, laughing their way to the next floor.

John led the way down two flights of stairs to the ground floor where the noise wasn't as loud beside the closed door of the stairwell. Still, it was only a matter of time before the mob flooded the stairs as they rushed toward freedom.

Ned paused and laid his hand on the door to the main hallway, as if checking the temperature in case it was hot. "Not many of them have made it this far down. Them guards'll be waiting on whoever comes through."

His back against the wall, John grasped the door knob. "It's the only way out!"

Tom Bell covered the stairwell above. "Careful."

"Cody, you gonna make it?"

The young constable squinted through his good eye and gave Ned a grin. "I'll be better when we get back to our side of the river."

John twisted the knob, cracked the steel door, and a bullet whistled through the narrow opening to pop into the opposite wall with a vicious splat. He shoved the door closed as more bullets rang against the steel.

"Now what are we gonna do?" Neither Cody nor Ned had an answer.

Tom Bell stepped forward, crouched on one knee, and held the BAR at the ready. "Open it again and get ready to run. They're expecting unarmed prisoners, not us."

"Let's go," Cody said.

John again cracked the door open and winced as bullets richocheted off the steel. With a low growl, Bell stuck the muzzle of the BAR through the opening. Like Vengeance on two feet, the dance began when the monstrous rifle opened up on full automatic. Powerful 30.06 slugs punched through concrete walls as if they were made of paper.

His aim was once again high, giving the guards a chance to decide whether they wanted to hang around. When he stuck his third magazine into place, he lowered the muzzle and hosed the area beyond the door in a roll of thunder. If they wanted to fight, then he'd give it to them. "Open the door!"

They burst into a corridor filled with the smell of cordite, smoke, and dust. Half a dozen Mexican guards sprawled in awkward positions, surrounded by their dropped weapons. Others retreated in a rout to be cut off by escaping prisoners suddenly appearing from the far staircase Ned, John and Bell had originally used.

The two groups converged. Guards were immediately engulfed with no time to beg for their lives. Screams, groans, and curses rocked the hall.

Taking advantage of the rapidly fading opportunity, Bell led the way and darted into the main reception area. The original guard was gone, the room empty, and the front entrance gaped open.

Outside, pale light revealed the cars parked nearby.

"Almost there," John said.

"They're most likely waiting." Shaking like a leaf from exhaustion and fear, Ned wondered at Tom Bell's calm and composed demeanor.

"We can't stay here." Breathing hard, seeing through only one eye, Cody checked the loads in his pistol for the first time, unable to remember if he'd fired the weapon. "I've had all this place I can stand."

Bell motioned for them to get against the wall. "Wait! Here they come."

In seconds, a flood of freed prisoners rushed from the corridor into the reception area. Ignoring the Texans and the arsenal pointed in their direction, they saw freedom in the open street. The tightly packed mass of rejoicing Mexicans burst into the street to be cut down in a withering hail of gunfire as soon as they emerged. Pushed from behind, a steady stream of men raced into the chaos of the street amid a hailstorm of bullets.

It was a slaughter.

The fusillade continued as bodies piled outside the doorway, tripping men trying to escape. Shouts and cries in Spanish were indecipherable to Ned and Cody, but the common language of pain was clear to everyone in that hellhole.

Surviving prisoners fell back in the reception area, well away from the open door, realizing a world of death waited outside. They continued to ignore the Texans against the wall, who ignored them back.

When the roar of gunfire fell off, John knew the men outside were reloading.

Ned had no time to prepare himself for what was about to happen. John kicked the door farther open and stumbled over a body. He caught his balance and ran outside, firing high and shucking fresh shells into his shotgun. He dropped to a knee behind a car.

Bell followed, the BAR hammering the dawn.

Chapter Forty-six

Surprised by the wall of gunfire coming from what they thought were unarmed men, the mismatched army ducked behind their cars, frantically thumbing shells into empty guns.

Instead of Mexican police or the military they expected, the Texans faced a well-armed gang loyal to a man they thought was still alive, Guerrera. Cody recognized the mock uniforms, the same ones that executed Whitlatch and his gang, and charged outside, vaguely aware of a ragged volley of return fire.

"These ain't the police! They're soldiers who work for the bad guys. They're the sonsabitches who took me! Pour it on 'em!"

John and Tom Bell lowered their aim. Hellfire erupted from their weapons in a continuous ear-splitting barrage. Ricochets yowled off into the distance.

Cody shook his head to clear his mind after so long inside the jail. Rounds cracked past his hair and one plucked at his pants. Bullets blasted chunks of sandstone and stucco from the exterior to sting his face.

It felt odd, as if Cody were running in a cloud of feathers.

In the midst of the barrage, he idly wondered how some hit right beside him, as if they'd passed through his body. Protective wings wrapped around him.

I felt something like this the day I wrecked in the snowstorm.

Outside of his cotton-like cocoon, the Texans' weapons continued to bark.

Men fell like rag dolls.

Ned was the last to exit under the covering fire. One of Guerrera's men had been caught near the entrance when the prisoners first reached the door. Pretending to be dead, he waited in the midst of the bleeding corpses. Seeing the old man, he decided it was time to fight. He raised his arm, jammed a rusty revolver into Ned's stomach, and pulled the trigger.

Ned grunted at the sharp pain, feeling like he'd been kicked by a mule. "Ohhh!"

The wind knocked out of him, Ned's stomach immediately felt hot and wet. He dropped his shotgun from the impact, but years of muscle memory took over. He yanked the revolver from its worn holster, cocked it with his thumb, and shot, and then shot again. Blood flew and the man soundlessly fell back and out of sight.

"Don't stop now!" Cody yelled and grabbed Ned's arm.

John and Bell directed their aim at specific targets. Limp bodies dropped and frightened men dove for cover as Cody and Ned almost collapsed between the two cars. Cody picked up the dropped shotgun and fired until it shucked empty.

John ducked to reload and saw Yolanda waving frantically from halfway down the alley, directly across from the jail.

Gunfire reverberated on the street. High-pitched screams ripped the air. "Go with her!" Ned gasped, holding his belly. Already, flies swarmed to his wound.

"Who?" Cody had no idea who he was talking about.

Official police cars slid to a stop and blocked both ends of the street. They knew of Guerrera's side business and were more than willing to let his soldiers handle the issue at the jail. Their job was to contain the situation and prevent it from spilling into town.

More prisoners ran through the door, drawing much of the fire, but the experienced soldiers focused their aim on the *Anglos* with weapons. Tom Bell ducked and smacked in a fresh magazine. "Do what he says, Cody. Stay with that gal and I'll keep their heads down."

John shook his head. "Uh, uh. We're all getting out of this."

"No, we ain't." Bullets whizzed overhead and punched the car with metallic rings. The windshield exploded, spraying glass in a glittering cloud. The volume of gunfire increased. "Y'all git!"

Ned buckled from pain, and Cody reacted in horror when he saw Ned's ashen face and the bloody wound. "Ned!"

"Not right now. I ain't got the wind for it."

Tom Bell cast his bright, wide eyes on Cody. "Get 'em out of here, son. My time was up when I got back to Center Springs with the cancer."

Cody immediately understood the statement. He knew why Tom had left Center Springs for an extended visit while he recuperated in the hospital from the wintertime ambush.

Bell plucked the badge from his shirt and pressed it into Cody's hand. "I didn't know why I had to come back to Center Springs, but this was the reason, for y'all. You'll find out the rest pretty soon. Now ya'll git, and when you make it across the river, tell the Rangers what happened. They'll take care of the rest. Show 'em this."

Saved for a second time by the man he hardly knew, Cody grasped Bell's arm and gave him a half smile. "I'll finish this back home, where it started."

"I know you will, son." Any other conversation ended when Bell coughed and doubled over from the savage punch of a bullet. "Oh!"

Another tore Cody's sleeve and he realized one of *La Guardia* had a fresh angle on them behind the car.

"Y'all, *run!*" With an effort, Bell twisted to face the fresh attack and opened up once again with the BAR.

One part of Cody's mind wondered idly, how a man of his age moved with such fluid ease. He seemed so young. The other part of his mind screamed for action.

Cody pointed Ned toward the alley and whacked John on the shoulder. "Go!"

The big deputy had tears in his eyes when he gave Bell one last look.

The Ranger fired a short burst. "Hang on a minute! They keep popping up on yonder side of that car." He lowered his aim and the slugs hit the concrete in a stream of hot lead, bouncing under the dusty Buick, barely raising more than six inches off the ground. The "barking" technique worked, and three gunmen fell to the ground.

"*Now!*" Bell shifted his aim, found another target, and shot again, using the last few rounds to keep the *federale's* heads down and their attention away from his friends. He whacked the last fresh magazine into the rifle. "Go!"

The Texans sprinted for the alley. Behind them, Guerrera's men threw shots toward the retreating trio. They ducked between buildings as the firing reached a crescendo, and raced toward safety.

The BAR ran dry behind them when they ducked into the alley, out of harm's way for the time being.

Tom Bell drew his .45, and the firing resumed.

Chapter Forty-seven

"Hurry, you're too slow," Yolanda hissed as they trotted in a ragged line behind her between two houses. Dogs barked, but this time no one hushed them. Neighbors watched as the heavily armed and bloody Americans passed.

A wave of gunfire crested at *Las Células*, already sounding far away, and then trickled off to silence. Led by a child, they rushed across an open, unfamiliar street, then darted into another weedy and desolate alley. Fifty yards away, they hurried down an even dustier lane.

One last shot echoed as they zigzagged through a maze of stucco houses, wooden shacks, and crumbling buildings gaping to the elements. The gasping men emerged onto the dirt street where they'd left the car. Ned was horrified to find it gone. "They done stole the care *we* stole." He panted and sagged to rest one hand on his knee.

Drenched in sweat, the battered troop paused in shock over the stolen car. George ran out of his aunt's house and waved at Yolanda in the same way she'd attracted the Americans' attention only minutes before. "Follow *Jorge*." Yolanda shooed them forward.

Cody blinked to see clearly through his one good eye. "Who the hell is Hor-hay!"

"That kid right there." Lightheaded, Ned kept his hand pressed against his bloody stomach that burned like fire as he staggered along, weak and drained. He was running out of energy. "Stay with him."

John hung back, watching. Relieved that the coast was momentarily clear and there was no pursuit, he shifted the shotgun to his other hand and grabbed Ned under the arm. He halfcarried him around the house and through a haphazard corral full of manure and mama cows.

A shackledy fence made of cast-off boards, doors, metal signs, and leaning posts momentarily slowed the adults. The young, wiry kids slipped past the obstacle and into what Cody thought of as a rickety cow shed. George opened the door and they rushed into the cool interior. The whole building leaned in on itself, ready to collapse at any minute. The filtered morning light brimmed with dust motes.

Ned settled gratefully onto an overturned barrel, his belly filled with pain. "This ain't safe."

"We don't stop." George knelt beside a small door barely three feet high on the far side of the cow shed. He twisted a wooden block and pulled it open. "In a moment we go through here."

Ned moved listlessly, his life's blood soaking his shirt and pants. Cody knelt and stuffed his filthy undershirt against the wound. "Hold this tight. You got to stay with us."

Ned nodded and closed his eyes.

Cody rummaged through Ned's pockets for fresh ammo. Thumbing new loads into his revolver, he squatted and peered outside at tall clumps of cane, a palm tree, and beyond that, a thick stand of cottonwoods. "That the river?"

George nodded. "*Si.*"

"How do we cross?"

The youngster raised his eyebrows. "You can swim, no?"

"I can swim, yes, but Ned's shot and I'm afraid we'll get seen. How about telling us where a car is so we can drive back across the bridge."

A strong voice spoke from the other side of the warped wall. "That is a bad idea, *mi amigos.*"

Cody was shocked upright. He cocked the pistol and aimed at the shape flickering between the never-before-painted boards.

George held up his hand. "Don't shoot. That is my Uncle Reynaldo. He is here to help you."

Shaking from nerves and fatigue, Cody stepped back as Reynaldo knelt and crawled inside through the small door. The handsome, dark skinned young man was in his early twenties. He peeked back through a gap in the boards to keep an eye on the outside. "It is embarrassing to use a door intended for sheep and goats. You can relax. I will not harm you."

Aware of the gun in his hand, Cody lowered the revolver. Reynaldo built a smile under his thick black mustache. "We don't have much time. Many police and soldiers will be waiting for you on the bridge where you will be arrested and taken to *Las Células*. They would welcome you back with open arms, I assure you. The river is the only way."

"You sure we can make it?"

"You have to."

Light filled the opposite end of the cow shed when Yolanda opened the door and slipped inside. "The shooting has stopped. You must go now."

Reynaldo was concerned over the condition of the three exhausted men who were breathing hard and nearing the end of their strength. "The children speak highly of you. We want to help."

"It'll get y'all in trouble."

"It will not. The *policia* here are corrupt, but they aren't stupid. We are all related. Many of *Los Guardias* are our relatives. They will look, but won't see…if there's nothing here to look at."

There wasn't time for a cultural discussion. John rose from his kneeling position and put his shoulder under Ned's arm. "C'mon, Mr. Ned. We got to go."

Face ashen, Ned struggled upright and allowed John to support his weight.

Reynaldo clapped once. "*Bien*. Quickly, across the pasture. Once you are in the tall cane, there is a path leading to the river."

"What do you get out of all this?" Cody waved his gun toward the jail.

Reynaldo spread his hands. "You have done us a favor, freeing many of our family from *Las Células.* They were falsely accused. Guerrera wanted *mas rescate* to get them out. I gave him almost all the money I earned in my bar, and it still wasn't enough."

"You have relatives in that shithole with other kinfolk guarding them?"

"It is complicated. You were in there. You know. They didn't took them for nothing, but no one deserves *Las Células.*"

While they talked, John ducked through the door, his bulk almost getting stuck in the small opening. Once free, he reached back to drag Ned into the open. Cody jiggled the pistol uncertainly in his hand. "They won't come here and hurt the kids?"

"No."

"All right, then. If they do, we're coming back to finish the job."

Reynaldo's eyes crinkled. "As would I. But do not worry. Now, come."

Cody dropped to his knees and crawled outside with Renaldo right behind. Once in the open, he felt horribly vulnerable. No one but the buzzards circling high overhead saw them cross the pasture and disappear into the thick stand of cane.

Reynaldo moved swiftly through the ancient cottonwoods lining their side of the river. Leaves rustled high overhead. Puffs of cotton drifted on the breeze like summer snow as the clusters of green grape-like seeds burst open to reveal their fluffy interiors.

The bank sloped sharply toward the river, thick with willows leaning over the water's surface. Cautiously working their way along a footpath, they came to the river's edge. Two men squatted on the bank passing a bottle back and forth. They leaped up and held their hands high in fright when Cody and John pointed their weapons. "No! *Estamos aquí para ayudarle.*"

We're here to help you.

"It's all right." Reynaldo patted the air. "They are my cousins. Lower your weapons."

"What are they doing with them jugs?" John asked.

"They are for to help you swim."

"I can swim."

"They say American *negros* cannot swim."

"I can swim!"

"Then they are for *su padre* who is hurt."

"It's a good idea, John." Cody eyed the cluster of plastic one-gallon jugs held together by rope. "Ned ain't gonna be much help."

"I can swim," Ned whispered and dropped down to sit in the Rio Grande mud.

"This'll help, Mr. Ned." John took the jugs from one of the young men and tied them to Ned's chest. Blood soaked his shirt and pants. His skin was pale and waxy. "That hole in your belly might cause you to fill up and sink." He grinned at his own weak joke. "Don't want that."

Without hesitation, John hoisted Ned to his feet and half dragged him into the muddy river. He stopped when they were waist deep. The morning mist had burned off, and the opposite bank stood in sharp relief. "Won't people see us in that open water?"

"Probably."

John and Ned splashed into the depths until the soft bottom fell away under their feet. They dog-paddled toward the north bank.

Cody tucked the revolver behind his belt in the small of his back, then stuck his hand out to Reynaldo. "Thanks."

"*De nada.* Nothing but a few jugs, and your *padre* and his *negro* bought the *ninos* new shoes."

"He's not my...John's not his...he did? Never mind. Thanks again."

Behind Reynaldo, the barefoot children stood in the mud beside the trunk of a huge cottonwood, their new shoes tied by the laces and draped around their necks. He waved, and they gave him wide smiles.

Without a backward glance, Cody pushed off and swam to take Ned under his free arm, allowing the wounded man to gratefully lean backwards and float. John supported him from the other side. Together they paddled across the Rio Grande as the current pushed them downstream toward the bridge.

In seconds they were swept out of sight and the five people on the Mexican bank were hidden by the willows. A wedge of startled teal shot overhead, wind whistling over their wings like tiny jets on their way to strafe *Las Células* one last time.

None of the trio noticed the dusty red and white El Camino pacing them along a dirt road on the Texas side.

Chapter Forty-eight

The smell of damp dust and sour mud made it hard for me to breathe as we cruised beside the Rio Grande in the back of Uncle Cody's El Camino, but my puffer did the trick.

Pepper punched my shoulder as I stuck it back in my pocket and pointed. "Look! There's some people in the water!"

We'd already made two passes on the road across the river from a cluster of houses and barns half hidden by cottonwoods, willows, and mesquites. Norma Faye said there was a town somewhere over there, but the only thing showing through breaks in the trees were worn out buildings. Something big was on fire, black smoke boiling into the still air.

We heard a lot of shots, and I knew it wasn't anyone taking target practice. The sounds were like we heard on the television show, *Combat.* I was scared, because nobody got through that much shooting without being hit and I knew Grandpa, Uncle Cody, and John were somewhere over there.

Norma Faye and Miss Becky had picked us up at daylight from Grandpa's motel room where we'd been watching television with a Spanish lady Mr. Tom paid to sit with us. She worked there, cleaning rooms.

When we pulled up in front of the motel that morning with Mr. Tom, he said we hadn't missed Grandpa and Mr. John but by a few minutes. He gave Miss Hernandez some money, told us to wait until somebody came and got us, and then hurried off to catch up with them.

I thought we were in for a butt whippin' when Uncle Cody's El Camino pulled up in front of the room, but when we realized it was only Norma Faye, Miss Becky, and Miss Sweet, I knew it would wait. It was strange to see the three of them puffing and wheezing to get out of that two-door car after riding so long all squished up like sardines. When they saw us looking out the window they ran into that little room, crying and hugging us like we'd been gone for a week.

Miss Menendez had a letter for Norma Faye in an envelope. I'd been admiring Mr. Tom's handwriting while we waited for them to get there. The big flowing letters reminded me of the signatures on the Declaration of Independence.

When she finished reading the letter, Norma Faye sat on the edge of the bed and stared at the pages in her hand. "Mr. Tom really was a Texas Ranger. He knows this area, and says that when they come back across the river with Cody, they most likely won't use the bridge. We're supposed to look for them...," she waved toward the west, "out of town."

"What does that mean?" Miss Sweet wanted to know.

"It means they had to break Cody out of jail and people will be chasing them."

Miss Becky hadn't set down. She'd been frowning at the room, her big purse hanging in the crook of her arm. "We need to get going."

Miss Sweet shook her head. "Laws, honey, I got to rest a spell. Y'all leave me here, and I'll be waitin' when y'all come back."

They left her resting on the bed and less than an hour later, me and Pepper saw three heads bobbing close together. The current carried them out of sight, but Norma Faye heard us hollering at her to stop and she finally caught a glimpse of them in the water. She paced them until they disappeared under the bank, and then idled along until the brown-green water pulled them into view again, this time much closer.

Norma Faye stopped us in the shade, and we waited for another glimpse.

Chapter Forty-nine

John was terrified they'd be swept under the bridge, but the sluggish current wasn't enough to carry them around the last bend to meet the watchful eyes of the border guards.

"Kick, Mr. Ned, kick." His order was more to keep Ned alert than for the assistance. Ned kept going limp and John was sure he passed out each time, but at his shout, Ned rallied and continued to fight.

John whispered under his breath. "Thank the good Lord them boys back there on the riverbank thought about these jugs. He sent us a couple of angels to hold Mr. Ned up."

They were completely out of sight from Reynaldo and the kids when Cody's feet finally once again touched the muddy bottom. He kicked a few more times, and with a grunt, planted his shoes and gave a heave. It was enough relief for John to set his own feet, and together they dragged Ned onto the shore.

"We made it." Cody flopped to the ground. "Back in good ol' Texas."

"Not yet, we ain't." John stretched out, holding Ned and scanning the landscape. "We gotta get up this sharp bank where them people back there cain't shoot at us no more, and down the road a piece, then we're home. Right now, it looks like a long way to the top."

Cody glanced upward, thankful the drop wasn't nearly as sharp as the Red River bank at home. "Look, there's trails leading to the top. They're either cattle or game trails, or made by folks that swam the river like us. They'll help us get up."

"Well, let's get to going. I want to get some cover between me and that sorry country over there. Them boys are still looking for us." With a grunt, John pulled Ned upright. "I want to unloosen these wet knots, but I can't get them undone to get the jugs off."

"Don't matter. We'll worry with them when we get to the top. You can work on them while I walk into town and try to find a car."

"No need for that. You look a lot worse than I do, and I know where we left Mr. Ned's car at the motel."

"Either one of us'll attract attention."

"That's a fact."

They let the idea rest and lifted Ned to his feet. For a moment he was almost dead weight. After their rough handling, he rallied enough to stiffen his legs and they supported him upright.

"Ned, stay with us a few more minutes. Then we can rest," Cody said. Still heavily armed, the two pushed and pulled him up a crooked trail through the grass and mesquite. Cody groaned in relief when they finally struggled to the top of the bank and level ground.

In the shade of a cottonwood, they carefully lowered Ned to the dry earth. For the first time Cody surveyed their surroundings while John cut the jugs free with his pocket knife.

The land to the north was an open, treeless expanse of pasture and cultivated land. A single dirt road paralleled the river and meandered its way around cottonwood groves and deep cuts eroding into the river. The wide open space revealed all. They'd know if anyone was coming, and there was.

A cloud of dust rose in the distance and drifted toward the river as a vehicle rushed toward them. Cody slumped. "Uh oh. I bet that's the border patrol. We have some explaining to do." He removed the pistol from behind his belt and laid it in a clump of grass. "John, put your guns down."

Instead, John squinted at the approaching car and flung the jugs into the thin trees behind them. "Do the border patrol drive red-and-white cars down here?"

"I don't have any idea…" he drifted off. "Why that's an El Camino like mine…" He stopped in wonder, not believing what he was seeing through his one good eye. "That *is* my car, and Norma Faye's driving it."

"Here comes another'n." John looked in the opposite direction. He soon realized that he recognized that one, too. "Somebody's driving Mr. Ned's car, too."

"What's going on?" Cody felt fuzzy as all of the energy suddenly drained out of his body. He looked down in wonder at hands suddenly heavy as cement.

Norma Faye slammed on the brakes when the men stepped out of the brush. The El Camino slid on the soft sand. Then both doors blew open. She jumped out of one side, and Miss Becky struggled from the other.

Top and Pepper rolled out of the truck bed and over the side. "Uncle Cody!" Top shouted.

"Mr. John!"

"Ned! Cody! Hallelujah!" Miss Becky shouted. She reached out to hug Ned and got a good look at his bloody shirt as he slumped to the side. John went with him and settled to the ground. He gently lowered Ned's head into his lap.

The rejoicing became horror.

"Oh my God, Daddy's hurt bad!" Miss Becky knelt beside him and placed her hand over the wound. The undershirt they used as a pressure bandage had slipped out of position and was soaked with blood and water. "Norma Faye, give me your slip right now."

Torn between Ned's wound and the almost overwhelming need to hold Cody, Norma Faye reached under her skirt and yanked her slip down. She stepped out of it, and hurried to Ned's side.

The bullet entered through the fat that rolled over his belt on the left side. Miss Becky opened Ned's wet shirt to reveal the ugly powder-blackened entrance wound. "Tear it in two, hon, he's got two holes in him."

Norma Faye divided the slip and handed it to Miss Becky. She rolled him to check the exit wound farther toward the middle of his back, where the .38 round crossed through his body. It bubbled with blood and water. Gobs of yellow fat protruded from the torn flesh.

"Help's on the way, Daddy. Just you hang on." Miss Becky packed the wound with the slip and laid him back. "This ain't no worse than the time you got your hand caught in the clutch on that John Deere. You remember, you walked all the way across the field to the truck and wrapped it in that rag soaked with coal oil and …"

Her face told those around her that it *was* worse, though.

Finished with all they could do for the moment, Norma Faye slipped her arms around Cody and held him tightly for a moment, then she ran her hands over his body, looking for wounds of his own.

"What'n hell are you kids doing here?" Cody, numb, wondered aloud. The whole event suddenly had the semblance of a dream.

To everyone's surprise, Ned's sedan rolled to a stop and Reynaldo slid from behind the wheel. It made Cody's head spin. They'd only left him minutes earlier, and here he was, driving Ned's car on the Texas side. Without a word, Reynaldo hurried around and opened the passenger door, struggling for a moment to help the passenger out.

John and Cody squinted at the newcomers as the kids dashed from one adult to the other.

"Laws! It's so hot down here I cain't get my breath, and that ain't helping these old knees of mine that are plumb wore out. Young man, give me your arm and get me over to that there dark complected feller."

Reynaldo held her fleshy arm as Miss Sweet lumbered toward the ragged group. The spreading bloodstain on Ned's wet shirt diverted the old healer's attention. "Oh, Lord help us, Mister Ned!"

Unable to move because Ned's head rested in his lap, John showed no surprise at the sight of his aunt so far from Lamar County. He blinked away the tears in his eyes. "Mister Ned's bleeding bad and 'bout dead. Can you help him, auntie?"

"I've done what I can," Miss Becky told her and moved aside.

With a grunt, Miss Sweet settled heavily to the sandy ground beside Ned and opened her muslin bag full of healing herbs and salves. "Hold that slip tight agin' his belly 'til I get ready, hon." She met John's gaze. "I'll do what I can with what I got, but it's up to the good Lord after that, John."

"We need to get him to a hospital." Cody turned too quickly and felt his head spin. He clutched Reynaldo's arm. "I'm as worried about shock killing him as that bullet hole."

Reynaldo shifted uncertainly on his feet. "Sit down. You're in shock yourself."

Cody sat, and turned to John. "How are you doing, partner."

"I've got a powerful thirst. My mouth is dry as cotton."

"Top," Miss Becky called. "You take and get that quart of water out of the car and give it to Mr. John."

The kids raced to the car. Pepper was the first to find the fruit jar of well-water in the floorboard and ran it to John. Instead of handing it to him, she gave it to Top who screwed the ring off and removed the lid. Only then did he pass it to John, who drained half a full pint in one long draught.

John held the jar up. "Why don't you give Cody a sip and then see if Mr. Ned can drink any of this."

Top handed the jar to Cody, who passed the water to Miss Becky as he looked up at Norma Faye from his seat on the ground. He was having trouble tracking. "Where'd y'all come from?"

She dropped to her knees and hugged him long and hard in relief. "We'll explain it all later."

Chapter Fifty

Hembrillo Sheriff W.M. Anderson and his enormous black mustache arrived five minutes after Miss Sweet stopped the bleeding. The sun-darkened, middle-aged lawman took quick stock of the situation. He radioed for the ambulance and called the border patrol.

Anderson wondered aloud at the marks on Cody's face and why many of them were several days old. He listened intently to Cody's story about fighting with an escaped Mexican prisoner who swam the river from *Las Células* before he shot Ned and disappeared into the thick mesquite that stretched for miles northward.

"You boys sure 'nough have a lot of guns," Sheriff Anderson said around a cedar toothpick.

Cody shrugged and kept his face impassive. "We're lawmen, vacationing a long way from home."

"Um hum. Where are your badges?"

"Musta left 'em home. You can call up to Chisum and talk to Judge O.C. Rains. He'll tell you who we are."

"I'll do that for sure. The three of y'all are soaking wet and you look like hell. The fight with that escaped prisoner carry all y'all into the river?"

"He was a rough customer."

Shirtless and unshaven, with his hair plastered with oil and water, Cody's appearance did nothing to gain the sheriff's confidence. "Your whole family in the habit of traveling like this?"

Emotionally and physically exhausted, Cody wanted nothing more than to lay down and sleep, but they needed to pass this one last hurdle, and he wasn't sure they'd be able to do it. "How do you mean?"

"You look like you've been lost out here in the scrub yourself for a week, while everyone else here looks like they slept in a bed last night. You know, this don't smell right, especially when I find a lawman with a hole in his belly while kids wander around looking for horny toads."

Pepper swelled up at the comment. "We ain't looking for nothing except a little shade."

"Hush, honey." Miss Becky kept pressure on Ned's wound as Miss Sweet wrapped a poultice in the remnants of Norma Faye's slip.

"Um hum." Anderson squinted at the young Mexican man standing nearby. "Don't I know you?"

Reynaldo flashed a wide smile under his thick mustache. "*Si, jefe.* I work on this side of the river, but *mi casa* is over there. You've seen me before."

"What are you doing here?"

"He's driving my auntie around for us," John answered truthfully, waving a hand at Miss Sweet, who was slipping the fresh poultice under the pressure bandage. Ned's color had returned after she gave him half a bottle of some dark liquid from her sack, and the waxy look was gone from his face.

Anderson cleared his throat. "That's another thing. I don't believe I've ever seen…colored and white families vacationing together. Y'all must do things a lot different in your part of Texas."

"Sheriff Anderson," John spoke softly, respectfully. "You ever been to Lamar County?"

"Nope, went to Eureka Springs once, but the rest of the time I've stayed right here in Hembrillo."

"Well then, sir, you don't know much about us or the way we live our lives up there."

Anderson glared a hole through John. The wail of an ambulance was far away. "That's true. We don't have too many niggers down here, but the ones I've come across have always been respectful, and they don't travel with white families."

Miss Becky shocked the kids when she joined the verbal fray. Her statements weren't quite true, but far from lies. "Sheriff Anderson, John and his family have worked for us for years. It shouldn't surprise you none that they come with us to do what needs doin'."

He recognized the significance of the bun on the back of her head. "So you sayin' they're…servants?"

"Nossir, and they ain't slaves neither. They're as close as family can get without bein' blood."

Anderson wanted to say more, but a station wagon from the town's funeral home came to a dusty stop beside the group huddled in the shade of a mesquite tree.

The driver and his assistant moved quickly to load Ned into the back. Sheriff Anderson was on his radio when Cody moved close to Reynaldo and whispered. "Where'd you come from?"

Reynaldo seemed surprised at the question. "Why, I walked across the bridge with everyone else coming to work this morning. They were looking for *you*, not me. I knew where Mr. Ned is staying. There aren't too many secrets here. When I got to the motel, this woman was waiting by the swimming pool. We don't have many *tias negras* down here, so I knew she was looking for the big *negro* hombre, so here we are."

"She didn't have keys to Ned's car."

"Keys? *Amigo*, I learned a long time ago how to start a car without a key. Like the one your uncle left in front of *mi tia's* house a couple of hours ago."

"A couple of hours." John watched them slam the ambulance's back doors. Miss Becky slipped into the back seat and motioned for Cody to come on. "Lordy mercy. Has it only been two hours? You go on with Miss Becky and Mr. Ned. We'll take care of the young'uns and meet you back at that mo-tel when you know something."

"*Bien.*" Reynaldo beamed at Top and Pepper. "You two remind me of my niece and nephew. Jorge is about your age, *algodon*, Cotton, and Yolanda is a little pepper, like you, *niña.*"

He wondered why John and Miss Sweet laughed.

Chapter Fifty-one

Television and newspapers the next morning were filled with news of the jailbreak across the river. For the first time since the late eighteen hundreds, *Las Células* was closed and all the remaining prisoners housed elsewhere.

Newspapers reported the rioters somehow freed themselves from the cells, took guns from the guards, and killed more than a dozen *policia*, including the *Capitán* himself, Fernando Guerrera, and nearly burned the place down.

Mexican officials hailed Guerrera as an honest, dedicated officer and a great man who would be missed by those who loved him.

Chapter Fifty-two

In a bizarre circle, this time it was Ned in the hospital bed with everyone gathered around. Out of danger two days later, he opened his eyes from a brief nap and for a long moment studied the large needle in his left arm. Shivering slightly because of his dislike of needles, he traced the tubing up to the glass bottle suspended above his head.

It seemed as if everyone he knew was gathered around his south Texas hospital bed. "We all made it?"

Cody felt empty. The man had given his life to save Cody a second time. "Tom Bell didn't."

"Have they brought him back over here?"

"No one has heard a word, but a lawyer and a Texas Ranger named W. B. Graves came by yesterday with some papers to sign. I don't know how he knew we were here in Hembrillo, but he did."

Ned closed his eyes and waited, recalling W.B. Graves as the Ranger who'd investigated Cody's attack back in the winter.

"Graves said Tom was a retired Texas Ranger for sure. He knowed him most of Tom's life and served with him here in the Valley for years."

Ned wondered why Graves had kept quiet about Tom's history. It didn't make any sense.

Cody continued, as if talking to himself. "The lawyer said Tom left a will, and for some reason, the house he almost finished, and the land in Center Springs, goes to me and Norma."

Miss Becky sniffled and wiped her nose.

"Where's John?"

Cody jerked his head toward the north. "They're out there in the waiting room. He's been there since your fever spiked and they thought you was gonna die from the infection you got from that river water. He's chomping at the bit to leave though, now that you're better…said something about visiting a new friend of his when they get back. Miss Sweet gave him a funny look, and then hugged his neck like they hadn't seen one another in a year."

"He has a girlfriend," Norma Faye clarified. She knew the road would be hard for the two of them, but time and understanding changes opinions. Miss Becky's new wedding ring quilt spread over the bed she and Cody shared was evidence enough for that.

Cody absently rubbed his throbbing split lip. "How do you know?"

"I heard."

Doing their best to stay out of the way in the corner of the hospital room, Pepper and Top scrunched together in a chair, looking through small yellow folders of pictures he dug from his back pocket. Kids deal with death differently. They were immensely sad their friend had died, but their response was to look back at happier times. Top had captured some of those moments with his spy camera.

Cody watched them for a moment. "Tom left a savings account for Top and Pepper's college."

When Cody stayed silent for a long while, Ned opened his eyes. "Anything else?"

"Yep. He left a folder with some information that makes me pretty sure Sheriff Donald Griffin is behind the drug smuggling. J.T. Boone's in jail, because O.C. caught him in a lie about when he was supposed to come help us in the army camp and he didn't. They found a thick envelope full of money in the trunk of his car and put the screws to him. He confessed to working with Whitlatch to keep the law away from what was going on. They may have him on the attempted murder of y'all, too, because of being in on the army camp ambush."

Cody paused, absently watching the kids. "I guess the last thing we need to wrap this up is more evidence against Griffin, but it might be a long time coming. None of what we have will stick right now, even though I have a strong suspicion he's behind everything that happened."

Ned moved the arm attached by a clear hose to the last of many bottles hanging above his bed. "We'll get him, when I get out of this damn hospital."

"That's a fact." For the first time in his life, Cody hoped he'd have a dream that would tell them what to do.

"Watch your language Daddy." Miss Becky patted his hand. "The kids are right over there."

They snickered.

Ned coughed and grinned at them. "What's so funny, you two?"

"The look on Pepper's face laying there in the snow." Top angled the little booklet to show the adults. "I took these with my secret agent camera when Uncle Cody was in the hospital." He passed the packet of photos to Cody. "Here's some of you when you didn't know I took 'em."

Miss Becky asked Ned if he was comfortable and Norma Faye rose to adjust his pillow. Distracted, Cody took the packet and absently flipped though the shuffled photos. There was one of him the day before the accident, walking across Miss Becky's yard in a blur of motion. He flipped past one of the kids playing in the snow outside of the hospital while they waited for their turn to visit Cody. His gaze lingered on a photo of Tom Bell standing in front of his house, staring upward at the new roof. Others were of Tom in his hat, in the yard littered with lumber scraps, and kneeling to pat Hootie. The next to last shot showed the snow-covered statue of the Confederate Soldier in front of the courthouse.

The last picture of two men standing at the base of the statue made Cody feel better than he had since the ambush. "Top, where are the films to these pictures?"

"In a shoe box in the bottom of Miss Becky's chifferobe."

"Do you like that one?" Norma Faye leaned over his shoulder. "Sure do!"

Ned adjusted himself in the hospital bed to settle his pillow. "Oh, I got something else for you to do, Cody."

"What's that?"

"Call and tell O.C. he needs to forget where them fruit jars full of money are buried."

As everyone laughed, Cody stared downward at the surprisingly clear black-and-white photo of Sheriff Donald Griffin handing a thick envelope to the recently deceased Whitlatch.

The hospital phone rang. Norma Faye answered, because she was closest. "Well hidy, O.C."

She fell silent and listened. Cody slipped the packet of photos into his shirt pocket. "I see. All right, I'll tell them."

Norma Faye gently replaced the receiver in the cradle. "I don't believe this."

"What?"

"Mr. Ned, you have kinfolk down here in the Valley?"

"I don't know. There's some family that split off and came down this way back in the Indian days. They mixed in with some colored folks, too, out near Hondo. We call them the Black Parkers."

"Well, I believe this is a different line. Mr. Bell's daddy was a Parker, one of your grandaddy's boys. Mr. Bell dug around these last few years and found all that out, and Judge O.C. figures that's why he came back to Center Springs after he retired."

"The good Lord brought him back to us for a reason, Ned. That's why you're a-layin' in that bed."

"Might be." Norma opened the blinds to let in a little more of the south Texas light. "Judge O.C. also said he left an envelope for you back home. Said it's what you're gonna need to clear all this up."

"Does he know what's in it?"

"Nope, just what's wrote on the outside. It said, 'To Ned. The dreams told me to find you. Inside is what you want to know about Griffin. It's signed by him in his legal name. Thomas Belton Parker."

To receive a free catalog of Poisoned Pen Press titles, please contact us in one of the following ways:

Phone: 1-800-421-3976
Facsimile: 1-480-949-1707
Email: info@poisonedpenpress.com
Website: www.poisonedpenpress.com

Poisoned Pen Press
6962 E. First Ave. Ste 103
Scottsdale, AZ 85251